Run For Cover

Graeme Hampton

hera

First published in the United Kingdom in 2022 by

Hera Books
Unit 9 (Canelo), 5th Floor
Cargo Works, 1–2 Hatfields
London, SE1 9PG
United Kingdom

A CIP catalogue record for this book is available from the British Library.

Print ISBN 978 1 80032 994 2
Ebook ISBN 978 1 80436 900 5

Look for more great books at www.herabooks.com

Printed and bound in Great Britain by Clays Ltd, Elcograf S.p.A.

I

Run For Cover

Graeme Hampton was born in Paisley and grew up in Stirling. The Denning and Fisher crime thriller series is inspired by his time living in London in his twenties. He now lives in Hastings, East Sussex.

Also by Graeme Hampton

D.I Denning and D.S Fisher

In memory of Charles Hampton, whose support and encouragement never dwindled.

Prologue

It's early March, but winter lingers like a dull ache.

Dougie Pyke hates winter. He longs for summer and a bit of sun to warm his ageing bones. By rights, Dougie should be retired. But he likes to work. He needs to fill his days with something. And besides, the money's not bad.

He's in the car park, leaning against the old battered works van, smoking a roll-up, watching as the thin trail of smoke disappears into the chilly air above his head. It's not his first smoke of the day, and certainly won't be his last. Dougie's job is to supervise the young lads that are paid peanuts to do the donkey work: ripping the guts out of old buildings and, if they're lucky, making a few extra quid by flogging anything of value left behind by previous owners.

Dougie likes his job. He gives those lazy sods their orders for the day, makes sure they meet their targets, and doesn't have to get his hands dirty by doing any of the real graft. Delegation, an ex-boss once told him, was an art, and one that Dougie had perfected to a tee.

White tufts of frost dust the overgrown verge that borders the car park. Dougie takes another drag on the rollie, holds it between his puckered lips for a moment while he rubs some feeling back into his brittle fingers.

They're gutting an abandoned hotel in Bromley. Solid and Victorian, Dougie thinks it's sad to see such a once-beautiful building fallen on hard times.

He blows out another thin line of smoke and casts a half-bored eye over the derelict property. It's been empty for years, and now the vandals and birds have made it their home. There are plywood boards where the windows used to be, and a fire has blackened one of the walls. A makeshift wooden ramp runs up to the once-impressive entrance, where one of the lads is currently pushing a wheelbarrow full of rubble towards an overflowing skip.

Some developer has bought the place and wants to turn it into luxury flats…

Dougie closes his eyes and takes another drag on his rollie. He can just about hear birds singing over whatever racket the lads are listening to on their radio.

Suddenly his thoughts are broken by someone screaming. He opens his eyes and sees one of the lads running towards him, shouting and gesturing, barging past the man with the wheelbarrow, who only just manages to get out of his way. It's Tomas, one of the younger lads who has only been with them for a few weeks. He's no more than a kid, so this is probably something and nothing.

'What's all the fuss about?' Dougie yells, tossing the withered remains of his cigarette into the tangled shrubbery.

'Come quick.' Tomas is waving at him, beckoning him towards the building. 'Quick!'

Dougie's first thought is that one of those stupid lads has injured themselves, and not for the first time. If so, they'll have Health and Safety all over them again, meaning delays; meaning Dougie could lose his bonus.

Sometimes, he thinks to himself, these daft lads are more trouble than they're worth.

Dougie curses, grabs his hard hat and follows Tomas into the building, already planning the bollocking he's going to give the lad for wasting his time. The former reception area beyond the entrance is covered in dust and debris. It is lit by large arc lamps that throw spikey shadows into empty corners. There's rubbish piled next to a wall where an impressive marble fireplace once stood. Tomas is gibbering something nonsensical and pointing to a corridor that leads to the former ballroom behind the reception area, which is really no more than a large conservatory tacked on to the rear of the building. They've just started working on it today but he hadn't imagined it was going to give them any grief. Dougie hurries along the corridor, panting slightly, still cursing to himself. As he pushes open the door to the ballroom, he thinks briefly of the happy times the room must have seen; the memories and the ghosts that still dance there…

But it's empty now. Derelict and forgotten, like the rest of the building. Many of the glass panels in the roof have been smashed, and the vast room smells of damp and rot.

There's a raised stage area at the far end. A few of the lads are standing around staring at something on the stage floor, which he can't quite make out. They're chattering excitedly to each other, but fall silent when they see Dougie approach. Their faces are pale.

Dougie crosses the room, his heavy boots crunching the shards of shattered glass that litter the floor. He climbs onto the wooden stage, ignoring the sharp twinge that shoots through his knee.

The lads part, and Dougie can now see what they've been staring at.

At first he can't believe his eyes. He thinks it's some kind of sick joke the lads are playing on him. But as he looks closer he realises this isn't a joke. The horror show in front of him is real.

Two men are lying naked and spreadeagled on the stage; a metal spike has been hammered through each wrist, each ankle. Another pierces their throats.

'The police,' he hears himself saying. He forgets about his bonus. He feels bile rising in his throat as panic seizes him. '*Someone get the sodding police!*'

He gazes at the bodies half in terror and half in bewilderment. Young men, probably in their early thirties. Their faces are black and purple. The wooden flooring around the bodies has been stained dark red. Dougie wonders what kind of monster could have done this.

And why.

The word that keeps running round his head is *execution*.

Chapter One

Three Months Later

DI Matt Denning was sitting in his DCI's office, glancing every so often at the clock on the wall. He had a 'capacity meeting' scheduled for eleven a.m. with the head of the ancillary support team regarding the outsourcing of IT provision, and he was aware that time was ticking. Ordinarily such tedium would have come under DCI McKenna's remit, but she'd graciously delegated this task onto his shoulders with neither explanation nor apology.

DCI Liz McKenna, known out of earshot as Betty Taggart, sat behind her desk, lips pursed and arms folded across her chest, staring at the contents of an open manila folder which spilled across her desk like a paper tsunami. This meeting was what she liked to call 'housekeeping': a weekly catch-up between her and her DI that was intended to bump heads over the current state of play with the Major Investigation Team she commanded. It was also a chance to fill her DI in on what was happening in the wider world of Met policing.

'DCS Harrison's replacement has finally been confirmed,' she said. 'It's a Brenda Ross. She was a DCI based in West London for a number of years, and is considered to be an "honest plodder" – not my words. Officially starts tomorrow; unofficially started last week.

Apart from that, I know jack shit about her.' McKenna's eyes lifted from the pile of notes and she shot Denning a withering look. 'It's hoped she'll last slightly longer in the job than her predecessor.'

Ian Harrison, their previous detective chief superintendent, had left the post earlier in the year under something of a cloud. It had been discovered he had links to a known criminal going back some time, which he had negligently omitted to mention when he was given the job. Despite there not having been a lengthy list of contenders queuing up to take his place – senior Met roles were always seen as something of a poisoned chalice amongst the rank-and-file officers – Harrison's resignation had been gratefully accepted by the Met's senior management. Had word of the reasons behind his hasty departure ever been made public, there would have been some very awkward questions to answer. Bad PR was in nobody's interests, especially those of a police force that found itself under constant media scrutiny.

'I expect we'll get a formal introduction at some point,' Denning said dryly. 'I know they like to be seen to be hands-on.'

McKenna managed a weak smile. There was something different about her today, he'd noted: a heaviness under her eyes and a weariness about her face. It was like she had lost some of her fire. In fact, thinking about it, she had been slightly out of sorts for a few days now.

She unfolded her arms and rested her hands on the desktop. 'And for the record, Matt, I'm pleased the IOPC inquiry has cleared you. Personally, I thought the whole thing was a waste of time and energy, but obviously we have to be seen to be doing things by the book.'

Denning nodded. He had recently been the subject of an inquiry by the Independent Office for Police Conduct after a suspect he had been pursuing had committed suicide by running into the path of an oncoming train some months back. There was nothing Denning could have done. The IOPC inquiry agreed, and had cleared him of any culpability. He was thankful for the outcome, and the fact he could get on with his life without it hanging over his head. But he hadn't told anyone he still had the occasional nightmare where he saw clearly the look on the man's face in the moment before the train smashed into him at around a hundred miles an hour. Or how it had taken several weeks for him to finally stop blaming himself for what had happened. The IOPC decision meant closure, at least so he kept telling himself. 'I'm happy to put it behind me and move on,' he told McKenna.

'Great, that makes two of us.' McKenna ran a hand unconsciously over the papers spread on top of her desk. 'Changing the subject, is there anything I need to know about the team?' she asked. 'Any grumbles of discontent amongst the troops that are in danger of becoming a full-blown revolt?'

He pulled a face and shook his head. 'We're still a DC down since Ryan Cormack left to join The Marine Policing Unit, and I'm not anticipating us getting a replacement this side of Christmas. Otherwise, it's business as usual.'

His DCI's focus had returned to the mess of paperwork. She seemed to be staring through it rather than at it, her mind somewhere else entirely.

McKenna originally hailed from Motherwell, just outside Glasgow, and had fought her way up through the ranks, earning a reputation along the way for not suffering fools willingly. She was something of a Jekyll and Hyde character – barking at her officers one moment then offering beer and cuddles the next. Yet, despite having got off to a slightly rocky start, they worked well together now: mutual respect – and at times admiration – had cemented their professional relationship.

'This Christmas or next?' Another weak smile. 'But seriously, if we're desperate we can ask to have someone drafted in from another MIT. Or even regular CID if necessary.' She rubbed a hand over her eyes. 'Though, obviously, it's going to leave them short.'

It was a familiar story: stretching limited budgets to breaking point. Doing more for less, as the politicians like to say, though never offering any examples of doing it themselves.

'We'll see how things go,' Denning said. 'They're a good team. I'm sure we'll muddle through.'

She nodded, still staring at the mess on her desk. 'Hmm...'

Denning didn't know much about McKenna's life outside of work, assuming she had one. Like so many long-serving coppers, the job had pretty much become his life, and hers too, he imagined. He was aware she suffered from insomnia, as he did himself on occasions, but this looked like something more than tiredness.

'Is there anything else?' he asked.

'Sorry?'

'It's just that I get the impression...' He shrugged and offered a vague smile. 'Never mind. Not important.'

'If that's it, I really should get back out there.' He nodded towards the main MIT office on the other side of the glass partition that separated McKenna's office from the main team's workspace.

She raised a hand in acknowledgement. 'Thanks, Matt.'

As he slid out her door, he glanced back at her. She was still staring absently at the papers on her desk.

—

Back in the main MIT office, his team were going about their business. A dozen desks, arranged in pairs, faced each other, only half of them in use. The room was a large expanse of beige walls and grey carpet, way too big for their needs. A couple of whiteboards sat at one end of the room; a photocopier and a water cooler at the other. Housed on the second floor of a former police station in East London at the point just before it becomes Essex, they were one of the Met's smaller Major Investigation Teams, and their numbers had been in steady decline for some time.

But Denning liked it that way. It meant he knew his team. He knew how they worked, how they thought, and where their strengths and weaknesses lay.

He glanced around the room. DS Deepak Neeraj was on the phone, looking serious, but Neeraj always looked serious, except on the rare occasions when he allowed himself a smile. DC Trudi Bell was typing away at her computer, quietly humming to herself. A show tune probably. Trudi liked her musical theatre. DS Dave Kinsella, at forty-five the oldest member of the team, was in court that day, giving evidence in a murder trial that was drawing to a close. He wasn't expected back until after lunch.

He was about to ask where DS Molly Fisher, the fourth member of his team, was when she suddenly appeared in

9

the doorway carrying a cardboard tray with four takeaway paper cups of steaming coffee. 'I've just been to the Costa across the road,' she said, handing a cup to Denning. 'I know you don't trust the machine in the basement. Americano, black with no sugar. Just how you like it.' She smiled at him.

Fisher had joined the team shortly after he had. Both had been in this particular MIT for just under a year. She passed another two cups to her colleagues at their desks. Neeraj nodded his thanks, still talking on the phone. Trudi looked up from her computer and uttered a 'Cheers, babe. No cakes?' She tucked a couple of loose strands of blonde hair behind her ear.

'Does that mean we're having a day off from the diet?' Molly joked.

'Too cruel,' came the response, followed by a throaty chuckle.

Denning took the cup and placed it on his desk. 'Thanks,' he replied. 'Much appreciated.'

'I wasn't sure if I should have got something for Betty Taggart,' Molly said, throwing a glance in the direction of McKenna's office. 'I don't even know what she drinks.'

'Blood, probably,' Trudi Bell replied. 'Straight from the neck of a virgin.'

The barb was met by a raucous laugh from Molly and a wry smile from Denning. 'Probably best to leave it,' he said. 'She's in a strange mood.'

'No change there then.'

'It's a different kind of strange...' He was about to elaborate on his meeting with McKenna, then decided it would be indiscreet. But if Molly Fisher's curiosity had been piqued, the matter was quickly brought to a halt. 'Boss!' Neeraj looked up from his desk, his forehead knitted into a train track of tight lines. 'I've just had a call from the local plod. The body of a young woman's been found in a churchyard in Leytonstone.'

Chapter Two

St George's Church was located on a quiet residential street just off Leytonstone High Road. The church was a grey stone edifice built in the late nineteenth century, with a squat central tower and a wide nave supported by a couple of narrow aisles on either side. At some point in the twentieth century an ugly brick extension had been stuck onto one side, slightly spoiling the building's symmetry. It was distinctive rather than attractive.

Denning slipped his Ford Focus into a space behind a squad car. Neeraj had undone his seatbelt and climbed out of the car before Denning had even applied the handbrake. He'd spent most of the journey noisily crunching an Extra Strong Mint and moaning about his lack of promotion prospects. Denning had tried his best to sound supportive, but the crunching of mints had slightly got on his nerves.

A thin band of police tape stretched between a couple of lamp posts, marking the boundary of the outer cordon. Already, a small group of onlookers had congregated by the cordon and were gawping at the scene. One or two bolder ones were questioning the uniformed officers standing guard but were getting the brush-off for their trouble.

Denning and Neeraj flashed their warrant cards at one of the uniformed officers standing by the cordon. He lifted the tape and they ducked underneath before heading towards the white-suited forensic team that had gathered in a huddle beside the main entrance porch at the front of the church.

It didn't take him long to spot a familiar face amongst the white suits. Sheila Gorton, the Crime Scene Manager, was already chatting to various colleagues. She raised her hand in Denning's direction when she saw him and Neeraj approaching. 'Photographer's in there now,' she said, pointing at a white forensics' tent about a hundred yards away. 'Shouldn't be long.' She smiled at Denning and nodded politely at Neeraj. 'Pathologist's on his way.'

Denning acknowledged Gorton and quickly took in the scene. The tent was situated beside one of the beech trees, its branches forming a canopy over the tent. Several CSIs milled around, searching the ground for clues. There was a coolness about the place. The sun didn't reach this part of the churchyard and the area was partially in shade, even in early June.

The churchyard itself surrounded the building, stretching off towards the rear of some houses to the north. Thin, straggly poplars lined the path that threaded its way through the churchyard, with the occasional sycamore and beech tree dotted around the place for good measure. Large, mossy gravestones poked above the grass, while birdsong filled the backdrop.

Denning climbed into protective booties and pulled on a pair of Nitrile gloves, while Neeraj headed over to speak to the uniformed officers.

Gorton led Denning into the tent where he saw the body of a young woman. She was lying on the grass, on her front; her left arm stretched out beside her, her right arm tucked under her body at an awkward angle.

She was dressed in a pair of jeans and a slightly torn T-shirt. Her arms were covered in lacerations, dozens of them. There were bald patches on her scalp, where it looked like her hair had been torn out at the roots. There were specks of dried blood on the grass.

'I suspect she was dumped here,' Gorton said. 'There's very little blood around the body, and the blood on the victim's clothing has mostly dried. There are numerous stab wounds to the body, so there would have been significant blood splatter if she'd been killed here.' It reminded Denning of the first time he'd met Gorton: the body of a young woman had been dumped in a London park. Her killer was behind bars now, but not before he'd killed again, and almost destroyed Denning's life forever.

'Any sign of sexual assault?'

'No…'

'But?'

There was an awkward pause for a moment before Gorton reached down and gently turned the body over. 'Be warned,' she said, 'this isn't pretty.'

Denning had been a murder squad detective long enough for death to no longer shock him the way it had when he first started looking at corpses. Even the sight of a dead body on the slab in a mortuary suite no longer held the same shock value as the first poor dissected corpse he'd gazed upon.

But even he had to suppress a twitching in his gut when he saw the state of their victim's face. 'What the hell happened to her?'

'Too early to say for sure at this stage, but that looks to me like burns. There are similar marks on her arms.'

'*Burns!*' He felt his stomach give another involuntary twitch. 'Was it done after she was killed?'

14

'We'll need to wait for the post-mortem, but let's hope so,' Gorton replied.

His mind was whirling, trying to make sense of what was in front of him. *Burned...stabbed...* The sheer brutality of what had happened to this poor girl was something beyond horrific. 'But you're ruling out sexual assault?'

'We'll know for certain once she's on the table, and we really should wait for the pathologist to check her over in situ, but an initial examination says not.'

'What about the cause of death?'

She screwed up her face. 'Judging by the amount of dried and drying blood on the front of the body, I'd say she was stabbed to death. But there's not a lot of point speculating this side of the post-mortem.'

Denning headed out of the tent and signalled for Neeraj to come over. 'Boss?'

'What did uniform have to say?'

'Not a lot,' Neeraj replied. 'She was found this morning by a couple of workmen who were here to cut the grass. They thought she was just some kid that had drunk too much the night before and was sleeping it off in the churchyard. It's happened before apparently. It was only when they tried to wake her that they realised she was dead.' He jabbed a thumb over his shoulder. 'One of the uniforms is with them now.'

Denning looked over at a police van, next to which a couple of men in grubby blue overalls were talking to a police officer. The men were ashen-faced.

'There was no attempt made to hide the body,' Denning said, returning his gaze to the tent. 'It's almost as though whoever left her here wanted her to be found.'

'I think the word you're looking for is "dumped", Inspector.' Sheila Gorton emerged from the forensic tent, mask round her chin, and came over to join them. 'I can't say if the location is of any significance. It could just have been convenient.'

'Then again,' Neeraj said, 'it is a churchyard. Perhaps their intention had been to bury her.'

It wasn't as crazy as it sounded. Dig a hole on top of an established grave and no one would think to look in there. Denning had heard of it happening before, but it seemed unlikely in this instance.

'What about witnesses?' he asked.

'Uniform are going to start on door-to-door as soon as we give them the nod,' Neeraj said. 'But this place isn't exactly overlooked.'

'With the exception of those houses over there.' Denning pointed to a row of sizeable houses whose back gardens ran along the perimeter of the churchyard several hundred yards away. There would be a good view of the churchyard from the upstairs windows. Whilst he wasn't holding out a great deal of hope, it was just possible someone might have seen something. 'We need to speak to the occupants. If we accept that she wasn't killed here, then we need to find out when and where she *was* killed.'

'Do we know who she is?' Neeraj asked.

'Ah, there we do have something tangible to work with,' Gorton offered. 'We found a bank card in the name of Frederica Hargreaves in her jeans pocket. It's bagged and on its way to forensics for examination.'

Denning shook his head. The name didn't ring a bell, but that meant nothing. 'Well, we'd better contact her next of kin.' He didn't fancy telling them what had happened to their loved one. Any murder was gruesome enough, but when someone had been so badly mutilated, it somehow made it so much worse. Even with the best skills in the world, a pathologist's team would be unable to make her face look anything less than grotesque. It was going to be traumatic for whoever was tasked with the unpleasant job of formally identifying her.

He asked Neeraj to contact the MIT office and get contact details for Frederica Hargreaves and find out where her next of kin lived.

Denning watched as Neeraj took his phone from his pocket and contacted the office. He looked around him. It was a peaceful spot. Birds overhead and the filtered sound of traffic from Leytonstone High Road a short distance away. Had the killer deliberately chosen this spot to dump the body? Was the church significant? Or was it, as Gorton had stated, simply convenient? Whatever the case, he had a feeling the girl had been meant to be discovered. It was like the killer was making a statement.

After a few minutes, he heard Neeraj end the call, politely thanking the person he'd been speaking to.

'Did you get a contact for Frederica Hargreaves?'

'Better than that, boss. I've just spoken to her.'

'Sorry?' He was never sure when Neeraj was taking the piss, and his slightly warped sense of humour often manifested itself at inappropriate times.

Neeraj shot him a cheeky grin. 'Someone stole her bag with all her cash and cards in it a few days ago. She reported it stolen.' He jerked his head towards the forensic tent. 'Whoever that is in there, it isn't Frederica.'

Chapter Three

The first briefing of a murder investigation was always the toughest. There was little to go on in the way of evidence, and they all had the gut-wrenching knowledge that, for the next few weeks, their lives would be on hold until the investigation reached its conclusion. That was assuming it *did* reach a satisfactory conclusion... Some cases were never solved; there was no chance of closure for the victims' families, and an overarching sense of failure for the detectives involved. Luckily such cases were rare, especially these days.

Molly made herself comfortable behind her desk until Denning started the briefing. He was standing by the whiteboard at the front of the room. Someone had stuck photos of the crime scene onto the board. There were several photos of the church grounds and a map of the surrounding streets. But it was the photos of the victim that were the hardest to stomach: close-up shots of the wounds on her arms and the back of her head; her face. Molly struggled to comprehend how someone could do something like that to another living creature.

Denning called for silence and started the briefing. 'We know very little about our victim,' he said, pointing at one of the photos on the board. 'Except that she *isn't* Frederica Hargreaves. Uniform have spoken to Miss Hargreaves, who has confirmed that her handbag was stolen from the

Duck and Drake public house on Upper Street a couple of days ago. She reported the theft and local CID looked into it. They have CCTV of the suspected culprit and, although it's too early to say for certain, the description is that of a young woman in her early twenties. And whilst we can't say for certain at this stage, it could very easily match that of our victim.'

'We're assuming our victim stole the card and still had it on her when she was murdered?' Trudi asked.

'That seems to be a logical assumption,' Denning said. 'But let's not jump to any conclusions until we have all the facts.'

'It would explain how she had someone else's credit card in her pocket,' Neeraj said.

'None of this actually helps us establish the identity of the victim,' Molly pointed out. 'Unless Islington CID have an idea who she is.'

'Neeraj has been on to missing persons,' Denning replied. 'And I've been in touch with someone from Islington CID to see if she can help.'

Molly briefly wondered who Denning knew at Islington, but this wasn't the time to ask. Instead, she said, 'If our victim is somehow involved in anything criminal, this could be some kind of revenge attack.'

'Revenge for what?' Neeraj asked. 'What could she have done to have warranted *that*?'

'I mean, it's a bit extreme,' Trudi said. 'Slap her around a bit, maybe. But this is just sick.' Molly glanced at the photos of the victim on the whiteboard. She had to admit that Trudi had a point: the level of brutality meted out to the victim suggested something more than revenge for some perceived slight. Then again, it wasn't unheard of for revenge attacks to get out of hand, especially if the wrong person had been slighted.

'But it is a possibility,' Molly said. 'And at this stage, we can't discount anything.'

Trudi nodded and threw a smile at Molly. 'I wasn't having a go, Moll. I'm just saying it's a bit extreme.'

'We have yet to ID the victim,' Denning said. 'The only distinguishing mark she has is a tattoo of a rose on her left ankle. We should keep an open mind as to motive. Let's not rule anything out until we have more facts. The streets surrounding the church are mostly residential, and there's very little CCTV in the area. Uniform are doing house-to-house, but there's nothing yet.'

He turned to the photos on the whiteboard. Molly tried hard not to look too closely at what was left of the victim's face.

'Obviously our first priority is to ID the victim.'

'I think I might have made some progress on the ID front, boss,' Neeraj offered. He waited until he had the room's attention. 'A Paul Chitterly has reported his girl-friend as missing. She didn't come home last night and there's no answer from her phone.'

'Do we have a name, Deep?' Denning asked patiently.

'Bryony Allen.' Neeraj smiled at his audience. 'And yes, I've just checked with the PNC: she's got previous for theft.'

-

Paul Chitterly had a problem with the police. That much was obvious. It had taken Molly and Trudi several minutes to calm him down and persuade him to let them in when they'd knocked on the door of his ground-floor flat in an ungentrified street in Upper Holloway and explained why they were there. His first reaction had been to accuse them of lying, insisting Bryony wasn't dead and they were trying to mess with his head. He'd stared at them aggressively from behind his front door, saying in a low hiss that he'd done nothing wrong and had refused to let them in. He'd seemed half out of it, and Molly suspected he'd taken something; probably skunk, which was resulting in his paranoia. Eventually, he'd given in, realising they weren't going to go away until he agreed to speak to them, and reluctantly acknowledged the immutable fact his girlfriend really was dead.

Molly and Trudi were now sitting opposite him in the living room of his dingy flat. He sat on an old armchair looking daggers at them; his left leg jigging furiously; his eyes darting from one detective to the other.

Forensics had confirmed that prints on the stolen credit card were a match for Bryony Allen. A phone call to Chitterly had established that Bryony had a tattoo of a rose on her left ankle. They still had to wait for a formal ID of the body – and Denning and Neeraj were speaking to Bryony's next of kin – but they were now confident the body in the churchyard was that of Bryony Allen.

'When was the last time you saw Bryony?' Molly asked.

He looked at her for a few seconds before answering. 'Yesterday. Lunchtime. She went out after lunch. Said she was meeting some friends.'

'Did she say who these friends were? Or where she was meeting them?'

He shrugged. 'She never said.'

'So, you don't know who she was meeting, or where?' Molly kept her tone light; inquisitive rather than inquisitorial. She had a feeling Paul Chitterly was going to have

21

to be gently prodded when it came to answering their questions.

'I dunno. I don't know all her friends,' he said.

'And you weren't worried when she didn't come home last night?'

He looked at Molly again before he answered. 'Sometimes she stays over with a mate. If they've been out somewhere. She doesn't like coming home by herself if it's late.'

Very sensible, thought Molly. Though ultimately that caution hadn't done her any good. 'Can you think of anyone who would want to harm Bryony?' she asked.

A quick look on the Police National Computer had told them Chitterly had a criminal record as long as Bryony's. If he and Bryony had pissed off the wrong people, then Molly and Trudi needed to find out who and why.

Chitterly shook his head. He was a thin, wiry lad, with a slight weasely look about his face, and dressed in scraggy jeans and a faded T-shirt. 'It wasn't me,' he said quickly. 'I would never hurt Bryn.' Despite the hardened exterior, it was clear he was struggling to rein in his grief. She knew the sort of person he was. He couldn't allow himself to show any weakness, not in front of police officers, especially not female ones. But Molly could sense his pain. One look at the flat told them he didn't have much in his life. And the one thing he valued more than anything had just been taken from him in the cruellest of ways.

'We don't think that, Paul,' Molly said calmly. But in truth she couldn't rule it out, at least not entirely. She had a feeling she was going to have her work cut out here. She was trying to muster some sympathy for him. After all, he had just lost his girlfriend in horrific circumstances.

If it were anyone else she would have been overdoing the tea and sympathy. But he just sat and looked at her with narrowed eyes. For a moment, she thought he was leering at her. 'I need to know a little more about Bryony. How long have you been together?'

'A few years. We was at school together.'

'And she lived here? With you?' Molly asked.

His eyes darted from Molly to Trudi, then back to Molly.

They'd agreed on the way there that Molly would ask the questions, while Trudi would take notes, flag up any inconsistencies.

'Yes,' Chitterly said after a gap. 'The council found us the flat.'

Molly looked round the room. There was nothing that made the place look even halfway homely: no photographs, no little bits and pieces that would have given the place a hint of personality or warmth. The flat stank of chip fat and unwashed clothes. Molly was certain she could detect the acrid stench of stale urine somewhere in the room, possibly originating from a cat or dog, though there was no evidence that the flat was home to any pets.

'How long have you lived here?' she asked.

'Why? We've got a lease. We're not squatting.'

She tried to smile at him; break down his defensive barrier. If they were to make any kind of progress here, they needed the victim's boyfriend on their side. 'I'm not implying anything, Paul. I was just wondering, that's all.'

Maybe it was the attempt at a smile, or maybe it was because he finally realised she wasn't going to arrest him just for breathing, but he seemed to relax ever so slightly. 'We've been here for almost a year.' He gave a little smile.

'The rent's cheap. We were living in a squat before we found this place.'

'What about Bryony? Was she happy here?'

He looked at her again. 'Of course she was happy. Why wouldn't she be? Look, I dunno who killed her and I dunno why they did it. She never harmed anyone, did Bryn. I mean, not really. She had a heart of gold, deep down. She was never in any trouble.'

'That's not entirely true, Paul. Is it?' Molly's voice had softened. 'You've both been in trouble with the police, haven't you? Theft, handling stolen goods. Drugs.'

'You're talking rubbish. You just want to fit me up for something I never done. Bryn wasn't a thief and nor am I.'

'That's not why we're here, Paul. All we want to know is who killed Bryony and why. And I think you can help us with that. Did anyone threaten you? You or Bryony? Did someone threaten to come after you for something one of you did?'

He was shooting her daggers again. The trust she'd built up had vanished as quickly as it appeared. 'Nobody's threatened us. Why would they? You're just trying to frighten me.'

He was becoming twitchy again, and the creasing of his brow said there was something he was holding back. Molly wanted to probe further, find out what it was he didn't want them to know. But this wasn't the time. He needed to get his head round what had happened to Bryony and come to terms with the fact she wouldn't be coming home. Maybe once that reality had sunk home he might feel like opening up. 'OK, Paul,' she said. 'I'm not going to push it. For now. But I may need to speak to you again.'

'What… what happened to her?' he asked. 'You said she was murdered, but you didn't say what happened?' He looked awkwardly at the floor for a second. 'Was she stabbed?'

Molly was curious as to why he'd asked this. 'We'll know more once the post-mortem has been done.'

He was still looking at her, biting his lower lip. She got the impression there was something else he wanted to ask.

'I'll be in touch as soon as we hear more,' she said. She handed him her card with her contact details. 'If you can think of anything that can help us find Bryony's killer, Paul, and I mean *anything*, please call me. I promise you all I'm interested in is catching Bryony's murderer. Nothing else.' She waited until he finally made eye contact and she could reassure herself that what she'd said to him had sunk in. He took her card, looked at it and nodded.

She and Trudi showed themselves out.

As soon as they were on the pavement, Molly breathed in some welcome fresh air. The flat had felt stuffy and unloved. And there was something about Paul Chitterly that had unsettled her.

'What did you make of all that?' Trudi asked as they headed back to her car.

'I don't know. We need to find these so-called friends, if that's really where she was. I suspect there's more to her staying out all night than he's implying.'

'Maybe they had an argument,' Trudi suggested.

'Maybe…'

'Potentially puts him in the frame then. If they had argued that is.'

'There's something else,' Molly said. 'I got the feeling he's scared of something.'

'His girlfriend's just been murdered. There's nothing to say whoever did it won't be coming for him next. I think I'd be worried if I was in his shoes. That's assuming he didn't do it.'

'It's more than that, Trudi. There's something else. There's something he wasn't telling us.' She glanced back at the flat. 'I think he knows who killed Bryony, or at least has a very good idea. And I think he knows why she was killed.'

Chapter Four

Liam Allen lived in a quiet street in leafy Hornchurch. The house was buffered from the street by a well-tended garden, mature shrubs and a neatly trimmed lawn. Denning parked the car in front of the tarmacked driveway.

'Nice place, boss,' Neeraj said. 'Are you sure we've got the right address?'

It was a curving avenue of smart 1930s semis that faced a near identical row opposite. Number nineteen was the address they'd been given for Bryony's parents. 'Let's not make any assumptions, Deep,' Denning said, locking the car with a bleep of his key fob. He hated the fact he'd made the same assumption himself as they'd turned into the street: a nice house meant a good family. So why had Bryony Allen ended up how she had?

Liam Allen opened the front door. He was a large man in his late forties, with a bushy black beard and a thick mane of hair, just starting to go grey at the temples. He looked at Denning and then Neeraj and blinked. They flashed their IDs, which he studied carefully.

'Liam Allen?'

'Yes. What do you want?' He seemed anxious, as though he was expecting bad news to come knocking.

'Is it OK if we come in?'

Liam Allen stood in the doorway for a moment, looking confused. Denning heard a woman's voice in the background asking who it was. 'Police,' Liam Allen replied, standing aside to let them in. A polished tiled hallway led through into the kitchen at the rear of the house, where a slim, blonde woman in a light summery dress was drying dishes at the sink. Denning guessed she was about ten years younger than Liam Allen, perhaps a bit more. She dried her hands on the dish towel and placed it on the worktop beside the sink. She was introduced as Allen's wife, Carly.

The house was just as the garden had hinted: warm and homely. Leafy house plants sat in brightly coloured pots along the kitchen window ledge, and a faint aroma of exotic food lingered by the stove.

Although there was no one sitting at the kitchen table, they all preferred to stand. Carly Allen leant against the sink, while Liam stood by the fridge freezer. Denning and Neeraj stood in the doorway.

'We're here about Bryony,' Denning said.

'Oh, Christ, what's she done now?' Carly asked. She shot her husband an exasperated look, suggesting this wasn't the first time the police had come calling with some tale of woe about Bryony.

'Can I confirm,' Denning asked, 'does she have a tattoo of a rose on her left ankle?'

Liam nodded. 'She had it done for her eighteenth. A bit of a joke, really. I wanted to call her Rose when she was born, but her mother insisted on Bryony.'

Neeraj looked at Carly Allen, who shook her head.

'I'm Bryony's step-mum,' she said.

'Bryony's mum died when she was ten,' Liam informed them. 'Suicide.'

'We brought Bryony up,' Carly said. 'Not that she appreciated it.' There was no trace of emotion in her voice. It was like she was discussing someone she hardly knew.

'What's this about?' Liam asked, as though suddenly sensing they weren't there because of something his daughter had done. 'Has something happened to her?'

'Why don't you sit down, Mr Allen?' Denning suggested. He nodded at Carly. 'Both of you.'

Liam Allen looked at them and then at his wife. 'This isn't good, is it?'

'We've found a body, Mr Allen. We believe it's Bryony,' Denning said. He was trying not to think about her injuries. 'At this stage we don't know the exact details, but we're currently conducting a murder inquiry.'

'Murder?' Liam looked like he'd been hit by a brick. He shook his head and sat down at the kitchen table, resting his head in his hands. When he spoke, his voice was barely more than a thin whisper. 'I wish I could say I'm surprised. I really wish I could...'

Carly Allen sat down beside her husband.

'When did you last see her?' Denning asked.

'Not for a while. We were estranged,' Liam said. 'The last time she came round here we argued.'

'What about?' Neeraj asked.

But he didn't answer. He shook his head and squeezed his hands together, trying hard to make sense of what he'd just been told about his daughter.

'She was always in trouble,' Carly Allen said, breaking the silence. 'If it wasn't one thing it was something else. Liam did his best for her. We both did. But she was always bringing trouble to our doorstep. We've got our other kids to think about.'

'Other kids?' Neeraj asked.

She nodded. 'We've got two boys. Twelve and thirteen. They're at an impressionable age. It wasn't good having Bryony around. I mean, they never got on, for a start.'

Denning spotted a freshly washed football kit poking out of a laundry basket waiting to be ironed. The house still served its role as a happy family home, just not for Bryony.

'That's not true,' Liam argued, but his wife carried on as though he'd never spoken.

'And I was always the bad one. I was always the one having to remind everyone that this whole fucking family didn't revolve around Bryony and her latest drama.' She looked at Denning. 'It's not easy being a step-parent, you know.'

Denning sympathised with Carly Allen. His own wife, Sarah, was step-parent to his ten-year-old son, Jake. Something he knew she struggled with. He had first-hand experience of just how difficult it could be bringing up someone else's child.

'You're saying that you hadn't seen her for a while?' he asked.

'Almost a year ago,' Liam confirmed. 'She turned up here having had an argument with her boyfriend and wanted somewhere to stay.' He looked at his wife, bitterness and regret imprinted on his face. 'We… I let her stay for a few days. But it didn't work out.'

Carly stared impassively at the fruit bowl on the kitchen table and shook her head.

'What happened?' Neeraj asked.

'Apart from her turning up here stoned out of her brain every other night?' Carly said.

'She was a drug user?' Denning asked.

'She was an addict.' Carly Allen said coldly. 'A hopeless addict.'

'She was trying her best to get off the drugs,' Liam argued. 'She'd been to rehab a few times. She promised me she was clean; that was why I let her stay.'

'That's because you wanted to believe her.'

'She was my daughter, Carly. What was I supposed to do?'

Liam Allen rubbed his hands over his face. When he removed them, Denning could see the redness round his eyes. His wife placed a sympathetic hand on his arm, but it looked to Denning like she was going through the motions.

'We argued,' Liam said sheepishly. 'Over her drug-taking, yes, but other stuff too. Nothing, mostly. She said we'd never loved her. It was mostly a rehash of old arguments, with some new stuff added in for good measure.'

'When you say drugs, what are talking about? Dope? Cocaine? Heroin?'

'Literally anything she could get her hands on,' Carly said. 'She wasn't averse to the odd spot of dealing either.'

Liam Allen shot her a look and her gaze shifted to the floor again.

'Once, Carly. Once, we thought she was dealing.'

'Selling shit to one of our neighbour's kids. I'm surprised they're still talking to us.'

Denning decided to move the discussion on. Family recriminations could wait until he and Neeraj had left, allowing them to conduct their grief and share their bile in private. 'Did she mention anything about anyone being after her for something? A drug debt maybe?'

'There was always someone after her for something,' Carly said. She sighed. 'Look, I don't want you to get the wrong impression. We loved Bryony, even though she would probably have claimed otherwise. But the truth is, she resented us – both of us. And the boys. We did all we could for her. But it was never enough. She resented me for not being her mother and she resented Liam because he walked out on them when Bryony was little, and then only agreed to bring her up out of guilt.' She looked at her husband, no longer pretending with the sympathy. 'I'm only saying it like it was. There's no point sugar-coating things for them. They'll find out the truth soon enough.'

Liam Allen ignored his wife's outburst. He looked up at Denning. 'When will they release the body?'

'I can't say,' Denning said. 'There will need to be a post-mortem and then...' He couldn't finish the rest of the sentence. 'We'll let you know,' he said.

Liam Allen nodded silently while Carly Allen offered to show them out. 'I'm sorry for what happened to Bryony,' she said when they were standing on the door-step, 'but I can't help thinking she's somehow brought this on herself.'

Denning wanted to reply, but found there was nothing he could say. He wanted to shout at her and tell her she was wrong: no one ever brought murder on themselves. Bryony Allen was a human being, and whatever trouble she'd found herself in, she hadn't deserved to die the way she had. Instead, he just looked at her and said, 'I think your husband's going to need all the support you can offer, Mrs Allen. Whatever your own personal thoughts, he's just lost his daughter.' With that he and Neeraj headed back to the car.

Chapter Five

'Have you chased up the PM yet?'

McKenna was sitting behind her desk. She seemed more focussed than the last time they'd chatted, but still looked like there was something on her mind that was taking up more thought space than it ought to.

'Dr Baker assures me it's top of his list of priorities,' Denning said. 'He's promised me first thing tomorrow.'

'Good. We need the time of death confirmed ASAP. At least then we've got something to work with.' McKenna was looking at copies of the crime scene photos that she'd laid out on her desk. She grimaced slightly when she saw what had happened to Bryony Allen's face. 'What does your gut say, Matt? Are we looking at the work of a nutter, or is this about something else entirely?'

For some, as yet unexplained reason, his gut said it was the latter. But without further evidence, he couldn't be certain. 'We can't, at this stage, rule out the possibility she was randomly targeted: a young woman; wrong place and wrong time. It wouldn't be the first time that kind of thing has happened.'

'But…?'

He thought for a moment, carefully shaping the words in his head before he spoke them aloud. 'Bryony Allen has an interesting history. It's possible she's made some enemies. And it's just possible one of those enemies has come after her.' He filled her in on what Liam and Carly Allen had told him. Part of him wanted to put some kind of positive spin on it; try and suggest Bryony's life hadn't been as grim and empty as the reality implied. But there was no point. It was always better to stick to the facts. 'It's clear there's no great love lost between Bryony and her step-mum. I got the impression her father wishes he'd done more for his daughter, but I accept he was in a difficult situation.' He paused. 'In short, I get the impression Bryony wasn't shy when it came to pissing people off.'

McKenna nodded. 'OK. Sounds like we've got something to work with. Let's get looking into her background in more detail. If she was dealing drugs, find out who she was selling to and who was supplying her. It's possible she's trod on someone's toes. Or it could be someone wanted her out of the picture to make way for fresh blood. And check out this boyfriend of hers, too. Looks like he's got previous. In fact, according to what's on the PNC, he and Bryony were not far off being East London's answer to Bonnie and Clyde.'

That was overstating it a bit, Denning thought. Judging by what he'd read on the PNC, most of their crimes were at the pettier end of the spectrum. But then again, it was possible there was stuff they didn't know about. There was one thing the PNC had flagged up that he felt was worth commenting on. 'There's nothing on file about drugs,' he said, 'dealing or possession.'

'There's nothing *yet*,' McKenna countered. 'We've both been around long enough to know that the kind of crimes they were involved in are usually indicative of drug use, and it's not uncommon for users to become dealers to fund their habit. And in light of what the parents have told us about Bryony, I think we have to assume both she and the boyfriend were dealing. Probably not big-league dealers, but it's all part of the same pot.'

'Fair point. It's certainly something we should be looking into.'

'If this is about drugs, and there's someone bigger behind them, then we need to find out who it is. The last thing we want is a drug-related turf war.'

But there was another possibility Denning felt they had to consider. 'If Bryony was a drug user, then we can't ignore the fact she could have been funding her habit through prostitution. If that's the case, then she might have unwittingly put herself in danger.'

McKenna nodded again. 'Which brings us back to the random nutter scenario.' She tapped her steepled fingers against her chin. 'Let's keep an open mind about potential motive. The PM results should answer some questions. At least once we know *how* she was killed, we might have a better clue as to *why*.' She was staring at the crime scene photos on her desk, but they didn't seem to be registering with her. Denning tried to make eye contact but without much luck. He decided to take a punt.

'Is everything OK, Liz?'

She seemed slightly taken aback by his question, shooting him a look that suggested he'd crossed a line. Then her face softened. She rubbed a hand through her raven hair again and pressed her lips into a thin smile.

'Everything's fine. Why wouldn't it be?'

It sounded more like a statement than a question. 'Sorry. I wasn't trying to pry...'

'I'm just tired. I'm not sleeping too great at the moment.' She massaged her eyes with her thumb and forefinger. 'Pressure of work. I'm sure I don't have to explain that to you.'

He wasn't sure he believed her. He waited for her to add something further, but she just continued to stare vacantly at the photos sprawled across her desk. Eventually, she looked up. 'Look, Matt: I'm fine. Just focus on finding Bryony Allen's killer, OK. I have a horrible feeling that whoever did it hasn't finished yet.'

'Why do you say that?'

A gimlet stare, followed by a sigh. 'Returning to my initial point: if this isn't a falling out between rival drug gangs, then there's every chance we are looking at the work of a nutter. Which in turn means we could find ourselves on the hunt for a serial killer.'

Chapter Six

'OK everyone, so far we know our victim was murdered elsewhere and dumped in the churchyard in Leytonstone. We need to find out when she murdered and where. The post-mortem results should give us a good indication of when, but we'll need to find out where.'

Denning was by the whiteboard at the front of the room, looking at the team.

The briefing had been called for straight after lunch. Molly had already been tasked with searching through the limited CCTV around the churchyard in the hope it might throw up something useful, which so far it hadn't. It was a thankless task, and she hadn't been looking forward to it. At least the briefing would serve as a welcome distraction.

Denning was scribbling information on the whiteboard. He was wearing what looked like a new suit. Molly wondered how he always seemed to have money for expensive clothes, which even on an inspector's salary was an extravagance. Then she remembered someone telling her his wife worked as a hedge-fund manager for a bank somewhere in the City. She suspected the Dennings didn't have the same financial worries as most ordinary people.

Kinsella was back from court now, sitting behind his desk, arms folded, a bored look on his weathered face. Yet, despite his gruff exterior, Dave could be a good laugh when the mood struck, and was never afraid to muck in with the rest of the team when it came to the crunch. When Molly had asked him how the court case had gone, he'd just grunted and said the correct verdict had been delivered. However, he had given no indication as to what the verdict was.

Molly was suddenly aware of Denning looking at her. 'Any luck with Bryony's boyfriend, Molly?'

'There's something not right there,' she said, quickly shifting her attention back to the matter in hand. 'He claims the last time he saw her was yesterday lunchtime, and she was meeting friends somewhere. Couldn't say who they were or where she was meeting them.'

'Sounds fishy,' Kinsella said. 'No pun meant, DS Fisher.' He grinned like an imbecile and Molly ignored him.

'He was certainly cagey, and I mean much more so than is normal for someone with a phobia of police. It's like he was frightened.'

'Probably shitting himself in case you arrested him for being a nasty little scrote.' Kinsella guffawed at his lame joke, though no one else seemed to appreciate his humour.

'His girlfriend's just been murdered,' Denning said. 'He's bound to be jittery.'

'It was more than that. I can't put my finger on it, but he definitely knows more than he's letting on.'

'You think he was lying?' Denning asked.

'More a case of not being entirely honest.' She glanced back at the photos on the whiteboard; a reminder of the kind of monster they were dealing with here. 'But I don't think he killed Bryony. I just don't think he's got it in him to do that to another human being, let alone someone he loved. I also have a feeling he was probably telling the truth about not knowing where she was, or who with.' She thought back to her interview with Paul Chitterly. He was pathetic rather than malicious, but there was always the possibility that could have been an act. 'I get the definite feeling there were a lot of secrets in that relationship.'

'OK, let's leave him alone for now,' Denning said. 'But we may need to speak to him again at some point, so he's not entirely off the hook. We need to find out where Bryony was between lunchtime yesterday and when she was killed. And who she was with.' Denning looked over at Neeraj. 'Deep and myself spoke with Bryony's father and stepmother. It would appear that Bryony has been estranged from them for some time, and they weren't particularly close. They alleged that Bryony had been dealing drugs from their house. This is potentially worth looking into further.'

'What was their reaction when you told them what happened to Bryony?' Kinsella asked.

'Her father took the news hard,' Neeraj said, 'but the stepmother seemed more relieved than anything else.'

'Are we ruling out the stepmother?' Trudi asked.

'She didn't hide the fact she's probably glad to have Bryony out the way – that would certainly give her a motive. But no, I don't think she would have gone as far as to actually kill Bryony,' Denning said.

'I checked on the girl's real mother,' Neeraj said. 'Jumped off a tower block about eleven years ago. Depression, apparently. But it was never confirmed. Liam Allen and his wife had separated by that time. There's no mention about what happened to Bryony.'

'It would have been shortly after that when Bryony moved in with Liam and Carly.' Denning seemed to give this matter some thought. 'Is it possible Bryony's problems started after her mother's death, as Carly Allen hinted? Let's speak to social services, and to Bryony's school. Find out if there were any issues in her childhood.'

'Why are we wasting time looking into her background? It's pretty clear this is the work of a nutter,' Kinsella said, echoing the words of McKenna.

Denning shook his head. 'There's no evidence to say this *was* a random attack. Until we know otherwise, we keep an open mind as to motive.'

'And what happens if he strikes again?' Kinsella sat back in his chair; beefy arms folded across his barrel of a chest.

Denning ignored him and brought the briefing to a close. But Molly felt herself tensing at Dave's words. Kinsella was always a glass-half-empty kind of bloke at the best of times. Sometimes she felt he actually got off on spreading fear and despondency amongst the team, possibly inflating his own sense of importance into the bargain. But on the other hand, they couldn't readily ignore what he was saying. The prospect of a maniac attacking random women was something they would have to consider until such time as they could rule it out unequivocally. She wanted Dave Kinsella to be wrong, but in her gut she knew there was a chance he was right.

The thought not only made her feel ill, but rekindled a memory that she'd tried hard to forget. It would be so much easier to blame Paul for Bryony's murder; label this whole thing as nothing more than a domestic that had got out of hand. She was certain he was holding something back. He was definitely worth another conversation.

Chapter Seven

Molly found the bar without too much trouble. From the outside it didn't look like anything special: a converted Victorian pub, painted black, with large windows and a couple of desiccated hanging baskets dangling limply either side of the entrance. The interior was no more inspiring, painted in different shades of grey with stripped wooden flooring and a slightly soulless feel. The furniture looked like it had been gathered from second-hand shops: there was even an old church pew resting against one wall. A billiard table occupied an area on the far side of the bar near the door to the toilets, while a TV screen above the bar streamed one of the sports channels on some kind of loop. It felt like everything jarred, as though the bar suffered from a split personality and couldn't decide what kind of clientele it should be aiming for.

The woman behind the bar had short, spiky blonde hair and a scowl on her face. She greeted Molly with an efficient smile. Molly ordered a sparkling mineral water.

'Does a Paul Chitterly ever drink in here?' Molly asked.

The woman pushed the drink across the bar and shook her head. 'Never heard of him.'

Chitterly had phoned her unexpectedly. He'd said he wanted to talk, but he needed to know if he could trust her first. She'd suggested meeting on neutral territory, and he'd suggested The Lydon Arms, a bar on Holloway Road, not far from Archway Tube station.

'Two pounds ten, please.' The woman behind the bar had her hand outstretched, and the same cold, efficient smile on her face.

Molly paid the woman and then wandered over to a table beside an exposed brick fireplace with a good view of the bar.

The place wasn't busy: a middle-aged couple sat in a far corner drinking and talking quietly. Another, younger couple – probably early twenties – had eyed Molly when she'd first walked in, then returned to their drinks. They were playing on their phones now, oblivious to her presence. Out of the corner of her eye, she spotted a young woman sitting at a table near the bar, casting occasional glimpses in Molly's direction. She looked as though she was nursing the dregs of a pint of lager, and Molly got the impression it wasn't her first.

Molly checked her watch: Chitterly was already late.

She sipped her mineral water and checked her phone in case there was a message to say he was on his way and to get him a drink, but there was nothing. She should probably have run this by Denning first. Made sure she wasn't taking an unnecessary risk by agreeing to meet a possible suspect in a murder investigation unofficially. But if Denning had decided to make this official then there was a chance Paul wouldn't have agreed to meet her. He'd already made it obvious he had trust issues with the police. If she was to get anything useful out of him, then this had to be off the record.

She was watching the door when a couple of men came in. Neither of which was Paul Chitterly. The men were tall and broad, and gave the impression they were no strangers to a gym. They spoke to the barmaid before briefly looking around the place, taking in Molly and the other drinkers. One of them gave Molly a second look and said something to the other man. She wondered if he recognised her as being a police officer.

Music had begun playing in the background; progressive rock, not too loud but enough to make it difficult to hear what they were saying, not helped by the fact they were keeping their voices low. Molly watched the woman behind the bar shake her head and shrug. She got the impression the two men were looking for someone.

The barmaid pushed a couple of bottles of beer towards the two men. One of them handed over a note and told her to keep the change.

'Excuse me.' The young woman who had been sitting near the bar nursing a pint had now sat down next to Molly. She was smiling at her through crooked teeth. 'I heard you asking her about Paul,' she said. 'You a cop?'

Molly shook her head. 'No. I'm a friend,' she said. 'We're doing a bit of business together.' She hoped it sounded convincing. She had a horrible feeling The Lydon Arms wasn't the most cop-friendly of drinking establishments.

The girl observed Molly for a moment, eyeing her curiously, then smiled again. She wasn't exactly scruffy, but it looked like she'd been wearing the same clothes for more than a couple of days. And the whiff of stale body odour hinted that she hadn't been near a bath for a while. 'I reckon you are a cop,' she said after a moment. Another smile. On someone else, Molly mused, it might have been quite endearing, but on this girl it made her look slightly feral.

'If you are,' she continued, 'you probably know what happened to Bryn.'

It was said as a statement as much as a question. The girl was still looking at Molly when she spoke; not unfriendly but looking like she wasn't a stranger to trouble.

The two men who had been standing at the bar had moved to a table nearby now. One of them looked to be in his late thirties to early forties, with pockmarked skin and a small scar running under his left ear. He reminded Molly of her uncle's Pitbull before they'd had it neutered. He glanced over in Molly's direction then said something to his mate. His mate was about the same age; thick set with a couple of days-worth of stubble round his chin. She had a feeling they were trying to listen in to her conversation with the crooked-toothed girl.

'I didn't know Bryony,' she said to the girl, 'but I heard about what happened to her. Terrible.'

The girl looked Molly at with a wariness in her eyes. 'I bet you don't know. I bet you don't know the half of it.' She smiled again at Molly, though this time it looked more like a smirk. 'Buy me another one of these and I'll tell you. All about Bryn and Paul. And Rob.' She waved her half-empty glass under Molly's nose.

'Who's Rob?' She noticed one of the men glance over at the mention of the mysterious Rob.

The girl just waved her glass at Molly and kept smiling. Molly was sure she was trying it on. Bluffing her way to a free pint with an empty promise of information she didn't have. Another quick glance at her watch told her Paul Chitterly was either very late or wasn't coming. It was beginning to look like the latter.

Bryony's murder would have been on the local news by now, though she hadn't been officially named yet. And it was possible the woman had recognised Chitterly's name because she'd overheard Molly speaking to the barmaid. But why would she mention the name Rob? If she *did* know something about Bryony's death, then Molly felt obliged to follow it up.

'What's your name?' she asked.

'Kelly-Ann.' She extended a trembling hand at the end of a skinny arm and offered Molly a limp handshake.

'I'm Molly.' She returned the handshake, feeling the girl's bones beneath the thin flesh of her hand. 'Would you like another drink?' She wasn't sure it was sensible to offer her more alcohol, but if she did have anything useful to say it was likely the only way Molly would get it out of her.

'Lager, please. Pint.' She smiled and drained the last of the dregs from her glass.

Molly took the empty pint glass from her and headed back to the bar, aware of the Pitbull and his chum watching her. She placed the empty glass on the bar top and ordered a pint of Carlsberg, convincing herself if this came to nothing, all it would have cost her was a drink in a depressing pub.

The woman behind the bar glared at her. 'She can have a half, and that's it. She's been here since lunchtime.'

Molly nodded her agreement. 'Fair enough. A half then.' She waited for the woman to pour the drink, and then paid her. She was tempted to say something about a smile costing nothing, but suspected the barb wouldn't be appreciated.

When she turned round, Kelly-Ann had gone.

So too had the men who'd been sitting nearby. Their half-drunk bottles of beer were still sitting unattended on the table. 'Did you see where she went?' she asked the barmaid.

'Toilet, maybe? Throwing up?'

Molly checked the ladies. She pushed open the two cubicle doors but there was no one in either of them.

'She's not there,' Molly said when she was back at the bar. 'Where else could she have gone?'

A shrug of the shoulders. 'I don't know. Maybe she's gone home. She's had a skinful.' The barmaid sighed and gave Molly a look. 'I know her. She's a pisshead. I should bar her, but I feel sorry for the poor cow. And she's mostly harmless.' The woman took the half-pint of Carlsberg and poured it down the sink. 'But I wouldn't take any notice of anything she tells you,' she added. 'She's full of shit.'

'She mentioned someone called Rob,' Molly said. 'Do you know who she was talking about?'

The woman shook her head. 'I've no idea. Like I said, she was pissed. She'd probably tell you the moon was made of cheese if she thought there was a drink in it for her.'

But Molly was curious. She had a feeling the unhelpful woman behind the bar knew exactly who Rob was, but she didn't want to make things official, at least not yet. Not until she'd at least spoken to Denning. She also wanted to ask about the two men who seemed to disappear at the same time as Kelly-Ann, but she knew she would just get fobbed off again. It could have been nothing, but it was strange that all three were no longer in the bar. Instead, she looked at her watch. There was still no sign of Paul Chitterly. It looked like he'd been wasting her time.

Chapter Eight

The Pear and Partridge, an oak-panelled, real-ale pub overlooking the river in Wapping, was slightly off the normal tourist trail, which meant it tended not to get too busy in the summer. It had plenty of character and a quirky charm, like a forgotten relic from a previous age that had somehow survived into the twenty-first century. It was rumoured that one of Jack the Ripper's victims had drunk there prior to meeting her grisly end, though Denning tended to take that particular rumour with a large pinch of salt. Besides, the last thing he wanted on this pleasant summer's evening was to be reminded of serial killers.

He'd been here a few times since he and his wife, Sarah, had discovered the pub by accident earlier in the year. She liked its convenience; he liked its total lack of pretension.

Denning took his drink outside to the patio that overlooked the river, and placed it on the wooden table.

'It's nice here.' His companion was already there, sipping something that looked like an alcohol-free cocktail, but could have been nothing more exotic than lime juice and fizzy water. 'Not what I expected.' She smiled at him as he sat down opposite her.

He didn't want to explain that he usually came there with his wife. It was probably easier to keep Sarah out of

47

things for the time being. He didn't want to risk complicating a situation that was already in danger of becoming more complicated than it should be.

Denning hadn't known Anna Klein for very long. She was a DS with Islington CID, and their paths had crossed a few months back when they'd found themselves investigating an attack on a retired academic which had turned out to be something else entirely. They'd kept in touch, even going as far as meeting up for the odd drink now and again.

She took a sip from her glass and visibly relaxed. 'God, that's hit the spot.' Anna was dressed in her work suit: a neat, grey pin-striped jacket and skirt, with a pale blue blouse underneath. A beige Burberry raincoat was draped over an adjacent chair, though there had been no sign of rain for days.

'Stressful day?'

'I don't need to tell you how it is. Three major investigations running simultaneously, and barely enough bodies to adequately cover one.' She pushed her glasses against the bridge of her nose. 'You?'

Denning told her about the body in the churchyard. 'We don't have a lot to go on at the moment,' he added. 'Post-mortem's tomorrow. Hopefully we'll have a clearer picture then.'

'I saw that on the local news earlier,' she said. 'Nasty business. Have you got a name?'

He sipped his drink. 'Bryony Allen. But we're not releasing that until the next of kin have done a positive ID.' Or as close as they can, he thought.

'Bryony?' He watched her nod her head slowly, like one of those nodding dogs that people used to have in the back of their cars. 'Horrible thing to say, but I reckon it was only a matter of time before Bryony came a cropper.'

It was strange to hear someone echoing the sentiments of Bryony's step-mum. The more he tried to piece Bryony Allen's life together, the more he began to feel some sympathy for the girl. 'You knew her?' He wasn't entirely surprised to hear that Bryony had flashed up on the local CID's radar, but he was curious to hear more.

'We all bloody knew Bryony and her gang. They've been terrorising the area for months. I was half expecting something like this to happen.'

'Gang? I thought it was just her and her boyfriend?'

'And the rest. They've been known to us for a while now.' Anna took another sip of her drink and sighed. 'Bryony and Paul initially started off with pretty low-level stuff: mostly handling stolen goods, petty thieving, that sort of thing. At least that used to be the case. They fell in with some dodgy individuals about six months ago. A really unpleasant bunch. They get their kicks targeting elderly householders.' She gave a slight shudder. 'The real worry is that the level of violence involved has been increasing lately. The last attack, just over a week ago, left one householder dead.'

'Dead?' He quickly looked round to make sure no one was listening to them. 'And Bryony Allen was part of this gang?'

She took another sip of her drink and shrugged. 'There was no real evidence linking Bryony to the attacks themselves, beyond a description from some of the victims that just happens to fit her to a tee. We also have CCTV footage of her and Paul Chitterly in the general vicinity of at least two of the robberies, but that's at best circumstantial. We did show Bryony's photo – along with some of the other suspected gang members – to the victims, but none of them were able to confirm that she was there. To be fair, most of them just wanted to forget about what happened. From what we can gather, Bryony mostly acts as either lookout or decoy.'

'Decoy?'

'She'll knock on the door one evening, claim she's been attacked or whatever, and that she's lost her phone – can she use theirs to call the police. The householder takes pity on this this poor little creature of a girl, then as soon as she's through the door, the gang bursts in and ransacks the place. At least that's how it started. Like I said, they're getting bolder now – either that or people are just more wary about who they open their front doors to, especially at night. Lately, they've been breaking in: either down-stairs windows or unlocked back doors, threatening the householder into handing over their valuables, sometimes even smacking them around for good measure.'

'What happened with the last victim?'

'A Valerie Heaton. She lived in Finsbury Park. Appar-ently the gang broke in one evening, there was a bit of a struggle, she was assaulted and later died in hospital. She had early-stage dementia, it seems, so it's possible she didn't know what was going on and the gang grew frustrated and attacked her. Of course, it's possible the assault was always part of the plan from the off.'

'Arrests?'

'One of the gang, a right little shit called Dylan Lee, was picked up a couple of days after the attack, thanks to some DNA he'd left at the scene. There was nothing to point the finger at Bryony and her dodgy boyfriend, and Lee refused to name the others. We're pretty sure Bryony and Paul were there, but without any evidence, we can't prove anything.'

'But you spoke to Bryony? And her boyfriend?'

'They were formally interviewed, but they alibied each other. So apart from the description of Bryony – which, to be honest, could fit about half a dozen other girls her age – we have nothing concrete that would have linked her to the robberies.'

Denning sipped his drink and thought about what Anna had just told him. He tried to fit all the pieces together in his head. 'What did you mean when you said it was only a matter of time before Bryony came a cropper? You thought someone was going to kill her?'

She gave an awkward laugh. 'No. Well, maybe not murder, admittedly. But I can't honestly say it's come as a huge shock.'

'Go on.'

She sipped some more of her drink and looked out to the river. 'Dylan Lee was attacked last week. He got a right pasting by all accounts: a few broken ribs, cracked skull; nothing life-threatening but he spent a couple of nights in hospital. Naturally enough he's keeping his nasty little gob sealed over who did it – and why – but we reckon he knows all right.'

'Suspects?'

'Clever money's on the other gang members. Lee being lifted for the attack on Mrs Heaton would have been enough to spook them. It's only a matter of time until we find something to link him to the others. We're almost certainly talking about a manslaughter charge. We'd ideally like to go for a murder charge, but we'd have to make sure the CPS would buy it.'

'You think the beating was a warning to make sure he keeps his mouth shut?'

Another shrug. 'That's a definite possibility.'

'And Bryony? Could the same people have gone after her?' If that had been the case, he thought to himself, someone had gone to pretty extreme lengths just to stop her talking to the police.

Anna shook her head. 'Who knows? There was no suggestion that they were likely to talk. We got nothing from either of them when we interviewed them and there was no indication they were likely to change their story. I mean, as soon as any further evidence came our way we'd have taken them in again, and maybe then there was a chance then that Bryony might have said something if we'd piled on the pressure. I would have argued that she was the weakest link in the chain.' She let out a sigh. 'We'll never know now.'

'Could there be a drugs connection?' he asked.

'Gangs like that, there's inevitably going to drugs involved somewhere. Either users or dealers. Or both. Bryony's been an addict since she was a teenager. Paul too. That's probably why they got in with the gang: the lure of easy money. At least it might have seemed that way at first. Valerie Heaton's death may have changed things. There's a good chance Bryony and Paul realised they'd got in over their heads and wanted out, and that wouldn't have gone down well with the rest of the gang.' She tilted her glass at Denning. 'Another possible motive for you.'

Denning sipped his pint and thought about this. The sheer brutality of what had been done to Bryony suggested there was more to her murder than a falling out between fellow gang members. But if drugs were involved, that meant big money. And more than likely there would be scarier and nastier people further up the chain who wouldn't take kindly to the gang attracting attention to themselves. If the attack on Dylan Lee hadn't had the desired effect, perhaps they'd felt the need to take things further with Bryony? Then again, it could just be a coincidence... 'How can you be sure Bryony and Paul were part of this gang?' he asked. 'You said yourself, all you really have to go on is a vague description of a young woman who might or might not have been Bryony.'

'Luckily that's not my worry any more. Bryony's your problem now, and good luck sorting that out.' She drained her glass and got up from the table. 'Time for another?'

He nodded. 'Yes, go on. I've nothing much to hurry home for.' He asked her to get him the same again.

'Why don't we get something to eat?' she suggested. 'There's a menu on the table.'

Denning watched as she headed back into the bar, then he turned and looked out onto the river. The sun was low in the west now, casting its warm glow along the Thames and turning it into a wide expanse of glistening silver. He should Skype Sarah when he got home. She was in New York, which was five hours behind, meaning it would be early afternoon over there. It might be better to wait until closer to bedtime...

He picked up a menu and perused the list of food on offer.

Chapter Nine

When Molly arrived home later that evening, Billie Eilish was playing in the living room. 'When I Was Older'. Not one of Jon's. Or hers. It meant they had company.

Home was a Victorian terraced house halfway along an anonymous street in Crouch End, which she shared with Jon. She closed the front door behind her and sighed. She had been hoping for a quiet evening. A glass of something chilled and *Emmerdale* on the telly. Instead, she was going to have to smile and chatter and make an effort to be sociable.

Jon was sitting on the bare wooden floor in the centre of the untidy living room. There was a young woman sitting opposite, her legs tucked under her body, her iPhone plugged into the sound system. She was in her early twenties and very pretty. They both looked up when Molly poked her head round the door.

'Hi, Molly. Rowan just called round to chat about the wedding plans and look through some old photos. I said she might as well stay for tea.'

Molly spotted a couple of old-fashioned, leather-bound photo albums lying open on the floor. Faded colour pictures looked up at her. One or two were even in black and white. They really were unearthing the family history in some detail.

She could smell the heady tang of dope in the air, even though Jon had promised to stop using it, for now. Or it could have been Rowan, but she didn't think so. Marijuana had always been Jon's drug of choice. At least he'd had the good grace to get rid of the evidence before she got back from work. The ashtray on the coffee table looked like it had recently been wiped clean.

Molly smiled back at Jon's daughter and asked how she was. 'Fine, thanks. Busy day. How are you guys?' She'd met Rowan, briefly, a few days ago when she'd knocked on the door and asked to speak to Jon, explaining awkwardly who she was. Quickly sussing out Molly and trying to guess how she fitted into her and her father's life. Molly had arranged to meet Trudi and some other friends for a drink in the West End, so their interaction had been brief. But now she was here again, making herself at home. She'd always known that Jon had a daughter, though she'd never been a part of their lives until now. Jon had been almost forty when they'd met, so it was to be expected he would have baggage. It shouldn't have bothered her, and yet increasingly these days she found herself thinking more and more about how little she really knew Jon.

'Come in and sit down,' Rowan said. 'We're discussing the wedding.'

Jon poured Molly a cup of tea.

'I've asked Dad to give me away.' Billie Eilish finished and Sam Smith came on. A song she didn't recognise.

Jon sat there beaming like a cat that had scoffed the cream; he passed Molly her tea. Molly perched on the edge of the sofa and took a sip. The tea was lukewarm and Jon had added too much milk. She'd much rather have opened a bottle of wine.

'Not long now,' Molly said. 'Have you got butterflies?'

Rowan laughed. 'More like blind panic. There's still so much to do. Eli seems totally calm about the whole thing, but then he's pretty chilled at the best of times.'

Rowan's fiancé worked for an insurance company doing something so dull Molly couldn't recall what it was. Molly had yet to meet him, though Jon had been out for drinks and done the whole 'concerned father' act shortly after Rowan had come back into his life. He had ended up liking Eli apparently, so his prospective son-in-law had received Jon's parental seal of approval. But Jon either liked someone or he didn't. There was no in-between.

Jon sat between the two of them, nodding his agreement. He was happy for now, but Molly knew his depression bubbled away beneath the surface, like a dark, slithering serpent waiting for its time to strike. It wouldn't take much to push him back into the abyss of despair and gloom. Molly would have to find the energy to lift him out of it.

Jon had been estranged from his daughter for a number of years. Rowan was a product of Jon's second – and longest – marriage. He had recently found out that she was getting married and had fought hard to be allowed back into her life, despite the insistence from her mother that Jon was no longer part of their lives, and hadn't been for some time.

'Jon tells me you're a detective,' Rowan said, still smiling. 'That must be challenging.'

Molly laughed. 'It's certainly that, all right. Some days more so than others.'

'You enjoy it though?'

She was unsure if that was a question or a statement, but she confirmed that she enjoyed the job, even if there were days when she wasn't sure.

Rowan now worked for a marketing company based in Covent Garden having spent several years living in France. That much Molly knew. Jon had been light about the details when he'd told her.

'Molly was promoted to the Major Investigation Team last year,' Jon said. She could tell he was proud of her achievement, even if he'd never actually said so. 'She spends her days catching murderers.'

'Cool,' Rowan said. 'Keeping the streets safe from psychos and serial killers.'

Molly smiled, even though she was sure the smile hadn't reached her eyes. 'It's not as much fun as it sounds. We found the body of a young woman this morning; murdered, tortured and mutilated in the most horrific manner,' she said coldly. 'And she wasn't much younger than you.'

Rowan looked at Molly and gave an embarrassed laugh. 'God. That's horrible.'

Molly immediately felt bad and wished she hadn't said anything. Rowan probably hadn't intended her remark to sound as flippant as it had. 'Sorry. I didn't mean that to come out the way it did.' She smiled again. 'Ignore me. Bad day.'

Although she was closer in age to Rowan than she was to Jon, Molly felt like she was chatting to a kid. But perhaps that was unfair. She didn't dislike Rowan – there was nothing about her that could provoke anything other than fondness – but it was hard trying to underplay the awkwardness they both felt around each other: two women fairly close in age who shared the very different affections of the same man, whilst pretending there was nothing strange about the situation. She really should take the time to get to know Rowan. If they hadn't just found themselves at the start of a murder investigation, then she might have been tempted.

'There was something on the news about that,' Jon said. 'Body was found in a churchyard, wasn't it? Sounds like this could be quite a big case.'

'Let's not dwell on it,' Molly said. 'I'd rather not talk about work.' When they'd first met, Jon had been a journalist with the *London Echo*. Redundancy a couple of years ago had left a hole in his life, which he now filled with writing and teaching. However, even though he was no longer a journalist, there were times she felt his antennae were still tuned to look out for a potential story. For so long in their relationship she'd had to be careful never to discuss work; or if she did, make sure she was always light on details.

'Suits me,' Rowan said.

Yet, despite her words, Molly found her mind wandering on to the murder investigation that had kicked off that morning. It felt uncomfortable to be chatting about murder as though it was nothing more than a prurient subject for gossip. In reality, it meant some family's life had been torn apart and would probably never heal, not properly. And this murder today... The brutality of it disturbed her. The photos pinned to the board in the incident room would occupy her dreams tonight. She had a bad feeling about this case.

'Mum's fretting about everything,' Rowan said, the conversation having moved on while Molly's mind had been occupied with more serious matters. 'She likes to worry, though. It gives her something to do.'

'How is Jenna?' Jon asked. Relations between him and his ex-wife were still chilly to say the least, but they had agreed to paint on a brave face at the wedding for Rowan's sake.

'Oh, you know Mum,' she said with an airy wave of her hand. 'Same old crazy woman.'

Molly smiled and stood up from the edge of the sofa. 'I think I'll make fresh tea. This stuff's pretty stewed.' She picked up the tea tray and headed into the kitchen.

In reality, she wanted to escape the claustrophobia of having to play happy families when she really didn't feel like it. She would be at the wedding, sitting there with Jon's family, trying her best to fit in despite feeling like an outsider.

She was happy that Jon's daughter was now back in his life. It was just what he needed to help keep the melancholy thoughts at bay. She still hadn't worked through her feelings about what Rowan's return to Jon's life meant for her. There was unlikely to be any real possibility of her being pushed out to make space for the daughter he had long since deleted from his life. But there was always the chance she would have to fight to be heard in the new family set-up. She instantly tried to dismiss the thought from her head.

She filled the kettle, switched it on and sat at the kitchen table.

Jon had welcomed Molly into his life and into his house. There was never a feeling that it was his house and she was the lodger. She'd suggested moving once, buying a place together that would be theirs rather than his. He'd been against the idea. The mortgage had been paid off, he'd insisted, so why go to all the hassle if they didn't have to? And besides, where would they move to?

She'd let the subject drop after that, settling into his house and gradually turning it into something that reflected her tastes as much as his: the odd throw here, a couple of pictures there; a smart, trendy rug for the back room, the one they used when they didn't have guests...

She'd always known about the previous wives. She even knew about the existence of a long-forgotten daughter. Jon was nearly forty when they'd got together. It was only natural he'd had a life before they'd met.

And she was happy to live with that, most of the time. But now things were changing. His family, for so long a buried part of his past, was now edging its way back into their lives. If she wasn't careful, Molly was going to find herself with a ready-made family. And she didn't know if she wanted that.

Not now.

And possibly not ever.

Chapter Ten

It was after ten when Denning arrived back at his flat; an airy loft apartment in trendy Shoreditch. He turned off the alarm and then headed up the spiral staircase to the main bedroom on mezzanine level, and then changed out of his suit and into something more casual.

He'd stayed at The Pear and Partridge for another couple of drinks after he and Anna had eaten. They'd chatted some more about work, but the conversation had inevitably moved on to the subject of Sarah and relationships. Anna had insisted she was happy being single and in no hurry to settle down. She'd said it with so much conviction it was as though she was trying to convince herself as much as Denning. But by the third pint he'd agreed to go to the cinema with her that Friday, a decision he was already regretting. He knew he had to make his feelings clear towards Anna. The only problem was that he had to get them clear in his head first.

He loved Sarah, and couldn't imagine them splitting up. Besides, he'd already lived through the pain and trauma of one divorce and hadn't the energy to relive the experience for a second time. However, he didn't want to throw out the wrong signals to Anna. He liked her. They had much in common. And it was always good to have someone to chat to about work issues. Someone who wasn't an immediate colleague.

He hurried to the laptop in the study and clicked on the Skype icon. He wanted to catch Sarah before she headed out to dinner, no doubt at some swanky restaurant. Once it was up on the screen, he quickly signed in, then found Sarah's name on the list of contacts and clicked the video button. It took a few seconds until her face appeared on the screen, her stylish and expensive hotel room forming a chic backdrop. She was looking harassed. Her gorgeous almond eyes flicking every so often to the clock at the bottom of her laptop.

'How's things?' he asked.

'Endless bloody meetings,' she said. 'But it looks like there might be an end in sight. I'm hoping I can get back this weekend, but I can't promise anything.'

'How's the Big Apple?'

'I haven't seen much of it so far, to be honest. Just the journey from the hotel room to the office. We went out for dinner last night, but it was nothing special. How are you?' Even though he could hear her clearly, she was still shouting. That was Sarah's default way of talking to people who weren't in the same room as her. And sometimes even if they were.

'Yes, good. Nothing exciting to report.' He didn't mention the murder investigation that had just been launched; there was no point. She was over three thousand miles away, and had never taken more than a cursory interest in his work anyway. But to be fair, he hadn't taken too much of an interest in hers either.

'How's Jake?'

Denning nodded and smiled. 'Jake's well. He sends his love.' In truth, he hadn't seen his son for a while. Claire, his ex-wife, had left a message asking him to return her call. But he knew what it was about and he knew it was going to lead to another argument. One that would inevitably use up a lot of spare energy he didn't have. 'I miss you,' he said, though he wasn't entirely sure why he'd felt the need to say it. They were neither of them especially needy, which had been part of the attraction between them in the first place. But the flat was large and he missed her presence about the place; someone to talk to when he came home from work; someone to eat dinner with, and someone to share the empty king-sized bed.

'Miss you too,' she said. 'I'll be home soon.' He sure he could hear another voice in her room. A woman's voice, at least, suggesting it belonged to a work colleague.

They finished the call, with Sarah apologising that she had a dinner meeting lined up with some American clients and had to change into something presentable before heading out.

He headed into the vast open-plan living area that took up most of the flat. He was tempted to grab a bottle of beer from the fridge but he'd already exceeded his quota for a weekday. Plus, his head was already starting to throb. The mortuary awaited first thing tomorrow morning: the post-mortem results. He would have to cut down on the booze. He needed a clear head for the next few days.

He wandered over to the french doors leading to the tiny patio and looked out at the view over East London. The flat was an airy loft conversion at the top of an old wine warehouse in Shoreditch, at the point where the City ran into the old East End. It was totally beyond his pay scale, and if it wasn't for Sarah heading an investment portfolio for a merchant bank, there was no way he'd be living there.

But he *was* living there. And he appreciated how lucky he was. Did he want to jeopardise this by having a silly fling? He couldn't deny his attraction to Anna. If circumstances were different he might have been tempted to go down that route.

He knew he would have to speak to Claire at some point. She wanted to talk about Jake and his future. Jake had autism and ADHD. He'd been coping well enough at a mainstream school for the past few years, but his interaction with other children was never good. His teacher had noticed a deterioration in his behaviour over the past year and had suggested the possibility of moving him into a specialist school. Claire was keen to explore their options, arguing that it was about whatever was in Jake's best interests. Denning, however, had his reservations. Special school meant singling Jake out as being different. They were going to have to have a proper talk about this, maybe even ask Jake what he wanted, assuming he knew. There were times he wished his domestic life wasn't so complicated. A little more 'picture perfect', like his brother's; a nuclear family cemented on the foundations of a strong marriage. He knew his parents looked at their two sons with a warm glow of admiration for one, and a secret note of concern and disappointment for the other.

He continued to gaze out over the view of East London. The last thin flickers of daylight had already faded, and London was awash with the artificial glow of streetlights now.

He thought about McKenna. There was clearly something troubling her and he suspected it was unlikely to go away. McKenna was a good DCI, despite her flaws. He relied on her as much as he relied on the rest of his team. She would need to be fully focussed on the job for the duration of the murder investigation, otherwise the entire house of cards would come crashing down. He was going to have to say something; tact being the operative word. But a distracted DCI wasn't in anyone's best interests.

It was getting chilly now, the warmth of the day evaporating as quickly as it had arrived. He went inside and closed the French doors behind him. He looked around the flat: it was airy and elegant, but without Sarah it just felt like a fashionable show home.

He thought again about Anna. They were getting close, no matter how much he tried to steer their friendship away from the choppy waters of something messy.

At some point he was going to have to make a difficult decision.

His thoughts turned to Bryony Allen. He kept thinking about Carly Allen's words: *I'm sorry for what happened to Bryony… but I can't help thinking she's somehow brought this on herself.*

How did someone bring torture, murder and mutilation on themselves?

He realised they were dealing with a dangerous psychopath, who was murdering young women. He had to find that killer as a matter of urgency. His private life would have to take a back seat for now.

Chapter Eleven

Denning pushed open the heavy glass doors to the mortuary suite after he'd been buzzed in. The mortuary was located in the basement of University College Hospital near Euston, where parking was always something of a lottery. He'd been lucky and had found a space that was less than a five-minute walk from the building.

The mortuary was air-conditioned to the point of being chilly. Denning had never quite managed to feel entirely comfortable in its antiseptic environment, or with the overpowering smell of disinfectant that somehow seemed to graft itself onto the skin whenever he had to visit.

Dr Baker was finishing off the post-mortem on Bryony Allen. He was talking into a microphone and issuing instructions to his assistants. The whole process was being videoed as per the new Home Office instructions regarding the autopsies of murder victims.

Denning tapped lightly on the glass partition that separated the main post-mortem suite from the outer viewing area. Baker nodded his acknowledgement and gestured for Denning to wait in the cramped office at the end of the corridor.

There were only two seats in the small space: Baker's, which was behind his desk, and another one against the wall. The room consisted of white-washed, breeze-block walls, a small sink. Apart from the desk and two chairs, the only other furniture was a metal filing cabinet that stood in a corner near the desk. The room was illuminated by a single strip light.

Liam Allen had come down the previous evening to formally ID the body. Her ankle tattoo and a strawberry birthmark on her lower back had been enough to confirm that it was Bryony. He'd been spared the horror of having to look at the damage to her face.

A few minutes later, Baker joined Denning in the office and took the seat behind his desk.

He'd removed his scrubs and mask, but hadn't yet changed back into civvies. It was very likely he had another post-mortem to perform straight after this one.

Baker was a heavy-set man in his late fifties, with a round, slightly pugnacious-looking head, topped with a mane of unruly greying hair, which was still tied beneath his protective headwear. Someone had told Denning that Baker had once played rugby at county level in his youth, something Denning – who had played for his school's First XV – appreciated.

'This was a nasty one, Matt. And believe me I've seen my share of unpleasantness over the years. Burns victims; road accidents, and the endless round of murders, stabbings and shootings. You name it, I've had them on my table. But *this*...' He searched for the word. 'This is just *vicious*.'

'Vicious?' Denning raised his eyebrows. 'Care to elaborate...?'

'I'll email you the video later today, along with my official report, which will detail my findings. There is one small crumb of comfort: I can confirm that our victim was not sexually assaulted before or after she was killed.'

'Interesting,' Denning said. 'That could be significant.'

'Unfortunately, that's where the good news ends,' Baker added, giving his eyes a massage. 'What *was* done to that poor girl was horrific. There are numerous burn marks on her arms and legs, most likely caused by a cigarette judging by the size and shape of the wounds, as well as several lacerations resulting from the arms and legs having been slashed by a bladed instrument, in all probability a knife of some sort. None of those particular knife wounds are especially deep, however, and the cigarette burns, whilst significant, are unlikely to have contributed to her death.' He paused for a moment, letting the full impact of his words sink in. 'Livor mortis tells us the time of death was between twenty-four and thirty-six hours ago. I can't be more exact because of the condition of the body, but if you had to pin me down, I would say closer to thirty-six hours than twenty-four. And definitely not more than thirty-six.'

'So sometime between late evening on June second and the early hours of June third,' Denning said, making a mental note. At least now they had an accurate window around which to work.

'Cause of death was a single stab wound to the heart,' Baker continued. 'A bladed instrument, non-serrated, approximately eight inches long. Almost certainly the same one that had been used to inflict the more superficial stab wounds. Death would have been mercifully quick, considering the amount of suffering she must have endured by then.' Baker took a deep breath before continuing. 'And then there's her face.' He shook his head slowly. 'That what really concerns me. The burn marks on the limbs are, like the stab wounds, mostly superficial, comparatively speaking I mean. But the marks on her face are indicative of something much more extreme.'

'More extreme than cigarette burns?' Denning wasn't sure where Baker was going with this.

'The condition of the flesh is consistent with a small but relatively intense application of heat administered at close range,' Baker said. 'And very probably done over a prolonged period of time. I'll be able to go into greater detail in the post-mortem report, but I would say those burn marks were caused by some kind of naked flame.'

'Specifically?'

Baker stroked his chin. 'I'm afraid I can only speculate there. A lighter maybe, or a Bunsen burner...'

Denning was incredulous. 'And this was done while she was still alive?'

'It's impossible to say for certain. It could have been done post-mortem as some crude attempt to remove any distinguishing features, though they clearly missed the birthmark and the tattoo elsewhere on the body. In addition, some of her hair has been pulled out at the roots, though this could have occurred when the body was moved to the disposal site.' He nodded gravely at Denning. 'Taking into account everything that's been done to her, I'd say our victim was extensively tortured before she was killed. We're clearly dealing with a sadist here, Matt.'

'A sadist, or a maniac,' Denning said, airing his thoughts aloud.

'Is there a difference?' Baker asked.

'A sadist does it for fun. A maniac doesn't know when to stop.'

But Denning had a niggling feeling that there was something else going on here. Something he was missing.

'You're certain the cause of death was a single stab wound to the heart?' he asked.

'Absolutely. She would probably have died from the torture-related wounds eventually, but the puncture wound to the heart would have resulted in a quick death.'

'Which is strange.'

'How?'

'Everything else was brutal, messy even. Almost as though whoever did it enjoyed inflicting pain for the sake of it. The actual killing itself feels neat. Almost prosaic by comparison. It's like our killer had had his fun and needed to end her life as efficiently and as unemotionally as possible.'

'I can only tell you what I found when I examined the body, Matt. Anything else is over to you.' Baker glanced at his watch, signalling to Denning that he had more bodies awaiting his attention. 'There is one more thing, though I don't know if it's in any way significant. I found evidence of historical drug use. There were needle marks on her wrists, but no evidence of heroin in her bloodstream. Nor any other illegal substance for that matter. None of the needle marks looked to be recent, so I'd suggest she'd either given up or had certainly not been using for the past few months.'

'So she was clean?'

'She had been for a while.'

Denning thanked him and made his way outside. As he left the mortuary, blinking at the sunlight that immediately greeted him, he couldn't help thinking that Bryony Allen's post-mortem had thrown up more questions than answers.

Chapter Twelve

The Lydon Arms was closed when Molly called round the next morning. She looked through the window and saw the same woman as the previous evening setting up the bar. She tapped on the window and waved. She could see the woman sighing, then reluctantly coming out from behind the bar to unlock the door.

'We're not open yet,' she said, looking Molly squarely in the eye, giving no indication that she recognised her from the night before.

'I was here yesterday evening,' Molly said, prompting her. 'I need to speak to you.' The woman stood in the pub's doorway; a defiant look on her face. When she could see the woman wasn't going to budge, Molly flashed her ID, adding: 'I'm a police officer, and this is in connection with a murder investigation.' She didn't say anything about being there unofficially, or explain that she was following up on a hunch. She would clear things with Denning if anyone in the bar were to take things further, but for now there was something about The Lydon Arms that made her want to ask some questions, even though she wasn't convinced she was going to get any answers.

It took a full moment before the woman stepped back and let Molly in. There was a cleaner pottering round near the toilets and a mound of deliveries waiting by the bar.

'Do you mind if I carry on with this?' the woman said, indicating the deliveries.

'No, that's OK, I just need to ask you a few questions about the woman I was talking to last night? She said her name was Kelly-Ann. Do you know who she is, or how I can get hold of her?'

'Not a clue,' the woman said, dumping a crate of beer on the bar top and removing the bottles one at a time. 'I've never seen her before last night.'

Molly didn't believe her. 'Really? You gave me the impression you knew her. You said you should bar her but you felt sorry for her. Why would you say that if you didn't know her?' Molly had a chance to fully acknowledge the woman now. She looked like she was slightly older than Molly, maybe mid-thirties. Her spiky blonde hair gave her a slightly impish appearance, and she wore large, gaudy earrings that looked like bright red ceramic foetuses. She was certainly no friendlier today than she had been the previous evening.

'I recognise the type, don't I?' she said. 'I've been working in pubs since I was eighteen. I know a ponce when I see one.'

'So last night was the first time you've seen her in this bar? She's never been in before?'

'That's what I said, didn't I.'

'OK. It's just I got the impression she'd been here before. She seemed familiar with the place.' She looked at the woman who ignored her and continued taking bottles from the crate. 'Did you happen to see if she left alone or if there was anyone with her?'

'I was too busy serving you at the time.' She put the bottles down and looked at Molly. 'Look, you're wasting your time here, love. She was just some sad old alky who was trying to blag a free pint off you. I expect you're not the first person she's tried it on with, and I doubt you'll be the last. I wouldn't take it personally.'

'I'm not taking it personally. I just need to speak to her again.'

'I've told you: you're wasting your time.'

'Thanks for the advice, but I think I'm the best judge of that.' Molly tried smiling at the woman. 'I'm so sorry, I don't think I got your name.'

The woman returned to her bottling up, trying her best to be oblivious to Molly. 'Deena,' she said eventually. 'Deena Jackson.'

'And how long have you worked here, Deena?'

She stopped what she was doing and looked at Molly: a no-nonsense look that said she'd dealt with everything from nosy cops to abusive drunks, and had yet to find someone who could intimidate her. 'I've been here three years. And I still don't know who that bloody woman was you was chatting to last night.'

'OK, Deena, what about the names Paul Chitterly and Bryony Allen? Do they ring a bell?'

She shook her head. 'Never heard of them.'

'What about the name Rob? Know any Robs?'

'I know a few. What of it?'

'Would any of them know Kelly-Ann? Or Paul Chitterly or Bryony Allen?'

'No they wouldn't. Why would they? I told you, even I don't know who these bloody people are.'

Molly didn't believe her. But she sensed she was unlikely to get any further information from Deena Jackson unless she were to formally question her, and even then it was unlikely she would get anything close enough to the truth to be of any use.

73

'I believe Paul Chitterly drinks here. He arranged to meet me here last night. And I suspect Bryony Allen used to as well. Until she was murdered.' She was starting to worry about Paul. She hadn't heard from him and there was a real concern something might have happened to him.

Deena Jackson's left eyebrow twitched slightly at the mention of Bryony's murder, but there was little else in the way of a reaction. 'I'm sorry to hear that someone's been murdered. And I'm sorry you were stood up last night, but I can't help you. I'm really busy, and unless you come back here with some kind of warrant or whatever it is you lot need to harass people in an official capacity, then I'm going to have to ask you to leave.'

She stood there, behind the bar, hands on hips, defying Molly to challenge her, letting her know she'd kick up all kinds of shit if Molly didn't do things by the book. Molly knew she was clutching at straws. What did she have on The Lydon Arms? A vague connection with Paul and Bryony, and some drunk woman who claimed she knew what happened to Bryony but – even if they did find her – would be anything but a reliable witness?

'OK,' Molly said, pushing her card across the bar. 'If you do think of anything, Deena, or you decide you'd like to start being more helpful, give me a call.'

She showed herself out. As the door closed behind her she could hear the sound of bottles clanking and she just knew the card was going to sit on the bar, ignored, until she was gone, and then find its way into the nearest bin.

She looked up and down Holloway Road. It was already getting busy: buses jostling with taxis and vans; a delivery driver dropping something off at a mini-supermarket on the other side of the road. She was certain

Kelly-Ann must live nearby, but with only a first name and a vague description to go on, what were her chances of finding her?

Chapter Thirteen

'It's now been confirmed that Bryony Allen wasn't sexually assaulted. However, there is evidence that she had been tortured before she was killed.' Denning was addressing the team. Baker had emailed through the post-mortem results, which had been printed off and copies handed to every officer in the room. Most pairs of eyes had scanned over the details and only digested the summary on the last two pages. It told them all they needed to know. 'We now know she was murdered sometime late on Sunday June second or in the early hours of Monday third. The level of brutality involved,' he continued, 'tells us that the person we're dealing with is ruthless and extremely dangerous.'

'And now we're counting down the days until this nutter strikes again,' Kinsella said, an I-told-you-so look spreading across his face like a nappy rash. There were times when Kinsella tried Denning's patience. Now was one of those times.

'While we remain alert to the possibility there's a serial offender out there,' Denning said coldly, 'we also keep all other options on the table.'

'Like what?' Kinsella asked.

'If we rule out a sexual motive,' Denning argued, 'then the whole torture scenario becomes about something else entirely.'

'What are you thinking, boss?' Neeraj asked.

'I don't know... Revenge? Punishment?' He looked around the team: Kinsella was shaking his head; Neeraj looked confused. Molly Fisher and Trudi Bell looked like they were waiting for a punchline.

'Whoever did this,' Denning continued, 'must have taken their time. Presumably Bryony was held somewhere soundproofed and not overlooked while she was being tortured. That takes planning and a degree of level-headedness. Our killer knew exactly what they were doing. They're organised.'

Molly Fisher raised her hand. 'From what you're saying, is it possible Bryony Allen could have been deliberately targeted in some way?'

Denning took this as his cue to share what Anna had told him about Bryony. 'I've spoken to someone at Islington CID,' he said. 'Bryony was part of a gang that deliberately targeted elderly people, assaulting and robbing them in their own homes. Their last victim was seriously injured and died in hospital just over a week ago. The gang was also believed to have been involved in drug dealing. We have to explore the possibility that's somehow connected to what happened to Bryony.'

'A falling-out among thieves?' Trudi asked. 'But to do *that* to her? It's barbaric!'

'Which is why my money's still on this being the work of a nutter,' Kinsella said. He cast his gaze around the room. 'I know no one sitting here wants to admit it, but we're looking for a psycho serial killer here, and we'd all better get used to the idea.'

Denning spotted Trudi muttering something under her breath, while Molly rolled her eyes. Denning waited for Kinsella to pipe down. But he wasn't finished yet...

'Just look at those injuries,' Kinsella continued as everyone in the room turned to look at the photos on the whiteboard. 'That isn't the work of someone normal. If we're going down the route of a revenge attack, or a falling-out between members of their scummy gang, then it would have been a beating, or a gunshot to the head. Someone who took their time mutilating that poor cow. This is down to a psycho.' He glanced around the room, ensuring he had everyone's attention. 'Come on, we're all thinking it.'

Denning fixed him with an impatient stare. 'Like I said before, Dave: until we know otherwise, we keep an open mind.' He noticed Molly was indicating she wanted to speak. 'Molly?'

'I don't want to piss on Dave's chips, but I have a feeling this does have something to do with the gang they were involved with.' There was a brief pause until she continued. Dave Kinsella gave another shake of his head. 'I was supposed to meet up with Chitterly again yesterday evening,' Molly said. 'He phoned me to say he had something to tell me. Unfortunately, he was a no show. I realise I should have made that official, but I was frightened about scaring him off.'

'OK, Molly, chase that up,' Denning said quickly. Molly Fisher was a good detective and he'd always admired her single-minded determination to follow up on a lead. But sometimes she cut corners and didn't do everything by the book. He had a horrible feeling it might ultimately be her undoing. 'Get back on to Paul Chitterly,' he continued. 'Find out just how involved he and Bryony were with this gang, and what the score was with them. Keep emphasising that we're only interested in Bryony's murder at this stage, and any crimes he and Bryony may or may not have been involved in are only relevant if they are in any way connected with her murder.'

'Does that include drug dealing, robbery and manslaughter?' Kinsella asked, the sarcasm clear in his voice.

'If any of it turns out to be relevant to Bryony's murder, Dave, then yes. Otherwise, it's not our concern. We can pass anything interesting over to the local CID and let them handle it, but at this stage our primary focus is finding Bryony's killer. I'll have a word with my contact at Islington CID, Molly. It might be worthwhile liaising with her. She's familiar with the gang's MO, and would be useful at providing a bit of background. But definitely speak to Paul Chitterly again. If he is frightened of someone, find out who and why. In the meantime, how did we get on with the house-to-house enquiries?' Denning asked. 'And have we found any usable CCTV footage from the streets around the church?'

'Nothing useful as yet,' Trudi said, surreptitiously slipping on her reading glasses in the vain hope no one else spotted her doing it. 'There's little or no CCTV in the streets next to the church, and any private door-cam footage only covers driveways and the pavements immediately in front of houses. It's almost as though our killer chose the churchyard to dispose of the body precisely because it's so tucked away. But we'll keep looking and we'll widen the search area if necessary.' She sighed and looked through her notes. 'According to uniform, the only faintly useful bit of info came from a man in his seventies who lives in the next street to the church. He claims he heard a car reversing in the early hours on the morning Bryony's body was discovered. However, he couldn't give an exact time, or confirm what kind of car it was. Or if it even was a car. It could have been a van.' She looked at Denning, quickly whipping off her glasses and slipping them back into the case on her desk. 'We'll extend the search area, but that's going to take time.'

'OK. Keep trying. Somebody has to have seen or heard something. What about social services and Bryony's school? Have we spoken to them yet?'

'I've spoken to Bryony's old school. It's the usual sad story: seems Bryony was a frequent truant. By all accounts, she used to hang around with a dodgy crowd that were constantly in and out of trouble, on the rare occasion when they actually attended school. Most of them were expelled at some point.'

'What about social services?' Denning asked.

Trudi looked at her notes. 'Just confirmed what we already know. She was placed in the care of her father and step-mother after her mother's death. As soon as she was sixteen she left and moved in with some friends in Walthamstow. That's when she fell off the radar. Social services checked with Liam and Carly Allen a couple of times, but all seemed to be well.'

'That does seem to contradict what Carly Allen told us,' Neeraj said.

'It's entirely possible she and Liam painted a rosier picture of family life for social services' benefit,' Denning said. 'Then again, I did get the impression they both tried to make things work with Bryony,' he added. 'At least at first.'

'We're overlooking another possibility, boss,' Neeraj said. 'If Bryony and Paul were involved with drugs, then we could be looking at a turf war. It's not unknown for these gangs to use torture as a means of controlling their own crew and threatening rival gangs.'

'Good point, Deep. Let's look over similar cases to see if there's anything to link this to a turf war over drugs. See if the MO fits any known gangs in the area. Also, let's look into this gang Bryony and Paul were part of. See if they have links to any known drugs gangs.' Denning turned to Kinsella. 'Dave, as you're so certain this is the work of a serial killer, get looking at any similar cases from recent years, particularly focussing on murders where torture or mutilation have featured. Also, check out any offenders who have recently been released from prison. See if their profile fits our killer. Deep can help.' He cast his eye around his team. 'But don't spend too much time on it. I think Bryony knew her killer, and I believe the reason she was killed has something to do with what was going on in her life, and was less likely to be down to her being the random victim of a serial killer.'

Of course, it was just possible he believed this because he wanted to. Because if he was wrong and Kinsella was right, then they were going to have to accept the possibility there was a dangerous psychopath at large in London, torturing and killing young women. And if that was the case, then their problems had only just started.

Chapter Fourteen

Denning tapped cautiously on McKenna's office door. There was no answer but he pushed the door open anyway.

McKenna was kneeling on the floor picking up pieces of a mug that was lying smashed on the floor in the middle of a tiny puddle of milky tea.

'Fuck! Fuck it! Fucking shit!'

He'd been at his desk when he'd heard the crash, followed by the swearing coming from the direction of McKenna's office. 'Look, let me do that.' He knelt down to help her. There was a red nick on her thumb where a sharp splinter had punctured the skin. A trickle of blood began to ooze out of it.

'The twatting thing slipped out my hand and smashed off the edge of the desk.'

The mug was in three pieces plus the handle. Denning placed the pieces in the wastepaper bin under her desk. He took a packet of paper hankies from his jacket pocket, opened it and handed her one.

'What's this for?'

'You've cut yourself.'

She looked at the blood on her thumb and started dabbing it with the tissue. Denning used another couple of tissues to mop up the spilt tea, most of which was already absorbing itself into the thin carpet.

McKenna sat behind her desk and took a deep breath through her nose. For a second, Denning thought she was going to burst into tears, but that would have been so out of character he would really need to call a doctor.

'It wasn't a favourite mug, was it?'

'Sorry?' She shook her head. 'No. Just something from the back of the kitchen cupboard.'

He sat opposite her, tossing the sodden tissues into the bin alongside the shattered shards of mug. 'It's just you seem…' He offered a smile. 'I can pop across to the Costa and get you another tea.' He knew this was going to involve tact and patience, but he wasn't going to leave her office until he'd found out what was biting her. This needed sorting.

'Look, Matt, I'm not bothered about the tea.' McKenna had a small kettle in her office, as – like most of the people who worked in the building – she didn't trust the coffee machine on the ground floor. On occasions, if she was in a generous mood, she would dust off the spare mug and make a cup for Denning.

'No.' He smiled again. 'Somehow, I don't think this is about a broken mug, either, is it?'

There was a pile of paperwork on her desk. She pushed it to one side. Monthly budget sheets and other admin. She'd ended up going to the tedious outsourcing meeting yesterday after all, while he was in a churchyard looking at what was left of Bryony Allen.

'Please tell me you've got some news about our latest ongoing murder investigation that's going to put a smile on my face.'

'We've got a couple of interesting leads we're currently pursuing. Bryony's boyfriend, Paul Chitterly, is of partic- ular interest to us. While we don't think he's responsible for Bryony's murder, DS Fisher suspects he knows more than he's admitting to. The drugs link is certainly worth looking into further.' He looked at her. He knew she needed to be kept up to speed with everything. Ultimately, as DCI, she was the one who took overall responsibility for the case. She was answerable to both senior management and the media, who would be chomping at the bit to know what was happening. 'But that's not why I popped in.' He leant on the desk and hoped he appeared relaxed, as though this was just two work colleagues having a friendly chat. 'Liz, is everything OK?' It felt strange calling his DCI by her first name, though she preferred it to guv or boss, or ma'am, which she specifically hated. To him, she was always McKenna, sometimes Betty Taggart, though he tended to avoid using the nickname if he could help it, out of some sort of nod towards respect for a superior officer.

'You mean apart from having a deranged killer on the loose?' she said, trying to make light of matters.

'Yes. Apart from that. Is everything OK?'

She sat back in her chair and rubbed a hand through her raven hair. 'I'm just tired. I'm still not sleeping well.'

'We've all been there. Being tired goes with the job.' He waited a moment before continuing. 'There's something else, isn't there?' He leaned forward on the desk and placed his hands on the edge, making sure he was looking her in the eye. 'Look, you can tell me to mind my own business. You can even tell me to fuck off if you like. But I get the impression there's something wrong, and if it affects you then it affects the team, and I think I have a right to know about it.'

A heavy silence filled the room. He waited for her to tell him where to go; to remind him that she was his DCI and whatever was on her mind was nothing to do with the job and therefore none of his concern. He was surprised when after a moment she simply said, 'Terry Myerson.'

The name didn't ring any bells, but she said it as though it should answer his question so fully that no further information was necessary.

'You're going to have to elaborate,' he said. 'Who is Terry Myerson, and what's he done to piss on your chips?'

McKenna shot him a gimlet stare, possibly taken aback by his out-of-character directness. Then she let out a heavy sigh, so heavy it bordered on being theatrical. 'You have to swear to keep this to yourself. I'll have your bollocks on a kebab skewer if this gets out.'

'I haven't developed a reputation as a gossip, and I don't plan to start now.'

She smiled. 'I'm sorry. I know you wouldn't discuss this with anyone, it's just…' She glanced round the office suddenly, and Denning thought it looked like she was worried the place might be bugged. 'Terry Myerson. He's with the National Crime Agency now. He is… *was* a friend.'

'Go on.'

She looked at him for a minute, fixing him with another of her gimlet stares that seemed to burrow into his soul. 'Myerson and I worked together years ago. We were based in Hounslow. He was a DS at the time I was promoted to DI. Terry specialises in undercover work. These guys are only supposed to go undercover for short periods, for their own mental health if nothing else. But Terry enjoyed the work. And he was good at it. He helped bring down an economic terrorist group about six years ago. They'd been planning to blow up a bank in the City somewhere. Real hardcore nutters. Terry had been with them for over a year, living with them, sleeping with them – literally in a couple of cases – all the time gathering enough information to bring them down...'

Denning was vaguely aware of the work of undercover operatives, but most of what they did was so shrouded in secrecy even their closest friends and family didn't know what the officers got up to half the time. He was also unsure what exactly qualified as being an 'economic terrorist', but he let that pass. 'So what's happened?'

'His handler contacted me last week. He's been getting in touch with everyone who knew Terry. Strictly on the QT. There's been no official contact with Terry for over two months now. He's supposed to report in on a regular basis.' Her hand ran through her hair again. 'His handler thinks it's possible he's got in too deep. It's not unheard of for undercover officers to drop off the radar for a time, especially if it's a big job. But not this long.'

'Do they know if he's still alive?'

'His mobile phone is no longer active. The last time it registered any activity was over a month ago.'

'So he could be dead?'

She shuddered slightly. 'He could be, though no body's turned up.' Her gaze shifted from Denning to the pile of papers on her desk. 'But that means nothing. If he is dead, then it's possible the people he's gone undercover with have been successful at disposing of it. Then again, he could just have got rid of his old phone and not got round to informing his handler that he's replaced it.'

'What about family?'

'He's divorced. Got a kid he rarely sees. Limited contact with his ex-wife. He's got a flat in Brighton which he's not been near for weeks. But that's not unusual for Terry; he often stays with friends in London when he's not working. None of them have heard from him either.'

'What does his handler say?'

'This is where it starts to get messy.' She frowned, then looked back up at Denning. 'This is all absolutely hush hush. Terry's been undercover with a notorious drugs gang for the past year. The bastard who runs that gang is called Jason Hart. The NCA have had an eye on him for some time, but he's clever and he's savvy. He runs it like a business: slick and professional. And ruthless.' Another heavy sigh. 'It gets worse. There's a chance Terry may have been involved in an incident earlier in the year.'

Denning looked at her, unsure where she was going with this. 'Incident?'

'About three months ago,' she continued, 'two members of a rival gang were found murdered in an abandoned hotel in Bromley. It had all the hallmarks of a gangland-style execution: slick and brutal. According to Terry's handler, this was Hart getting rid of the last of his competition.'

'What's the connection with Myerson?'

'His DNA was found on one of the victims.'

'That doesn't mean he was directly involved with their murders. There could be any number of reasons as to why his DNA got there.'

But he didn't believe that himself, and even McKenna didn't look convinced. 'Terry was always... *unpredictable*. There had been concerns that he might...' She tugged at her hair again; a sure sign of internal anxiety. 'There was always a real fear amongst some senior officers that he might eventually go rogue. He was something of a loose cannon. And we're talking about drug dealing on a massive scale here. There are huge sums of money involved in this operation. A decent-sized backhander could tempt even the straightest of cops over to the dark side. You've got to admit, it's quite an incentive.'

Denning felt some sympathy for McKenna. She was clearly worried, and perhaps with good cause. But apart from offering words of support, there was little he could realistically do to reassure her.

'My advice is to speak to his handler again,' he said. 'It's possible they've been in contact with him. Or at least, spoken to someone who has.'

He could tell from the look on her face she wasn't buying it.

'I reckon you're worrying about nothing,' he added.

But he wasn't sure he really believed that. Assuming Terry Myerson was still alive, there was a very real chance he was now in the employ of a dangerous criminal. Denning thought about the significance of this for McKenna. Did she feel any misplaced loyalty for Myerson? Would this compromise her? She was first and foremost a professional copper, and not one to let emotion muddy her decision making. Yet she was clearly behaving out of character. Perhaps he should take this further and mention it to their new DCS. Although that seemed unfair, and he wasn't comfortable at the thought of going behind McKenna's back, he couldn't have this investigation jeopardised because their DCI's mind wasn't fully on the job.

Denning offered her a reassuring smile before he headed back to his desk. 'Look, Myerson's probably just keeping his head down for a while. The murder in Bromley will have attracted attention from one of the South East London MITs, and he'll be waiting until the heat's off before he gets in touch again. Either way, you losing sleep over it isn't going to help anyone. Least of all yourself.'

Her focus had returned to the stack of paperwork on her desk. 'Let's hope you're right,' she said. 'Because the alternative doesn't bear thinking about.'

Chapter Fifteen

Paul Chitterly's face twisted itself into a pained expression the moment he opened the door and saw Molly standing on the threshold.

'What do you want?'

'Can I come in?'

He seemed to give the question some thought, then reluctantly pulled the door open.

'Have you caught Bryn's killer yet?' he asked when they were sitting in the messy living room. There was no offer of tea or coffee.

'We will,' she said. 'But we need a bit of help to fill in some of the gaps around Bryony's life. And I think you can help there, Paul.'

He affected a blank look. 'I've told you everything I know. I can't tell you what I don't know, can I?'

'I don't believe you, Paul. If that were true, why did you say you wanted to meet me yesterday after work? I waited for you in The Lydon Arms but you never turned up. How come?'

He picked at a loose piece of thread on the tatty armchair. 'I forgot.'

She shook her head. 'When are you going to start telling me the truth, Paul? I'm investigating the murder of your girlfriend and I gave you that card because I hoped you'd get in touch if there was anything you wanted to tell me that might be relevant.' She waited for her words to sink in, but there was no response. 'You told me you had information for me.'

'I lied,' he said a little too quickly. 'I just wanted to meet you for a drink. That's why I said the Lydon.'

Molly could tell from his body language alone that he was lying. There was some other reason why he'd changed his mind about meeting her last night. Or more likely, someone had changed it for him. One of the scummy gang members, probably; threatening him with a fate similar to Bryony's if he spoke to the police.

On the one hand, she should be glad nothing *had* happened to him and he was still in one piece. But on the other hand, she was tempted to arrest him for wasting police time. Instead, she thought she'd try a little psychology. She knew that Denning had a degree in psychology, which he always claimed helped him read people and second-guess how they were thinking. She'd spent enough time with him to know it was worth a try, especially if she had little else to work with. 'Paul, I think you do know something. OK, perhaps you don't know who killed Bryony, but I think you have a pretty good idea as to why she was killed. Am I right? And I think you wanted to tell me this last night. That's the real reason you phoned me and arranged to meet me at The Lydon Arms.'

He stared at the patch of carpet in front of the tatty armchair for so long he was in danger of burning a hole in it.

'If I'm wrong, tell me and I'll walk out that front door and won't bother you again. But if you want us to find whoever killed your girlfriend – and not just killed, Paul, but tortured and mutilated as well – you need to start telling me the truth about Bryony and the gang you both found yourselves entangled with. Because this isn't just going to go away. And if you have any fears that the person or people who did that to Bryony will come after you, then you have to stop treating me like a twat, Paul. I want to help you, but you have to meet me halfway.'

'I don't know who killed Bryn, or why. If I did, I'd tell you.'

'I went to The Lydon Arms last night, Paul. I spoke to a woman called Kelly-Ann. Does that name ring a bell with you? She seemed to know you and Bryony. She mentioned someone called Rob, but she left before she had a chance to tell me anything more. Who's Rob?'

He gave a low, guttural laugh. 'Kelly-Ann's off her head. No one takes any notice of her. Did she try and ponce a drink off you?' He looked at her, read her mind and smiled. 'Yeah, that sounds about right. She'd tell you the moon was made of cheese if she thought you wanted to hear it.'

'OK, so she persuaded me to buy her a drink. And she probably was trying it on, but she mentioned you and Bryony. Then she mentioned this bloke, Rob. She implied the two of you knew him, so who is he?'

There was more staring at the carpet, but Molly was patient. She wasn't going anywhere until she'd got the answers she'd come for, and Paul Chitterly knew it. It was just a question of calling his bluff.

Chitterly finally looked up from the faded carpet and looked at Molly. 'His name's Rob Jardine. He owns The Lydon Arms, and I think he owns another place in Harlesden somewhere. We used the Lydon to fence stuff we'd nicked.'

'And this Jardine bloke knew about this?'

'He'd take a percentage. The bar staff would turn a blind eye.'

'When you say you used The Lydon Arms to sell stolen goods, are you talking about the things you stole from the elderly householders you robbed?'

He looked sheepish. A slow nod of the head and his gaze dropped to the carpet again. 'That and other stuff. Bryn used to lift stuff from shops. Sometimes we'd nick from people's bags in pubs and on trains and the like.' He lifted his gaze from the floor and looked pleadingly at Molly. 'We were never really part of that gang, not seriously. Bryn knew Dill from way back. He said he'd cut us in for a piece if Bryn agreed to act as bait. When she told them she didn't want to do it anymore, they said she could act as lookout.' He shook his head. 'It was easy money.'

Not so easy for the people it affected, Molly thought. Their homes invaded; their peace of mind shredded forever at exactly the time in their lives when they needed it most. And by a bunch of kids who were too stupid or too selfish to care about the damage they inflicted on innocent people. 'How can we get hold of Rob Jardine?' she asked.

He shrugged. 'I dunno. He lives in North London somewhere. We only ever used to meet him at the Lydon. I think Bryn might have been to his house a few times.'

'Why would Bryn visit his house?'

He looked at Molly like she was an idiot. 'She was shagging him, wasn't she?'

'She told you this?'

'She didn't have to. I knew. At first she went with him when she needed to score and didn't have the cash. Then she just went with him because he would give her stuff. Nice stuff. Sometimes money, if we were short.'

'He's a dealer?'

'Not exactly.'

'What then?'

'He knows the dealers. Dylan put Bryn on to him. That's where they used to get their gear from. But Bryn wanted to come off that shit. She wanted to have kids. She knew she had to stop putting that shit inside her if she was going to be a mum.'

Molly's first thought was to pity any child that was brought up in this kind of environment: two petty criminals for parents, living in a dump. But then she knew it was unfair to judge. Bryony and Paul deserved just as much of a chance as anyone else to make a go of their lives. Now someone had deprived Bryony Allen of the chance to be a mother, and that was cruel. The thought of Bryony having prostituted herself to Rob Jardine, and Paul not only knowing about it but having no choice but to accept it, was a depressing one.

'So, just to confirm all this, you're saying The Lydon Arms was used for selling stolen goods and drug dealing, all with the owner's consent?'

He nodded. 'That's where she was. On Sunday. The day she was murdered. She was meeting Rob.'

'At The Lydon Arms?'

'I don't know. She just said she was going to meet Rob.'

'Did she say why?'

'She was going to ask him for money. She said he owed her.'

Suddenly a lot of things were making sense. They needed to speak to this Rob Jardine, and quickly. She reckoned he was someone who could offer a lot of answers.

All they had to do was find him.

Chapter Sixteen

The ball thudded off the wall an inch above the serve line with such ferocity that Denning nearly missed the return shot. He hadn't played squash for a good few years, and it showed. He hadn't seen Steve Marsh for almost as long. He hadn't changed much: thicker set; a bit greyer around the gills. Hair receding ever so slightly...

It had been Marsh's idea to meet for a game of squash, after insisting Denning had promised him a game the last time they'd met. Denning had once been a keen squash player, but either the game had got tougher or his fitness levels weren't as sharp as they used to be. His companion, though a couple of years older than him, was clearly in much better shape.

'You're getting slow, old man,' Marsh said, hitting the ball comfortably within the touchline to score the winning point.

Denning, who felt a noticeable twinge in his right shoulder, willingly conceded defeat.

Once in the changing room, they had a chance to properly catch up.

'How's life in MIT?' Marsh asked, stepping out of the shower and wrapping a towel round his waist.

'Yeah, still good,' Denning said. 'There's never a shortage of murders to keep us on our toes.'

Marsh laughed and began drying himself. 'And Claire?'

Denning realised it really had been a while since they'd last been in touch. He turned off the shower, grabbed his towel from the hook and joined Marsh in the changing area.

'Claire and I split up.' He opened his locker and removed his clothes and his gym bag, placing them carefully on the bench, then started drying himself. 'I'm married to Sarah now. She works for a merchant bank in the City. She's over in New York at the moment – work.'

Marsh was still drying himself. 'Cool. I'm with Freya these days. Can't remember if you met her. She was a SOCO based out in the wilds of Romford a few years back. Back in the days when they still called themselves SOCOs, rather than the sexier CSIs they prefer now. She's a university lecturer now: forensic science at UCL. Less money but better hours.' Marsh finished drying himself. He flicked a few droplets of water off his towel before throwing it over his shoulder. He began hauling his clothes from his locker then dumping them in a heap on the bench next to Denning's. 'We should all get together sometime.'

Denning recalled Marsh having had an endless string of girlfriends on the go at one time and refusing to commit to any of them. But then everyone had to grow up at some point.

Denning and Marsh had been DSs together with one of the South East London MITs based in Lewisham, until Marsh's ambition had taken his career in a different direction.

'How long have you been with the NCA now?' Denning asked.

'About four and a half years, give or take. Still being treated like a new boy.'

It was Denning's turn to laugh. The National Crime Agency had only been up and running for less than a decade. Set up by the then Home Secretary Theresa May, its remit was wide, covering everything from organised crime to child abuse. Although the NCA often worked in tandem with regional crime units and individual police forces, it was an autonomous body, answerable to its own director general. It was seen by some as being the UK's answer to the FBI.

Denning shook his towel, folded it and placed it neatly in a plastic bag before putting it into his gym bag. Marsh was already pulling on his clothes. 'Am I right in thinking Terry Myerson is one of your lot?' He tried to make it sound casual.

'Myerson? Dunno. Why do you ask?' Marsh sounded convincing, but the slight flickering around the eyes suggested he knew exactly who Denning was talking about.

'His name came up in conversation the other day. Someone mentioned he was with the NCA. I thought you might have heard of him.' He stood and watched as Marsh buttoned up his shirt. 'And I think, maybe, you have…'

Marsh finished buttoning up his shirt, then climbed into his trousers. He gave Denning a wry grin. 'Liz McKenna's your DCI, isn't she? Do people still call her Betty Taggart behind her back?'

Denning laughed again. 'They make sure it is behind her back.'

'You know she and Myerson had a thing?'

Denning hadn't. But it explained a lot. 'Really?'

'I'm going back a good few years now. Tel was still married at the time, and I think she might have been too.

98

I can't remember the details. I only met her once. She looked like she ate bollocks for breakfast, but Tel seemed keen enough on her.'

Denning slipped on his trousers, followed by his shirt.

'According to McKenna, nobody seems to have heard from Myerson for a while. There are rumours he might have gone rogue.'

Marsh laughed. 'There are always rumours about undercover officers. Why should Tel boy be any different?' Marsh was dressed now. He stuffed his sports gear and damp towel into his gym bag, zipped it shut, then leant against the lockers waiting for Denning to finish dressing.

'What are your thoughts on Myerson? Trustworthy? Dodgy?' Denning stood in front of the mirror massaging gel into his thick, blond hair. He wasn't going to mention what McKenna had said about Myerson's previous character. He wanted a fresh opinion from Marsh. 'Could he have gone rogue?'

Marsh sighed. 'You know I can't talk about an ongoing case, Matt.'

'But just say… Just say you had concerns. What then?'

Marsh laughed again. 'This is Betty Taggart, isn't it? She's heard a rumour and put two and two together to make twelve.'

Denning wiped his hands on a paper towel, then put on his linen jacket. He was keeping quiet about Myerson's DNA pitching up at a murder scene. Let's see how much Marsh knew. 'But if this isn't just a product of DCI McKenna's paranoia, what then? He wouldn't be the first undercover officer to go rogue. They're either brainwashed by some persuasive ideology or tempted by the prospect of making some seriously easy money. Some of them even have kids with the very people they're supposed to be keeping tabs on.'

Another laugh. 'I don't think Tel's the paternal type somehow. He's already got one kid he never sees. I doubt he'd want to be saddled with another.'

'But the prospect of earning some serious cash by helping a drug dealer keep one step ahead of the law would be a tough offer to decline?'

He shrugged. 'Would you be tempted?'

'No. I joined the police because I believe in right and wrong.'

'Same here. And there's nothing to suggest Terry Myerson is any different.'

Denning zipped up his bag and threw it over his shoulder. They left the changing rooms and headed out through the sports centre's smartly carpeted reception area to the car park.

Once outside in the cool evening sunshine, Marsh turned to Denning. 'I'd drop this if I were you, mate. Whatever the score with Terry Myerson, it's not for you to break sweat over. Until my governor says there's a problem, then I'm cool with it all.' He touched Denning on the elbow. A gesture of friendship, but it could also have been seen as a tacit warning. 'Take a bit of free advice, Matt: don't go looking for problems. Wait until they find you, and then decide if they're worth stressing over.' He offered Denning a final smile before heading to his car. 'Can I persuade you to join me for a post-game pint? There's a not-too-shabby pub down the road, and I think we've earned it.'

Denning fumbled in his jacket pocket for his car key. 'Sorry, Steve, I've got to be somewhere. Catch you another time.' He watched as Marsh headed back to his car. A metallic grey Toyota Corolla parked under a tree. He waited until Marsh got into it and then drove off, raising his hand in acknowledgement as he passed.

He took his phone from his pocket and noticed there was another missed call from Claire. He couldn't keep putting off the inevitable. Sooner or later they were going to have to get together and come to a decision about Jake. But he had something else to do first. Another untidy part of his life that needed the creases ironed out.

As he got into the Focus, he wondered how his life had suddenly managed to become so complicated.

Chapter Seventeen

Anna Klein lived in Harringay, on a narrow one-way street that looked like it mostly consisted of flats and bedsits. Wheely bins sat in concreted gardens, and a continuous row of parked cars ran along one side of the road, while a faded double-yellow line ran down the other. He'd squeezed his Focus the full length of the street without seeing anywhere to park, before eventually finding a tight space in the next street.

Number 25b Bridgewater Road occupied the first floor of a pale-brick, flat-fronted terraced house situated roughly halfway along the street. Denning pressed the buzzer beside the main door and waited to be let in. The door to her flat was already ajar when he reached the top of the stairs. He lightly tapped on it and pushed it open.

The door opened onto a long rectangle of hallway. A part-glazed door to the left led to the living room at the front of the flat, while another two doors led, presumably, to a bedroom and a bathroom.

When Denning entered the living room, Anna was pottering in a tiny kitchen area in an alcove in the corner. The whole space was barely larger than the guest bedroom in his Shoreditch apartment.

'Do you want something to drink?' Anna asked. She'd changed out of the formal business suits she wore for work and was wearing a striped T-shirt and baggy jeans. Her hair was loose around her shoulders. 'I've got beer in the fridge.'

'No thanks. I'm driving.' He cast another eye round the room. 'Nice place.'

She appeared from the kitchen area, which was separated from the living room by a worktop at which sat a couple of hard wooden bar stools. The flat was subtly decorated in tame pastel tones, with some interesting abstract artwork peppered around the walls.

'It's hardly a palace, but it's home.' She smiled at him. 'Can I get you a tea or coffee instead? I'm making one for myself.'

'No, thanks. I can't stay long. I really only popped round to ask a favour.'

'Sit down.' She indicated a sofa beside a bookcase. 'I won't be a minute. Kettle's just about to boil.' Denning sat and glanced through her book collection. Classics mostly: *Jane Eyre*, a couple of Dickens novels, a faded copy of *Vanity Fair*. There was a contemporary crime novel by an author whose name he didn't recognise that nestled incongruously amid the more vintage works. Someone once told him you could judge a person by the kind of books they read. He mostly liked reading biographies and books about history. He wasn't sure what that said about him.

Anna reappeared with a mug of tea for herself. She sat on an old-fashioned-looking, wooden-framed armchair opposite Denning, pulling her legs up and tucking them under her body. 'What's this favour?'

Denning explained about Molly and how she'd been tasked with looking into Bryony Allen's gang. 'We're not sure where, if at all, it fits in with her murder, but if there is a connection, it would be helpful to find it.'

She nodded. 'The press seems to be running with the idea that this is the work of a serial killer. According to the *London Echo* it's only a matter of time until he strikes again.'

Denning spotted a copy of the *Echo* on the coffee table, half hidden under a TV listings magazine. He picked it up and read the story on the front page:

Girl Slain in Churchyard Horror, read the lurid headline. Denning scanned the rest of the story.

> *Police seem clueless as to who was responsible for the brutal murder of Bryony Allen, whose body was discovered in the grounds of a church in East London yesterday, amid rumours there might be a deranged serial killer on the loose in London. One woman who lived nearby and asked not to be named, said, 'It's horrible that something like this can happen here. I have two young children and worry about what's happening in the world.' The Evening Echo understands that Bryony Allen had been tortured prior to being murdered and that her body was mutilated after she had been killed. Police are refusing to say whether she was sexually assaulted before being killed. Detective Chief Inspector Elizabeth McKenna of the East London Serious Crime Command Unit insisted they were following a number of important leads, but she refused to speculate on whether this was the work of a serial killer. However, it's clear there's a dangerous individual out there. And the longer this individual remains at large, the greater the possibility they could strike again.*

Denning threw the paper back onto the table. It was typical tabloid crap, but it wouldn't help their investigation. McKenna's press briefing had been deliberately vague, keeping to the barest minimum of facts and shouting down any idle speculation about deranged killers on the loose in London. However, she'd looked like she'd delivered the press briefing on autopilot and hadn't fully acknowledged the media's need to twist reality in order to sell papers. But it worried him how the paper had discovered facts about Bryony's murder – specifically relating to her having been tortured prior to her death – which hadn't been made public. He didn't like to explore the possibility there could be someone on his team that was leaking information to the press. He trusted his team.

Anna came back into the living area. She nodded at the newspaper. 'Sometimes it feels like they're one step ahead of us,' she said.

'I don't run murder investigations for the benefit of tabloid editors,' Denning said. 'Unfortunately, the truth isn't always as prurient as the readers of the red tops would like it to be.'

She gave a lame little chuckle. 'So, what direction is the current line of enquiry taking?'

'You know I can't go into detail. And I can't allow you to join the murder investigation, at least not officially. But I think you and Molly would work well together.' He wasn't entirely convinced on that last point, but he thought it was worth a try. In many ways they were very similar, but in other ways they could almost be considered total opposites. Both had worked their way through the ranks, rather than being fast-tracked like he had been. Both were dedicated and professional to a fault. But Molly was impulsive; she listened to what her gut told her about a case. Anna was totally by-the-book, and would no more act impulsively than he would.

'She's a good officer,' he added, feeling the need to slightly oversell Molly's merits for Anna's benefit rather than the other way around.

'But you do think there's a possibility Bryony Allen's murder has something to do with the burglary gang?' Anna asked.

'It can't be ruled out.'

She sipped her tea and adjusted her legs, stretching the right one in front of her body, and flexing her foot. Unpainted toenails… 'We've been investigating the burglaries for some time now,' she said. 'While I couldn't swear Bryony's gang were behind all of them, the evidence seems to suggest they were. As for the drugs angle…' She pulled a face. 'Bryony and Paul Chitterly were certainly users. The others most likely see dealing as a rite of passage as far as gang membership goes.' She looked at Denning, offering up a weak smile. 'It's as much about gangs proving themselves, asserting their authority, as it is about making money. Members have to prove how tough they are, and the envelope is always being pushed that little bit further every time a new gang wants to exert its authority.'

It all boiled down to gangs, Denning thought: ASBO gangs on council estates trying to mark their territory and million-pound drug gangs like Jason Hart's marking theirs. The same principles applied to both, only the stakes were higher the further up the ladder you went.

'According to Molly a dodgy bar in Holloway called The Lydon Arms seems to be central to all this. Has that come up on your radar?'

She wrinkled her brow very slightly. 'Can't say it rings a bell. But it might be worth checking out.'

She took another sip of tea. 'Anyway, thanks for popping round. I was going to ask if you still wanted to go to the pictures on Friday. There's a new Coen Brothers comedy just out. It's got mostly positive reviews.'

'Yeah, sounds good.' He paused just long enough to give his brain a chance to change gear. 'Might have to wait a while, though. At least until we start to make some progress with this case.'

She nodded and sipped her tea. 'Sarah's still in New York, isn't she?' A pause, which hung in the air for a moment too long. 'You must get lonely when she's away.'

He made sure his face remained impassive. 'I'm too busy to worry about getting lonely. Besides, she'll be back in a few days.' His right hand had decided to tap out an unconscious morse code on the arm of the sofa. She only seemed to notice when he stopped.

'Just the same...' The rest of her sentence was left to wither in the air between them. Anna finished her tea and placed the mug on the bamboo coffee table with a delicate thud. 'Have you eaten? You could stay for dinner. I can easily make something.'

He smiled. 'I'm all right, really. And I have to be going.' He stood, willing his body to relax. 'I really appreciate your agreeing to work with Molly. I'll email you her details. And, obviously, I'll clear it with your boss first. As a courtesy.'

'There's really no need. I'm sure he'll welcome the extra support. Like I said, we've been after this gang for months. Another foot soldier chasing the loose ends will always be appreciated.'

He knew Molly wouldn't see it that way, and part of him wondered if the prospect of them working together was as good an idea as it had first appeared.

'OK. Maybe we could meet for a drink sometime?'

'Maybe.'

As he left her flat and returned to his car, he had a horrible feeling that rather than making a difficult situation better, he had just made it ten times worse. He liked Anna, but he needed to make it clear to her that this was never going to be anything more than a friendship. He knew he was going to have to be fair and blamed himself for unintentionally leading her on, if that was how she'd interpreted his behaviour.

Chapter Eighteen

When Molly opened the front door, she could hear Jon's raised voice. He was on the phone to Jenna, Rowan's mum. She could hear her voice on the other end of the line, muffled yet audible. It was strange hearing the voice of someone she'd never met but who had somehow managed to loom large in their lives; much larger than she ever should.

Molly headed into the kitchen and poured herself a glass of water.

She could still smell Paul Chitterly's grubby flat about her clothes and in her hair. It was as though his sad, tawdry life was rubbing itself off on her.

Jon's voice was coming from the other room. He wasn't shouting now. He just sounded defeated. She took the water into the garden. She needed some fresh air and silence.

She sat at the rusting table and chairs, sipping the water and watching a sparrow scudding amongst the weeds in the tangled grass of the lawn.

Her real fear was that this whole situation would plunge Jon into another well of depression, which, each time it struck, got harder and harder to shake off. And she seemed to be the one to pick up the pieces. But she felt guilty. As his partner, she should support him. At least that was what she kept telling herself. It was great that

Rowan was back in his life, and for all the time things were going well, Jon would be on a high. Then, when things would go wrong, as they inevitably would, Jon would take it badly.

Neither she nor Jon were particularly enthusiastic gardeners, and the back garden was something of a wilderness. She convinced herself this was a good thing as it attracted wildlife and insects and everything else that was good for the environment, but in reality she envied their neighbour's garden, with its neat oval patio and manicured foliage.

A light breeze wafted the pleasant scent of their neighbour's jasmine, which was still in bloom. It hung over the fence and had tangled itself in some unknown shrub.

At the bottom of the garden was Jon's shed, his refuge from the madness of the world. Sometimes she yearned for something similar.

After a moment, she was suddenly aware of Jon standing at the back door.

'What's up?' she asked, already knowing the answer.

'Jenna's being difficult.' He sat at the table next to her, scraping the metal chair against the flagstones. 'She says I'm trying to turn Rowan against her. Apparently Rowan's done just fine without me all these years, and she doesn't need me messing up her life now.'

Molly wasn't sure what the real story was, and wasn't sure she wanted to know.

'A bit harsh,' she said. Though she did quietly wonder if there was a sprinkling of truth in it. She sighed.

'What's the matter?'

'Nothing.' She rubbed a hand over her eyes, trying to massage the tiredness out of them. 'I'm just worried this whole situation with Rowan is getting out of hand.'

'What do you mean?'

'Let's have something to eat and we can chat about this after dinner.'

Jon folded his arms on the table, clearly wanting to talk about it now. 'She claims all this bellyaching is having an effect on Barry's health. That's bullshit. Barry wants me at the wedding. He said as much.'

'Jon, getting angry won't help. Talk to Rowan again. Maybe she can have a word with Jenna, get her to back off a bit.'

He shook his head. 'I don't know. I don't know if it's worth it.'

Molly sipped some more water. 'You've got two choices here: give in to Jenna, or fight your corner. Rowan wants you there, so stand your ground.'

'I know you're right. But I only wish it was that easy. Barry's ill. This whole wedding was brought forward to make sure it happens before he dies. Rowan wants her grandfather there.'

'Well, of course she does. That's understandable. But she can have both, can't she? Her father and her grand-father?'

Jon just shrugged. 'Not according to Jenna. She said the only reason Rowan asked me is because she's being polite.' He looked at Molly. 'I don't know who to believe. I want to believe that Rowan wants me back in her life. Though if she's just doing all this because she feels she has to keep everyone happy...'

'Do you want me to have a word with Rowan? At least I'm slightly detached from the situation. She might respond better to someone outside of the immediate family.'

He shook his head, staring at the rusting top of the garden table, picking at loose bits of ochre green paint. 'This is down to me. She's my daughter. And perhaps Jenna has a point, maybe I wasn't there for Rowan when she was growing up. I sure as hell want to be there now.' He looked at Molly. 'Besides, you *are* family. You're my partner. That means you're on my side.'

Molly didn't know what to say. She didn't want to find herself forced to take sides in someone else's family dispute. She'd wasted enough time over the years having to take sides in her own family arguments. Luckily that was mostly behind her now.

She opened her mouth to say something, but closed it again before any words had a chance to come out. She had a feeling that whatever she said, it would be the wrong thing.

'Can we change the subject?' she asked. 'It's been another long day.'

'Sorry. I shouldn't be dumping all this on you.' He threw her a smile. 'How's your murder investigation going? Any closer to catching the bastard?'

'Slow progress to be honest, but we're confident of a breakthrough.' She drank the rest of the water and realised she was still thirsty. 'Look, I'm going to get some more water. Do you want anything?'

He shook his head. She went into the kitchen, headed over to the sink and poured herself a glass of water.

As she turned off the tap, she was suddenly aware that Rowan was standing in the room. 'Parents…' She let the rest of the sentence hang in the air.

'I know. They're hard work at times. But I suppose we've got to remember they're human.' She smiled at Rowan, feeling some sympathy for her. 'How they feel about each other doesn't have any bearing on how they feel about you. In fact, I suspect the main reason they're still fighting after all these years is because they both care about you. You're the glue that will always hold them together, and if the only way they can manage that is by yelling at one another, then there's not much you can do about it.'

Rowan took a sip of water. 'I get that. I really do. I just wish they air their resentment when I'm not around. I feel I ought to insert myself into their conversation and act as mediator.' She shrugged. 'But, you know, it's probably not worth wasting the energy.'

Molly watched her. She couldn't help thinking about Bryony. They were roughly the same age; one had a loving family, the other had been cast out from hers and her life snuffed out in the most brutal manner. The difference was stark.

She thought about what she'd just said to Jon. *Slow progress to be honest, but we're confident of a breakthrough.* It was a standard response uttered during any murder invest-igation. Except they weren't confident that any break-through was coming their way soon.

She chewed things over in her head. Deena Jackson was clearly holding something back. And although she couldn't be certain, she had a feeling the two goons from The Lydon Arms were connected somewhere along the line.

And then there was the mysterious Rob Jardine. Whatever role he played in this, they had to find him and speak to him. There were so many unanswered questions. The Lydon Arms seemed to be the key to everything. Only she couldn't quite figure out how.

Chapter Nineteen

As soon as Denning arrived home, he phoned Claire.

'At last, Matt. I've been trying to get hold of you for the past few days.'

'I'm sorry, Claire. I'm in the middle of a major investigation. Things are pretty hectic at the moment.' He always seemed to be apologising to Claire these days. 'I promise we'll get together and sort out the schooling situation as soon as I can.'

He thought he heard a sigh coming from the other end of the line, but it was possible she was just taking a deep breath. 'Look, Jake really isn't happy at his current school. And I'm the one who has to go up there and talk to his teachers. Not that it makes any difference. It's the same problem every time: he says he's being picked on by the other kids and the teachers don't care. And to be honest, Matt, having spoken to some of them, I think he might have a point.'

It was Denning's turn to sigh. He knew Jake was unhappy at school. But not all the problems were down to the other kids. In fact, if he was being brutally honest with himself, a lot of the problems were down to Jake. And it wasn't just that he just didn't like school. Deep down, Jake wanted his parents back together again, and that wasn't going to happen. 'Can I talk to Jake?' he asked.

'I'm trying to get him ready for bed. I don't want him over-stimulated. He's been too over-stimulated lately as it is.'

He knew they needed to get together and sort out Jake's schooling situation. Jake was his son as much as he was Claire's. He felt guilty at passing so much of the responsibility for their son's welfare on to her shoulders. His job made it difficult to spend as much time with Jake as he wanted to, but how did he explain that to a ten-year-old boy who just wanted to be like other children: normal and settled. Despite being SIO on a major murder investigation, he was going to have to make time for his son. 'OK. Tell him his daddy loves him, and I'll see him soon.'

'Yes. I'll tell him. But we need to talk. I've been in touch with a school in Southwark that specialises in children with Autism and ADHD. I think it would be good for Jake. I'll email you a link to their website. They said we can call round one evening and the head teacher would show us round.' There was a pause from the other end of the line. 'I think we should go.' Another pause. 'For Jake's sake.'

Despite his reservations about sending Jake to a specialist school, Denning knew it was something they were going to have to seriously consider. As Jake got older, his schooling would become more important. Their son's welfare and future education were not something to be taken lightly.

'OK, Claire. You sort it out with the school and I'll meet you there. Just let me know the day and the time.'

He ended the call. He was too tired for idle pleasantries with his ex-wife. He thought about Skyping Sarah, but it was still the middle of the afternoon over there and she'd be working. Working. Working hard so they could afford the luxuries of life, like a loft apartment in Shoreditch.

The flat felt lonely without Sarah, yet her presence was everywhere; her personality was so imprinted on the place, from the plump linen sofas to the tasteful artwork on the walls.

He realised he still hadn't eaten, having hurriedly declined Anna's offer of dinner. He went into the kitchen and looked in the freezer for something to eat, settling on a frozen lasagne that had probably been skulking in there for months.

Then he took a beer from the fridge, opened it, and headed over to his laptop sitting on the coffee table. Curiosity had got the better of him. He logged on to the internet and typed the name Jason Hart into the search box. There was very little there to go on. Hart seemed to be someone who was adept at flying below the radar, which probably explained why he was as successful as he was. The only piece he could find was an arrest for assault while Hart had been working as a bouncer at a club in Liverpool ten years ago. Hart had pleaded self-defence, claiming the person he'd allegedly assaulted had tried to attack him with a knife. The jury had clearly believed Hart's version of events because he'd been found Not Guilty and subsequently acquitted. Since then, there was nothing to suggest he had come into contact with the police.

Denning read the article a couple of times, though it told him very little about Jason Hart. There was a photo of Hart looking directly at the camera; attractive, well-groomed, with an air of arrogance about him. His dark hair was immaculately sculpted, and he had a peppering of designer stubble around his chin. There was a small nick of a scar running down one side of his forehead. The article gave his age as twenty-six, meaning he'd be around thirty-six now.

Next, he checked out the story about the two bodies found in Bromley back in March. A quick Google search led him to a story on the BBC News website. Two men had been nailed to a floor in a derelict hotel that was due for redevelopment as luxury apartments. They had been named as Kelvin Moore and Adie Carter, and described as 'local drug dealers'. Further details were sketchy and there was certainly no mention of Jason Hart or Terry Myerson, though Myerson would almost certainly be going under an alias while he was undercover. The case was described as 'active', which meant the investigation had stalled, but the local MIT hadn't officially moved it onto the back-burner yet. In reality, the case had probably been passed over to the NCA, especially if there was a suggestion that Hart and his gang were behind it.

He used his remote log-in to access the PNC, and typed in their names. Both men had links to organised crime, and both had previous convictions for assault and drug dealing. But they were, reading between the lines, bit-part players. Moore had a connection with county lines in north and east Kent, but was clearly no Mr Big; Carter was mostly known as an enforcer – cracking the skulls of the street dealers whenever they stepped out of line. So why had they been killed? What was Hart's game-plan, assuming the intel was correct and he was behind it?

And where exactly did Terry Myerson fit into it? Was he acting on orders from Hart, or he was acting off his own bat, without Hart's knowledge? If he was planning to usurp Jason Hart, then as an officer with the NCA he was well placed to do so.

Then there was the question that really concerned him: How much did McKenna really know about Myerson and what he was up to?

Denning was certain there was more going on here than his DCI was admitting to. He thought back to what Steve Marsh had said about McKenna and Myerson having once been lovers. McKenna had always kept her private life to herself. And could he really blame her? This was probably none of his business. All he had was supposition and a gut feeling that she was holding something back. There was certainly nothing to suggest she'd had any involvement in the Bromley murders, and her relationship with another officer had no bearing on how she did her job. But police teams were close. He knew more than he liked about his colleagues' domestic dramas. They *were* a team, with McKenna at the helm. Even if she wasn't directly involved with the day-to-day management of a murder investigation – such matters were inevitably the responsibility of officers at his level and below – she was still in overall charge of the investigation. If she was connected to a rogue police officer and was somehow complicit in his actions, the damage could infect the entire MIT. There was already a nasty rumour doing the rounds that they were going to be merged with another East London MIT to save cash. A new DCS would be looking to make a good impression and sacrificing a poorly functioning murder squad could be one effective way of doing that.

The whole team needed to be focussed on this case, and that included their DCI. A complex murder investigation brought with it a unique set of problems, and if your head was somewhere else, then you were no use to anyone.

Bryony Allen's killer was still out there. Dave Kinsella's words were still echoing round his head about the possibility of it being the work of a serial killer. It was a thought that filled him with dread. Because he knew that if they didn't catch the person responsible then they would almost definitely strike again and people would be looking to him and asking why.

He would speak to McKenna in the morning. Though he had to admit, it wasn't a prospect he relished.

Chapter Twenty

Denning wasn't altogether surprised when McKenna was late in next morning. She was clutching a coffee from the Costa across the road, while half her face was obscured by a massive pair of sunglasses. Another morning where she looked like she hadn't slept.

He followed her into her office and sat on one of the two chairs opposite her desk. 'Liz...?'

'I'm fine.' She placed the coffee on the desk and threw her sunglasses on top of the filing cabinet. 'And I don't need the kid gloves treatment from you, however well intentioned.' She removed the lid from the coffee cup and took a sip. 'Do something useful. Give me a progress report on the Bryony Allen case.'

'Not much more to add to our conversation yesterday, I'm afraid.' He hoped the comment didn't sound too pointed; just enough to let her know she shouldn't go expecting miracles. 'Forensics have come back with a zero. They reckon Bryony was carried to the disposal site in some sort of polythene sheeting. It's the worst kind of material for leaving any useable DNA traces. We've spoken to both social services and Bryony's old school. Both have told us more or less the same story.' He gave her an account of yesterday's briefing, emphasising the possible link with The Lydon Arms.

McKenna nodded and took another sip of her coffee. 'Any joy tracing the "friends" Bryony was supposed to be meeting the night she was killed?'

'DS Fisher is going to speak to the staff at The Lydon Arms again. She seems to think they know more than they're letting on.' He paused, waiting until he had eye contact with his DCI. 'I've asked a DS I know from Islington CID if she would work alongside Molly Fisher on this. She's already familiar with Bryony Allen and her gang's activities. I think she could bring some useful intel to the case.'

McKenna looked at him and for a moment he thought she was going to question his decision, or ask how he knew this DS from Islington. Instead, she just looked up at him. 'Whatever you think. You're Senior Investigating Officer on this. It's your call.'

A silence fell over the room. Eventually, Denning found the courage to say what was on his mind.

'Look, I know I might be speaking out of turn here, Liz, but have you thought about taking a bit of time off? Get your head together.'

'I would have thought this was the worst moment to take time off.'

'I know the timing could be better, but if we're honest, it's never good.' He threw her a half smile. 'At least think about it. We can draft someone in from another MIT, or even CID if necessary.'

'I don't know...' She rubbed her hand through her raven hair. 'I'm not sure I can see upstairs agreeing to it.'

'There's only one way to find out...'

She sighed. 'OK. If it gets you off my back, I'll think about it. But in the meantime, I want to be kept up to speed with the Bryony Allen investigation. Let me know the minute there's any news. Yesterday's press statement should start yielding a promising response. Especially now we've named Bryony as the victim.'

He nodded, waited for a moment, then changed the subject. 'I take it you still haven't heard from Terry Myerson?' He didn't want to mention his chat with Steve Marsh. Not until he felt obliged to bring it up.

She sat back in her chair. 'I've left messages. He hasn't got back to me. And I don't think he's going to.'

Denning looked over at McKenna. 'Look, this isn't really our call. Let the NCA sort this out. By all accounts, Adie Carter and Kelvin Moore were a pair of lowlifes. I don't suppose there were too many tears shed over their unfortunate demise.' He raised a hand. 'OK, I know that's the wrong attitude: every victim's someone's loved one, and we're not paid to judge. But a couple of drug dealers were eliminated. The world still turns.'

'I think you might be choosing to miss the point here, Matt. Irrespective of their character, it's just possible an undercover officer was involved in their – as you so eloquently put it – "elimination". That has implications. Pretty bloody big ones.'

Denning was already all too aware of this. What he needed to know was how much McKenna knew about Myerson's relationship with Jason Hart. 'That's assuming Myerson *was* involved,' he said. 'And even if he was, there's no evidence to support the suggestion he's gone rogue.' He leaned his elbows on the desk. 'Unless you've heard otherwise.'

She clenched her teeth and gave a thin smile. 'I know you're right. It's just…'

'You and Terry,' he said quietly. 'This was more than just a friendship, wasn't it?'

She looked at Denning for a moment before dropping her gaze. 'No flies on you, DI Denning.' She sat back in her chair and sighed. 'Yes, Terry and I were… close. It was a long time ago, and it's been well and truly consigned to the history books now.' She sighed again. 'This was before I'd joined MIT. We'd worked together and found we liked each other. He was still married and I was going through the final stages of a messy divorce. His marriage was on the rocks anyway, though I admit that was no excuse.'

'How long did it go on for?'

She shot him a stern look, then dropped her gaze. 'A couple of years. And it was very on and off. More off than on, to be honest.'

Denning suspected there was more to it. He decided to take a punt. 'But you still have feelings for him?'

She raised an eyebrow. 'The moment my sorry-arsed love life becomes your concern, I'll let you know. For the record: I haven't spoken to Terry for some time, and I don't know where he is. If he gets in touch, I'll inform his handler. In the meantime, maybe you'd like to focus on what you're paid to do, namely find out who the fuck murdered and mutilated that girl. And, ideally, catch the bastard before he decides to do it to someone else.'

Denning could tell their conversation had come to an end. He was in danger of overstepping a boundary and pushing his luck too far. Whatever else was going on here, McKenna was still his boss. She said she'd had no contact with Myerson and until Denning knew otherwise, he had to believe her.

'OK,' he said. 'Point taken. But at least think about asking for some time off.'

'Thank you, DI Denning,' McKenna said firmly. 'Meeting over.'

Chapter Twenty-One

The Lydon Arms was quiet again. Molly wondered if the bar was ever busy, or if the whole place was just a cover for the criminal activities that went on under its roof, apparently with its owner's consent.

Deena Jackson was on duty behind the bar again. She initially pretended she hadn't seen Molly when she and Anna Klein walked in, but she couldn't keep the pretence up for too long, especially when Molly leant on the bar and smiled in her general direction. She was wearing her ceramic foetus earrings again.

'Back again?' Her mouth formed a tight line. 'What's it this time?' She didn't even bother to acknowledge Anna's presence.

'This is DS Klein from Islington CID,' Molly said. 'And you'll be pleased to know we've finally managed to identify the mysterious Rob that Kelly-Ann mentioned the other night.'

She waited for Deena's reaction. 'Oh yeah?'

'And I'm surprised you had never heard of him, considering it turns out he owns this bar.'

She pulled a face at Molly. 'Look, I just work here. I haven't even met the owner. As far as I know, he hardly ever comes in here. He just lets the staff get on with it. Which, frankly, suits me.'

'What about a bar manager?' Anna asked. 'Presumably he pays someone to run this establishment.' She said the word 'establishment' the same way some people said 'dog turd', and the inference wasn't lost on Deena. She stared at Anna for a couple of seconds, with a look that dripped acid, but Anna didn't flinch. Molly suspected she didn't even notice.

'Sam runs this place,' she said, still ignoring Anna and only looking at Molly.

'Is Sam the manager?' Molly asked.

'Yeah. Well, that's his official title.'

'Can we speak to him?' Anna asked.

'He's upstairs in the office.'

'Well, would it be too much trouble to ask him to come down and speak to us?'

Deena shot Anna another poisonous look, but Anna just smiled her response. 'This is a murder investigation, after all.'

After a moment, Deena turned slowly towards a phone next to the till, lifted the receiver and stabbed in a three-digit number.

While she was talking into the mouthpiece, Molly looked round the bar. What looked like the same young couple from her first visit were there, sitting at a different table this time and occasionally glancing in Molly's direction while trying hard to pretend they weren't. An older man sat by himself near the door to the toilets, supping what looked like a pint of Guinness and staring into space. There was no sign of either Kelly-Ann, or the two thick-necked muscle-bitches who had been there the other night.

'He's on his way down. He wants to know if you two want something to drink.' Deena had come off the phone and was standing at the bar, her hands digging into her sides and a pissed-off look stapled to her face.

'Thank you,' Anna said, smiling back at her. 'I'll have a black coffee. DS Fisher?'

Molly wasn't sure if she trusted Deena Jackson not to put strychnine in their drinks and then afterwards claim it had been an accident. But she asked for a sparkling mineral water, on the assumption she would be able to taste anything suspicious on the first sip.

They wandered over to a table near the entrance, far enough away from the splattering of punters to ensure their conversation wasn't overheard.

'What do you make of her?' Anna jerked her head at Deena Jackson.

'It's like she's been on one of those customer care courses and then deliberately renounced everything she was taught.'

Anna chortled. Molly threw a glance towards the bar. Deena had her back to them. She was fussing with a coffee machine, which was making a noise suspiciously like someone clearing their throat...

She still wasn't sure what to make of Anna. She seemed efficient, almost friendly. Almost, but there was something she was holding back.

A few minutes later, Deena sidled over with their drinks. Molly was just on the point of pouring the fizzy water into her glass when a young lad, who looked no more than late teens, approached their table. He was slim and very handsome, with smouldering dark eyes and a smooth complexion. A gold stud glinted in his left ear.

He extended a hand in Molly's direction. 'Sam Okojie. Deena said you wanted a word.' He shook Molly's hand, then Anna's.

'We're looking for Rob Jardine,' Anna said, immediately taking control of the conversation. 'We know he owns The Lydon Arms, but he seems to be a difficult man to get hold of.' A PNC check had flagged up nothing. The most recent activity was six months ago when his licence renewal applications were granted for The Lydon Arms and his other bar in Harlesden.

Okojie slipped onto the vacant seat between Molly and Anna. 'I wish I could be of some help to you, ladies. Unfortunately, Rob is rarely around. He just comes in now and again, checks the place is still standing and helps himself to whatever he fancies from behind the bar. He pays me to run the place for him.'

'You seem quite young to be running a bar, Mr Okojie,' Anna said, without any hint of tact.

He smiled at them. A warm, winning smile that could have easily passed for charm. 'I'm twenty-eight,' he said. He looked from Anna to Molly, adding, 'Yes, maybe that is young…'

'When was the last time you saw Mr Jardine?' Molly asked.

He pressed his hand to his mouth. 'I haven't *seen* Rob for nearly a week. Not since last Thursday when he came in to take some money from the safe. He said he needed cash for a new supplier and he would transfer the money into the company account. He never did, but that not uncommon. Rob sometimes treats this place like his own personal bank, especially if he needs to get his hands on large amounts of cash. At the end of the day, it's his bar so he can do what he likes I suppose.'

'That's the last time you spoke to him?'

'Actually, I spoke to him on the phone the following day.'

'Friday?' Molly asked.

'Yes. I called him to let him know there was a problem with the new tills. He said he'd send someone round to sort them, but he never did. I called him again on Monday morning, and again yesterday to remind him about the tills and the cash he borrowed, but I had to leave a message on his answerphone both times.' He frowned slightly. 'He still hasn't got back to me.'

'A problem with the tills?' Anna seemed puzzled.

'The tills are computerised,' he explained. 'They should be automatically backed up every evening. Except they haven't been doing it. Rob seemed to think it was dodgy software.' He smiled at them. 'I expect he got them cheap.'

'Is that unusual?' Molly asked. 'Rob not getting back to you if there's a problem?'

He nodded. 'Actually, it is. Especially if there's a problem involving money.' He glanced round at the bar, where Deena was serving the elderly man. 'If the system doesn't store the information from the tills, then it's possible to fiddle them. I mean, none of the staff here would do anything like that, but Rob's paranoid he's being ripped off.'

But he was happy to turn a blind eye to all the criminal activity that went on in his bar, Molly thought. 'How did he seem?' she asked. 'When you spoke to him last Friday?'

Okojie shrugged. 'Yeah, fine. Well, actually, he seemed slightly harassed, as though I'd caught him at a bad time.'

'Harassed?'

Another shrug. 'Well, distracted, maybe. I think it's possible he's having problems with the other bar. I imagine their tills are playing up too. It's the same system.'

'So he definitely wasn't here on Sunday? Early afternoon?' Molly asked.

'No. I wasn't here on Sunday, but Denna would have said if Rob had been in.'

Molly didn't trust Denna Jackson to tell her if it was Tuesday or rice pudding, but she let it drop. 'What about the time he came in, on the Thursday?' Molly asked 'How was he then?'

He looked at them again, a slight frown creasing his youthful brow. 'He was all right. We had a drink and a chat. The tills weren't playing up then, so he just took the money and told me he'd repay it the following week.'

'And was he with anyone?' Molly asked.

'No. He was by himself. He only stayed for about half an hour, then left. I didn't really have much of a chance to chat to him as I had to go upstairs to redo the staff rotas. One of the girls is off sick, so I had to spend ages phoning round people to get cover.'

Molly made a note of all this. 'By the way, do you have an up-to-date mobile number for him?'

She handed him a pen and a piece of paper from her bag, and he scribbled down a mobile number. 'Like I said, it's going straight to voicemail.'

Molly thanked him, then asked, 'Do you know if a Bryony Allen was here on Sunday afternoon? And if she met anyone?'

He shook his head. 'Can't say I recognise the name. Though...' He paused, pursing his lips together. 'Wasn't that the name of the girl who was murdered the other day? The body found in the churchyard in Leytonstone?' He looked at them again, confusion wrinkling his otherwise smooth forehead. 'It was on the local news. Did she drink here?'

'We believe that she not only drank here, but that she and her boyfriend used this pub to sell stolen goods. It's also possible they used it for drug dealing too.' Anna looked directly at him, but he didn't so much as blink.

'I'm sorry, but I don't know anything about that. If we were aware of such behaviour, we would notify the police and bar the individuals responsible. We have a zero drugs policy, which is vigorously enforced.'

It was difficult to say if he was being sincere, or was just a good actor. Either way, he was obviously determined not to reveal anything potentially incriminating about The Lydon Arms. Rob Jardine had clearly employed a good bar manager.

'One last question, Mr Okojie,' Molly said. 'Would it be possible to look over your CCTV from Sunday?'

'Ah, that might be a problem.'

'We can come back with a warrant, if that helps,' Anna said.

He shook his head. 'It's not that. The CCTV is linked to the same computer system as the tills. Whilst it's been recording, it hasn't been saving the recordings.' He offered them another smile. 'I can let you have what we've got, but I'm almost certain nothing from the past few days will be there. Not since the system started playing up.'

'Can we have a look anyway?' Molly asked.

He headed back upstairs, saying he'd be a few minutes. Molly finished her drink, while Anna toyed with her coffee, stirring it with the spoon, but not actually drinking it.

'I don't believe that crap about the CCTV,' Anna said. 'He's trying to pull a fast one. It's all a bit convenient it starts playing up the same weekend Bryony is murdered and Rob Jardine disappears.'

'Let's wait and see what he comes up with,' Molly said.

Okojie returned several minutes later holding an envelope, which he handed to Molly. 'I've copied what was on the DVR to a flash drive. It's a week's worth of footage, up until last Friday when the system started playing up.'

Molly thanked him and slipped the envelope into her bag. She passed him her card and asked him to notify her immediately if Jardine got in touch.

As they left the bar, Molly threw Deena a polite smile, earning a narrow-eyed glare in response.

'Well, that was a shithole,' Anna said as soon as they were outside. 'I feel I should wipe my feet. And the coffee was rank.'

'Interesting, though,' Molly added.

'What was?'

'Rob Jardine seems to have disappeared at around the same time Bryony was murdered.'

She glanced at Anna, and judging by the look on her face, she thought that was interesting too.

Chapter Twenty-Two

Back in the office, Molly shared her thoughts with Denning. Anna had returned to Islington to update her DI on the situation and the possibility of organising a raid on The Lydon Arms if resources could justify it.

Denning and Molly were staring intently at her computer screen, scrolling through the CCTV footage from the week leading up to Bryony's murder. The screen had been split into four, showing images covered by the camera by the entrance, one directly behind the bar and two covering the bar area itself.

Denning was looking over her shoulder as she fast-forwarded through hours of people drinking, buying drinks or heading to the toilet. So far there was no sign of Bryony, Paul or Rob Jardine. There was also no evidence that the bar was being used for either selling stolen goods or drug dealing, but they'd only skimmed through two days' worth of footage, with plenty more to go.

'We can pass this on to Islington CID when we're finished,' Denning said. 'If there's any evidence of criminal activity, it'll be their call.' He smiled at Molly. 'Incidentally, how did you get on with Anna?'

'Yes, good,' she said, a little too quickly. 'She seems really on the ball.'

'Do we have any photos of Rob Jardine yet?' Denning asked.

Molly opened the folder on her desk and pushed a couple of photos over towards Denning. They'd been taken from the internet and showed an overweight man in his late fifties, trying his best to look younger. The thinning hair was combed over just a little too vigorously and his face looked slightly more youthful than his neck. It turned out Jardine had something of a chequered work history, with a career that covered everything from taxi driver to nightclub promoter. A timely inheritance a few years ago had saved him from impending bankruptcy and enabled him to open The Lydon Arms, followed two years later by a second bar in Harlesden.

'I take it we've spoken to the manager at Jardine's other bar,' Denning said.

'Same story as The Lydon Arms,' Molly said. 'No one has seen or heard from Jardine since the weekend Bryony was killed.'

Denning continued to stare at the screen. 'Could be coincidence. But obviously we can't rule him out as a suspect until we've interviewed him. And we can't interview him until we know where the hell he is.'

Molly had to admit it didn't look good. Now the recent story in the *Echo* had forced them to go public with Bryony's name sooner than they'd originally intended to, it raised the obvious question: why hadn't Jardine been in touch? He must have seen or heard the news, and the appeal for witnesses. So why hadn't he come forward to rule himself out, if nothing else? Even if he was someone who operated on the fringes of the law, this was a murder investigation and sooner or later they would catch up with him. The later that was, the worse it was going to look for him.

The footage from The Lydon Arms flashed by; sometimes the bar was busy and sometimes it was quiet. Molly was surprised by the clarity of the images: Deena scowling at customers; someone who looked like Kelly-Ann hassling punters; the same young couple who always seemed to be in there… But still no sign of Paul or Bryony, or the two burly blokes who'd appeared and then disappeared in the bar the other evening. Or Rob Jardine.

She was sure if she slowed things down and went through the footage frame by frame, she would find evidence of dodgy dealings, and no doubt some poor sod at Islington CID would have that particular privilege to look forward to in the not-too-distant future.

Denning returned to his desk. Molly saw him throw a glance in the direction of McKenna's office. According to Trudi, Betty Taggart had been acting weird of late. Molly hadn't noticed, but then she tried to keep out of their DCI's hair. Betty Taggart could be unpredictable at the best of times, and experience had taught Molly it was best to keep her head down.

Suddenly, something caught her eye. She checked the date stamp on the bottom right of the screen to confirm the date and time. It was from early evening on the Tuesday: two days before Okojie said he'd last seen Jardine. It was unmistakably him, breezing in like he owned the place, which – to be fair – he did. Even Deena managed something resembling a proper smile. There was someone with him who looked suspiciously like Bryony. Jardine bought drinks for everyone. Bryony headed over to a table near the fireplace. She watched as Kelly-Ann tottered over to the table and chatted to Bryony, though it didn't look like Bryony wanted to engage her in a conversation. She kept glancing back at Jardine who was standing at the bar.

After a few seconds, Kelly-Ann disappeared into the ladies and Bryony busied herself with her phone, still throwing the occasional glace at Jardine.

Jardine was talking to Deena, and the conversation didn't seem too intense. Molly even saw Deena laughing at one point.

Then two men suddenly appeared at the bar. She was certain the taller of the two was one of the gorillas from the other night. The other man, younger and slimmer and with an air of self-assurance about him, approached Jardine and placed his hand on his shoulder in what looked like a gesture of affection. Except Jardine's body language suggested otherwise. No longer laughing with Deena, his face tensed very slightly. He smiled at the man whose hand was still on his shoulder, but it looked awkward, as though Jardine was trying too hard to appear relaxed. On one of the other screens, she could see Bryony had abandoned her phone and was watching the scene unfold.

Deena served the two men with what looked like whiskies. No money changed hands. Jardine was talking with the two men, but his attention was mostly focussed on the younger man. Jardine was nodding at whatever the man was saying. Annoyingly, there was no audio with the CCTV footage, and Jardine had his face turned away from the cameras, so it was impossible to know what they were saying.

The whole exchange only lasted a few minutes. As soon as the men knocked back their drinks they left, the younger man saying something to Jardine and grabbing his shoulder again, much firmer this time, causing Jardine to glance nervously in Bryony's direction, though he carried on nodding. Then the two men left and Bryony joined Jardine at the bar. He indicated for Deena to bring them more drinks. He and Bryony looked like they were deep in conversation, with Bryony looking worried and Jardine trying to reassure her. Then they were laughing and joking again as though the incident with the two men had never happened.

But what had the incident at the bar been about and why had Deena lied to them about Bryony and Jardine? Either she was scared, or money had changed hands to ensure she acted deaf and dumb if anyone came into the pub asking questions.

She asked Denning to come over. She rewound the footage to the point when Jardine and Bryony entered the bar. Denning watched in silence. When the two men entered, he asked her to pause the footage, then enlarge it. He spent a good few seconds staring at the picture, craning his neck and screwing his eyes.

'I don't believe it...'

'Do you recognise them?'

'I don't know the stockier man, but I recognise the younger man with him. And if I'm right, this case has just turned in a very disturbing direction.' He spent a few seconds staring at the screen, seemingly oblivious to Molly's presence. Then he said, 'I'm sure the man with his hand on Jardine's shoulder is Jason Hart.'

136

Chapter Twenty-Three

Denning was running over the facts in his head as he waited to start the team's next briefing. He was trying to make sense of what they'd learned so far. Hart clearly knew Jardine, though the body language on the CCTV footage suggested they weren't exactly best buddies. The obvious link was drugs, but was that *too* obvious? Was there another link, and how did Bryony fit into it?

McKenna had called him in to her office earlier to confirm that she had taken his advice and had requested some time off after all. She agreed she needed to clear her head and get some space. She was at this moment sitting in an office at New Scotland Yard having her request rubber-stamped by their new DCS. This meant Denning would be taking over as acting DCI in her absence. McKenna said she would put in a formal request to have additional support drafted in from one of the other MITs, but she'd advised him not to hold his breath. At best, these things took time; at worst, they never happened.

But he couldn't escape the other bleak thought dancing round inside his skull: if Hart was involved, then there was a very real possibility Myerson's DNA could be all over this sticky mess too. Perhaps it was just as well McKenna was going to be spending the next few days at home with her feet up.

'OK, team, let's get started.' The room fell silent as all eyes turned towards the whiteboard. There were two photographs pinned to it now: a victim and a missing person.

'Robert Malcolm Jardine,' Denning said. 'We now know he has a connection with Bryony Allen. We also know he has various criminal connections. And more worryingly, he hasn't been seen or heard from since around the time of Bryony Allen's murder. Therefore, we need to find him.'

'Does this now mean we're ruling out her murder being the work of a serial killer?' Kinsella asked. 'We're now saying this Jardine geezer killed Bryony?'

'Not necessarily, Dave. We're saying we have to be prepared to explore other avenues while ruling nothing out. You've been looking into past cases with similar MOs. Anything come up that chimes with what we're looking at here?'

Kinsella shook his head. 'Nothing as extreme as this. There was a case about a decade ago: a trophy killer operating in and around West London. Bloke used to cut off one of his victim's ears and keep it as a souvenir. But he's been in Broadmoor for the past nine years.'

'Could be a copycat?' Trudi offered. 'Only more vicious just to show he's got some originality.'

Denning thought about this. 'The MO's similar, but noticeably different. And why start killing now?'

'Has there been anything on the telly about this bloke?' Neeraj asked. 'Or maybe he's got a book out.'

'Not that I know of,' Kinsella said. 'But it's easy enough to find these nutters if you look hard enough on the internet.'

'OK,' Denning said. 'The serial killer theory remains on the table for now. But maybe we need to start thinking along different lines, and Jardine is definitely a person of interest. We know – or at least we believe – Jardine and Bryony were involved in a sexual relationship. It's possible that relationship turned sour, and Bryony was killed as a result.'

'But she was more than just killed,' Trudi added. 'She was tortured and mutilated. Why would he go to those lengths if this was just simply a couple of lovers falling out? This suggests a deep, targeted rage.'

'Agreed, boss. This doesn't feel like it was done by someone who was close to our victim.' Neeraj looked around the room for support. A couple of heads nodded.

'That brings us back to the serial killer theory,' Kinsella said. 'Trust me, this has all the gut-feel of a psycho getting his rocks off by attacking random women. We just want there to be an obvious connection between victim and killer because it makes it easier to find the fucker.'

'It's been three days since Bryony's murder, Dave, and there have been no reports of any similar killings anywhere in the capital,' Denning said. 'I accept it's still early days, and serial offenders don't necessarily work to an obvious timetable. But taking that into account, as well as the lack of sexual assault on Bryony, I really don't think we are looking at a serial offender. At least not one that's attacking random women.'

Kinsella was like a dog with a bone. 'But we can't rule out the possibility, can we? We could be dealing with a nutjob, and there's a real chance he *could* strike again.'

Could… could… They were dealing with so many imponderables here, it made Denning feel uneasy. He preferred to structure his investigation around facts rather than supposition. Supposition meant they ran the risk of chasing shadows down blind alleys, and they had neither the time nor the resources for that.

Trudi Bell had her hand in the air. Denning nodded at her. 'But if Dave's right – and I accept it has been known – then we should put out a warning. Make women aware that there could potentially be a psychopath out there, and at least warn them to be careful. Err on the side of caution.'

'We don't want to cause panic,' Denning advised. 'And we don't want to start victim-blaming either. Until we have hard evidence that confirms this is the work of a serial killer, we investigate Bryony Allen's murder on its own merit.'

'What hard evidence do we need?' Trudi asked. 'Another young woman turning up dead? *Mutilated?*'

Denning sympathised with Trudi's concerns, but it would be dangerous to make a public statement until they were sure of their facts. 'Ideally, Trudi, we find this man before he has the opportunity to kill again.'

'Not easy if we have no bloody clue who he is,' Kinsella added. 'Or where to look for him.'

'Like I say, we rule nothing out. But we keep looking into Bryony's personal life. We look for anything that directly connects Bryony Allen with Robert Jardine. What about Bryony's social media accounts? Have they been checked?'

'Might help if we had her phone,' Trudi said. 'So far, all we can tell is that she was an infrequent user on Facebook, and had been known to use Snapchat, but hadn't been active on either for some time. There's the usual suspects on her timeline: mostly people she knew from school; a couple of her fellow gang members, but nothing incriminating. There's no sign of any communication between her and Jardine.'

Denning looked around the team. He wanted to canvass opinion and make sure they were all on board with the direction of travel the investigation was heading in. They were a team, and right now they needed to work as one. 'What do we all think?' he asked.

'What happened to Bryony,' Molly said, 'the burn marks and everything else… that suggests that this whole thing could be personal. I'm not saying that necessarily means Jardine is our killer, but I do have a feeling his relationship with Bryony is relevant.'

'If someone found out about him and Bryony,' Trudi added, 'they could have acted out of jealousy…?'

'Jardine's hardly God's gift, is he?' Kinsella countered. 'You'd have to be pretty desperate to murder someone because you've got the hots for a middle-aged lothario like him.'

'It takes all sorts, Dave,' Trudi said with a sardonic smile. 'Beauty is in the eye of the beholder, or at least so someone told me.'

Kinsella flicked his middle finger in Trudi's general direction, as Trudi and Molly exchanged looks. Neeraj laughed, and Denning waited until they all calmed down before he spoke.

'There is something else we should be aware of,' he said, once he had their attention. 'We have evidence to suggest that Robert Jardine was a possible associate of Jason Hart. Hart is a known and dangerous drug trafficker.' He wrote Hart's name on the whiteboard. 'As yet, there's nothing to suggest Hart has any involvement in Bryony Allen's murder, in fact there's nothing to suggest he even knew her. But we know Bryony had been a drug user, and as Hart's name has been flagged up as having a connection with Jardine – and therefore Bryony – we can't ignore the fact he might somehow be involved.'

'How, exactly, does Hart fit into this?' Kinsella asked.

'I don't know, Dave. Right now, I don't even know if he *does* fit into it... What we do have is CCTV footage taken from the pub Jardine owns showing the two men together; shortly before Bryony was murdered, and shortly before Jardine disappeared. We suspect Jardine is either directly or indirectly responsible for supplying drugs, as The Lydon Arms is rumoured to be used for dealing. Jardine has to be getting them from somewhere, and Hart is the obvious candidate.'

'So, we're more or less back to square one.' Kinsella had folded his arms across his barrel of a chest, indicating he had nothing further to add.

'We need to explore any links between Jardine and Hart,' Denning continued, ignoring Kinsella yet again. 'And – if they exist – any links between Hart and Bryony. But our main priority right now is finding Jardine. Uniform have been round to his house but there was no answer, and none of his neighbours have seen him for the past few days. Similarly, the manager of the pub he owns in Harlesden has had no contact with him either.' He looked at Molly. 'I've left a message on his voicemail urging him to get in touch with us as a matter of priority.'

'Do we know if he's even still alive?' Neeraj asked.

'At this stage, Deep, all we know is that Robert Jardine seems to have disappeared. There are two likely reasons for his disappearance: he's a suspect in Bryony's murder and is lying low, or he's come to harm either as a result of Bryony's murder, or for some other reason.'

'I think we should bring the bar staff at The Lydon Arms in for questioning,' Molly said. 'I'm pretty sure Deena Jackson knows more than she's letting on.'

'In terms of the criminal activity that was going on in The Lydon Arms, perhaps, but it sounds like she's as much in the dark about Rob Jardine's disappearance as everyone else. And I'm not convinced she's involved in Bryony's murder.'

'There's always the possibility Deena and Jardine were an item and she was jealous of Bryony,' Trudi offered. 'In which case, that would back up the possibility this is down to a jealous lover.'

'And then there's the mysterious Kelly-Ann,' Molly said. 'She seemed to know what was going on in The Lydon Arms. We still don't know what happened to her.'

'Maybe she was knobbing Jardine too,' Kinsella said, stifling a chuckle. 'Perhaps they've run off together.'

'Not helpful, Dave,' Denning said, throwing him a stern look. 'Let's add Kelly-Ann's name to the board. At the very least we should consider her to be a potential missing person. Though without a surname, we haven't got a lot to go on. Molly, have another word with Paul Chitterly, see what he has to say for himself. Do we have an address yet for Jardine? It's possible he's just lying low at home with the curtains drawn hoping all this will go away.'

'I've got an address for him here, boss. He lives in Essex,' Neeraj said. 'Although local uniform have been round knocking and no one's seen him for days.'

'But has anyone actually been inside the house?' Denning asked. 'Because it's just possible there might be some clue as to where he is.'

Denning ended the briefing and let his team get back to work. As he pinned Hart's photo to the whiteboard, he hoped Jardine was simply lying low, because if his suspicions were correct, then Jardine could be in serious trouble.

Chapter Twenty-Four

Paul Chitterly eyed them nervously. Molly introduced Anna and explained why they were there. After some hesitation, he cautiously opened the door and let them in.

Molly caught sight of Anna casting a critical eye around the flat, clearly making the same value judgements she'd made when she'd first met Chitterly. The same judgements she was trying hard to overcome now, having convinced herself the poor sod deserved a break.

'Have you found who murdered Bryn yet?' he asked as they sat on the crumpled furniture. It was the same question every time, and he would no doubt go on asking it until they had an answer.

Molly sat opposite him, Anna beside her, looking like she thought the fabric of the sofa was going to burn her arse cheeks. 'We need to ask you a few more questions, Paul,' Molly said. 'I know this feels like we're going over the same ground again, but until we get some answers, we're not going to make any progress with the case.'

He nodded, looking from one to the other. 'What else am I supposed to tell you?'

'How about the truth, Paul? I know you lied to me last time we spoke. You were both involved in petty crime, including drug dealing. If you want us to find Bryony's killer, you need to tell us the truth about you and her.'

She waited until he made eye contact with her. 'And you need to tell us everything you know about Rob Jardine.'

He didn't speak.

'We know you used to sell stolen goods in The Lydon Arms and Jardine knew about it,' Anna said. Molly shot her a look that told her to be quiet. They had agreed that Molly would lead on this. Anna clearly had ideas of her own. She'd asked to tag along because her boss was pressurising her to get a result on the burglaries case and on Valerie Heaton's death. But Molly had insisted Bryony Allen's murder took priority. She thought Anna had agreed.

'Robert Jardine, Paul. Do you have any idea where he is?' Molly prompted.

He shook his head. 'I haven't seen Rob for ages. And anyway, Bryn was closer to him than me. I never even liked the bloke.' He looked at Anna and then back at Molly. 'It's the God's honest truth. He was a ponce.'

'He's disappeared,' Molly said calmly. 'And we need to speak to him. It's just possible he might know something about what happened to Bryony.'

'How come?'

'He was having an affair with Bryony. And now she's dead and nobody can get hold of him. It could be nothing but until we speak to him, we can't rule him out.'

'I told you last time: it wasn't an affair. She would go with him for money and stuff. But it wasn't like she was in love with him or anything.'

'OK,' Molly said, gently raising a hand to calm him down. 'It wasn't an affair.' She waited until he was less agitated, then continued. 'But he sold her drugs?'

'Kind of.'

'What do you mean, "kind of"?' Anna asked.

He shuffled awkwardly in his chair and scratched at a scab on his nose. 'We used to score off Dil, but he started to get shitty with us, claiming we owed him money. Then Rob put us in touch with a couple of blokes he knew who used to drink in The Lydon Arms. They'd let us have stuff on tick, then if we couldn't pay, Rob would help us out.'

'What about Dylan Lee? Did he come after either of you for money?'

'No. Rob sorted it with him and the others we owed money to.'

It made sense. Molly knew how things would have gone: Jardine letting them sell stolen goods in The Lydon Arms in return for commission, Bryony being part of the payment in lieu of cash. But there was something that bothered her.

'I thought Bryony was clean?'

He shook his head and stared at the floor, saying nothing.

Then the penny dropped. 'The drugs were for you.' She was shocked at realising the lengths Bryony was prepared to go to for her deadbeat boyfriend.

'I've tried giving up that shit, but you've no idea what it's like.' He looked at Molly, then looked daggers at Anna. 'Neither of you have any idea what it's *really* like.'

'We're not here about that,' Molly said. 'We're not the drugs squad. We just want to know about Rob Jardine. He had access to drug dealers, but he didn't actually deal in drugs himself?'

He nodded. 'Rob didn't like to get his hands dirty. He was only in it for the money.'

'Is that why you took part in those robberies?' Molly asked.

'That and some other stuff,' he said. 'We nicked stuff, but we never hurt anyone.'

'What about the last robbery, Paul?' Anna asked. 'The one where Valerie Heaton was killed. What happened there?'

'We didn't attack her, honest. She fell and hit her head. We legged it after that.'

'Only after you'd ransacked her house.' Anna wasn't letting it drop. 'You still took the opportunity to rob a dying woman. Her sons said there were a number of valuable items missing.'

'It was just a few bits and pieces. Rubbish, mostly. Dil said there was some expensive stuff in that house, but we never found nothing seriously worth nicking.'

'Why did he think there was anything really valuable in the house?' Anna asked. 'Valerie Heaton wasn't particularly well off?'

Molly agreed. She had scanned the crime report Anna had given her. Valerie Heaton had lived in a modest terraced house in Finsbury Park. She certainly wasn't rich. According to her sons, a few items of jewellery had been taken along with some ornaments and a watch belonging to their father. Mrs Heaton hadn't been the kind of woman to keep her money in a box under the bed, and the stolen jewellery was worth a few hundred pounds at most.

Chitterly shrugged. 'I dunno. Dil reckoned someone told him there was stuff worth nicking in there, and it would be worth our while going in.'

'What kind of stuff?' Molly asked 'Antiques? Cash?'

'I told you, I dunno. He just said it would be worth our while doing the place over. He persuaded me and Bryn to go along with it. If we'd known what was going to happen we would never have said yes. It was a big mistake.' Molly thought he looked like he was going to cry.

'There's a good chance you could end up being charged with manslaughter, possibly murder,' Anna said. 'But if you tell us what really happened – who pushed Mrs Heaton – it may well go in your favour.'

He clasped his head in his hands. He was breathing quickly, like he was going to have a panic attack.

Molly didn't think this was to do with Valerie Heaton's death, at least not directly.

'What is it, Paul? What are you not telling us?'

'Nothing. I never hit the old woman and I don't know who killed Bryn.'

'But you know something,' Molly said quietly. 'And whatever it is, you don't want to tell us. Is it because you're scared?'

He didn't answer. Anna opened her mouth, but Molly raised her hand.

'Who is it you're scared off, Paul?'

'It's Dil…'

'Dylan Lee? What's he done? Has he threatened you?'

A violent shake of the head.

'What is it then?'

'Those men went after him. They probably did for Bryn too.' He looked up; the whites of his eyes seemed large; a bead of sweat trickled behind his ear. 'They're going to come for me next.'

'Which men?' For a moment Molly thought he might be talking about the two goons from The Lydon Arms, and maybe that was why he hadn't turned up the other night, frightened they might be there and were going to come after him for some reason.

He mumbled something they couldn't quite hear. She asked him to repeat it.

'That old woman,' he said, so quietly the words were barely audible. 'The one who died. Her sons went after Dil. They put him in hospital. Because of what we did. They half-killed him, and they're going to come after me next.' He looked at Anna and Molly. 'I'm going to end up dead.'

Neither woman spoke. Possibly because they didn't want to alarm him. But also because they thought there might be some truth in what he was saying. Denning had mentioned to her about the attack on Dylan Lee. Until now she hadn't connected it to Bryony Allen's murder, but what if the people responsible were escalating the violence they were prepared to use? And if that was the case, then Paul Chitterly had every right to be worried.

Chapter Twenty-Five

Rob Jardine lived in a large, semi-detached house on a tree-lined avenue in Becontree. One or two front gardens had been converted into driveways.

A neighbour had phoned the local nick, and they had passed it onto Denning: Rob Jardine, it seemed, was at home. To be more accurate, the next-door neighbour had heard someone moving around in Jardine's house, and had assumed the owner of the property had returned.

Denning and Neeraj had parked further down the street. Neeraj, ever wary of taking unnecessary risks, had suggested asking the local uniform along as back-up, but Denning didn't want to waste time. The call had come in almost twenty minutes ago, and it had taken them almost that long to get there. If Jardine's intention was to pop back to collect some belongings before vanishing into the night again, they needed to be quick.

They walked up the tiled pathway and rang the door-bell. The house was probably late-Edwardian: solid, with a wide, double-height bay window jutting out the front. Denning briefly noticed a curtain twitch at the downstairs front window of the house next door. They waited a moment, but there was no answer. Denning could hear movement coming from inside. He pressed his finger against the doorbell again then rattled the letterbox. The movement from inside the house stopped suddenly. 'It's the police, Mr Jardine. Can you open the door, please?'

'There's definitely someone in there,' Neeraj said. 'I could have sworn I heard someone moving about.' He turned the brass door handle. The front door wasn't locked. Denning nodded at Neeraj and he pushed the door open. A wooden-floored hallway stretched out behind the front door, with a staircase off to the right. Denning was sure he caught a glimpse of a shadow darting out of sight behind the bannisters on the first-floor landing.

'Mr Jardine, it's the police. We need to speak to you.' Denning wasn't shouting, but he made sure his voice was loud enough to be heard.

'I think we should call for back-up, boss,' Neeraj said quietly. 'How do we know that whoever is up there *is* Jardine?'

He had a point. Denning knew from experience that going into a possibly dangerous situation without the appropriate back-up was potentially asking for trouble; whoever was up there could be armed, or they could even find themselves about to rush headlong into a hostage situation. But time was against them.

He shouted up from the bottom of the stairs, announcing who they were and implying there were more than just two of them. There was no answer. He nodded at Neeraj and they slowly ascended the stairs, the thick carpet muffling their footsteps. But as they did so, Denning had a horrible feeling that Neeraj was right, and whoever was up there wasn't Robert Jardine.

He gestured for Neeraj to get his radio out, just in case they had to hurriedly call for help.

At the top of the stairs, there were three doors, all of which were open. Two of them looked like they led into bedrooms, but the room facing him – a box room above the front door – looked like it was used as an office. The room was a mess. Folders and papers littered the same deep-piled carpet that was on the stairs. There was no sign of any life about the rooms, and he briefly wondered if he'd imagined the shadow he'd spotted at the top of the stairs.

He glanced at Neeraj, who had removed his radio from his jacket pocket and was ready to use it if needed.

Without warning, two men suddenly appeared from one of the bedrooms. Both were dressed in black: one wearing a leather jacket; the other a bomber-style jacket. Their appearance fitted the description of the two men Molly said she'd seen in The Lydon Arms. There was a momentary pause while both pairs of men eyed each other, then all hell broke loose.

The men ran towards Denning and Neeraj. One of them punched Denning in the face, throwing him against the wall, while the other raced down the stairs, barging into Neeraj and knocking the radio out of his hand. Neeraj lost his balance and tumbled down some of the stairs before grabbing hold of the bannister to steady himself. Meanwhile, the man who had punched Denning was charging down the stairs after his mate, whacking Neeraj on the shoulder as he ran past him. Neeraj made an 'oomph' sound and clung onto the bannister with both hands to prevent himself from falling any further.

By the time Denning had got to his feet, he heard the front door slamming shut followed by the sound of footsteps running on the tiled path. He checked Neeraj was OK: he seemed to be slightly shaken and a bit bruised but otherwise unhurt. His radio was lying smashed on the wooden hallway floor.

Denning then raced out of the house to see the two men running in the direction of a grey BMW parked across the road from the house. Denning reached the low metal gate at the end of the tiled path just as they climbed into the BMW, closed the doors then sped off.

He made a note of the number plate and reached into his jacket pocket for his radio. He managed to give a description and the number plate before the car disappeared round a corner almost colliding with a Tesco delivery van that was turning into the street.

The BMW turned right, heading towards the heartlands of Essex.

He glanced behind him to see Neeraj slightly staggering out the front door.

'You all right, boss? What the hell was that all about? Who were they?'

Denning suddenly realised this was the first time he'd seen Neeraj without his hair immaculately gelled into place.

'Probably safe to say that wasn't Robert Jardine,' Denning said. He noticed the neighbour from the house next to Jardine's had come out and was approaching them with a worried look on his face.

'I've phoned the police,' he said. 'They're on their way.'

'We are the police,' Neeraj replied, without looking at the man.

Denning introduced himself. 'I take it you're the neighbour who reported this?'

'I'm Andrew Clements,' he said. 'I live next door to Rob. A police officer called round the other day asking about him. He said to get in touch if Rob came back.'

Clements had a faint trace of a Welsh accent. One or two of the other neighbours had come out now to see what the commotion was. Clements handed Denning a handkerchief. 'You're bleeding.' Denning took the handkerchief and thanked him.

'I take it you've never seen those men before?' Denning asked.

Clements shook his head. 'I don't think they're friends of Rob's.' He looked at Denning, who was dabbing the handkerchief against his face. 'Is Rob in any trouble?'

'We just need to speak to him, that's all. If you have any idea where he is, it would be helpful if you could tell us.' He made to return the bloodied hanky to Clements who gave another shake of his head. 'It's OK, you can keep it.' He offered Denning a weak smile. 'As I told the officer yesterday, I don't really know Rob, and I have no idea where he is. I do know he owns a couple of bars somewhere. It might be worth your while asking there.'

Denning thanked him. A squad car was pulling up outside the house now, blue light strobing, but luckily no siren. Two officers got out: one male and one female. The male officer nodded an acknowledgement at Clements, then began ushering him and the other neighbours away from the front of Jardine's house.

The female officer approached Denning and Neeraj. 'PC Hale,' she said by way of introduction. 'No sign of the vehicle. Traffic cameras have been alerted and hopefully the ANPR should flag it up before it gets too far.' Denning nodded his thanks and pocketed the bloodied hanky, while Neeraj gave her a wide smile.

'I reckon they're well gone by now, boss,' Neeraj said, watching PC Hale return to her colleague and help him secure the front of Jardine's house with police tape.

'We need to get forensics down here, and get them to go over Rob Jardine's house with a fine-tooth comb.' Denning was looking at the house. Those men were obviously looking for something or someone. And judging by what had just happened, it was clear they hadn't found it.

Chapter Twenty-Six

They found the Heaton brothers in a snooker hall in Dalston. For some reason, Molly always associated Dalston with snooker halls. Her boyfriend before Jon – a work-shy, wannabe musician – had spent most of his days and a fair number of his evenings hanging around various snooker halls in Dalston.

She couldn't believe how much the area had changed. She'd remembered the place as being slightly down-at-heel, a part of London that the developers had overlooked. It seemed they'd found it now: smart new apartment blocks had suddenly sprung up like flowering crocuses, and the main street was now awash with trendy bars and coffee shops. The arrival of the overground station a few years back had clearly helped to stimulate this urban regeneration.

But some parts of Dalston remained stubbornly ungentrified; Motley Road and its snooker hall being one such part.

The place had the air of a 1920s speakeasy, minus the nicotine fug of cigarette smoke. As soon as Molly and Anna entered the premises, a leaden hush fell upon the place, punctuated by the cheerless dirge of Country and Western music playing in the background.

There were four snooker tables, two of which were being used. A long, thin bar ran along one wall, where a group of men stood drinking and watching their approach with a mixture of amusement and anticipation. The presence of women seemed to be as unwelcome as it was uncommon.

'We're looking for Blair and Connor Heaton,' Molly announced to the man behind the bar, showing him her ID. One of the standing drinkers eyed her up and down and then gave her a tacit nod of approval. She wasn't sure whether she was flattered or offended.

The barman pointed to two of the men playing at the nearest table. Both glanced over at the bar, then carried on with their game.

Molly and Anna approached and she introduced them. The Heaton brothers were in their mid-to-late thirties, gym-toned and dressed in smart jeans and short-sleeved shirts. It was obvious they were brothers, but the older-looking one had a self-assurance about him, like a man who was used to getting his own way. The other brother seemed more subdued, as though he was accustomed to living in his brother's shadow. Both men were attractive, but in a rough and unmanicured kind of way.

The older man paused his game and extended a hand. Bare forearms were adorned with tattoos. Molly remembered reading in the case notes that both men had served in the military in their twenties. There was no indication of what they did for a living now. He introduced himself as Blair Heaton. Jerking his head in his brother's direction, he said, 'This is Connor. He doesn't say much.' His younger brother merely nodded his acknowledgement. He clutched his snooker cue and looked anxious to get back to his game. 'How can I help you, ladies?' Blair asked. His smile seemed plastic, as though it was something he added for effect. He looked at Anna but said nothing. Her return handshake had been limp, as though done merely out of politeness. She seemed awkward, as though she didn't want to be there. Perhaps she was intimidated by Blair Heaton, but Anna didn't strike Molly as being the kind of person who was easily intimidated. She knew Anna felt this was a waste of time, and her body language seemed to be confirming this. They only had Paul Chitterly's word that the men had been responsible for the attack on Dylan Lee, but it wasn't something they should casually dismiss. At least not until they had formally spoken to the Heatons.

'We're here about Bryony Allen,' Molly said.

'Who?' he asked.

'Bryony Allen was found murdered three days ago.'

'Well, I'm sorry to hear that, but I've never met her and I've no idea who she is.'

'*Was*, Mr Heaton.' She looked at both brothers, trying to gauge their reactions. She waited until she had his full attention. 'She was part of the gang that we suspect may have robbed your mother's house on the evening she died.' Molly knew she had to tread carefully here. Irrespective of the circumstances, the Heaton brothers were victims here too.

'Have you caught the rest of those murdering scum?' Connor asked.

'We're not here about that,' Molly said. 'We're here about another possible member of the gang: Dylan Lee. We think there might be a connection between the attack on Dylan and Bryony's murder.'

Blair looked at both of them. Anna remained unusually quiet. She had been against approaching the men in the first place, arguing that the Heatons needed to be treated with tea and sympathy rather than accusations, especially accusations that had come from someone as unreliable as Paul Chitterly. But Molly had insisted. Dylan Lee had been assaulted shortly before Bryony had been murdered. There was an obvious connection and the Heaton brothers were clearly in the frame for Lee's assault.

'So what? I can't say I'm sorry, but it had nothing to do with me.' Blair Heaton stood his ground. Defiant, rather than threatening.

'But you and your brother went after Dylan Lee?' Molly asked.

'Is that what he told you?' He smiled at them. 'Then that's crap. And if you're going to make those allegations, then you need to have a bit of proof to back them up.'

'OK. Leaving aside the assault on Dylan Lee, let's focus specifically on Bryony Allen. Can you tell us where you were on the evening of June second and the early hours of June third?'

It was Connor Heaton who spoke. 'You're not fucking serious, are you? You're not just saying we beat that little fucker up, but that we actually murdered some tart? You're off your fucking heads.' The aggression was clear in his voice. Molly realised she was going to have to adopt a conciliatory tone. Blair Heaton reached over and silenced his brother with a firm grasp of his wrist. Connor took the hint and fell immediately silent.

'We have to consider all the options, Mr Heaton. And you must admit, you have a motive. You blamed Bryony's gang for your mother's death. It would be perfectly understandable if you felt you wanted revenge.'

'Look, lads, we don't want any trouble, and we're certainly not accusing you of murdering Bryony Allen, or of assaulting Dylan Lee.' Anna had finally found her voice. 'But your names have come up in the course of our investigation. If you tell us where you were on the night in question, we can be out of here and let you get back to your game.'

Blair Heaton looked at Anna for a good few seconds. It was almost as though he resented her for speaking. 'We were here on fourth June,' Blair said. 'Playing in a tournament. Anyone who was here will vouch for us. Then we went home to bed. Our other halves will vouch for that.' He offered them another smile. 'Now, is it OK with you if we return to our game?'

Molly nodded. She thanked them and left. Once they were outside, she turned to Anna. 'Well, you weren't much support back there.'

'I told you what I thought about speaking to them. At best, we have tenuous evidence linking them with Lee, and zero evidence to suggest they had anything to do with Bryony. We just made ourselves look stupid back there.'

They walked back to where Anna had parked her car. 'I think there's something else going on here, Anna.' She looked at the DS, whose face creased in a worried frown. 'I think you resent being asked to work with me. You think I'm treading on your toes and on your case. Well, I'm sorry, but we're investigating a murder here. A young woman has been brutally murdered, and we seem to have bugger all to go on at the moment.'

It was Anna's turn to sigh. 'I think you're being unfair, Molly. Denning asked me to help with this, and I'm happy to do so, but that doesn't mean I have to agree with you.'

'You were the one who asked me if you could tag along,' Molly said. 'You insisted you wanted to get answers on the robbery case.'

Anna opened her mouth to say something else when she stopped. 'Look, we passed a half decent-looking wine bar a couple of streets from here. Why don't we go for a drink and try and bury the hatchet?' She was already heading towards the bar before Molly had a chance to answer.

Chapter Twenty-Seven

Steve Marsh greeted Denning with a raise of the hand as he entered the pub. Marsh already had a bottle of Italian lager waiting for Denning on the table.

'Blimey,' Steve said, pointing at his face. 'Which door did you walk into?'

'Got in the way of some thug's fist,' Denning said. 'But anyway – cheers.' He raised the bottle to his lips. 'This is very welcome.'

'This is a bit of an unexpected pleasure,' Marsh said. 'Don't get me wrong, it's good to see you again. But there's nothing for the best part of six years, then suddenly I hear from you two days on the trot.'

Marsh was drinking a bottle of Becks. Denning suspected it wasn't his first. 'OK. Fair enough. I need to ask another favour.'

'Look, if this is about Myerson again, then forget it. Like I told you last time, I can't discuss an ongoing operation with you, even if I knew jack shit about it, which I don't. So get that beer down your neck and let's change the sodding subject.'

'Things have changed, Steve.' He told him about McKenna's leave of absence, which had now been authorised by their DCS. Denning was now heading up an under-resourced team of detectives who seemed to be chasing their tails. 'We have evidence that suggests Jason

Hart might be involved in the ongoing murder investigation. And that, by inference, suggests Myerson might be, too.'

'Woah, Matt. That's a pretty serious allegation. Are you suggesting an undercover police officer might actually be involved in a murder? You need to be very careful who you go sharing those kinds of wild theories with.'

Denning sipped some more beer. He told Marsh how McKenna had suspected Myerson might be involved in the murders of Adie Carter and Kelvin Moore. 'I think this is all somehow connected.'

Marsh didn't look convinced. 'Matt, mate, you really need to learn when to back off. View the bigger picture.'

'You still haven't told me what that bigger picture is.'

Marsh drank his lager, then swilled what was left around in the bottle. 'You fancy another?'

Denning shook his head. 'I've got to be somewhere after this. Best keep a clear head. Let me get you another, though.' He headed to the bar and ordered another bottle of beer for Marsh and a fresh orange for himself.

When he returned to the table, he could see Marsh was clearly chewing things over in his head, unsure how much he could share with Denning. Unsure, perhaps, if he could even trust Denning. 'Adie Carter and Kelvin Moore ran a drugs cartel based in Kent. They controlled the import through various access points along the south coast and distribution throughout Kent and other parts of London and the South East. They weren't the biggest, but they were ambitious.' He took another swig of beer. 'That was until about six months ago. Six months ago, Jason Hart decided he wanted a piece of the action. He offered Carter and Moore a deal. He claimed he had secured what he called "distribution rights" throughout London. There were no names and no details, but he assured them he could guarantee supply if they could meet demand.'

'We're talking county lines?'

Marsh gave a raw laugh. 'We're talking more than just county-fucking-lines, mate. We're talking about a very well-organised, very slick operation that is readily comparable with that of a major multinational corporation. Import and distribution on a massive scale. We're potentially talking millions of pounds.'

'So, what happened? Why did Carter and Moore end up nailed to a floor in a hotel in Bromley?'

'They wouldn't cooperate. We don't know the details; either they didn't believe Hart, didn't trust him, or simply weren't interested in the deal. Whatever the case, Jason Hart isn't the kind of businessman to take no for an answer. Hart already had access to the distribution, he just needed to get the import side sorted out. If Carter and Moore wouldn't offer him that willingly, he would remove them from the equation and take it anyway.'

'And Myerson?'

He tutted. 'This is more than my job's worth, Matt. This is all hush hush. If my boss finds out I've been talking to you, I'll be out on my arse. At best back in CID – if lucky – and at worst, out the job altogether.'

'We're dealing with a murder here. Possibly more than one. Jason Hart is now linked to one of our suspects. Hart seems to be the connection to all this. Which means there's a good chance Myerson is involved somewhere along the line. If he's gone bad, we need to know.'

'Myerson's been undercover with Hart's gang for over a year now. Two of Hart's former business associates were arrested about eighteen months ago. One of them did a deal in return for immunity. He told us what Hart was planning. He'd never come up on our radar prior to this intel. We put Myerson in to find out if there was anything in it. Turns out there was.' He looked at Denning. 'Tel's good. He's got a solid track record, as McKenna no doubt told you. For the first six months or so it worked great: we knew what Hart was planning; we had a list of his contacts. We even knew what his favourite brand of malt whisky was.'

'What happened?'

'We don't know. As soon as the true scale of Hart's plans became known, the intel began to get sketchy. Myerson was either feeding us duff info or not telling us about stuff that was going on. Carter and Moore was the final straw.'

'You think he's gone rogue?'

Marsh shrugged. 'Your guess is as good as anyone's. But it's clear McKenna thinks it's a possibility, and she probably knows him as well as anyone.'

But it wasn't just McKenna. The fact they were having this conversation now suggested there was a real concern high up in the NCA that Myerson was now toxic. The big question was, if Myerson had sold his soul for thirty pieces of silver, how much damage could he potentially do? Hart was a criminal: they would catch up with him at some point. But Myerson was an officer with the NCA. If it were to get out that one of their officers was corrupt, it would not do their reputation any good. There was even the possibility of an inquiry into some of Myerson's previous undercover jobs, and who knew what kind of can of worms that could potentially open.

'You know for certain Hart is responsible for the murders of Carter and Moore?' Denning asked.

'It can't be a coincidence. But he's too clever to incriminate himself.'

Clever enough to let an undercover officer with the NCA incriminate himself, Denning thought. But was that intentional?

'The obvious answer is to bring Myerson in. Arrest him for the murders of Carter and Moore, then find out just how deep his involvement goes.'

'Easier said than done. If Hart gets even the faintest suspicion we're on to him, then it's game over.'

'But if Myerson's gone rogue, then Hart knows he's been under surveillance anyway. At least that way you rein in a bad officer.'

'Matt, this is a whole different ball game to what you're used to. We don't know for certain Myerson's gone rogue. Undercover officers do have to bend the rules sometimes. He has to convince Hart that he's for real, and that means occasionally having to do things he would prefer not to.'

'Does that include murder?'

Marsh ignored him and carried on talking. 'There could be any number of reasons why he's not been in contact for the past few weeks. If he thinks his cover is in danger of being blown, then he's going to keep his head down. If Hart even suspects there's someone in his organisation that he can't trust, Myerson's finished. We have to tread very carefully here. We're talking about one of the biggest drug gangs in the UK, quite possibly in Western Europe. Drugs, on a major scale. Illegal money, which will have to be laundered. Not to mention the damage done by drugs swamping our streets, schools and housing estates. If we go after someone like Jason Hart, we need to make sure we bring him down completely. This needs to be watertight.'

'But if Hart's involved in a murder…?'

'And like I said, we can't link him to Carter and Moore, not directly.'

'I'm not talking about Carter and Moore. I'm talking about Bryony Allen. I think Hart had something to do with her murder. I don't know why, or how, but we know Bryony was involved with someone who was a middle-man for drug dealers and who has a connection with Jason Hart. That man is now a missing person. None of this is a coincidence.'

Marsh grinned at him. 'This is all irrelevant, Matt, because this case is totally off limits to you. I'm sorry about this girl's death, but even if you could find a connection between that and Hart – which is extremely unlikely – there's not a hope in hell of you being allowed to risk screwing up this case.'

Denning knew when he was being fobbed off. They didn't have enough evidence to approach the NCA officially. And with McKenna out of action, he had no one to fight his corner higher up the chain of command. But he couldn't just let this go. Three people had already been murdered. Denning had always been the kind of detective who dealt in evidence and hard facts, yet his gut was telling him these murders were linked and Hart was more than likely behind them. Perhaps it was time to listen to his gut?

And then there was Myerson. If there was even the remotest possibility that a serving police officer was directly involved, he had to take things further. Even if it ended up costing him his job.

Chapter Twenty-Eight

The wine bar was tucked down a side street just off the busy thoroughfare of Dalston High Road. It was busy with post-work drinkers when Molly and Anna entered, but they found a table in a corner, which was partially obscured by a large fake fern.

The bar was awash with wooden flooring and chrome fixtures, and subtle tones of jazz oozed over the speakers. The atmosphere was as fake as the plastic fern. It wasn't exactly where she'd choose to go for a drink, but it was a huge improvement on The Lydon Arms.

Anna ordered a large gin and tonic for herself and a pint of Kronenbourg for Molly.

'What did you make of them?' Anna asked.

Molly sipped her pint. 'The Heaton brothers?' In all honesty, she hadn't given them much thought. 'Typical ex-army, I suppose. Blunt to the point of rudeness. I can understand their anger towards Bryony and her gang, though. Losing their mum like that must have been tough. These kind of boys always dote on their mothers.'

'They're not the Krays, Molly. And anyway, that doesn't mean to say they killed Bryony.'

'We couldn't rule them out until we'd spoken to them. And I'd lay odds on them being responsible for the attack on Dylan Lee.'

'Not the same thing at all. Besides, there's no proof they attacked Lee. I still think another gang member's responsible for that.' Anna swirled the ice around her glass.

'Well, until we can confirm their alibis, we're obliged to keep an open mind.'

Molly was certain she saw Anna roll her eyes when she said this. She was on the point of saying something, when she decided it wasn't worth it and decided to let it drop. This was supposed to be a 'team-building' exercise, so it might be better to bite her tongue. 'Anyway, I didn't think we were here to talk about work.' She tried a smile and hoped it came across as convincing. 'Why don't you tell me about yourself.'

Anna spluttered a laugh, spitting a few droplets of her gin and tonic onto the glass tabletop. 'Jesus, anyone listening in is going to think we're on a date.'

Despite herself, Molly laughed.

'Well, there's not too much to tell,' Anna continued. 'Single and married to the job. Just like so many of us. You?'

'Actually, I have a partner.' She told Anna about Jon, lightly skimming over the trickier bits. 'His daughter's about to get married,' she said. 'They've been estranged for a few years, so it's all more than a little awkward.'

Anna just looked at her. 'God, I think you're very brave.'

'Brave? I'm only living with the bride's father. It's not like I've got to give her away or make any embarrassing speeches.'

'I didn't mean that.' She didn't speak for a minute; instead, she looked at her gin and tonic. 'I mean you and Jon. He sounds like a nightmare.'

Molly was taken aback by her comment. Her initial thought was anger: how dare this bloody woman she'd only just met make a value judgement about her relationship? Then she stopped herself. Anna wasn't the first woman to be surprised when Molly described her relationship with Jon. Not that long ago Trudi was trying her best to persuade Molly to leave him, claiming she would be better off away from him. That had been under very different circumstances: Molly and Jon had temporarily separated, and Molly had moved in with Trudi and her partner, Charys. She and Jon had reconciled, eventually...

'I'm sorry,' Anna said. 'I didn't mean to sound critical about your relationship. I'm sure Jon's a lovely guy. Maybe it's the age thing. I just can't imagine being in a relationship with a guy who's already had four wives and is almost twenty years older than me.'

Molly was about to point out it was closer to thirteen than twenty, but what was the point? Anna had clearly already made up her mind about her and Jon. 'It works for us,' was all she could find to say. But deep down she had been wondering if there wasn't something about their relationship she was missing. Something about her and Jon that other women could see and she couldn't? It was an uncomfortable thought.

'Right, let's stick to safer territory: why did you become a cop?'

Molly groaned. She told Anna about her best friend from school, Bex, being murdered after they'd been on a night out. Molly's guilt at feeling responsible for not ensuring her friend reached home safely. How becoming a police officer had felt like giving something back and making some kind of amends for Bex. 'But also there's the money and the pension,' she said, not entirely joking. 'And I could never work in an office.'

Anna nodded. She told Molly her reasons for joining had been similar: a sense of giving something back, plus a strong belief in right and wrong.

'Tell me about Denning,' Anna said suddenly. 'Why don't you fancy him?'

'Matt Denning? You are kidding?' You couldn't think of anything more inappropriate. If people thought she and Jon were a bad match, then she and Denning was wandering into the realms of insanity. 'I don't fancy Matt Denning.'

'I think he's rather cute.'

'He's also married.'

'Twice over, so I hear.'

Molly found herself trying not to laugh. Did DS Anna Klein really fancy Matthew Denning, or was this a wind-up? 'Why don't I get us another couple of drinks?' Molly said, getting to her feet.

When she returned a few minutes later, Anna clearly wasn't ready to let the matter drop. 'So, you think it's a happy marriage?' she asked. 'Matt and his wife? I mean they never seem to spend much time together. From what I gather, she's always over in America. Work clearly matters more to her than their relationship.'

Molly wasn't comfortable with the direction of the conversation. She knew Denning's wife worked in finance and had a high-powered job, but that was their business. Denning seemed happy enough, as far as she could tell. What was it about this woman that she seemed hell-bent on dissing other people's relationships? Was it because she didn't have one of her own? And how come she knew so much about Denning? It wasn't like they'd ever been on the same team. She knew Anna had helped with an investigation into an assault case a few months back, but that didn't explain why she seemed to have taken such an interest in his life. 'Look, Anna, I really don't know that much about Denning's private life, and if I did, I'm pretty sure I wouldn't be discussing it with someone I hardly know over a couple of drinks.'

Anna gave an awkward laugh. 'Oh, god. Absolutely. Forgive me, I'm just curious about people. I always wonder about what makes them tick. And you have to admit, Denning is something of an enigma.'

'Not really.'

'OK. Forget I said anything.' She tipped her glass at Molly. 'And I admire your loyalty to a senior officer. Acting DCI, I gather. He's certainly not shy in hiding his ambition. Wasn't he just promoted to DI a year ago?'

'These are very different circumstances. Betty Taggart's taken some annual leave for some reason, and it's hardly worth bringing in a new DCI, assuming they could find anyone. You need someone who's already well up to speed with the case, and Denning seems the sensible choice.'

She smiled. 'Of course. But that doesn't mean to say he isn't ambitious. I'm saying that as a good thing. I can see him getting to DCS within a few years.'

Molly nodded. 'Maybe. He's a good boss. And that's really all that bothers me.'

They carried on chatting for a while. Molly tried to move the conversation on to Anna's personal life, but it seemed she wasn't joking when she said her job was her life. Molly imagined she lived alone, with only a cat for company. However, it seemed she didn't even have a cat. The job really was her life.

When Anna finished her drink, she asked if Molly wanted another, but she didn't. She'd had enough. She'd tried to get to like Anna Klein, but even with the alcohol smoothing the waters, she had found the woman to be hard work. She made her excuses and left.

It was still light when she left the bar, though only just. A wide band of amber was already slowly thinning in the west, throwing lengthy shadows along the roads and pavements.

Anna would presumably have to get a taxi home as she was over the limit, and she wasn't the sort to risk her job for a drink driving conviction.

The overground station was only a few minutes away. From there Molly could catch a train to Highbury and Islington and then a bus home.

As she headed towards the station, she was suddenly aware of footsteps behind her. She quickened her pace and the footsteps speeded up too. She was a woman and a cop, so she knew when footsteps behind you meant someone was following you. It wasn't late and just ahead of her she could see the fag end of the rush hour commuters trickling home from the train station and bus stops. She knew in a few moments she'd be on Dalston High Road, then a two-minute fast walk to the station.

She was still aware of the footsteps behind her. Part of her wanted to turn round and confront whoever it was. She was a police officer, trained in how to look after herself. But she had also just had a couple of pints and who was to say her pursuer wasn't armed with a knife?

She glanced behind her and was aware of a presence – male, she assumed – about two feet behind her. She felt in her pocket for her house keys – an impromptu weapon should she need it – when from a doorway to her left a figure almost collided with her.

She opened her mouth to say something but he apologised, smiled and asked if she was OK. It was a man coming out of a newsagent's carrying a copy of the *London Echo*. Part of her wanted to laugh. Instead, she just said she was fine and waved him on his way. It was then that she felt a hand on her shoulder. House keys gripped in her right hand, she turned round, only to find herself face to face with Paul Chitterly.

Chapter Twenty-Nine

As usual, the house was spotlessly clean. Claire liked cleaning. It was almost like a form of therapy for her. In hindsight, Denning should have taken it as an indication of the deteriorating state of their marriage: the longer he worked late on a case, or found some other excuse for not spending too much time at home, the tidier the house seemed to get.

Jake had been looked after by their neighbour while Denning and Claire had looked round the school. He greeted Denning with an enthusiastic hug when he saw him standing in the living room.

'How are you, little fella?' Denning ruffled his son's hair. He wanted to pick him up and hug him, but Jake didn't like being picked up. He wasn't overly keen on being touched, but accepted it from his parents, as long as it didn't happen too often.

Jake had a new computer game his grandparents had bought him, which he wanted to play, but Claire insisted it was too close to bedtime. Luckily he was already tired out from playing with the neighbour's dog. Claire said he could watch some cartoons on TV before bedtime. 'Mummy and Daddy have to talk,' she said.

'Can we get a dog?' he asked.

'We've already had this conversation, young man. No, we can't get a dog. Mummy has enough to do, looking after you.'

'Daddy would let me get a dog.'

Denning ruffled his son's hair again. 'Hey, little fella, Mummy's already said no.'

Luckily the subject of a dog was soon forgotten and Jake busied himself with the cartoons on the telly.

Claire showed Denning into the kitchen/diner and they sat at the neat little dining table that smelled of wood polish. He declined her offer of tea or coffee.

The house was in Surrey Quays, built in the 1980s and totally indistinguishable from every other house in the bland development that had engulfed that part of South East London. Denning was still paying the mortgage on it as Claire only worked part-time as a teaching assistant at a local primary school. This, she claimed, gave her an insight into the inadequacies of trying to accommodate a child like Jake in mainstream education.

Despite his initial reservations, Denning had been impressed with the school. The headteacher, Dr Bedford, had been younger than Denning had expected: in her late thirties, early forties at most. She'd shown them round the school, emphasizing their ethos and core values.

Denning reread the flashy brochure Dr Bedford had given them:

> The school specialises in meeting every child's
> educational and social needs, which includes
> all aspects of ADHD and Autism Spectrum
> Continuum. We provide an Autism-friendly
> environment, tailoring our teaching to our pupils'
> abilities, developing their skills and helping prepare
> them for the challenges of adult life.

It all sounded so good. Perhaps too good... Turning out perfect-tuned children who would conveniently blend into wider society without drawing attention to themselves. Where were all the negatives? The acknowledgement that children like Jake had behavioural issues that could be challenging, and even the best school in the world was going to struggle to meet his needs.

'Dr Bedford was right when she said it's kids like Jake that suffer when resources start dwindling in mainstream schools,' Claire said, reading his thoughts. 'We've lost two support staff this term, and they're not going to be replaced.'

'I sympathise, Claire, but I'm still not convinced this route is right for Jake. He'll have to face adult life eventually, and he won't be able to do that if he hasn't spent his formative years in a conventional environment. Yes, it's a good school. I just feel uncomfortable at the thought of singling Jake out as being different.'

She shook her head. 'I thought the exact opposite. The school will prepare him for what's ahead and help him to find the best way of dealing with whatever life will throw at him. He needs the best chance for a good start and I think he'll get that from a school like that.'

Denning wasn't sure. Part of him agreed with her that it was a good school, but that didn't mean it was right for Jake. Ever since he'd received the diagnosis of Autism, they'd tried to keep things as normal for him for as long as possible: not making him feel different to other children. But as time had gone on, it had proved to be harder and harder to keep things normal. His behaviour had become more challenging.

'We need to discuss it with Jake,' Denning said. 'Ask him what he wants. Maybe take him along to the school to meet the staff and get used to the place. But it has to be his call.'

Claire looked at him as though she was about to disagree, then smiled. 'Yes. That makes sense. At the end of the day, it's got to be his decision.' She sighed. 'It's just... I sometimes feel we're placing too much on his young shoulders. He just wants to fit in and get on with other children. I really think this is the best place for him to do that.'

Denning didn't reply. A silence fell upon the table. Eventually Claire changed the subject. 'How are you coping without Sarah being around?'

He smiled. Hadn't Anna asked him that same question just the other day? 'To be honest, I've been so busy, I haven't really had time to miss her.'

'Oh yes. That young woman's murder. Is that one of yours?'

'You know I can't talk about it.'

'I'll take that as a yes.' She smiled. 'It was always work with us, wasn't it? You were so ambitious, and that ambition somehow got in the way of us.'

He could sense they were about to start raking over very old coals. Reliving the final days of their marriage as though another bout of naval-gazing would somehow result in a different outcome. It happened so often it was almost like it was on a loop. 'It wasn't just that,' he said. 'On reflection, we probably married too young. Then again, perhaps there were other issues too.'

'But you're happy now? You and Sarah? I think she's good for you.'

'Yes. We're happy.' He paused, wondering whether he should ask the next question. 'What about you? Is there anyone?'

She shook her head. 'After my last experience, I think I'll give dating a miss for a while.' Claire's last boyfriend was currently in prison after being found guilty of murdering several women. Claire had nearly become one of his victims herself. 'It's always difficult with Jake,' she added, keen to avoid mentioning the events of the previous year again. 'I would need to find someone who could understand him, and more importantly, someone he would accept in his life. And that's never going to be easy.'

Chapter Thirty

Molly approached Paul Chitterly with caution. He was still wary of the police after all, and it was more than a little disturbing to find him hot on her heels in a street in East London when she was technically off duty.

She tried to stop her heart from leaping out her mouth.

'Paul… What the fuck are you doing?'

He seemed flustered and was shaking. She wondered if he'd taken something. 'I wanted to speak to you. I saw you outside the snooker hall and I followed you to that bar. I wanted to wait until you were alone. I don't trust that other woman.' He looked at his feet. 'I don't like her.'

'But what are you doing here?'

'I was scared you were going to tell them it was me that tipped you off about them.'

'Tell who?' Then it dawned on her. He was talking about the Heaton brothers. 'How did you know where they'd be?' She shook her head. 'Look, let's go somewhere to talk. There's no sense in having this conversation on the street.'

There was a coffee shop halfway along a modern-looking square next to the station. It was still open. She led him in there, sat him down on a faux leather sofa and ordered two coffees and a couple of cinnamon muffins. He seemed nervous and hungry, and dug into his muffin straight away.

'How do you know the Heatons?' she asked. 'And how did you know where they'd be?'

He spoke through mouthfuls of muffin. 'They're always there. They spend more time there than at home. There, or there's a pub on the Balls Pond Road they go into sometimes.'

She waited until he'd finished eating. 'What I actually meant is – how do you *know* them?'

He'd finished the muffin and looked eagerly at Molly's. 'Aren't you eating yours?'

She pushed the plate over to him, wondering how long since he'd last had something proper to eat. 'You can have it,' she said. 'I'm not very hungry.' She sipped her coffee and watched him eat. 'I repeat: how do you know Blair and Connor Heaton?'

'Dil knows them,' he said eventually, through mouthfuls of muffin.

'Dylan Lee knows Blair and Connor Heaton?' She was aware that her voice had just risen an octave. 'Then why the hell didn't he name them as his attackers?'

'I don't know. But he knew them. That's why he said there was valuable stuff at their mum's house.'

'Except there wasn't, was there?'

He shook his head. 'But Dil swore he knew for sure there was.'

This was getting them nowhere. 'We didn't mention you to the Heatons, Paul. And if it's any consolation, I don't think they killed Bryony. And I don't think they'll be coming after you. You can relax.' She wasn't sure if either of those statements were factually accurate, but it was what Chitterly needed to hear right now. And if that reassurance would stop him following her down side streets, then it seemed like a good idea. 'Paul, I'm aware that I'm beginning to sound like a broken record, but you really do need to stop bullshitting me and tell me the truth here.' She was aware that she'd raised her voice, and actually shouted the word 'bullshitting' much louder than she intended to. The bloke behind the counter plus a couple of other customers were looking over at her, accompanied by a general wrinkling of brows.

'There's nothing more I can tell you,' Chitterly insisted.

'I think there is, Paul. And I think that's the real reason you hung around waiting for me to come out of that bar. Alone.' She stressed the word 'alone' as though emphasising that this wasn't acceptable behaviour for any man, let alone one with a criminal record, but it seemed to be lost on him. She wanted to shake him, except she couldn't stop herself feeling sorry for him. He reminded her so much of someone she'd met not too long ago who had been vulnerable and lost. She had ultimately ended up letting him down. She couldn't allow herself to do the same with Paul Chitterly. 'I want to help you, Paul. Honestly. But I can't if you keep messing me around.'

'I've told you everything.'

'OK. Well, let's go over it again. Jardine: we know he allowed The Lydon Arms to be used for criminal activities… for buying and selling stolen goods and for drug dealing. I think it's possible Bryony's death is linked to something Jardine was either directly involved in, or something he allowed to happen at The Lydon Arms and deliberately chose to turn a blind eye to.'

'The Heaton brothers,' he said eventually. 'Why are you so sure they never killed Bryn?'

Did he know that she wasn't really certain? Was he calling her bluff? If she was demanding honesty from him, why was she not prepared to offer it herself?

'We've spoken to Mrs Heaton's sons, Paul, and they have alibis for the night Bryony was killed. Obviously we'll check their alibis, but if it turns out they didn't kill Bryony, then we need to look at other possibilities.' She was aware that Denning was already convinced Jason Hart was responsible for Bryony's murder, but he'd also told them to keep an open mind. 'Do you think they did it?'

He picked at the crumbs on his plate, then took a sip of his coffee, holding the mug with both hands. 'I don't know. I know they attacked Dil. And I think they went after Kelly-Ann as well.'

'Why?'

'She told me two blokes came into the Lydon when you were there that night. She thinks Deena tipped them off. They wanted to know who you were and warned Kelly-Ann not to talk to cops. They told her leave, or else. She says she's never seen them before, but from the description she gave me, I'm pretty sure it was the Heaton brothers.'

Molly thought back to the night in question. She was certain the two men she'd seen in The Lydon Arms that night weren't Blair and Connor Heaton, though she had to admit there was a certain resemblance. Could there be a connection? She couldn't see it somehow.

'When did you speak to Kelly-Ann?'

He looked sheepish. 'This afternoon. Just after you and that other copper left. I bumped into her hanging round outside the Lydon. She looked like shit, claimed Deena's barred her. Said she'd break her legs if she ever saw Kelly-Ann in there again.'

'How was she? Kelly-Ann, I mean.'

'She tried to borrow a tenner off me, but I'm skint. That's when she told me what happened in the Lydon that night. She knew you was Old Bill.'

So Kelly-Ann was still alive. That was something. 'I'm going to need her full name and address, Paul. I need to speak to her.'

He shook his head. 'There's no way she's going to speak to you lot. Not after they threatened her. They told her she'd end up the same as Bryn if she spoke to the cops. She might be an alkie, but she's not stupid.'

Molly was reluctant to let Kelly-Ann off the hook entirely. It was just possible she knew something, though finding her sober and persuading her to tell them anything useful was going to be a challenge. 'OK. But if we decide we need to speak to her, you'll have to give me her details.'

He nodded. 'I dunno where she lives. Someone said she lives with her brother, who's as off his head as she is. There's no point talking to her anyway. She doesn't know shit. She just makes stuff up all the time. For attention. Or for booze.'

'What about Rob Jardine. What can you tell me about him?'

'You think he killed Bryony?'

'I don't know. But I do think there's a good chance he knows who did, and why.'

Paul drank his coffee, but grimaced slightly as though it wasn't something he was used to. 'I wanted to get married,' he said suddenly. 'Bryn needed someone to take care of her. Her mum died when she was a kid and her dad and step-mum never gave a shit about her.' He looked at Molly, a flick of the hand wiping away a tear. 'You lot probably thought she was just another scumbag who got what she deserved. But she was a good person who deserved a better chance in life. And people took advantage of her. That's why she wanted off the drugs. She wanted to live like normal people. She knew she could never do that as long as the drugs were fucking with her head.'

'To do that, you would have to have been clean too. As long as she was around drugs, there was always a danger she would give in.'

'It was Rob,' he said. 'Rob could get hold of anything you wanted, or put you in touch with someone who could.'

'I know all this, Paul. What I don't know is how it ties in with Bryony.' Molly thought for a moment, trying to focus and kick her brain back into work mode. 'Right: how did Jardine know all these dealers?' She decided to take a bit of a punt. 'What about a man called Jason Hart? Does that name ring a bell?'

He shrugged. 'Maybe? Rob had lots of friends. There were always people hanging around the Lydon.'

'Drug dealers?'

'Sometimes…'

'Look, Paul, I'm not interested in that. I just want to find out who killed Bryony. When you said Jardine could get hold of any kind of drugs. How exactly did he do that?'

'He had contacts.'

'What sort of contacts?'

'A list of local dealers. He knew them. Most of the big London dealers he either knew, or knew of.'

'A list? Are we talking about a physical list? Like, on a piece of paper?'

Another shrug. 'Perhaps. Bryn told me about it. She said it was on his computer.'

'A computer?'

Chitterly shrugged again, but Molly was thinking aloud. Jardine's house: when Denning and Neeraj had gone round and disturbed those two men, they'd been looking, not for some*one* as they initially thought, but for some*thing*.

She reached into her bag for her phone. She needed to speak to Denning.

Chapter Thirty-One

The Parkland Walk stretched between Highgate and Finsbury Park. A scenic tree-lined ramble that was a haven for wildlife and a popular route for walkers and cyclists. But not today.

By the time Denning arrived at the scene early the following morning, there were already several CSIs milling around a car park at the back of a drab 1970s block of flats. A police cordon had been placed at the rear of the car park, where a low brick wall bounded a steep shrub-encrusted embankment. The uniformed officer at the cordon waved him through when he showed his ID.

Sheila Gorton was standing at the top of the embankment. She chatted to him as he changed into his protective boots and overalls.

'Why couldn't our murderer have found somewhere a little more accessible?' she said. She'd dropped her mask so that it dangled by her chin, and Denning noticed a wry grin on her face. 'We haven't got a hope in hell of getting a forensic tent down here.' She was holding on to the trunk of a tree. 'I barely managed to get myself down here.'

'What is this place?' Denning asked, nodding at the steep cutting, at the bottom of which ran a cindered path that was bordered on either side by dense greenery.

'Used to be a railway line,' Gorton said. 'Originally ran between Alexandra Palace and Finsbury Park according to

Google Maps. It was converted into The Parkland Walk sometime in the 1980s. Apparently it would have been part of the Northern Line if the Second World War hadn't got in the way.' Another grin. 'Rumour has it, Stephen King was once inspired to write a ghost story about the area.'

Denning could easily believe it. There was something slightly eerie about the place: desolate and abandoned, yet slap bang in the middle of a major city. He was continually being surprised by these hidden pockets of London that felt like they belonged somewhere else.

'Who would know about this path?'

'Anyone who lives round here. Anyone who's familiar with the area. Anyone with a map of London. The walk is popular, though mostly at weekends.' She nodded down the steep cutting, where silver birches and sycamores grew in abundance. 'Baker's already down there having a poke around.' Another little grin. 'He wasn't happy at having to climb down there, I can tell you. But I insisted, under the circumstances, that he should see the body in situ.'

Denning was climbing into his suit and not looking forward to clambering down the banking himself. 'Circumstances...?'

'You'll know what I mean when you see the body.'

'Who found the body?'

'A passing cyclist spotted something in the under-growth. Seems he cycled past and was almost into Highgate when he thought he should turn back and double-check it was what he thought it was.'

Denning was suited up now. He held onto a tree branch and slid down the grassy slope. The body was roughly halfway down the bank, lying against a tree trunk, at right angles to the path and partly covered in leaves. A mass of flies were already making their presence known.

The victim was dressed in a smart jacket and a pair of skinny Levi's. The right shoe was still attached to the foot. The other shoe lay about a metre away, further down the cutting. A CSI grabbed Denning's arm to help steady him when he slid on some loose earth: the plastic shoe covering not being the ideal footwear when scrambling down an old railway cutting.

He greeted Baker with a nod of the head, receiving something that sounded like an annoyed grunt in response. Baker was very red in the face, probably from the effort of climbing down the steep slope to look at the body.

'Is it OK if I have a look?' Denning asked.

'Fill your boots,' Baker said. 'I just need a word with Lady Gorton, then I'll be on my merry way.'

Denning knelt down to examine the body, glancing over his shoulder to see that Gorton had scrambled down the cutting behind him.

'You'll have seen the injuries,' she said.

He looked at the victim's face: the same burn marks; the same signs of torture. He couldn't escape the fact there were uncomfortable parallels with Bryony Allen's murder. This wasn't good. Whilst it didn't exactly prove Kinsella was right about the serial killer theory, it certainly gave it some further credibility.

Baker had braced himself against a tree now. 'I can guess what you're both thinking, and at this stage it's not something we can discount. Killed elsewhere and then dumped here. Just like Bryony.'

'Except this time the victim's male,' Denning said.

'Well spotted.' Gorton smiled.

'Despite that,' Baker said, 'the similarities would clearly suggest a connection. But you're the detective: I just cut them open and tell you how they died.'

Denning finished examining the body, and looked at the surroundings. On one side of the cutting was the seventies block of flats, the other side looked like the back gardens of decent-sized houses. The area wasn't overlooked. Again, like the churchyard in Leytonstone, there would be little or no CCTV and few, if any, witnesses. 'How do we think they got the body here?'

'We still need to finish conducting our search,' Gorton said, 'but I would say it's likely he was dumped at the car park behind us then rolled down the slope. There are shreds of clothing snagged on some branches halfway down the bank. Also, signs of the earth having been disturbed. There's dried blood on the ground.'

'When—'

'Body's not been in situ long, so probably dumped sometime yesterday evening, or very early hours of this morning,' Baker said, before Denning had even finished asking the inevitable question about time of death. 'It was a warm evening last night. Looking at the state of the hands, it's possible a fox, or some similar animal, has had a go at him. Though, of course, that could have been done pre-mortem. Obviously that, plus an approximation of time of death, will be established during the post-mortem. And yes, Inspector, before you ask, under the circumstances I will do the PM as a priority.'

It was clear the significance of another body turning up wasn't lost on anyone. Denning looked up as the forensic photographer slowly made his way down towards them.

'One consolation,' Baker said dryly. 'We do have an ID.' He nodded towards Gorton, who was waiting to greet the photographer.

'Oh, yes,' she said. 'I nearly forgot. There was a wallet in his jacket pocket. Cash and cards in there, so we're ruling out robbery.' She nodded at the body. 'Not that any of us thought for a minute that's what this was.' She held onto the photographer's arm as he steadied himself.

'The ID?' Denning prompted, already wondering how the hell he was going to clamber back up to the car park without risking sliding back down on his arse.

'It's a Robert Jardine,' she said. She guided the photographer to where the body was, ensuring he had found his footing. She looked up at Denning. 'And I can tell from the look on your face that you recognise the name.'

Chapter Thirty-Two

Denning was at the front of the room about to start another briefing. Faces around the room were grim.

'Obviously we'll need to wait until there's been a formal identification,' Denning began. 'But it's almost certain that our victim is Robert Jardine.'

He gestured at the photos on the whiteboard. They were hard to avoid. The same as those of Bryony: brutal and visceral.

'As with Bryony Allen,' Denning said, 'our victim has been murdered and tortured.' He looked over at Dave Kinsella. 'The only consolation here is that we know we're now not looking at a random killer. These two individuals have been deliberately targeted and killed for a specific reason.'

'Which was?' Kinsella asked.

'Molly, you think you may have found that reason?'

'According to Paul Chitterly,' she began, 'Rob Jardine had a list of London-based drug dealers. It was on his computer, but very likely he'd saved it to some kind of device, probably a pen drive. There's a strong chance the men who were at Jardine's house the other day were looking for it, or something similar. We still don't know if they found it. We still don't have his phone, but it's possible whoever was in the house has that too.'

'Forensics haven't come up with anything, and they've been over that place twice,' Denning said.

'It's possible he hid it somewhere clever,' Neeraj said. 'Then again, it's also possible those goons found it.'

'There's still a cordon round Jardine's house, and a continued police presence,' Denning added. 'If they didn't find it and come back to look for it, they'll find it hard to gain access to the property.'

'Do we know where Jardine's been for the past few days?' Kinsella asked.

'Not yet. It's possible he was in hiding somewhere, knowing his life was in danger. It's also possible he was being held somewhere against his will.'

'It's certain he must have been held somewhere while he was being tortured and murdered,' Kinsella said. 'Presumably the same place Bryony was done. But whoever did that to them must still have been a psycho.'

'Boss?' It was Neeraj, eyebrows raised. He was clearly thinking the same as Molly: Denning knew something and was deliberately holding it back from the team, which wasn't like him at all.

'Jason Hart,' Denning said, gesturing at Hart's photo on the whiteboard. 'It can't be a coincidence. We know he knew Jardine, and we can assume Jardine had something he wanted.'

'But why was Bryony Allen murdered?' Trudi looked around the room. 'If Jason Hart was after this list of suppliers, why go after her?'

Denning shrugged. 'I don't know that, Trudi. Possibly to get to Jardine.'

'We know Bryony and Jardine were sleeping together,' Molly said. 'Maybe Hart thought there was something more to it, and he could use Bryony as leverage to get Jardine to play ball.'

'Then when that didn't work, he offed her and then offed him too for good measure,' Kinsella added.

Denning didn't answer. He wasn't sure if he had any answers right now, just a lot of difficult questions.

'So, Jason Hart's the man we're after?' Neeraj asked.

'He's the most likely suspect,' Denning said. 'He needs a good distribution network to get his drugs out there. Jardine had that. We can probably assume Jardine wasn't willing to offer this up and Hart decided to take matters into his own hands.'

'Right then,' Kinsella said, 'We go after this Jason Hart character and see what he has to say for himself.'

'It's not that simple, Dave. We have to tread cautiously around Jason Hart, and I can't go into details as to why at present.'

Denning was trying to sort things in his head. He felt like there were several pieces of the jigsaw lying on the table, but at least a couple of important pieces were missing.

'Where do we go from here?' Molly asked.

'Well, I've got a press conference coming up,' Denning said. 'And we need to keep Hart's name out of the picture for as long as possible. In the meantime, we look for anything that specifically links Hart with Jardine. Molly, you can keep on that. I think Bryony's boyfriend might be worth keeping tabs on. But also keep an eye on The Lydon Arms. That seems to be the one place that links Hart, Jardine and Bryony. We have uniformed officers asking at the residents of the block of flats. It seems the lights in the car park were vandalised a few weeks ago and haven't yet been repaired, so whoever dumped the body had the advantage of the cover of darkness. It's possible there might be some CCTV to work with, but I'm not holding out much hope.'

As his team dispersed, Denning wondered about the links between Bryony and Rob's murders, and the execution-like murders of the two men in the abandoned hotel in Bromley. They all had one thing in common: the link to Jason Hart. Both Marsh and McKenna were certain Hart was responsible for the murders of Carter and Moore, but he was going to have to speak to someone from the NCA to get more information, and there was no guarantee they would be forthcoming. Not unless he could persuade someone higher up the chain of command that there was a definite link, and without proof that wouldn't be easy.

He felt rather than getting closer to Hart, they were actually getting further away from catching him.

Chapter Thirty-Three

Molly had agreed to put her reservations about Anna to one side. They still had much to discuss about the case. She found herself agreeing to meet her for a walk along the canal in Islington. It was another gorgeous summery day and the houseboats that bobbed along the side of the canal looked cheery in the sunshine. Anna was licking away at an ice cream, trying to finish it before it melted. Molly had declined her offer of one; she didn't want to pretend this was social. Despite it being a warm day, Anna was wearing her raincoat. Molly was beginning to wonder if she slept in it.

'That's Noel Road over there,' Anna said, pointing at the back of a row of tall houses whose leafy gardens backed on to the canal path. 'The playwright Joe Orton lived there.' A pause. 'And was murdered there by his partner. There's a blue plaque on the front of the building.'

Molly hadn't agreed to meet to discuss murdered sixties playwrights. 'What's this about, Anna? We're in the middle of a murder investigation. A double murder investigation now, as you've no doubt heard.'

She nodded. 'Yes. Rob Jardine, isn't it? It must be a difficult time for Denning.'

'He's a big boy, Anna. I think he'll cope.'

Anna stopped to look at a brightly painted houseboat called *City Boy*. A fat ginger cat that had been sleeping on the deck suddenly woke up and blinked at them for a couple of seconds, then returned to its slumber.

'I always wanted to live on a houseboat when I was younger,' Anna said. 'I thought it would be romantic. I could steer it wherever I wanted to go. Just up and leave whenever the mood took me.' She looked at Molly, a dribble of ice cream trickling down her chin. 'Don't suppose it appeals to you. You seem to prefer the more mundane approach to life's pleasures.' She dabbed the ice cream on her chin with a paper hankie.

'I hope you didn't ask me here to rake over my private life again,' Molly said dryly. 'I thought we exhausted that conversation last night.'

Anna sat down on a bench on a grassy stretch that bordered the canal path. She indicated for Molly to sit down beside her. The leafy branches of a chestnut tree offered some welcome shade as they filtered the sunlight through their foliage. 'Sorry about that.' She smiled at Molly. 'Sometimes I'm just too nosy for my own good. I really didn't mean to offend you.'

'You didn't.' She was tempted to tell Anna she was pissed off rather than offended, but what was the point? It was said and done with. Perhaps it would be better to keep their relationship on a professional footing from now on. 'But I'm sure you didn't ask me here to talk about last night.'

'The Heaton brothers' alibis check out,' Anna said. 'They were at the snooker hall playing in a tournament all evening then went home to their respective partners, just as they claimed. They didn't murder Bryony. And you'd really have to clutch at straws to suggest they had anything to do with Rob Jardine's murder.'

'You didn't need to drag me all the way out here to tell me this, Anna, lovely as it is. And this still doesn't let them off the hook for the attack on Dylan Lee.' She waited until a couple of joggers had run past before she continued. 'I did a PNC check on the Heaton brothers. It turns out Connor Heaton has a record for assault. There's not a huge leap from that to what happened to Dylan Lee.'

'The assault charge is from years ago and is hardly relevant. And besides, this isn't actually your call, is it? As you've already pointed out, you're investigating a murder. The attack on Dylan Lee comes under local CID's jurisdiction and is part of an ongoing investigation into the burglaries. Nothing for MIT to soil their hands with.'

But Molly wasn't convinced. There was something else going on here. Something Anna wasn't telling her. 'All this could have been said in a phone call.'

'I really wanted to apologise for last night. And to your face. I'm not really a drinker and those G&Ts may have gone to my head.' She offered Molly a sheepish smile. 'I'm sorry if I said anything inappropriate. You should have told me to shut my mouth.'

Molly certainly found the idea appealing. She watched as Anna finished her ice cream, wiping her fingers on the paper hankie as she munched down the last of the cone.

'Let's just forget about it,' Molly said. 'I've already told you I wasn't offended.'

'I trust you got home safely? I had to get a taxi back, then come for the car this morning. Luckily it was still there. And with all four tyres still attached.'

'Actually, I bumped into Paul Chitterly after I left you last night,' Molly said. She was keen to gauge Anna's reaction.

'You're not serious? What was he doing there?'

Molly shrugged. 'I don't know. Just passing, he said. I felt a bit sorry for him. There's just something of the victim about him. It's as though life's kicked him around and he's lost the will to fight back.'

'He's a hardcore recidivist,' Anna said. 'I'd save your sympathy for the people he's robbed over the years.'

'Whatever else, Anna, he's lost his girlfriend, and in pretty horrific circumstances. They were planning to get married, you know. Him and Bryony. Or at least, he was planning on asking her.'

'Oh, come on, Molly. We both know he's playing games with you. You can't help people like that. They just go on committing crimes. It's all they know, and it's an easy option for them.'

Molly wanted to disagree but her heart wasn't in it. 'What's your point, Anna?'

'I think we should take everything Chitterly's told us about the Heaton brothers with a very large pinch of salt. There's nothing to connect either of them to the attack on Dylan Lee. And if Lee really did know it was them who attacked him, why didn't he name them? The whole thing is just a load of crap.'

Molly couldn't understand why Anna was so keen to let the matter drop. There was something she wasn't being told. Some agenda that was being kept from her. 'You seem very sure. Why are you so quick to dismiss Paul Chitterly and believe the Heatons?'

'Perhaps because Chitterly is a known criminal and the Heaton brothers are respectable members of the community.'

'One of them having a criminal record for assault.'

'I've told you: that was years ago, and wasn't serious.'

'Connor Heaton put a man in hospital.'

'He was eighteen and he was drunk. It was a silly pub brawl that got out of hand. The bloke he hit dropped it before it went to court. He as good as admitted he was the one who'd started it. If the army didn't think it was relevant, then I don't see why we should.'

'Then there's the attack on their mum. It stands to reason they might want revenge, and that would certainly give them both a strong motive so we should bring them in for questioning.'

'You're clutching at straws here, Molly. Let it go.'

Molly could sense the direction of travel here and felt she was fighting a lost cause. Anna had made up her mind and that was that.

There was a brief pause in the conversation, then Anna said, 'How's Denning? I've tried phoning him a couple of times but he's not answering his phone.'

'He's working a double murder investigation, Anna. He's likely got other things on his mind.'

'I appreciate that. I just thought he might have got back to me. I've left a couple of messages.'

'Probably best to leave it for now.'

This clearly wasn't what Anna had wanted to hear. She got to her feet and threw the tissue into a nearby bin. Another couple of joggers ran past, followed by a cyclist. 'It was good to chat,' Anna said. 'I would still like us to be friends. I don't have many friends on the force. It's always nice to chat to someone who understands where you're at.'

Molly nodded, unsure what to say.

'Let's do drinks again,' Anna said.

'Yes. OK.' Molly reminded Anna that she had her number, asking her to call if she wanted to arrange drinks.

She watched as Anna headed up a slope that led from the canal path to the road that bridged the canal.

Molly still wasn't sure what was really behind Anna's request to meet. To apologise for the night before? Anna Klein didn't seem like the kind of person who made a habit out of apologising for anything. To try and steer her clear of the Heatons? That seemed to make more sense. But why was she so keen to warn her off? Yes, it now looked likely they had no involvement in Bryony Allen's murder, and the assault on Dylan Lee was – as Anna had been so quick to remind her – not part of her remit. Did she want to bag the Heatons for the assault and claim the victory for herself? Or did she secretly think they were justified in assaulting Dylan Lee? Or maybe, just maybe, it was really all about Denning? If Anna Klein really did have the hots for Acting DCI Denning, then she was barking in the wrong forest, never mind up the wrong tree. Denning wasn't the sort to cheat on his wife. But then again, how well did she really know him?

She waited until she felt sure Anna would be out of sight and, narrowly dodging another passing cyclist, she headed up the slope to the road, where she hoped to flag down a passing taxi. She saw one approaching and raised her hand. Just as it pulled up alongside her, she found herself wondering why Anna was really so keen to protect the Heaton brothers.

Chapter Thirty-Four

A bank of journalists and news crews were staring at Denning, waiting for him to speak. They were in the conference room on the ground floor, where the briefing could be contained. There were a dozen rows of padded chairs, comfortably filled, and a couple of TV cameras at the back of the room to catch his every blink.

He rubbed a hand nervously through his hair and relaxed his shoulders; a technique McKenna told him always worked for her whenever she had to deliver a press conference. The first time she'd had to deliver one, she'd confided in him once, she'd thrown up both immediately before and after. Nowadays, although she wouldn't have said she enjoyed them, she'd pretty much learned to take them in her stride. They brought with them a vicarious kind of celebrity if you did them often enough. Some old bloke in a pub had even asked for her autograph once, having recognised her from an appearance on an ITV evening news bulletin, where she'd been outlining the distressing circumstances concerning a murdered child. He'd even offered to buy her a drink. 'I thought I'd be doing *Strictly Come Dancing* before the year was out,' she'd joked.

It had been agreed with upstairs that he would reassure the media there wasn't a maniac on the loose torturing and killing random strangers, but he was to give little else away about their ongoing investigation, except to confirm that they were making solid progress: a lie he was expected to deliver with conviction.

'We can now confirm the identity of the victim found next to the Parkland Walk in Islington earlier this morning is that of Robert Malcolm Jardine, aged fifty-six, of Acorn Road, Becontree. We cannot at this stage speculate as to why or how Mr Jardine was murdered. But our investigation is progressing and we're currently pursuing a positive line of inquiry.' He remembered McKenna had also told him to keep it brief and only tell them what he wanted to read on a newspaper's front page.

'Is there a link to the murder of Bryony Allen?' someone asked.

'Bryony Allen and Robert Jardine were known to one another, but we are unable to confirm what – if anything – the significance of this is at this stage.'

'Has Bryony Allen's boyfriend been questioned in relation to their murders?' Another voice, male, from one of the middle rows.

Denning confirmed that Bryony's boyfriend had been questioned, but was not currently considered to be a suspect. There were another couple of questions about suspects, and possible connections to any unsolved murders in recent years. Denning managed to fend them off without too much difficulty.

So far the questions were reassuringly predictable, and he felt like he would soon be home and dry. Then came the curveball.

'Can you confirm whether there's any truth in the rumour that Jardine was involved in organised crime?' A woman at the back asked the question. Denning couldn't tell who she was with. She had short blonde hair and was wearing a tailored navy pinstriped suit, but he didn't recognise her.

'There's no evidence to suggest Robert Jardine was in any way involved with organised crime,' Denning said.

'Both victims were tortured before they were killed,' the woman said. 'That suggests either a sadistic maniac, or something along the lines of an execution.'

'We're still awaiting the post-mortem results for Robert Jardine,' Denning said, 'so it's too soon to speculate on the exact cause of death.' He hoped he'd said enough to fob her off. He quickly took another question.

'What about motive?' someone else asked. 'Can you discount robbery?'

'We've ruled out robbery as a motive, but we can't comment at this juncture as to what the possible motive was.'

'What about drugs?' It was the blonde-haired woman at the back again. Denning hoped the cameras wouldn't pick up the slight throbbing in his temple that had suddenly started. Denning tried to ignore her and hoped another hand would go up. None did. 'Can you comment on the rumour that Robert Jardine's murder is in some way connected to an ongoing investigation into an organised drug cartel, and the murder of two known drug dealers in Bromley back in March?' the blonde-haired woman asked.

'At this stage, I can't comment on that.' Denning hoped his voice sounded more confident than he felt.

'But you're not denying that there is a connection?' The woman was staring straight at Denning. The other journalists were looking at him too, waiting for an answer. There was a silence that was in danger of turning into a vacuum. He knew the longer he said nothing, the more their suspicions would be aroused.

'I repeat, there's no evidence to suggest any link between Robert Jardine and drug dealing or any other kind of organised crime,' Denning said. 'I wouldn't go believing rumours.'

'But you don't deny that one of the bars Mr Jardine owned was regularly used for drug dealing as well as other criminal activities. And Mr Jardine was an associate of a known drug dealer?'

Denning took a deep breath and tried to stop his stomach from doing flip-flops. The questions, along with the article in the *London Echo* made him fear there could be somebody on his team leaking information. This journalist seemed worryingly well informed. 'I can't comment on operational procedures, but I can reassure you that we are doing everything we can to find the killers of both Bryony Allen and Robert Jardine. Beyond that, I'm afraid I can't say any more.'

He watched the woman at the back smile. 'I'll take that as a yes.'

Chapter Thirty-Five

As soon as Molly got back to the office, she phoned a friend at Putney CID. DI Susan Gorman had previously worked in Islington, although it had been some time ago. It was, at the moment, nothing more than a hunch, but there was something niggling away at her. Anna Klein's insistence that there was no reason to go after the Heaton brothers didn't sit right with Molly.

'Susan, it's Molly Fisher. Have you got a minute?' After a brief exchange of pleasantries, she shared what was on her mind.

'Oh yes, I remember Anna Klein. She was always a bit of a dark horse. Kept herself to herself. You know the sort: turns up late for works drinks then leaves early, that sort of thing. But a good copper, as I recall. Solid, hardworking. Why do you ask?'

Just like Denning, Molly thought. Perhaps that's what lay behind the attraction: Anna saw them as being kindred spirits. 'Did you ever think there was something strange about her?' Molly asked.

'Strange?' She could imagine Susan raising her eyebrows, curiosity pricked. 'In what way?'

'I don't know, and it's probably nothing. There's just something about her that doesn't sit right.' She filled Susan in on the Bryony Allen murder case, lightly sketching over the more lurid details, but mentioning the vague connection with Blair and Connor Heaton. 'I can't read her,' Molly added, 'and that's what I find most strange.'

'I can have a word with her DI at Islington, if you like. But if you're searching for any dirt on her, I doubt you'd find anything. She struck me as a bit of a Goodie Two-Shoes, if I remember. She even used to boast about how she'd been head girl at her school.' There was a pause followed by a slight chuckle. 'What exactly is it you don't like about her?'

Susan Gorman was as perceptive as ever. 'What makes you think I don't like her?'

'You wouldn't have called me unless there was a good reason, and you're a good judge of character, Molly.'

'I don't know what it is exactly. There's just something I don't trust about her.' Molly wished she could say more than that, but she had still to fully figure it all out in her head. 'It's this whole thing with the Heatons. OK, I get that she sees them as victims, but even so, I can't get away from the feeling there's more to it than that. Her insistence that we back off from them strikes me as out of character for someone who does everything by the book. And there's something else...' Molly wasn't sure: it really was just a flickering moment that she had thought was a bit odd at the time but hadn't really appreciated the significance of.

'Go on.'

'When we interviewed the Heaton brothers, I got the impression there was something about them that made her feel uncomfortable. I thought maybe she'd had some kind of run-in with them before. But there's nothing on the PNC to suggest they've come up on the local CID's radar, and I'm sure she would have said if she'd had any previous dealings with them.'

'So, you've checked these Heaton brothers out, then. I take it they're not big-time gangsters or anything?' She heard Susan laugh.

'One of them has a record for assault, but it was almost twenty years ago. I mean, they're a pair of bruisers and both are ex-army, but I wouldn't describe them as intimidating.'

There was a silence where she was sure she could hear Susan Gorman's brain ticking over. 'Look, I'll have a word with David Gillies, he's her DI. Don't worry, I'll be discreet – David and I go back a long way. If there's anything that rings alarm bells, I'll get back to you.'

'Thanks, Sue. And I appreciate the offer of discretion. I really hope this is nothing more than paranoia on my part.'

'You're probably right. Let's be honest, sometimes we just don't get along with certain work colleagues, no matter how hard we try.'

Molly looked around the MIT room: Dave Kinsella got on her nerves sometimes, and Neeraj could be a prick when the mood took. Trudi clearly had a rod up her arse at the moment whenever she was around Molly, and Denning blew hot and cold depending on the mood he was in. And, OK, she and Betty Taggart were never going to be best mates, but there wasn't one of them she could honestly say she *disliked*. At least not the way she felt she disliked Anna Klein. 'Yes,' she said. 'I think that's it.' But there was something else that niggled at Molly. 'Just one last thing, Sue: when you said she'd been head girl, you don't happen to remember what school she went to?'

A pause from the other end of the line. 'God, now you're asking. I know she said she was local; that was partly why she was happy to be based at Islington, because she knew the area.'

'So she's from Islington?'

Another pause. 'Finsbury Park, I think, but it's all the same, isn't it?'

Molly thanked her and promised to buy her a pint sometime.

She ended the call and thought about what Sue Gorman had just said.

It's all the same, isn't it?

No, it wasn't, not the same at all.

Chapter Thirty-Six

When Denning returned to the office after the press conference, Neeraj slapped him on the back and told him it had gone well and not to worry, but he spotted the quick exchange of looks that shot between Neeraj and Kinsella, which they obviously thought he hadn't noticed.

'Who was that bloody journalist?' he asked. He was still smarting from having been caught out.

'Helen Tranter,' Neeraj said. 'I think she works for the *London Echo*. She's fairly new.' His mouth curved into a smile. 'And very sharp.'

'How the hell did she know about the link with Jason Hart? We haven't gone public with that.' He was thinking about the potential shitstorm the NCA would be throwing his way now, especially if Steve Marsh got wind of what had happened. 'Someone's leaked this.'

There was silence from the rest of the team. But he couldn't believe someone on his team would do that. He'd worked with these people for a year now. They were good detectives; honest and trustworthy. But who else could it be? If the leak hadn't come from his team, then it must have come from someone at the NCA.

'I suppose the only thing we should be grateful for is that she didn't mention Hart by name,' Denning added.

'Maybe she's been asking around,' Kinsella said. 'It's possible someone's said something without realising its significance and she's put two and two together.'

Denning wasn't convinced. 'Maybe. I still think she was well informed. She knew what she was talking about.'

'There's some news on the BMW from outside Jardine's house,' Neeraj added. 'Found burnt out in a layby on the B147 near Romford. Forensics are going over it for prints and anything else useful, but they're not holding out much hope of finding anything. Turns out the plates were fakes.'

His day was getting worse. He headed into McKenna's office, aware that the team were muttering about him, not loudly enough for him to hear what they were saying but loudly enough for him to know they were doing it.

It felt strange thinking of it as McKenna's office when technically it was his office for the foreseeable. There was no word on when McKenna was planning to return to work, suggesting she was taking this break as sick leave rather than annual leave. He sat at her desk, feeling uncomfortable about being on the other side of it.

The PM report on Jardine had been emailed through. Denning opened and read it. It confirmed the manner of death was the same as Bryony Allen's. Jardine had been tortured before he was killed. There was evidence of numerous stab wounds – Baker had counted at least forty-two – and the cause of death was likely either a stab wound to the heart, or one of two to the neck; the same method of execution as Bryony.

Execution. His mind kept returning to the disastrous press conference, and Helen Tranter's use of the word. He couldn't understand how he'd been so unprepared. So much was down to nerves, but it was more than that.

Baker had put the time of death at more than twenty-four hours ago but less than forty-eight, suggesting Jardine had either been held somewhere prior to his death, or had been in hiding before his luck had finally run out. The signs of torture had been as brutal with Jardine as they had been with Bryony, only this time – in Baker's opinion – more prolonged. His further opinion suggested he thought the torture had a 'professional' feel about it, as though it had been clear and methodical. This implied it was done for a reason: the extraction of information rather than out of some sick sense of enjoyment. Denning reread the report. It pretty much confirmed what they already suspected: they weren't dealing with a maniac who tortured and killed random victims out of some sick pleasure, but somebody calculating and ruthless who was prepared to kill and mutilate someone in order to get what he wanted. Jason Hart fitted that description.

There was another email, this time from Sheila Gorton. She had the report back from forensics. There was nothing of note, except that there were traces of DNA evidence that matched some that they already had on record that was coming up as unidentified. Gorton had flagged this as being odd. He focussed on this section, not quite believing what he was reading. The faint traces of DNA found on the victim matched that which had been found on Adie Carter. They couldn't identify the DNA as yet, but Denning knew it belonged to Terry Myerson. He decided to keep this information to himself for now. For Myerson's DNA to pitch up on one murder victim was careless. On two, it was more than unfortunate; it was alarming.

He was hit by a sudden note of panic. He grabbed his phone and selected McKenna's number from his contacts list. He called her number but it went straight to voicemail. He left a message asking how she was and apologising for bothering her. He asked her to get in touch, saying he needed a word. She had said he could contact her if there was anything important.

He sat at McKenna's desk and thought about it. He was in danger of over-reacting. There was nothing to suggest McKenna was in any kind of danger. She was probably relaxing on a beach in some Spanish resort somewhere, sipping a bucket of sangria and forgetting he and the rest of the MIT even existed. But he couldn't be sure… If he had contact details for her ex, he could get in touch to ask if he'd seen her, or had some clue as to where she was. But it was clutching at straws. As far as he knew, McKenna hadn't spoken to her ex for some time. In fact, he got the impression she was closer to Myerson than she was to her ex-husband.

Probably relaxing on a beach… And yet that niggling voice of doubt kept whispering in his ear. What if she was determined to try and track Myerson down? She may still have contact details for him, or at least have some idea as to how to get hold of him. Myerson's DNA had been found on Robert Jardine's body. Whoever had killed Jardine had very likely killed Bryony Allen too.

Myerson was potentially dangerous and that made McKenna vulnerable.

And why wasn't she answering her phone?

Chapter Thirty-Seven

Molly waited for Anna. She'd suggested meeting up at the same wine bar as the previous evening. It wasn't exactly convenient, but it felt like neutral territory.

Anna was late getting there and Molly was beginning to wonder if she was going to turn up. Much the same feeling she'd had waiting for Paul Chitterly to pitch up at The Lydon Arms that night. But Anna was reliable, so she'd be here. Reliable, and curious.

The bar was quite busy for a week night, and considering it was ever so slightly off the beaten track. A handful of post-work drinkers and a couple of what looked like students were spread out over half a dozen or so tables. Molly was sitting at the same table as the previous evening, so Anna wouldn't have any difficulty spotting her.

She'd already ordered a pint of Kronenbourg for herself and a large gin and tonic for Anna. She was going to need it when Molly confronted her with what she'd now found out.

There weren't that many secondary schools in the Finsbury Park area, and it had only taken a quick internet search and a couple of emails to confirm her suspicions.

Anna entered the bar looking harassed. She spotted Molly and headed over to join her.

'Thanks. It was good of you to suggest meeting up again. I wasn't sure how we left things earlier.'

Molly pushed the gin and tonic over to her and Anna took a sip.

'And cheers for this, though I'm pretty sure it was my round.'

'My treat,' Molly said. 'Busy day?'

'Pretty much, yes.'

'The burglaries, any progress?'

Anna wrinkled her brow. 'A bit. I am working on another couple of other cases at the moment as well as the burglaries, but they're certainly taking up a fair amount of my time.'

'Have you spoken to Dylan Lee again?'

Susan Gorman had sent her an email just after lunch. Not quite a smoking gun, but enough to raise some questions that needed answering. By the time she'd finished reading the email for a second time, she had a clearer idea of what Anna Klein had been up to.

'Why would I speak to Lee again? We already have a statement from him.'

Molly sipped her pint and watched Anna to see if there was any suggestion she knew where Molly was going with this. If she did, she was giving nothing away. 'Because, apparently when you and a DC from Islington CID first interviewed Lee after the assault, he indicated in his statement that he recognised his attackers. When asked if he was willing to name them, he said he was frightened about possible reprisals. OK, maybe he didn't use those exact words, but that was the basic gist of it. DI Gillies felt it would be sensible to give Lee some time to think things over, then approach him again once he was out of hospital. You offered to speak to him – without the presence of a detective constable this time – and in his second statement, he claims that he was mistaken. He was now saying he didn't recognise the men who assaulted him and gave a description of two men who don't even bear a passing resemblance to Blair and Connor Heaton. You also took charge of checking any CCTV footage from the night of the assault, which, conveniently, failed to show anything that might incriminate the Heatons.'

Anna raised her gin and tonic to her lips, but didn't take a sip. There was a slight clinking of ice in the glass, then she placed it back on the table. 'Not this hoary old chestnut again.' She sighed heavily through her nose. 'We've been over this. I don't know what you've got against the Heaton brothers, but this is beginning to get rather boring.'

She took a swig of her G&T this time, possibly more confident that she'd fought back sufficiently to throw Molly off the scent. But if she thought that, then she really didn't know Molly.

'The reason there's nothing incriminating is because you made sure anything that could have pointed the finger at them was deleted. Just as I imagine you persuaded Dylan Lee to change his mind about naming the Heatons as his attackers. I don't think that would have been too difficult: point out that they were both in the army, one of them has a conviction for assault and if they were to get hold of him again, they would do more than simply give him a good pasting next time. Am I warm?'

Anna just looked at Molly, her lips narrowing to a tight line. 'That's rubbish. Why would I deliberately jeopardise a major police investigation?'

'Because you know Blair Heaton. The two of you were at school together. Probably the same year.'

It hadn't taken Molly long to find the relevant inform- ation. Blair Heaton's Facebook page listed his former school, while DI Gillies had confirmed via Susan Gorman which school Anna had attended. It was the same school.

Anna just shrugged. 'It was a big school. There were over a thousand pupils there. Blair Heaton could well have been one of them.' She leaned in closer to Molly. 'But if you're suggesting that I've been doing favours for him simply because we happened to be at the same school at roughly the same time, then you're insane. And more to the point, if you told anyone about this, they would laugh at you.'

'Perhaps. But you've got to admit, it explains a hell of a lot. And it can't just be a coincidence, can it?'

Anna was almost talking through clenched teeth now. Molly was pleased to see she'd got her riled. 'That *is* all it is: a coincidence. I have no reason to do Blair Heaton or his ape of a brother any favours, except that – yes – I feel sorry for them. What happened to their mum was horrible. Nobody should have to go through that. We should be charging those little thugs with murder, but as it is, we'll be lucky to get a manslaughter charge to stick.' She clasped her gin and tonic glass so tightly Molly thought she was in danger of breaking it. 'In fact, do you know, if the Heatons did go after Dylan Lee, or any of the others, then I'd say good on them. Because that's the only kind of justice they understand. It's more than the courts will ever dole out to people like that.'

She said *people like that* as though they were some form of sub-human species. Whilst Molly would never condone what they'd done, it wasn't up to her or Anna to stand in judgement, or to decide what passed for an acceptable mode of justice.

'You're lying. There's something else.' She sipped her pint, turning things over in her brain. 'I could go to your

DI, tell him what I know and ask for you to be taken off the case.'

Anna laughed. 'What good would that do? Chitterly's already admitted he, Lee and Bryony were part of a gang that broke into the homes of elderly residents, robbing and terrorising them. We've got other names too. We now have enough to bring them in and charge them with burglary and, in the case of Valerie Heaton, manslaughter. Lee isn't going to change his story, whatever you might think. The case is as good as closed.'

Molly felt like she was in danger of losing the upper hand here. Anna was fighting back strong; stronger than she'd expected her to. She finished her pint and dumped the empty glass on the table. 'There is something I can do. I might not like it, and it might not lead anywhere, but it's worth a try, because if you have lied and tried to manipulate justice, then I'm damn sure I'm not going to stand back and watch you get away with it.'

She left the bar, taking her phone from her pocket and dialling Paul Chitterly's number. It was a long shot, but it was all she had.

Chapter Thirty-Eight

McKenna's flat was on the third floor of a modern apartment block in Limehouse. She'd moved here after her divorce, apparently, preferring somewhere small and easy to clean. She'd also got it cheap because the previous owner had committed suicide in the spare bedroom. Denning hadn't been sure she was serious when she'd told him the last bit, but it hadn't surprised him.

He'd been buzzed in by a neighbour, after explaining who he was and flashing his ID at the screen.

The same neighbour was waiting for him in the carpeted vestibule when he came out of the lift. The neighbour introduced himself as Jim, and told Denning that he barely knew his neighbour. In all the years they'd lived next door to each other, he'd probably exchanged no more than a couple of dozen words with her. He did, however, have a spare key for her flat, just as she had a spare key for his.

Jim was in his early sixties, with a sharp angular face and neat little goatee beard. He was dressed in a pair of neatly creased chinos and a thin woollen cardigan. He observed Denning with wary eyes.

'I'm still not sure I should be doing this,' he said as he unlocked the front door to McKenna's flat. 'She told me the key was for deliveries and emergencies. I'm still not convinced this qualifies as the latter.' He stepped aside to let Denning enter the flat. 'I should really phone the station and double-check you are who you say you are.'

Ordinarily, Denning would have commended his vigilance, but right now he just wanted the man to shut up. He could see why McKenna and her neighbour rarely spoke.

The flat had a Spartan feel about it – not unhomely, just not overly fussy. Magnolia walls and laminate flooring, with a large, square blue and green checked rug on the living room floor. A pale grey IKEA-style sofa, complete with fluffy blue cushions, faced an over-sized telly, while a glass-topped dining table and two chairs occupied a corner. A pair of un-curtained picture windows looked out onto the quiet suburban street below.

There were some generic prints on the wall, but no photographs or ornaments dotted around the room to make it feel like something other than an anonymous show flat. There wasn't even a house plant to offer a note of cheer.

'Well, she keeps it tidy,' Jim said, having followed Denning in, either to keep an eye on him, or more likely to have a good nose round his neighbour's flat.

There was a galley-style kitchen off the narrow hallway, which was as pristine as the living room. Further doors led to a couple of bedrooms and a bathroom.

He looked in the bedrooms. The larger of the two, which he took to be the master bedroom, had a standard-sized double bed, a chest of drawers and a couple of built-in wardrobes. He opened the wardrobes, but nothing seemed out of place: mostly work clothes, or jeans and blouses. There were gaps in the rail where he guessed there were clothes missing, but it was impossible to say what, if anything, she'd taken. A row of heeled Chelsea boots sat along the wardrobe floor. There was a large, wheeled suitcase on top of the wardrobe, though there was nothing to say it was her only suitcase. He remembered seeing her favourite biker-style leather jacket hanging on a hook on the coat rail in the hallway. At first he'd thought it strange that she hadn't taken it with her. Her ex-husband ran a bar in Majorca and Denning had wondered if she'd taken herself off there. They were still on speaking terms, though McKenna found it hard to stomach her ex's new partner. If she had gone to Spain, she was hardly going to need a warm jacket at this time of year. But there was nothing to say she *had* gone to Spain. And if she had, why hadn't she been in touch?

The other bedroom, where the alleged suicide had taken place, was laid out like an office-come-spare-bedroom, with a solid-looking sofa bed against one wall, and a desk against another. McKenna's laptop sat on the desk, the lid closed. Denning looked at Jim, expecting him to make some comment about the rumoured suicide that had taken place in the room, but he just stared back at Denning. Either he didn't know what had happened, or McKenna had invented the story for effect.

He closed the door and returned to the living room, Jim hovering at his heel.

This wasn't how he'd imagined McKenna lived. He'd expected her to be messier for some reason, more chaotic. He'd assumed she was the sort of person who left things lying around so they were easy to find whenever she needed them. But she obviously liked order, and a tidy home was, after all, a sign of a tidy mind.

'She didn't say if she was going away anywhere?' Denning asked Jim. 'Or when she'd be back?'

He shook his head. 'Like I told you, our conversations are mostly limited to hello and the odd request for taking in packages. I hardly know her. Apart from her telling me that she was a cop – and she only told me that because I asked what it was she did for a living when I first met her – I know very little about her.'

Denning thought about this. It was possible she took herself off somewhere at the last minute, and hadn't bothered to tell anyone where she was going, and certainly not a neighbour that she was on little more than nodding terms with. It was not as though there were plants needing to be watered or a cat to feed.

Equally, there was no sign that McKenna had left the flat by force, or that anything sinister had happened to her here. But it was out of character for her to just disappear without saying something to someone. He wanted to try her mobile again, but was there any point? He'd already left a couple of messages asking her to contact him, and she hadn't.

No matter how hard he tried to stop his brain from going there, he couldn't stop thinking about the comparisons with Robert Jardine. Missing, until he turned up dead...

All roads led back to Terry Myerson, and that made his skin bristle.

'Seen all you want?' Jim asked.

He took one last look around the cold flat and wondered what kind of life McKenna lived away from work. Perhaps it was understandable that if she came back to this lonely abode every night she would be tempted to turn to someone who had once brought her warmth and happiness.

Denning nodded. 'Thanks, Jim. You've been very helpful.'

There was nothing else to see, and certainly no clues as to where McKenna was or what had happened to her.

Chapter Thirty-Nine

There was laughter coming from the living room. Molly didn't need to open the door to see what was going on. Rowan was round again. She and Jon were looking to rebuild their father and daughter relationship over a bottle of wine. Molly didn't want to disturb them but at the same time she didn't want to appear rude. She gently pushed open the living room door and waited until one of them noticed her. They were both sitting on the sofa looking through a family photo album Rowan had uploaded to her tablet. They both looked up and smiled when she entered the room. Molly glanced at one of the photos: it was Jon and Jenna on their wedding day. Jon quickly slid to the next picture when he spotted that Molly had clocked the photo. He smiled up at her. 'We're just reminiscing.'

About your life before me, Molly thought. But she smiled back. 'Would you like something to eat?' She was addressing Rowan but the offer was being made generally.

'We've already eaten.' Rowan nodded towards a pile of empty takeaway boxes lying beside the sofa. 'But thanks.'

Jon offered Molly another weak smile. 'Sorry. I wasn't sure when you'd be back.'

She nodded and said it was OK. She headed into the kitchen and opened the fridge. Luckily, she wasn't very hungry. She was still chewing over her bruising encounter with Anna. She was sure she was lying, or at least keeping something back. She'd barely flinched when Molly had confronted her about her connection with Blair Heaton. Perhaps Molly had got it wrong. Perhaps it really was just a coincidence? But no; she was certain it was relevant, somehow. She just didn't yet have enough information to connect all the dots. At least not yet. She'd left a message with Paul Chitterly to get back to her.

She found some leftover quiche on the top shelf and gave it a sniff. It had been in there for at least three days, maybe four, but it was probably still edible. She rummaged in the salad drawer, where there were some tomatoes and a piece of cucumber. If she mixed them with some salad dressing, that and a slice of quiche would be enough to keep her going.

The takeaway incident shouldn't have rankled as much as it did. Jon's focus was on Rowan right now, and Molly's work hours were unpredictable. She was home late again this evening, and she hadn't bothered to phone Jon to let him know. It was understandable that he and Rowan shouldn't have to wait for her to pitch up before they had dinner.

But still…

There were times she found herself defending Jon, even though she knew in her heart he was being selfish and thoughtless and taking her for granted. She went on excusing his behaviour because she loved him. But there had been times recently when she found herself wondering if she really wanted to be part of a relationship, and if so, did she want to be in one with Jon?

There was so much spinning round inside her head at the moment. The lack of progress with the murder investigation worried her. This hadn't been helped by Denning making an arse of himself during the press briefing. Granted it was his first one, but by the time you got to inspector level, you were expected to have the necessary skills to deflect an inquisitive journalist.

A journalist, like Jon…

She turned round suddenly as Rowan came into the kitchen. 'Hi. I just wanted to see if you're all right.'

'I'm fine, thanks,' she said, a little too quickly. 'Just a bit zonked. Things are a bit full on at work at the moment, and sometimes it's hard to switch off. But thanks for asking.'

Rowan took a glass from the draining board and filled it with water from the tap. She took a sip. 'It's difficult for Dad right now. I'm not making excuses for him; he can be a selfish prick. And that's me talking, by the way, not my mum.' She sat down at the kitchen table while Molly mixed the salad. 'To be honest, I had mixed feelings about asking Dad to be part of the wedding, and believe me, I had to put up quite a fight on this.' She shrugged. 'But he's my dad and family is important, yeah?'

Molly wasn't sure if she was asking her a question or making a statement. She smiled back and sat down opposite Rowan to nibble her dinner. 'I know it means a lot to Jon,' she said. 'He's been estranged from you for so long I think he feels it's time to make amends. And this is the obvious way of doing it.'

'He's very lucky having you. Perhaps it's time the two of you thought about getting hitched?'

It was said in jest, but the slight twinkle in her eye suggested there was a serious hint to what she said. Did Molly fancy being the fifth Mrs Kavanagh? It was a question she'd asked herself from time to time but had never come to a fully satisfactory answer. Four failed marriages on his relationship CV was hardly a ringing endorsement for commitment on Jon's part.

Jon appeared in the doorway, grinning at both of them like a schoolboy. 'I've just found some pics of us, Molly. When we first met: Glastonbury, about six years ago. You haven't changed. I can't believe how much slimmer I was then. Rowan, you want to see these.'

Rowan shot Molly a humorous look and followed her dad back into the living room. Molly finished her dinner in silence, musing on Rowan's comments. They shared a love of music; it was what had brought them together and was a bond that kept their relationship from going sour. But there was more to a marriage than shared interests. Stability, security. Reliability. Mutual consideration…

Did their relationship really tick the boxes? Right now, she just wasn't sure.

And then there was the question of who was leaking the information to the press… Denning had flagged this up during a briefing. Jon still had contacts in the media. There was nothing to say he was the one who had leaked the story, of course. She hadn't discussed the case with him as far as she was aware. She always took care never to mention anything indiscreet outside of work; however, when you lived with someone inevitably work matters came up.

But Rowan coming back into his life had changed things. He'd been reminded of how life was in danger of passing him by.

She knew he wanted to get back into journalism. He taught it part time in a local college, but the job wasn't inspiring him anymore. She didn't want to believe he would have gone behind her back, but she also knew it was a possibility she couldn't entirely dismiss.

And a betrayal that would hurt, very much indeed.

Chapter Forty

'DI Denning?' He turned when he heard the voice, placing his teacup back in its saucer with a loud clink. Helen Tranter was standing there with her hand outstretched and a beguiling smile on her face. He shook her hand and she slipped into the seat next to him.

They'd arranged to meet in a café near Victoria Station. He'd got there early and had spent the past five minutes watching evening commuters scurrying into the station, oblivious to everything except their trains home. Normal people living normal lives.

'Thanks for coming,' he said. 'Can I get you something to drink? Tea, coffee?'

She shook her head. 'I can't stay long. What's this about?'

'I just wanted a chat. About the other day.'

Another beguiling smile. 'I take it this is off the record?'

He nodded. 'An informal chat, that's all.'

'In which case, I don't have to tell you Jack. I could just walk out of here right now.' However, she didn't look like she was about to walk anywhere. She was obviously intrigued by his request to meet and, as a journalist, that would mean having to sit there until she knew what it was he wanted. Though he suspected she'd already worked that bit out.

Helen Tranter was clearly as sharp as his first impression had suggested. She was immaculately dressed: a smart business suit and polished hair. Her accent was educated, what could even have been described as posh. He'd looked into her background before asking her to meet. Her LinkedIn profile said she'd been educated at Roedean, though it appeared she'd left school at sixteen, and there were a few years unaccounted for.

'About the press conference the other day…'

She watched him sip his tea. 'Yes, I thought that might be the reason you asked me to meet.' She folded her arms across her chest, which reminded Denning of Dave Kinsella when he was in one of his petulant moods. 'It's my job to ask questions, Mr Denning. And it's your job to answer them. If there's a dangerous individual on the loose, then the public has a right to be party to all the relevant information. The police have been known to keep information to themselves, and that's in no one's best interest.'

'That's not the case. We obviously withhold certain pieces of information during an ongoing investigation for very good reasons. And in this instance, we have no evidence to suggest that the wider public was in any danger. But you already knew that, didn't you?'

'I'm a journalist. And a bloody good one. I have to be in order to survive in what's left of this profession. And being a good journalist means finding out the truth, rather than simply accepting what you're told.'

'I'm not denying any of that. All I want to know is how you came by the information. Information that wasn't in the public sphere.' He lowered his voice and met her eye. 'I need to know if I have someone on my team who's leaking information to the press.'

She returned his gaze, but took her time answering. 'You know the old saying about journalists and their sources...'

'I'm not asking you for names. Just tell me if there's someone on my team that I can't trust.'

She sighed. 'Look, you can relax. I was tipped off by an old contact. Someone who used to work for the *Echo*. They're keen to... re-establish contact with the newspaper industry and thought it might be worth doing me a favour. Don't panic, they didn't tell me anything about operational matters, only that there was more to the Bryony Allen murder than first appearances suggested. The rest I was able to work out for myself.' She was glancing at her phone; probably waiting for a call or a message. 'I followed one of your officers to The Lydon Arms and then spoke to a member of staff. The staff member was more than willing to share the contents of her discussion with your officer in return for cold, hard cash. Your officer had been asking about Robert Jardine. A bit of research online about Jardine, and I was able to join the dots. It's what I do.' She stopped glancing at the phone and looked him in the eye. 'It's not all that different to what you do, just with different end results. But at the end of the day, we both want this maniac caught.'

'What about the links to murders in Bromley?' Denning asked. 'That would have taken more than educated guesswork.'

'Adie Carter. He and Jardine used to run a van hire business together years ago. Very probably a cover for money laundering, but that's not really relevant here. I checked with Companies House. The business is long-since dissolved, but there's always a trace.'

'I'm impressed,' Denning said. 'You should consider becoming a detective.'

She checked an incoming text on her phone. 'You never know, if my career in journalism ever goes tits up, I might consider it.'

'OK,' he said. 'I'll do you a deal. When we've worked all this out, you can have an exclusive. On condition you run any story by me between now and then.'

She looked like she was thinking about it, then after a moment said, 'What's the catch?'

'No catch. Straight up. You get the full background to the investigation, names, etc, but no more leaked info until then.'

Her phone beeped with a message. She took it out of her pocket and read the message. 'Deal.' She slipped the phone back into her pocket. 'Look, I'm sorry to run out on you like this, but I need to be somewhere.' She handed him her card with her name and contact number. 'If you're serious about giving me the heads up, then get in touch.' She slipped her bag over her shoulder and stood. 'It's been good talking to you, Detective Inspector, and I hope we can work together in the future.' Before Denning had a chance to answer, she'd headed out the door. As he watched her leave, he wasn't entirely sure he could trust her. He glanced at her card, then slipped it into his jacket pocket. She'd told him all he needed to know. Educated guess work had pointed her in the right direction, and that was her job. But his primary concern at the moment was who had put her onto this in the first place. He remembered her words: *I was tipped off by an old contact. Someone who used to work for the Echo. They're keen to… re-establish contact with the newspaper industry and thought it might be worth doing me a favour.* That fitted the description of someone he knew. Or to be more accurate, the partner of someone he worked with. He didn't blame Molly, at least not directly. A careless word here, talking about a high-profile murder case to your partner was something they were all guilty of from time to time. Except most police officers weren't married to a former journalist. He would have to broach the subject carefully with Molly. Carefully, and with some reluctance.

–

As soon as Denning got home, he decided to go for a run. He changed out of his work clothes and into his running gear, found his iPod, and headed out of the flat.

It was another warm evening and he couldn't bear the thought of being stuck indoors, especially when it was still light. There was a stillness in the air. The noise and bustle of London seemed to be filtered through some kind of sultry gauze that made it feel distant. He would head north, to the scratch of scrubland that passed for Shoreditch Park.

Away from the main roads that ran through Shoreditch, the side streets were mostly quiet. A couple of cyclists passed him, and a man and a woman, both smartly dressed and looking like they were heading out for dinner.

He kept thinking about McKenna. He was certain there was nothing to worry about. She could look after herself. But it felt odd – unsettling, even – to know that she was out of reach. Even just a text to say she was fine and to stop being a prat would be welcome.

He ran up Pitfield Street, where another new luxury apartment block was growing out of the ground. Something had stood there before but he couldn't for the life of him remember what it was. A board announced that eighty per cent of the new flats had already been sold. Who bought them, he wondered, and why? Were they investments, or actual homes for real people to live in?

He crossed over Pitfield Street and entered Shoreditch Park. The park never seemed to be busy. On the few occasions he'd run round it before, he was lucky if he spotted another jogger, or a random dog walker. He'd suggested going there for a picnic one Saturday with Jake and Sarah, but Sarah had worried about ants, and Jake wanted to stay inside and play on his computer.

He stuck to the paths that criss-crossed the park. It hadn't rained for several weeks, and the grass was yellow and arid.

He was trying hard to put McKenna out of his mind; to convince himself that she was fine and he was over-reacting. But he kept thinking about Jason Hart, and what Steve Marsh had told him. Two people murdered in the most horrific of circumstances, both possibly somehow connected to the deaths of two drug dealers in Bromley three months ago. It all bounced around inside his head, somehow jumbled up with other things: Anna Klein; Sarah; Jake and his schooling. His thoughts turned to Bryony Allen and Rob Jardine: lovers, but not lovers. Was Bryony killed to get to Jardine? Or was there more to it than that?

He couldn't ignore the fact they still had no proper leads. Usually, at this point in an investigation they had something concrete to work with. Right now, all they had was the name Jason Hart, who had no obvious connection to either victim and little or no evidence to prove his involvement.

He could feel the pressure. The media would be on his back now, as was evidenced by the pointed question at the press conference. As acting DCI, the top brass would be looking at him to get a quick resolution to this case. He had been given a chance. He had to show he was up to it.

He stopped for a moment, aware he had a stitch. He breathed slowly and stretched. Looking up, he saw a plane high overhead, heading northwest, probably to America, possibly New York. He reminded himself Sarah would be home soon and the flat wouldn't feel so empty.

The answer to this investigation lay with the NCA. Jason Hart was the best lead they had at present; he was their only lead. In spite of what Steve Marsh had told him, he was going to have to approach the NCA, regardless of the consequences.

Chapter Forty-One

'Are you making this formal?'

Doug Callaghan wasn't the kind of man to take prisoners. He glowered at Denning from behind his desk, his furrowed face making it clear he wasn't happy about this meeting being arranged at such short notice.

Denning had been unable to sleep the night before. As soon as dawn broke, he was making arrangements to meet with Myerson's handler and start demanding some answers. It had involved an early morning phone call to his new DCS, which hadn't endeared him to her at all, but she had succeeded in pulling numerous strings with the NCA's Director General.

Callaghan was a thickset man in his mid-forties, with a slightly receding hairline and a haggard face, as though he was someone who enjoyed spending time outdoors. He was Steve Marsh's boss – the equivalent grade within the NCA to a DCI.

'Not unless I have to,' Denning said in response to Callaghan's question. He felt bad going behind Steve's back, but he needed to speak to someone who was in a position to make things happen. The game had changed now; the ante had been upped. 'I need to get hold of Terry Myerson. I believe someone's life might be at risk, and Myerson is our best chance of sorting out this mess. You're the only person who has the first clue as to how I can get hold of him. Or at least, give me a good idea of where to look.'

Denning had already explained about McKenna having disappeared, having deliberately underplayed the link between McKenna and Myerson. He'd also mentioned the DNA link between Myerson and Jardine's murder. He knew they were already aware of Myerson's possible link with the murders of Adie Carter and Kelvin Moore. Callaghan was SIO on this case; he was Myerson's handler. The buck stopped with him.

'I can't let you speak to Myerson,' Callaghan said firmly. 'Anything that risks his cover could potentially bring the whole pack of cards crashing down. I'm not prepared to let that happen. Not now.'

'According to DCI McKenna, you haven't spoken to him for some time?'

'My conversation with DCI McKenna was in the strictest confidence,' Callaghan said coldly. 'She had no authority to discuss the matter with you.'

'That's not really the point here,' Denning said. 'I can't get hold of DCI McKenna. Her disappearance is out of character and I think Myerson knows something about it. McKenna and Myerson were... close.' Denning tried to underplay McKenna's connection with Myerson. She wouldn't thank him for discussing her private life with another officer, but he had to make it clear that there was a connection, and that this connection potentially placed her in danger.

'Look, there's no evidence that Liz McKenna has come to any harm. And nothing to suggest she's been in contact with Myerson. According to your DCS, she's taken herself off for a few days and is incommunicado. And who can blame her? Frankly, if I had the opportunity to do the same, you wouldn't see my feet for dust.'

'There's more to it than that.' He had to think about what he was going to say next. He didn't want to drop Steve Marsh in it by admitting that the two of them had spoken. Callaghan was right: there was no real evidence to suggest anything had actually happened to McKenna, and he had little more to go on than gut instinct. But something felt wrong and all roads led back to Terry Myerson. 'What about his DNA being found at two different murder scenes? You can't just overlook that.'

Callaghan rubbed a hand over his chin, clearly uncomfortable at the mention of one of his officers being potentially linked to a couple of murders. 'Myerson's mixing with some pretty unsavoury characters,' he said. 'It's understandable if his DNA were to get mixed up with theirs.'

'His DNA was found on three murder victims. And I'm sure if we examined Bryony Allen's body again, there's a good chance we might find some on hers too.'

'That doesn't mean he killed them.'

'A court of law might take a different view. And that's where this whole mess could end up if we don't start cooperating with each other.'

Callaghan gave him a long look. If he'd been a cartoon character, Denning was sure there would have been steam coming out of his ears.

'I'm not saying he is involved, but even if he was, they were criminals. Why the concern?' He leaned on his desk. 'Ever heard the expression "a sprat to catch a mackerel"? This is what we're dealing with here, Denning. These people you mention are unimportant in the grand scheme of things. Jason Hart, on the other hand, is a dangerous and ambitious criminal. We need to bring him down, and we should be prepared to do that by whatever means necessary. Myerson is a good officer. He's done undercover work before, and been commended for it. I trust him.'

'Except you haven't heard from him for weeks. You can't say for certain he hasn't gone rogue.'

'And we can't say for certain that he has. It's not uncommon for operatives to lie low at times, especially if they think there might be a risk of their cover being compromised.'

'They're supposed to report in regularly,' Denning said. 'That's operational procedure.'

'For Christ's sake, Denning, this isn't the Met, where everything's nice and cosy and runs by the rule book. We're dealing with serious hard cases and dangerous villains. That's why the NCA was set up in the first place. Operational procedure doesn't always cut it in these kind of situations. We don't have the luxury of playing by the rules.'

'If I could just speak to him. Ask him a few questions. I'll be the very embodiment of discretion.'

'I repeat – there's no chance at all of you speaking to Myerson. The risk is too great. If Jason Hart gets even a passing scent of Myerson being an undercover cop, he'll be on a mortuary slab faster than you can blink. And the past eighteen months have been pissed down the pan.'

'Just how much do you know about what Myerson is up to? You admit it's been some time since you last spoke with him. There must be a part of you that thinks it's just possible he could have gone rogue. It happens. More often than any of us would like to admit.'

Callaghan looked at Denning. If he was hoping to psyche him out with a stare then he was out of luck: McKenna had the gimlet stare perfected to an art form.

'That's bullshit,' Callaghan said. 'Myerson's a professional. There's no way he'd put his career on the line for a psycho like Jason Hart.'

'Not even for hard cash? The chance to retire on his cut of whatever Hart might have offered him. No one can say for certain he wouldn't be tempted. He's human, after all.'

'You're talking crap, Denning. I know Myerson: you don't.'

'Then get him on the phone. Ask him about McKenna and about the two murders. At best, he's a witness; at worst, he's a suspect.'

'Forget it, Denning. This conversation is over. The matter is closed.'

Denning could sense Callaghan wasn't going to budge. He *could* take the matter further; go over Callaghan's head, but what would be the point? Callaghan was right when he said Denning had little evidence to suggest McKenna's life was in danger, and nothing – apart from an unsubstantiated rumour – that Terry Myerson had gone over to the dark side. The presence of Myerson's DNA at two murder sites suggested he was dangerous, possibly even out of control, but it wasn't enough to prove he had gone rogue. And even if that was the case, it was clear to Denning that Callaghan wasn't going to budge.

Denning stood to leave. 'This isn't over.'

Callaghan didn't speak.

Denning left his office, hoping he could remember his way along the rabbit warren of corridors back to the main entrance. He found the lifts and pressed the button for the ground floor. He was suddenly aware of a voice behind him. He turned round to see Steve Marsh walking along an identical corridor to the one he'd just been down.

'Matt. What the fuck are you doing here?'

He nodded a greeting at Marsh. 'I had to speak to Callaghan. Things have moved on since we last spoke.' He explained about McKenna's disappearance.

'You've spoken to Callaghan? Are you mad?'

'Don't worry, I kept your name out of it. But I really need to speak to Myerson.'

'Seriously, though, Matt, you can't go running to Callaghan with tales about police corruption. This could get a lot of people into a lot of trouble.'

'I can't ignore what's happening. I think Myerson has become a liability and I think you – at the very least – suspect that too.' He looked directly at Marsh. 'Tell me I'm wrong and I'll drop this.'

But Marsh just looked at him, his face saying nothing. After a few seconds, he rubbed a hand over his eyes, then indicated to Denning to follow him into an empty office. 'Look, this doesn't go outside these four walls.' He sighed. 'We haven't heard from Myerson for some months. He hasn't reported in and none of his fellow undercover operatives have seen him.'

Denning nodded. 'I know all this, Steve. Callaghan as good as confirmed it. He doesn't seem to think it's a problem.'

'Probably because he would do anything to avoid having to admit something might have gone wrong with Myerson.'

'But there might be?'

'There's a safe house the undercover blokes meet up at from time to time. It gives them a chance to unwind, drink beer, play pool and talk about any kind of crap apart from work. Myerson was always a regular there. Every week, regular as clockwork. He said it was the only thing that kept him sane while he was on a job.' A twitch of the eyebrows. 'He hasn't been near the place in months.'

'And nobody thought this was strange?'

'In itself it doesn't prove anything, but it does hint at one of two things: either he's keeping his head down because things are getting tricky, or...'

'That tells me all I need to know,' Denning said.

He didn't bother waiting for the lift this time, just took the stairs to the ground floor, then a lengthy corridor led him to a set of doors that opened onto the car park at the side of the building.

His phone rang just as he was leaving: it was Neeraj. He pushed open the door to the car park and put the phone to his ear.

'Deep?'

'Another body's been found,' Neeraj said, his voice sounding heavy. 'It's a woman.'

Chapter Forty-Two

Monkswood Golf Club was located roughly halfway between Loughton and Buckhurst Hill. Denning was certain he and Sarah had once met friends for dinner there, and if memory served, the club prided itself on its exclusiveness. Not that that made too much of a difference when it came to the matter of a dead body being found in its grounds.

Technically, this was slightly outside their patch. It officially fell within the jurisdiction of Essex Serious Crime squad, but under the circumstances, Essex had willingly passed it over to them.

Denning parked the Focus outside the clubhouse, where the outer police cordon had been placed. There were already a couple of squad cars there, plus the various CSI vehicles. He spotted Neeraj's battered old Golf GTI – rather appropriate, he thought to himself, despite the fact this was not the time for humour.

A couple of indignant golfers were standing by the cordon remonstrating with one of the uniformed officers, insisting they had a game booked for that morning and demanding to speak to someone in charge.

Denning hurriedly flashed his ID and ducked under the tape, not wanting to get dragged into the argument and unsure he would be able to show sufficient restraint under the circumstances.

Neeraj, Gorton and the CSI team had congregated by the inner cordon about five hundred meters away. The golf course covered a wide area; a sea of carpeted green stretched into the distance, ending at a line of dwarf conifers that separated the golf course from the main Epping to Chigwell road.

He crossed the manicured turf, feeling his shoes sinking slightly into the soft grass.

Neeraj tipped his chin in Denning's direction by way of a greeting.

A weed-choked brook ran along one edge of the golf course. The body had been dumped in it. Her legs were partly submerged in the shallow water, while the upper half of her body was lying on the small bank that sloped down to the brook. The face was a mess, just like the others. Identification wasn't going to be easy. Or pleasant.

'Good morning, Inspector,' Gorton said, a sombre look on her face. Even her dry sense of humour had abandoned her today. She passed him a spare set of coveralls. 'At least this location is rather more accessible than the previous one. I don't want to move the body until Dr Baker gets here. I've been told he's on his way. He did mutter something about us trying to find someone closer, but I insisted. It's best if we can have continuity, assuming we're dealing with the same killer.'

Baker's main role was to confirm the victim was deceased, and to offer some indication as to time and probable cause of death. The latter they could already surmise. This wasn't a coincidence. Time of death was always approximate at this stage, but it gave them a window to work with.

'In the meantime, we're about to start a detailed search of the area,' Gorton continued. 'There are no signs of tyre tracks on the grass, so let's assume she was carried from the car park and dumped here.' She looked at Denning and Neeraj. 'The rest is up to you guys.'

'What you thinking, boss?' Neeraj asked.

Denning knew the importance of keeping morale high amongst his team. They had to remain positive until the victim had been officially ID'd and they could say for certain this wasn't McKenna. 'I think we need to get the post-mortem done as a priority, Deep. Then and only then can we even start to look at possibilities.' He glanced over at the car park. 'The clubhouse must have CCTV. Let's get hold of it. We're due a decent break at some point in this investigation. Hopefully, it's the CCTV that delivers it.'

'Sure, boss,' Neeraj said. 'I'll get on to them now.' He slipped out of his protective overalls and headed back towards the outer cordon.

'We need to ID our victim as a matter of priority,' Denning said to Gorton. He looked at the body: dark hair, black like McKenna's, but like lots of other women too. A smart grey jacket and a pair of skinny jeans. Denning was certain he'd never seen that particular jacket on McKenna, but as he knew from his brief look in her wardrobe, she had plenty of clothes she never wore to work.

'And in the meantime, we shouldn't go jumping to any conclusions,' Gorton added, as if reading his thoughts. 'The body of a middle-aged woman. It could be anyone.'

Anyone who had a connection with Jason Hart and Terry Myerson, Denning thought. That narrowed the field a bit. Word had already spread around the team that McKenna had to all intents and purposes disappeared. Just as Robert Jardine had…

Denning looked at the body. Gorton was right: it *could* be anyone, but it was hard to avoid jumping to the obvious conclusion.

'But there's a clear link to the other murders,' Gorton said. 'Both in terms of the MO and the fact the body was dumped. This isn't a coincidence. There is the possibility this could be a copycat, but that's highly unlikely.'

Denning watched as Neeraj ambled towards the car park. Dr Baker had just arrived and was getting out of a dark green Audi. He opened the boot and took out his coveralls and a large briefcase. The angry would-be golfers had obviously now given up and either gone home, or had repaired to the clubhouse for an early libation.

'Like I said, we get the post-mortem results in and then we consider the options.'

Gorton was looking up at him. 'DNA should help confirm the identity of the victim.' She sighed through her nose. 'Or at least rule out possibilities.'

One thing was becoming obvious to Denning: Jason Hart was dangerous and getting out of control. He thought about contacting Callaghan again and making things official. Go over his head if need be. All he knew was that they were going to have to go after Hart and stop him before more people got hurt.

Chapter Forty-Three

A heavy silence hung over the room like a dark veil.

Molly was trying not to make eye contact with Denning. At the front of the room, pinned to the whiteboard, was a photograph of the most recent crime scene, a blank square where the victim's photo would have been. There was a whisper going round that it could be Betty Taggart. No one had yet dared to utter anything out loud on the subject but the look on Denning's face said he wasn't ruling out the worst.

Whilst Molly had never had the easiest of relationships with their DCI, she respected her. McKenna stood up for her team and would always cover your back, even when you'd fucked up. And they all fucked up from time to time, even Denning. His embarrassing balls-up at the press briefing the other day was already a talking point amongst the team. They might have called her Betty Taggart behind her back, and Molly still wasn't sure where and why the nickname had originated, but she was certain it had been at least partially meant as a compliment.

It was inconceivable to think someone had murdered a serving DCI, but it was hard to ignore the possibility.

'At this stage, we have to keep an open mind,' Denning addressed the room. She could tell he was out of his comfort zone. Not only had he been thrust into the role

of Acting DCI without much notice, he was clearly struggling with the unwelcome possibility that the job might
now become permanent. He looked like he hadn't slept.
'We've asked for the post-mortem results ASAP. And,
obviously, there will need to be a formal ID.'

'The body was in a bit of a state,' Kinsella said. 'Any
identification is going to take time. And we haven't got
that, have we?'

'We can't make assumptions, Dave. Until we know the
score, we can't assume anything.'

Kinsella opened his mouth to say something further
then just shook his head. Of all the detectives in the room,
he had known McKenna the longest. He was the first
detective she appointed when she was approached to head
up their particular MIT, at a time when Major Investigation Teams were still a novelty. If it did turn out that this
latest victim was McKenna, he would take it worse than
anyone.

'Where do we go from here?' Trudi asked.

'I've been in touch with Missing Persons,' Denning
said. 'I've asked for the details of anyone even faintly fitting
our victim's description who has been reported missing
over the past few days. Once we have some possible names
to play with, we can start eliminating people from that list.
Neeraj has got hold of the CCTV from the clubhouse.
It's not ideal as there are only two cameras focused on
the car park: one on the main entrance to the clubhouse
and another on the storage area behind the bar. Neither
is particularly helpful, but at least it's something. We will
check ANPR to see if any vehicles are flagged up in and
around Monkswood Golf Club last night and early this
morning.'

'The golf course isn't a million miles from where the BMW was dumped,' Neeraj pointed out. 'Could be a coincidence, of course.'

'Or it could mean someone is familiar with the area,' Denning said.

'What about this Jason Hart character?' It was Kinsella again. 'Surely we at least bring him in for questioning.'

Molly watched as Denning nodded. 'At the moment, there's nothing that specifically links this to Jason Hart.' He glanced at the whiteboard, his eyes seeming to fall on Hart's photo. 'Hart is part of an ongoing NCA investigation. We have to tread very carefully here. We need to be one hundred per cent sure of our facts before we go blundering in with both barrels and run the risk of screwing up a major NCA investigation. This needs a kid-gloves approach.'

Kinsella shook his head. 'Seriously? The geezer's got blood on his hands. And if he is responsible for the murder of a senior police officer, we need to go after him with everything we have. Fuck the NCA and their investigation. This is a murder inquiry.'

The room fell quiet after Kinsella's outburst. He had said it. Referenced the stinking great elephant shitting all over the neat beige carpet of the MIT suite. Acknowledged out loud that their DCI was quite possibly lying on a mortuary slab being cut open as her inner organs were weighed and measured while they sat around playing Top Trumps over who had final say when it came to arresting the man allegedly responsible.

'We have no proof Hart *is* involved in the murders, Dave. If we go after him with nothing to back up our theory, Hart walks on the murder charge, and the NCA's case against him falls apart.'

'So what then? We just sit around and hope the NCA can get their shit together before someone else gets offed?'

'I'm sorry, Dave, but yes, that's basically it.'

Chapter Forty-Four

Molly could sense that Denning wasn't in the mood for talking, but there was something she had to get off her chest. She tapped cautiously on the door that still said "DCI E McKenna" on the nameplate, and tentatively pushed it open. Denning was sitting behind McKenna's desk with a pained look on his face.

'I wouldn't take Dave's outburst too much to heart, Matt. He's just frustrated.' She sat down unprompted on one of the two chairs opposite the desk, something she'd never have done if Betty Taggart had been sitting on the other side of the desk. 'I imagine it's easier if you're aware of the bigger picture.' She offered Denning a smile. He needed a friend right now, and she was probably the closest thing he had to one. 'Do you fancy going for a pint after work?' She hoped he'd take that offer in the manner it had been intended. What with Anna Klein trying to set her cap at him, he was probably wary of post-work drinks with female colleagues. 'I could ask Deep along if you like...'

Denning returned her smile, but without much enthusiasm. 'Thanks for the offer, Molly, but I'm probably going to work late tonight.' He indicated the pile of paperwork neatly stacked on McKenna's desk. He would have all that to wade through as well as keeping all the plates spinning on the multiple murder inquiries now under his responsibility. She really didn't envy him. 'And I don't blame Dave for his outburst. I understand his frustration, but as long as I'm being stonewalled by the NCA, there's not a lot we can do.'

'Then we get the evidence that allows us to go after Hart. There's nothing the NCA can do if we have a strong case.'

'Not quite that simple, Molly, but thanks for the support. And thanks too for the offer of a drink. Next week, definitely.'

'That's not the only reason I'm here.' She threw him another smile, but wasn't offered one in response this time. 'It's Anna Klein, Matt. I just don't trust her. She's been lying to me about the attack on Dylan Lee – he was one of the gang of burglars that Bryony Allen belonged to.'

Denning nodded. 'Yes, I know who he is, Molly. I've read the report.'

'I'm sure she's covering for one of the suspects. Well, two of them, actually.' She looked at Denning, hoping she didn't sound like she was making a fool of herself. 'Blair and Connor Heaton. She knows one of them. I don't know how well, but I'm certain she's manipulated evidence to ensure he and his brother get away with it.'

'Look, Molly, right now, the whole burglary gang connection isn't worth pursuing. We've got other, bigger fish to fry at the moment.' He gave her a stern look. 'You're going to have to walk away from this and leave it to CID to sort out.'

'Couldn't you have a word with her DI? He needs to know she's hiding something. If we do nothing, then a couple of dangerous thugs are going to get away with a serious crime, and a serving police officer is going to get away with aiding and abetting them. That can't be right?'

'Molly, I just don't need this right now. If things were different we could take this further, but this isn't our fight. Let it go.'

She could see that he wasn't convinced. And who could blame him? It sounded crazy. Anna Klein may not be the most popular member of Islington CID, but she was acknowledged as being a good detective. They would have a hard time trying to persuade her superiors she was anything else.

'It's not just that.' She bit her lip, knowing she should stop while she was slightly behind, and not stray into territory that wasn't strictly speaking any of her concern. 'She seems very interested in you.' She glanced awkwardly at her feet. 'At first I thought it might be a bit of a crush. But I actually think she might be some kind of obsessive.'

She expected him to either laugh at her, or tell her to get out of the office. But she could tell by the look on his face that she wasn't as far off the mark as she'd thought she might be.

'It's no secret that Anna and I have been out for a drink after work on a couple of occasions. She helped me with a case a few months ago and we struck up a friendship. There's nothing more to it than that.'

But Molly knew, from the slight twitch behind his ear, that there *was* more to it than that. 'Maybe you could have a word with her then, Matt. Let her know we're on to her. Or at least help me find out what it is she's hiding.'

Denning sat back in the chair, much as Betty Taggart used to do, and looked at her. Perhaps he was trying to perfect the hard stare that McKenna would give whenever she was attempting to psyche someone out. Or perhaps he just didn't know what to say.

Eventually he spoke. 'I've made my thoughts clear on the matter, Molly. You leave everything to do with Bryony's gang to CID and concentrate on what we're paid to do.' He managed a thin smile. 'Now, is there *anything* else, as I really have a lot to do?'

Chapter Forty-Five

Detective Chief Superintendent Brenda Ross had only been in the job for a few days. She was still finding her feet after the sudden resignation of her predecessor, but she was sharp and shrewd and knew the job well enough to hit the ground in her running shoes. Like McKenna, she'd joined the police in her late teens and steadily worked her way up the ranks. And like McKenna, she was probably counting the days until she could retire on a comfortable pension.

Ross was trying her best to be approachable and open. She'd been on courses, or so she'd told Denning, about how to work with colleagues in a non-confrontational way.

'It's good news,' she said, staring at the report in front of her. 'Of a sort.'

Denning had read the report. The post-mortem had understandably been done as a priority. It confirmed that the body wasn't that of Elizabeth Jayne McKenna, rather it fitted that of Karen Penfold, who had been reported missing by her ex-husband two days ago.

'Karen Penfold worked for the Border Force,' Ross said. 'Until she was sacked a week ago for alleged misconduct. She's been on the NCA's radar as someone who was possibly in Hart's employ. They knew Hart had someone on the inside, and a tip-off led them to suspect it was

Penfold. Dental records are expected to confirm the body left at the golf course is her, but the description fits her well enough for the NCA to now be taking an interest in the case.'

Ross continued reading over the notes. 'The preliminary post-mortem report has indicated that the level of torture appears to have increased. There's also evidence to suggest she was tortured over a longer period of time. The level of violence meted out to her is a sign of the increasing desperation with which Hart is ridding himself of anyone who either gets in his way, or who lets him down. He's getting more ruthless and more dangerous. The DNA test has come back negative, which is a shame as it would have given us a definite link with the other murders, but I think based on the MO, we can comfortably assume we're dealing with the same killer or killers.'

'Do we know why she was killed?' Denning asked.

Ross shook her head. 'The NCA are chomping at my heels to be allowed to take over on this. They suspect the Border Force got wind she was deliberately overlooking illegal shipments of drugs and then forging the requisite paperwork to ensure Customs didn't get suspicious. I've agreed that the NCA can come on board, but with a recommendation we work together.'

'And they've agreed to this?' Denning couldn't imagine Callaghan accepting this without a fight.

'I've spoken to my opposite number at the NCA, and she's agreed it's in everyone's interests to share resources and intelligence. They're never shy when it comes to asking us for a favour, or assistance with a major operation. Perhaps it's time to remind them that arrangement should be quid pro quo.'

'It doesn't address the bigger issue, namely Myerson. If it's true he's on the payroll of both the NCA and Jason Hart, how do we know the rot doesn't seep into the NCA itself?' He was remembering Callaghan's dismissal of his concerns about Myerson, and the vehemence with which he insisted there wasn't a problem. 'If Myerson is corrupt, he's going to ensure Hart's gang remains one step ahead at all times. I'm not sure Callaghan's taking that concern seriously.'

Ross nodded her agreement. 'I expect there's an element of them covering their own backsides over Myerson. They're never going to admit publicly that he's gone bad. But I'm betting if it turns out he has, then there's going to be some kind of internal investigation as to what went wrong. As his handler, Callaghan could potentially find himself in all sorts of shit.'

'In which case, are they going to welcome our involvement with open arms?'

'They're used to working with local forces as and when appropriate, so it's not like this is something new for them. We can bring some localised knowledge. That's always to their advantage. They can either have us inside the tent pissing out, or run the risk of us getting in the way of their investigation.' A twitch of a smile danced round her lips. 'And remember, kid-gloves approach with the NCA, Matt. They're not like us: they play by different rules, and unlike us, they're not directly answerable to the public.' The smile disappeared. 'This is Callaghan's call, so you'll be answerable to him?'

Ross attempted another smile. 'It might be better to think of it as working with him rather than for him, but – yes – ultimately Callaghan will have direct responsibility for this. They've been tailing Hart for some time. They're familiar with his movements and his modus operandi. This is and will continue to be their call, but it'll be a joint operation from now on. You will liaise directly with Callaghan and his team. Deepak Neeraj will take over the day-to-day handling of the ongoing murder investigation, which I believe is mostly now just a case of chasing up witness statements and checking over any outstanding CCTV. It's dull legwork, but it will help to ensure we have a watertight case when this whole shebang goes before the CPS. I've asked one of the other Major Investigation Teams if they can lend support as and when required, and they're prepared to do so. Callaghan says he trusts Myerson and is certain Myerson will lead us directly to Hart. It's not up to me to question an officer over whom I have no authority, but if he's called this wrong, then it's his career on the line and no one else's.'

'Neeraj is a good officer,' Denning said. 'You can rely on him.' Denning knew that Neeraj had been pushing for a promotion for a while now. With a bit of luck this would go in his favour the next time he applied for a DI's post.

'I understand you've got someone chasing up the loose ends regarding Bryony Allen and Robert Jardine. How significant is their involvement in all this?'

Denning explained about Molly Fisher and what she'd discovered so far. He left out the bit about her concerns about Anna Klein. 'We believe Jardine had links with a rival drugs gang. He had a detailed list of suppliers. Obviously this would be of use to Hart. Once he gets his hands on it, he's got a ready-made supply chain.'

'Do we know where this list is now?'

He shook his head. 'We suspect Hart probably has it, or at least has a pretty shrewd idea where it is.'

'And once he has it, all he has to do is introduce himself to the names on the list and make it clear what will happen to anyone if they refuse to cooperate. There must be enough whispers doing the rounds for people to know by now that Hart is responsible for what happened to Jardine and the others.'

Denning nodded. 'There's a journalist called Helen Tranter who seems to be very on the ball. I've had a word with her; offered her a deal. With a bit of luck, she'll play along. But you can never be sure with journalists – I'd certainly never trust one entirely. We may still need to keep an eye on her.'

Another smile appeared on Ross's face, fleeting but noticeable. Naturally she'd seen the press conference, but was gracious enough not to comment on it. 'There will have to be another one once Karen Penfold's identity has been officially confirmed, but I'm happy to cover that, especially if you're going to be tied up with Callaghan and his merry band.'

'I'd appreciate that, thanks.'

As Denning left her office he realised that he'd just dodged one bullet but was potentially about to walk straight in front of another.

Chapter Forty-Six

'I would say "welcome on board", but we both know you're hardly that.' If Callaghan was trying to hide the contempt he felt for Denning, he was failing miserably. Ross had done as she'd said and gone above his head, pulled some strings and insisted on having Denning seconded into the NCA's official investigation into Jason Hart. Callaghan, rather than welcoming the addition to his team, was determined to make his voice of disapproval heard loud and clear. Steve Marsh looked on, his face as impassive as a granite rock, determined to give nothing away.

'Noted,' Denning said dryly as soon as Callaghan had ended his rant. 'Now maybe all that's out the way, we can actually see how best we can work together.'

Callaghan's face burst into a broad smile. 'You're a wanker, Denning, but Marshie here tells me you're whip-smart and good at your job, so I'm prepared to have you as part of this team – just as long as you promise not to piss me off too much.' He sat back in his chair, keeping his gaze fixed on Denning. 'Not, it seems, that I have much choice in the matter. Karen Penfold's murder has considerably upped the ante. That, combined with what we already suspect about Hart, means the situation is in danger of going critical.'

They were in Callaghan's office, just Denning, Callaghan and Marsh, for what Callaghan called a 'chinwag'. Denning had been introduced to the others on the team on his way in; a flurry of names and faces which had been thrown at him in quick succession and only a few had actually registered. Some of the others he would get to know over the next few days, but Callaghan was clearly determined to let Denning know who was in charge.

'Border Force have confirmed that Karen Penfold was in Hart's employ. There have been payments made to her bank account over the past six months totalling more than twenty thousand pounds. Quite a nice little earner for her,' Callaghan said. 'As soon as her employers found out what she was up to, she was suspended pending a full investigation. Presumably Hart wanted to know how much she'd already told them.'

'Hart's going to find it tougher getting stuff through Customs now he's got rid of her,' Marsh said.

'Don't you believe it. He'll have had someone lined up to replace her before her corpse was driven off in the mortuary van.' Callaghan smirked. 'When you're throwing round that kind of cash you're never going to be short of takers.'

'Our priority should be finding DCI McKenna,' Denning said. 'It's possible Hart could be holding her somewhere as some kind of bargaining tool.'

'From what I remember of Betty Taggart,' Marsh quipped, 'I think Hart's the one in bigger danger.' He managed a weak laugh, but his face quickly dropped when he saw that Denning wasn't sharing the joke.

'If there's even a hint that McKenna's in real danger,' Callaghan said, 'we'll go in after her, but at the moment our priority is Hart. We know he's planning something big. We don't know what it is yet, but it's imminent and it's going to shift this whole game up a gear.'

'So you have other operatives watching him? Not just Myerson?' Denning asked.

Callaghan looked over at Marsh, still unsure how much he could actually share with Denning. 'Hart is under twenty-four-hour surveillance,' he said. 'But our strongest asset remains Myerson. He knows Hart, he knows what he's planning. It's via him that we can stay one step ahead of Hart.'

'Except no one has spoken to him for months, so no one knows for certain what's going on with Hart.'

'Not this again, Denning. I thought I'd explained it to you last time you were sitting uninvited in my office: Myerson is none of your business. I'm his handler. He answers to me and me alone.'

'Great. Well, let's get him here and listen to what he has to say. If anyone knows what's happened to McKenna, it's Myerson.'

'Not happening. Forget it.'

There was another heavy silence in the room. Denning looked at Marsh who just shrugged, then at Callaghan who sat impassively behind his desk with his mouth firmly shut.

'If this is to work,' Denning said slowly, 'we need to start trusting one another. And one of you needs to start telling me the truth. I don't want to take this further, but I'm prepared to do so if I have to. And if that means there's a risk this whole operation goes pear-shaped then of the three of us in this room, there's only going to be two men left with their careers intact.'

'You're bluffing, Denning,' Callaghan said, his poker face giving nothing away. 'You go running upstairs to report a fellow officer, you'd last five minutes in the job.'

'You have an undercover officer who is quite possibly corrupt, and there's a strong chance he's either directly or indirectly involved in the murders of five people and the possible disappearance of a senior Metropolitan Police officer. If you're covering for him, Callaghan, it won't be me getting cold-shouldered by my colleagues, it'll be you. That's assuming you're still in the job.' He looked at Marsh, who in turn was looking at Callaghan, a deep frown on his face. 'One of you had better start telling me what the hell's really going on here.'

It was Steve Marsh who spoke. 'Off the record, concerns were raised about Myerson. There have been problems with him in the past.' He looked at Callaghan. 'Sorry, Doug, but there's no use pretending everything's hunky dory, when it clearly isn't.'

'That was years ago and in very different circumstances,' Callaghan said. 'It has no bearing on this current case.'

'Go on, Steve,' Denning prompted, ignoring Callaghan. 'What sort of problems?'

Marsh looked over to Callaghan. After a moment, his eyes dropped. 'He was undercover with an environmental group about ten years ago. He was with the NPIOU at the time. They were a right bunch of headcases.'

'The NPIOU?' Denning had never heard of them.

'The National Public Order Intelligence Unit,' Callaghan explained. 'They deployed undercover officers to infiltrate groups that were deemed to be a threat to public order. They were funded directly by the Home Office and their remit was to target anything that came under the heading of "domestic extremism". Myerson was one of their first officers. Disbanded now, but their legacy lives on like a nasty stain on a pair of underpants.'

Denning wasn't sure he believed what he was hearing. He'd heard rumours about state-sponsored spying on political organisations, but to know that such activities had been sanctioned by the government with the willing assistance of the police was something he felt deeply uncomfortable with. 'What happened?'

'Myerson became involved with one of the women in the group. Long story short, he told the group who and what he really was. The group threatened to sue the police. Myerson was pulled, compensation paid out to the individuals involved and the whole sorry episode was hushed up.' Callaghan sighed. 'It could... *should* have been the end of Myerson's career, but he was good at what he did. He got results. One fuck-up wasn't considered enough to bring him down. He'd just got in over his head. He actually started believing in what they stood for. It's not unusual. These guys are embedded in the groups so deeply they actually start to think like them. They live, eat and sleep alongside the very people they're supposed to be investigating. It's understandable that there are times when it's easy to become brainwashed by the world you've effectively become a part of.'

'And you think that's what's happened with Jason Hart's gang? He's been persuaded by the glamour of a drug dealer's lifestyle? By the money?'

'He wouldn't be the first,' Marsh commented. 'Would he?'

They all knew it happened: sometimes entire forces became riddled with corruption, the situation so endemic that other forces had to step in. Police officers were human, the same as everyone. They had mortgages to pay; debts to settle. Ex-wives and children wanting their share of a not-too-impressive salary. That, coupled with the endless bureaucracy and politics both big and small that seemed to become more prevalent the longer you stayed in the job, meant it was tempting to take what seemed at first glance to be an easy option. But the costs were high. A corrupt cop's life would be made hell in prison. There was the loss of pension. But there were police officers who thought the risks were worth it; the chances of being caught so slim that the pluses outweighed the minuses. The question was: was Terry Myerson one of those cops?

'It was a different ball game back then,' Callaghan said. 'Those guys were never given the training or the support they should have received. We've all learned lessons since then. Things have changed. Like I said, the NPIOU has been officially wound up.'

'We took over a significant part of their remit,' Marsh added. 'Unofficially, of course.'

'Myerson learned his lesson,' Callaghan said. 'He's had half a dozen undercover assignments since then, and there have been no further problems.'

'Yeah, but nothing on this scale,' Marsh said. 'There were people questioning the merit of putting Myerson undercover on something this big again.'

'Questioning *my* judgement,' Callaghan said. 'I stand by my decision. I know Myerson and I trust him.'

'So when, exactly, did you last hear from Myerson?' Denning asked.

'We haven't had any official contact with Myerson since March,' Callaghan replied, refusing to meet Denning's eye.

'What do you mean, "official"?' Denning asked.

Marsh cleared his throat, then said, 'I received a call from Tel back in April, about a month after Kelvin Moore and Adie Carter were murdered. Tel said he was worried that things might be starting to get out of hand and Hart was more of a danger than we'd initially anticipated. He asked if I would meet for a pint and talk things over.' He looked at Callaghan, who was slowly shaking his head. Marsh ignored him and continued. 'He didn't want to make things official. He just wanted to sound me out. I told Doug. He agreed that I should meet Tel, talk things through with him then report back any concerns.'

'What happened when you met?'

'We didn't.'

'Why not?'

Marsh sighed. 'He never turned up.'

'But you tried to contact him?'

'Well, obviously,' Callaghan interjected. He looked at Denning like he was an idiot. 'I left a message urging him to get back in touch immediately. If it looked like he was in danger, or there was any chance his cover was about to be blown, then he had to get out fast. But there was nothing. I never heard from him.'

'But you've tried since?'

'He's using a burner phone. He's supposed to change it every couple of weeks so it can't be traced. That's standard procedure.'

'And you're OK with this?'

'Not initially, no. That's when I started contacting people Myerson knew, including McKenna. It was an act of desperation and, in hindsight, of stupidity. I didn't anti-cipate her overreacting the way she did. I could probably have handled things better. We did think about putting someone else in undercover, but it's too risky. It's probably too late now anyway. It took the best part of a year or more to get Myerson accepted by Hart. If we start beggaring around with things now, Hart might smell a rat. I talked things over with our Director of Investigations, and together we decided that the best thing to do under the circumstances was to wait. Give it time and see what happened.'

'What happened was that another three people were murdered.'

'That was unfortunate,' Callaghan said. 'But we considered that to be collateral damage.'

Denning thought back to the look on Liam Allen's face when he'd told him his daughter had been murdered. To him, Bryony was more than collateral damage.

'You should have pulled Myerson straight away,' Denning said.

'There was a real risk Hart might suss what we're doing,' Marsh added. 'That's assuming Myerson hasn't gone rogue.'

'Can we stop saying he's gone rogue,' Callaghan said.

'But it's a definite possibility,' Denning argued. 'And one that we can't ignore.'

'Admittedly, there could be other reasons as to why he's not getting in touch,' Marsh said. 'If there's even the remotest possibility that Hart suspects him, he'll be keeping his head well and truly below the parapet. If his cover is blown, then months and months of undercover work is down the toilet.'

Denning looked at Marsh. His face was telling a different story to that of his boss. 'Steve?'

'But then again, if he has gone rogue, then we really are stuffed. And as nobody's heard from him since our non-meet back in April, we can't help thinking the worst.'

'You're wrong,' Callaghan said quietly. 'I've heard from Myerson.'

'When?' Denning wasn't sure he believed him. 'If that's true, why are you only telling us now?' He struggled to keep the anger from his voice.

'A couple of days ago. He couldn't talk for long. Sounded like he was in a pub car park.'

'What did he say? Did he mention McKenna?'

Callaghan still wouldn't give Denning eye contact. 'No, he didn't mention McKenna. But he did mention Karen Penfold. I can't go into detail right now, but let's just say if what he says is true, then the shit's about to hit the fan.'

Chapter Forty-Seven

Molly had tried her best to ignore the text message that had arrived from Anna Klein suggesting they meet. As far as she was concerned, they had nothing further to say to one another, and as she'd been told to step back from the burglary investigation, she had no reason to maintain any contact with DS Klein. But Anna was insistent. She'd texted Molly, suggesting they meet at what was by now becoming their usual haunt: the plastic-coated wine bar in Dalston. She promised to tell Molly the truth about her involvement with the Heaton brothers, but she was only willing to do it face to face.

Although every nerve inside her was screaming at her that this was a bad idea, curiosity got the better of her. And besides, there were things she wanted to say to Anna.

When she got to the bar, there was no sign of her. She stood at the bar waiting to be served when she suddenly felt someone standing next to her. Heavy breath on her neck. She turned round to see Blair Heaton standing behind her with a bottle of lager in his hand. Even though he was smiling, she found the experience unnerving.

'What are you doing here?'

'Having a drink. Can I get you one?'

'I'm waiting for someone.'

'Then let me buy you a drink until she gets here.'

Molly wasn't sure what he wanted, but his presence was unsettling. 'Thank you, but no, and you still haven't told me what you're really doing here.'

'Why don't we sit down?' He gestured towards a banquette near the window.

'I'm all right here, thanks.' Despite her apprehension, she stood her ground, looking at him, defying him to challenge her, or worse still, threaten her. One foot out of line and she'd have no hesitation arresting him on the spot.

'Well, that isn't very nice.' He took a swig of lager from the bottle and made a theatrical 'aahhh' noise. 'I'm only suggesting a drink. You see, I've got a lot of respect for the police. You guys do a hell of a tough job for little or no thanks. You can never win, can you? You arrest criminals, you're accused of being fascists. You show a bit of leniency, and people accuse you of being soft on crime. I wouldn't want your job, not for anything. And you're talking to someone who's been in the army. I could go on and on about how I've had it tough, but, do you know, I don't think I've had it as tough as you guys have it.'

'Cheers for the kind words. Now you've said your piece...'

He took another swig of lager. 'See, we were so grateful when you lot came round after our poor ma was killed. Lots of promises about how you'd find the people responsible and they wouldn't get away with it. Then the next thing we know is you've found one of them, and you're going to charge the piece of scum with manslaughter. Manslaughter! We couldn't quite believe that at first, because surely when you attack an elderly woman in her own home and she dies as a direct result of it, then that's murder and not manslaughter? But then again, I can't pretend to be an expert on the law, like yourself. But OK, we decide to go along with this manslaughter charge because we're promised that that will most likely result in a conviction. And then the next thing we know, we're no longer the victims in this whole thing. No, suddenly we're being treated like suspects. All because one of the little bastards that attacked our poor old ma has himself been the victim of violence. I mean, nothing too heavy because he's still walking around and not six feet under like our ma, but serious enough for that same police who were so kind and supportive to us, to have now decided to treat me and my little brother like we're criminals. And we don't think that's very nice or very fair.'

Molly was determined not to be intimidated by him, even though her heart was now beating so loudly she was sure the entire bar could hear it. 'What's your point?' she asked, hoping her voice didn't sound as squeaky and high-pitched out loud as it did in her head.

'OK. I'll come straight to the point.' He lowered his voice so she had to struggle to hear him over the background noise in the bar. 'I hear you've been asking questions about me and Connor. We told you we had nothing to with that little girl's murder, or the attack on her scummy mate, but you don't seem to want to believe that. Connor wants us to contact our solicitor, make a formal complaint of harassment against you, but I told him that wasn't fair: you're only doing your job. That's what I told him. I've managed to persuade him to go along with that. And he's agreed. For now. However, Connor's not like me – I'm the patient one. My brother...' He closed his eyes and shook his head. 'Not so much.'

'You do know you shouldn't even be talking to me,' Molly said. 'Irrespective of whatever you might claim, you and your brother have both been named suspects in a serious assault.' And more besides, she thought. 'I could arrest you for this.'

Blair Heaton leant a beefy, heavily tattooed arm on the bar and grinned at Molly. 'That would be very silly.'

'Really? I'm not so sure.' She hoped she sounded more confident than she felt. 'This feels very much like you're trying to intimidate me into dropping an investigation.' She was aware that it wasn't her investigation to drop.

'Intimidation?' He gave a throaty laugh. 'That's charming. I've offered to buy you a drink and told you I just wanted to chat, and you go and accuse me of something like that. I might be speaking out of turn here, officer, but maybe you ought to brush up on your people skills. But I'll cut to the chase as you're obviously keen to get on your way. You have no evidence and you're not likely to find any, either. If this ever got as far as a court of law, you'd be laughed at. Take a tip from me: let the whole thing drop before it backfires and leaves you looking like a silly little girl.'

Molly fought the overwhelming urge to knee him in the bollocks. Instead, she said, as calmly and as politely as she could manage: 'I've been patronised by bigger and uglier men than you, Mr Heaton, so unless you have something useful to say, I would like you to fuck off.'

'That's fine, sweetheart. I'm just offering you some sensible advice. It's up to you whether or not you take it.'

'Well, that's very sweet of you. But if you don't leave this bar in the next ten seconds, I *will* arrest you for harassment and I'm pretty sure once you're down the nick we can find something else to charge you with. So, thanks for your kind words. I've taken them on board, now it's time for you to piss off.'

Heaton smiled at her, deliberately waited more than ten seconds, placed his almost-empty lager bottle on the bar, and slowly turned and left the wine bar.

Once she'd made sure he was out on the street, Molly took her phone from her bag. Her hand was shaking so much she had to leave the phone on the bar until she could feel her pulse return to normal. The barman came over and asked if she was all right, and did she want something to drink? She shook her head and told him she was fine. Luckily, he took the hint and left her alone.

After a couple of minutes, she picked up her phone and texted Anna:

Where the fuck are you?

She didn't have long to wait until the phone pinged with a reply:

Soz, something came up. Was just about to text you. Can we make it another time?

Molly didn't bother to reply. Whatever the hell was going on here, she now knew Anna Klein was involved with it right up to her scrawny little elbows. And, despite Denning's insistence that she ceased her involvement with the case, she was determined she was now going to drag the truth from Anna and hopefully bring her and Blair Heaton down in the process. Threatening a police officer, – and she was certain this had been a threat – suggested something big. She was sure the Heatons were responsible for the attack on Dylan, but now she was convinced there was something else going on. Something bigger.

Whatever the Heatons were up to, she was determined to find out. And she was sure Anna Klein knew the answer to that question.

Chapter Forty-Eight

It was early and the road was quiet. Only a handful of vehicles had been down it in the past ten minutes: a couple of cars, a van and a supermarket lorry. A light splattering of overnight rain had left wet patches on the tarmac, though none of the drivers had bothered slowing down. Denning imagined this would normally be a busy road as it linked London with the south coast, although circuitous and twisty.

He was sitting in an unmarked police car in a layby on the A21 not far from Hawkhurst, dressed in a padded flak jacket and trying not to keep glancing at his watch. It had been just over a week since Bryony Allen's body had been found in the churchyard in Leytonstone. As yet, nothing was happening. Marsh was parked in another layby about a quarter of a mile south of here, presumably doing much the same as Denning. Their target was on its way, and until it reached them, all they could do was count the passing minutes.

There were a dozen police vehicles waiting in a nearby garden centre car park, ready to move as soon as they got the word. The whole thing had been planned with near military precision. Marsh was leading the operation with the tactical support of the South East Regional Organised Crime Unit. He was in constant radio communication with Callaghan, who requested a continual update as events unfolded.

So far, there was nothing to report. And it was the waiting around that was the most frustrating.

Callaghan had been vague when pressed about his recent chat with Myerson. When pushed, he'd informed them that he had been given specific information that Hart was planning something big, and it was happening today. A major shipment of drugs was coming into the country. Hart was planning to flood the local markets and undercut his competition. Callaghan had organised a raid to stop him in his tracks.

Denning had specifically asked to be involved in this shout. Ordinarily, he wouldn't have been allowed anywhere near a major NCA-led operation like this, but he had insisted that if he was seconded to the team, then he had every right to be involved. Marsh had argued that the extra manpower might come in handy and Callaghan had reluctantly agreed.

Relations with Callaghan were still frosty, though a thin veneer of civility now existed between them. Denning thought Callaghan had had a defeated look about him at the last briefing, as though he knew they were being outgunned and outmanoeuvred by someone who invariably seemed to be one step ahead of them.

Jason Hart was a clever cookie. Had he been a legitimate businessman, Denning would almost have admired him. But he was a criminal, and one who quite possibly had a serving police officer on his payroll, in spite of anything Callaghan was arguing to the contrary.

Denning was sitting on the back seat of a Vauxhall Insignia, two taciturn NCA officers in the front pretending he wasn't there. He wanted to get out and stretch his legs, but it wasn't going to happen just yet. To his left, on the other side of a low hedge, was a field full of grazing sheep. The field ran down to a small lake, which was surrounded by further fields. In the distance, he spotted a large, pitch-roofed house topped with absurdly tall chimneys and beyond that, a row of two-storey cottages. He didn't know the area. It felt like it was beyond the back of beyond, yet they were less than fifty miles from London, and less than half an hour from Tunbridge Wells. Not so long ago, Sarah had mentioned the possibility of moving to the country, insisting it would improve their quality of life. Luckily, she'd soon forgotten the idea and it was never mentioned again…

The radio suddenly crackled into life informing them their target had just turned off the junction for Hawkhurst and was heading in their direction. It would be passing Marsh in a matter of seconds.

The turn-off at the next roundabout had already been closed by the local traffic police, and the previous junction would be closed as soon as the lorry had fully entered that stretch of road.

Their target was avoiding the quickest and most obvious route into London, the M20, preferring to stick to the quieter A roads that threaded their way along the south coast and then ran north through East Sussex and the High Weald of Kent, before entering London unobtrusively from the south east. This was one of the few straight sections of the road and had been considered the best spot for the target to be intercepted.

The target sped past them just as Marsh gave the word for the police convoy to move out. Within two minutes they had surrounded their target: a Dutch container lorry supposedly carrying dog food. There was a hiss of hydraulics as the brakes were applied and the lorry slid to an abrupt halt. The car Denning was sitting in immediately pulled out of the layby and stopped just behind the lorry. A second later, Marsh's car screeched to a halt beside them. Marsh and his team jumped out of the car and ran towards the front of the lorry, Marsh shouting orders to surround the lorry and get the driver. Armed officers had already poured out of the police vans and were pointing their Glock 9mm semi-automatics at the lorry's cab. It was unlikely the driver was armed, but they had to take the necessary precautions.

The driver climbed out of the cab and stood with his hands raised, looking confused, clearly not understanding what was being shouted at him. A couple of armed officers gestured at the road. He knelt on the damp tarmac while they checked him for weapons. One of them, a young woman in her twenties, looked over at Marsh and shook her head, confirming that the driver wasn't armed. He was immediately pulled to his feet and ordered to open the back of the lorry. Denning held his breath, unsure what was going to happen next. The driver still looked confused. Either his English wasn't very good, or he was so overwhelmed by everything that was going on his brain was unable to compute what he was being asked. Eventually, he got the message and slowly unlocked the rear doors. Marsh was at the back of the lorry now, with a group of armed officers covering him as the doors were pulled open.

Two NCA officers climbed into the back of the container. Marsh was relaying the whole thing back to Callaghan as it happened.

One of the two officers appeared at the back of the lorry. 'Nothing,' he said. 'It's clean.'

'Shit,' said Marsh. 'It can't be. Get back in there and have a proper look.'

He reappeared a few minutes later, again shaking his head. 'There's nothing in there. The wagon's empty.'

Marsh turned to the driver. 'What the fuck's going on? Where are they?'

The driver, a short, stocky man in his fifties, shrugged and rambled something in a foreign tongue, nervous eyes darting from Marsh to the armed officers surrounding his lorry.

Marsh was shouting at the driver in English. The driver was making a big show of not understanding a word Marsh was saying, shaking his head and looking bewildered, as though everything that was happening to him was some kind of nightmare that was beyond his comprehension. Marsh directed a couple of officers to handcuff the driver and put him into the back of one of the cars. The same female officer who had checked the driver for weapons moved towards him, unclipping a pair of cuffs from her belt. Suddenly there was a loud bang and the side of the driver's head exploded in a cascade of red, covering the female officer in an abstract spewing of blood and brain matter. A second later, the lorry driver was on the ground, unmoving, the bloody gore from his shattered skull soaking into the cold hard grey of the tarmac.

In the tsunami of confusion that followed, Denning remembered diving behind a car, trying to figure out where the shot had come from. Marsh was shouting at everyone to get under cover, while simultaneously relaying the incident to Callaghan over his radio. Another shot rang out, hitting an officer. A couple of them were firing into a line of trees at the top of a slope on the other side of the road, from where Denning now reckoned the shots must have come. Marsh was screaming down the radio, demanding that Callaghan deploy a helicopter. There was a rustle of movement from the top of the leafy slope opposite, and another volley of shots was fired into the trees.

Denning was still lying low behind a police car. The injured officer had been pulled to safety by a colleague and was clutching a bleeding wound to his upper arm, but indicating that he was otherwise OK. The lorry driver was lying motionless a few meters from his lorry. A crimson pool of blood was spreading out from what remained of his head, trickling down the camber of the road and staining the grassy verge with splashes of red.

A group of armed officers was heading up the slope in the direction of the long line of trees. Denning, squinting into the low morning sun, couldn't see anything except shadows dancing between the trees. Over the din of Marsh's shouting, he heard what sounded like a car accelerating from somewhere beyond the line of trees at the top of the slope. After a few minutes the officers returned, shaking their heads.

Marsh was swearing down the radio. He and Callaghan seemed to be having a heated discussion about the deployment of the helicopter. The general consensus now being that it was too late; the shooter would be long gone.

The blare of distant sirens began to filter through the chaos; presumably further police and an ambulance for the injured officer. There was nothing that could be done for the lorry driver.

Denning looked at the mess around him. It was difficult to say what had gone wrong. But it was clear that something had gone very wrong indeed. The grim expression on Marsh's face said someone's balls were going to end up in a vice. He couldn't see how Callaghan was going to talk his way out of this mess. He'd claimed he'd received good intel, but this was clearly not the case.

But there was something else here. Denning was beginning to regret having asked to come along on this. He wasn't sure this was why he had joined the police force in the first place. Solving crimes and catching murderers was one thing, but being caught up in an armed stakeout, especially one that had clearly gone very badly wrong, wasn't his bag. This hinted at something else; something that had less to do with policing and more to do with bravado. He was beginning to ask himself some very serious questions.

Chapter Forty-Nine

'Well, that was a fuck-up. A fuck-up of almost monumental proportions. In fact, as far as fuck-ups go, I think that's probably worthy of an award.' Callaghan wasn't happy. And he wasn't being shy about it.

They were in Callaghan's office in the NCA's headquarters near Lambeth Bridge. Denning, Marsh, Callaghan and a bloke from the South East Regional Organised Crime Unit, whose name Denning hadn't caught. Callaghan had to report to his superiors later that afternoon and offer up a credible explanation as to why things had gone wrong on such a spectacular scale. Denning still wasn't entirely sure why he was at the meeting. He'd been little more than an objective observer during the whole proceedings. But Ross had phoned him immediately after the event insisting that as one of her MITs had been involved, she wanted to make sure none of the oncoming shit was going to land on her desk. She planned to stay in the job marginally longer than her predecessor, and had her pension to think about. Policing was as much about politics as it was about catching criminals.

Denning was sitting at the back of the room, trying to keep his head down and say very little. What was there to say, anyway? He'd watched the entire thing unfold in front of his eyes like some kind of horror show. Callaghan hadn't wanted him on the team in the first place, and certainly hadn't wanted him on the operation, so he knew he had to keep quiet until the shit had been chucked at the fan. He would fight his corner if he had to, but until then, the best approach was to remain silent.

'We were obviously played for a bunch of twats,' Marsh barked. 'The whole thing was a set-up from the off. The lorry was clearly a decoy. I can't believe we were stupid enough to fall for it.' He said 'we', but he was directing his ire firmly at Callaghan. This had been Callaghan's call from the off.

Callaghan was trying his best not to look uncomfortable. Denning didn't envy him having to explain his actions to the senior bodies at the NCA, or for that matter, the Home Office.

'We had good intel,' Callaghan said, though the wobble in his voice suggested even he didn't believe that right now. 'We were told that Hart had arranged to have a significant consignment of drugs transported into London from the coast via a specific route. The route was chosen because it was unlikely to attract attention.'

'Where did this intel come from?' someone asked.

'I can't say,' Callaghan replied.

'Can't? Or won't?' he was asked.

Callaghan shuffled awkwardly in his chair. 'All that matters is that we had good intel and we were duty bound to act on it.' His voice had lost the wobble and he was clearly trying to come across as more in control of the situation than he felt. The look on Marsh's face said he wasn't buying it, but Callaghan was still his senior officer and so he had to watch his step.

They were still trying to unpick exactly what exactly had happened.

A map pinned to the wall in Callaghan's office showed the lorry's route between Dover and London, along with some aerial shots of the scene. A minor B-road ran almost parallel to the A21 at the point where the lorry had been stopped. At that exact point, it was only a few meters away from the section of the A21, immediately beyond the line of trees at the top of the slope. It had been an easy job to position a gunman there, unseen, and then for him to make his escape the moment he'd made the hit. He'd been clever; hitting the armed officer had been enough to let the rest of them think they were potential targets too. The momentary confusion between retaliating and diving for cover had given him enough of a window to make his escape.

'We suspect the shooter used a long-range AI sniper's rifle. Probably an Accuracy International, 7.62 x 51mm NATO/.308, or something similar, and likely ex-army issue,' the bloke from SEROCU said. He was a quietly spoken man in his forties, wearing gold-rimmed glasses, and dressed in an ill-fitting grey suit. He looked like he'd be more at home teaching geography in a secondary school, but he spoke with authority and neither Callaghan nor Marsh had dared to challenge him. If they were looking for a convenient scapegoat, it was unlikely they were going to choose him. 'Two bullets fired,' he continued. 'Both of which are with our forensics team, but they're probably not going to tell us much, except to confirm the age and make of the gun. Even if they do manage to connect it to a specific gun, the chances are it was brought into the country illegally and has more than likely been sold on or destroyed by now.'

'It's too late now anyway,' Callaghan said. 'It did what it needed to do. Our chances of catching the shooter are less than zero. This was clearly a professional hit.' He puffed his cheeks out. 'But all this is just window dressing. We know who's behind it. Hart's the man we should be focussing on.'

'You've almost got to admire his balls,' Marsh said.

'Yeah, well, when we've got him in custody, you can do what you like with him,' Callaghan retorted.

Marsh ignored him. 'Hart goes to all that effort to stage manage an elaborate distraction, ensures we're given duff intel and eliminates the one person who could potentially tie it all back to him. That takes some skill.'

'What *do* we know about the driver?' Denning asked.

It was the turn of the bloke from SEROCU again. 'An Austrian national called Kurt Lenya. He's clean. Been driving lorries all his adult life, though not for the past six months due to a heart complaint. Was based in Europe. This was only his second time in the UK. Very probably hired by a third party, and it's more than likely he was completely ignorant as to what was going on and only took the job because he'd been out of work for so long and needed the money.'

Denning tried not to think of what had happened to the poor man. Driving a lorry through an unfamiliar country, oblivious to the cruel twist fate had in store for him. 'Did he have family?' Denning asked. He was determined to remind everyone in the room that despite the focus being on the clever administrations of a drug dealer, there were real people whose lives were being destroyed.

'An ex-wife,' the Kent and Sussex Police bloke said. 'Not known if he had any children.'

'Look, can we forget about the sodding lorry driver,' Callaghan barked. 'It's shit-awful what happened to him, but let's keep focussed on the bigger picture here.' He was looking directly at Denning when he spoke. 'If Jason Hart isn't stopped we're looking at hundreds, perhaps thousands of lives being ruined by the poison he's going to be flooding the streets with. We know he's got the import side well and truly covered, and from what Denning's told us, it's now likely he's got access to a sound distribution network.'

'And the drugs are definitely in the UK now?' Denning asked.

'We reckon the real delivery was made this morning whilst we were playing silly buggers on the A21,' Marsh said. 'Either via another back-road route, or directly up the M20. It doesn't make much difference: Hart did what he needed to do to get the stuff in here. As yet, we don't know the quantity, but we know it's a lot. We're arranging with Border Force for a detailed itinerary of all container lorries that arrived in UK ports in the south of England today, but it will take weeks to track them all down.'

'By which time the next consignment will be on its way,' Callaghan said. He looked round the room. 'Do you ever feel like that little Dutch boy? The one who stuck his finger in a dyke. No matter how quickly he plugged one hole, another one appeared.' He rubbed a hand over his face. 'We're fighting a losing battle here. There are days I can't help thinking if they were to just legalise this shit we could all turn our priorities to fighting real crime.'

'It's not our call,' Denning said. 'You said it yourself, once these drugs find their way onto the streets, it'll cause misery for thousands.'

'Maybe,' Callaghan said, still not convinced.

'Still doesn't help us,' Marsh said. 'What went down today isn't going to make us look good.' He looked round the room. 'Any of us.'

It made Denning think. Think about how they'd got into this mess in the first place. 'Where did the original intelligence come from?' he asked.

'Unimportant,' Callaghan said. 'We had reason to believe it was reliable.'

'But it wasn't, was it?' Marsh said.

Then it dawned on Denning. 'It was Myerson?' he said. 'The tip-off: it came from him? This is what you meant when you said the other day that the shit was about to hit the fan. This is why he got in touch after all this time. He was deliberately giving you dodgy intel, getting you to look the other way while the real consignment got into the country, through Customs and shipped up to London, or wherever the hell it's gone, all with safe passage. This is your fuck-up, Callaghan. You need to own it.'

Denning could see Marsh was silently agreeing with him, but biting his lip to make sure he still had a job at the end of this.

Callaghan got to his feet. 'Look, Denning. You might not trust the officers under you, but I've still got some faith in mine. Myerson got in touch. He said things were difficult and Hart was watching him the whole time. He thought there was a danger his cover was about to be blown. He didn't say how, or why he felt like that.' Callaghan sat back down. 'Then he told me about the lorry. He gave me all the details.' He rubbed a hand over his face again. 'I believed him. I had no reason not to. We already knew from other sources that Hart was planning to bring a large quantity of illegal drugs into the country, we just didn't know the details. I trusted Myerson.'

'Except he let you down,' Marsh said eventually. 'And because of that we all ended up in shit creek. One man's dead and another one's in hospital.'

'He deliberately misled you,' Denning said. 'Thanks to that, Hart's got away with it. He's played you for a fool, and you've let him. And thanks to your balls-up, I suspect DCI McKenna's life is probably now in even greater danger.'

'Not this again, Denning. You've got no proof that Hart's gang have got McKenna. Or even that anything has happened to her. You're chasing shadows here and we don't have time for that.'

He knew Callaghan had a point. He had nothing more than a hunch that something had happened to McKenna. But her continued silence unnerved him. There were too many things happening here that he didn't like.

'There's another issue here,' Callaghan said. 'We've got to ask ourselves why we received this duff intel in the first place. I assume it was done on Hart's orders. Mainly to make us look like a bunch of twats and ensure our attention was focused elsewhere when the real drop-off was being made. But we can't ignore another possibility. If Hart has got suspicious about someone in his gang, he could have deliberately planted the duff intel knowing it would lead us in the wrong direction. It could be that Myerson, rather than having double-crossed us, is actually in real danger himself.'

Chapter Fifty

Islington police station was a characterless box of a building. It had been built in the late 1980s, but superficially made to resemble something from an earlier age. Except it didn't. It looked like what it was: bland and utilitarian and stubbornly modern.

The woman on the desk had smiled enthusiastically at Molly when she'd explained who she was and why she was there. She'd phoned up to CID to ask if DS Klein was free, only to be told she was in a meeting. Molly said she'd wait. She wasn't going to let Anna Klein off the hook quite so easily.

After about ten minutes, she decided to cut to the chase and sent Klein a text, insisting if she didn't come down right away, Molly would contact her DI and tell her what she knew about Anna and the Heatons. Maybe she wouldn't be able to prove any of it, but it would leave Anna with a lot of difficult questions to answer.

The reply wasn't long in coming. Just over a minute later, the door by the reception desk buzzed open and a slightly harassed-looking Anna Klein stood there. If she was happy to see Molly, she didn't let it show. 'What do you want, Molly? I'm busy.'

'You and me both. But we need to talk.'

There was a coffee shop on Upper Street, not far from the police station. Molly ordered a latte, while Anna had an Americano. They sat at the back near the door to the toilet so they wouldn't be overheard.

Molly told her about her run-in with Blair Heaton. The implicitness of his threat. The sinister nature of the conversation. 'But the thing that bugs me the most,' she said, 'was, how did he know I was going to be there?'

Anna stared into her Americano, as though the answer to Molly's question could be found somewhere in the black oily liquid. 'Maybe he followed you, like Paul Chitterly did that night. Or maybe he just got lucky.'

'Or maybe you told him I'd be there?' She looked directly at Anna, hoping the woman would have the decency to give her a bit of eye contact, but she continued to gaze into her coffee like she was hypnotised by it. 'It was you who suggested that wine bar,' Molly said. 'And I don't believe in coincidences. So, either you start telling me the truth, or I have a little heart-to-heart with your DI and tell him what I know.'

Anna looked up at Molly, her face a sallow wash of guilt. 'All right. You've guessed most of it.' She drank some of her coffee, placing the cup back on the saucer with a thud. 'I was at school with Blair. He was in the year above me, but we had a few friends in common. We used to hang out together. By the time I bumped into him again, we hadn't seen each other for years. But he recognised me. When I went to speak to them, after the burglary at his mum's, I recognised him, of course, and I'd already sussed from the name there might be a connection. He hasn't changed. A bit rougher round the edges, maybe, but still the same old Jack-the-lad. He and his brother used to be cocks of the walk at our school. All the girls were after them.' She took another sip of coffee. 'It seems they'd both left the army at around the same time.

I don't know the exact details but Connor was involved in some kind of incident and Blair tried to cover for him. Anyway, whatever the story, they'd either left by choice or been chucked out. They were earning a living doing whatever came their way.' She tutted to herself. 'They weren't exactly criminals – at least not proper villains – but they weren't afraid of ignoring the law when it suited them. From what I can gather, and it was all courtesy of rumour and hearsay, they were fencing stolen goods, that kind of thing.'

'OK, you knew them from school, you fancied one of them, and now you suspect they may be involved in criminal activities. That still doesn't come close to explaining why you've been covering for them now.'

She paused while someone headed into the toilet, waiting until the door closed behind them before she continued. 'It was years ago. Blair used to go out with my best friend, Nadine. We were teenagers at the time: young and stupid. A group of us were coming back from a nightclub in Essex. It was someone's birthday. We were drunk and ended up packed into a BMW I later learned was stolen. I can't remember the exact details because I was half asleep at the time, but we hit someone. It was pissing down with rain and he was standing in the middle of the road. Blair was driving, and he'd had a few. It was all over in a second, and to this day I can't really remember any of it.'

'What happened next?'

'We all got out the car. The bloke we hit was still alive, but unconscious. We could smell the booze on him. There was hardly any CCTV in those days, and because the weather was so awful, there was no one around, so we hadn't been seen. Blair phoned an ambulance from a phone box rather than risk the call being traced back to his mobile. They still had phone boxes on street corners back then.'

'I'm not interested in phone boxes, Anna. I want to know where this story's going.'

She sighed again as it all came back. 'We abandoned the car and legged it. Nadine and I ended up waiting in the rain for a night bus a couple of streets away. We had ages to wait for one to turn up. I remember hearing the sound of sirens and throwing up. I don't know what happened to the others. They either got a taxi back or nicked another car. I don't know. I never asked. I heard that the bloke we hit died in hospital the next day. We all agreed to keep quiet about it. Then we all just got on with our lives. It was the kick up the backside I needed to sort myself out. I'd been heading off the rails for a while; rebelling against my parents, I suppose. Anyway, I decided to sort myself out. I became head girl the following year and worked at getting some decent qualifications. I left school the year after and eventually joined the police. Maybe as a way of making up for what had happened, I don't know… I heard from Nadine that Blair had joined the army; Connor followed him a couple of years later. If it had got out about what we'd done, both our careers would have been stuffed.' She gave a dry chuckle. 'It's like what you said, that time in the wine bar, about your friend who was murdered. We all do things we regret when we're young. Things we wish we could go back in time and change. Or maybe not. Maybe these things shape our character as we get older. We're not so different, you and me.' She was looking at Molly now. Trying to suggest they were somehow kindred spirits because they were both still haunted by a moment of stupidity from their youth that had left an ugly scar on their insides, even years later. 'You fucked up when you were a teenager and so did I. We're neither of us perfect. It doesn't mean that fuck-up should define the rest of our lives.'

'Bex was murdered by a maniac, Anna. You covered up a crime. The two things are not even remotely similar.'

'I had no choice. Blair insisted we had to agree to keep quiet about it. If it got out, then we were all in the shit. There was a police investigation, naturally, but there was nothing linking us to the stolen car or to the accident. We got away with it.'

'Until now.'

'You can't tell anyone. You can't make this official, Molly. I'd lose my job. A job I love and am good at. For what? Something that happened almost twenty years ago?'

'I think you're missing the point, Anna. It's obviously affected your judgement. Connor and Blair Heaton are suspects in a crime. You have a moral – not to mention legal – obligation to report them.'

'They had nothing to do with that girl's murder, we know that now. And, OK, so they may have given that little shit a pasting, but so what? Do we really join the police to protect people like Dylan Lee? He's got a criminal record going back to his days in primary school. Society would be a better place without people like that running around.'

'We don't get to pick and choose the people we police, Anna. We uphold the law. The law applies equally to everyone, not just to the people with good jobs and nice manners.'

'This is somebody who broke into the homes of elderly people and terrorized them. Someone decided to teach them a lesson. It's more than the courts would have done.

It's more than any prison sentence would have taught them. People like Dylan Lee and the rest of that bunch of thieving, robbing scum have got away with it all their lives, and go on getting away with it. They know how to play the system, and it's innocent people who suffer. Our job is to tidy up their mess. We put a sticking plaster over the wounds, then sit back and wait for it to happen all over again.'

Molly shook her head and fought back her anger. 'It's not up to you to decide what happens to the criminals we catch. The moment we decide it's OK to mete out our own brand of justice is the moment we know we shouldn't be in the job.' She looked at Anna, trying to figure out what was going on in her head. But Anna didn't speak. The silence was filled by the hum of chattering from the other customers and the gentle throb of a radio behind the counter.

'What happened?' Molly asked eventually, to fill the silence if nothing else. 'Did Blair get in touch with you? Ask you to turn a blind eye to whatever he and his brother were up to or else he'd tell the world what you'd done? Is that how it went?'

The woman came out of the toilet. Anna stayed silent until she was out of earshot. 'Pretty much. He was waiting for me when I left work one evening. Took me for a drink and told me he wanted to reminisce about the "good old days". He asked if I remembered what happened that night. I tried to underplay it, knowing exactly where he was going with his "reminiscing". Dylan Lee was out of hospital and keeping his mouth shut. It seemed easiest just to forget about it. But then you kept digging. You wouldn't let it drop. Insisting there was more going on than just some petty criminal getting the shit beaten out of him. Even once we knew they weren't involved in Bryony Allen's murder, you just kept on and on about it.'

'But we didn't know, did we? We still don't know for certain they're not connected to her murder, even indirectly. Or Rob Jardine's, for that matter. They're officially still suspects. Suspects you've done your best to protect. And as for getting them to threaten me, that only makes them look even more guilty of something.'

Her face tightened. 'Blair didn't leave me with much choice. I'd already told him I'd persuade you to drop the whole thing, but when you wouldn't, he insisted on taking a more direct approach.' She looked at Molly pleadingly. 'Look, if I thought for one second that Blair or his brother were guilty of murder, I would have them both arrested no matter what had gone on between us. But they're not involved. They may be many things, but they're not murderers. I know they're not. You have to believe me and you have to let this go.'

Molly had finished her latte. She didn't want another one. She didn't want to spend another minute with Anna Klein listening to this crap.

'At least promise me you'll keep everything I've just told you to yourself. Please?'

Molly didn't reply. Anna changed tack. 'If you make this official, I'll simply deny it. There's nothing to link me to what happened back then, and little to connect me to Blair Heaton. So I was at school with him. That's not relevant and nobody would take that seriously.'

Molly left the coffee shop without saying anything. As she walked out the door, she was certain she could hear Anna still pleading with her.

Chapter Fifty-One

Denning had returned to the MIT office for a briefing and a catch-up.

Molly had gone over to Islington to tie up a couple of loose ends, according to Trudi. She, Kinsella and Neeraj were checking over witness statements for the three murders they were still responsible for investigating, as well as double-checking all the available CCTV. So far, they'd found nothing useful. CCTV from the golf club had shown a grey van pulling into the car park in the early hours, but no registration number was obvious. However, they would contact the DVLA to check with ANPR sightings of anything that fitted the description from the surrounding area. 'Even if we do find a match,' Kinsella said wearily, 'chances are the vehicle in question will have been torched by now, or have been through at least one respray and a change of plates, then sold on to some unsuspecting sod for cash.'

According to Trudi, a woman living in the flats that backed on to the Parkland Way recalled being woken by a noise shortly after midnight on the day Jardine's body had been found, but she was partially sighted, and when she'd looked out of her bedroom window, she hadn't seen anything beyond a blurry shape loitering by the wall. She'd assumed it was an animal of some kind, and gone back to bed thinking it was unimportant.

'It's like trying to push water uphill, boss,' Neeraj said. 'We just can't find anything that directly links Jason Hart with these murders.'

Denning agreed. They were dealing with pros here. And with Myerson advising Hart on their expected moves at every juncture, their chances of catching him out were diminishing by the day. Myerson had been a cop for a long time. He not only knew how they worked, he knew how they thought. And now Hart, if his suspicions were correct, had all that intel handed to him for nothing.

Denning headed into McKenna's office and sat behind her desk. There was still continued radio silence from their DCI, and with each passing day, his occupancy of her office was beginning to feel more and more like a permanent fixture. At which point, were they all going to have to give up hope and accept the inevitable?

He checked his watch. Callaghan would be in a meeting with his superiors now. There would be someone from the Home Office asking difficult questions. He was going to struggle to spin what had happened. If he told them the truth, his career would be over. If it could be proved that Myerson was corrupt, Callaghan could be seen as having been complicit. He would be lucky to escape with his pension intact.

They had been lucky in so far keeping the raid out of the media. It was simply referred to as 'an incident', and the finer details underplayed. There were the inevitable rumours doing the rounds on social media, but no one had yet come close to guessing the truth.

The bigger story was what would happen next. A large consignment of drugs had reached its destination and would shortly be entering the supply chain, making Jason Hart a very wealthy man and establishing him as a major player in the South East's drug market. And as word leaked out in the criminal community that he had successfully got one up on the NCA, thanks in no small part to the services of a corrupt officer, he would begin to feel he was untouchable. And, for a while, he would be. They'd catch up with him eventually, even if it took years and more botched attempts like this morning's fiasco. Too many botched attempts like this morning, however, and it wouldn't just be Callaghan's career on the line.

His phone rang. He glanced at the caller ID, but it came up with *number unknown*, the second time in the past hour that had happened. Strange… His first thought had been that it might be McKenna calling from another phone, but she'd have left a voicemail message. As would Claire if she'd been doing the same. He did briefly think it might be a senior officer from the NCA trying to contact him to get his feedback on that morning's botched raid, but he'd already submitted an official report in writing, which had covered everything in detail, or at least as far as he remembered it, events having unfolded so fast.

It was likely an unwanted sales call, or a scam telling him he'd missed a postal delivery and could he contact an anonymous number to pay a small fee. He'd received a few of these calls recently. They always seemed to come in spates.

He tried to put it out of his mind and concentrate on tying up the loose ends with the murder investigation. The only piece of evidence they had that even vaguely connected Hart with the murders was CCTV footage of him talking to Rob Jardine in The Lydon Arms shortly before Jardine disappeared. It was so tenuous as to be worthless. There had to be a smoking gun somewhere; something that would blow this whole case apart and signal the beginning of the end for Jason Hart. Right now, that moment felt very far away.

His phone rang again. He stared at the screen for several seconds: *number unknown* staring back at him. Another few seconds and the call would automatically divert to voicemail. This time, the caller might leave a message. Might, or might not…

He swiped to the 'answer' icon, and put the phone to his ear.

'Who is this?'

'Denning?' The voice was barely more than a throaty whisper.

There was a pause and Denning thought that whoever was on the other end of the line had hung up. Then, 'It's Terry Myerson. We need to talk.' Another pause. 'I'll text you when and where we meet. You tell no one about this call.'

Then the line went dead.

Chapter Fifty-Two

Molly felt nervous as she walked along the road. She was sure that she was giving off signals advertising the fact she was a police officer. And then there was the very real possibility someone might actually recognise her. Someone she'd arrested.

The estate was in one of the rougher parts of east Hackney and had a reputation as a rats' nest of roads and walkways inhabited by criminals, but she knew the reputation of a place never told its true story. Forty years ago, it had been a pleasant enough place to live. Her grandparents had briefly lived there in the late sixties and, whilst crime wasn't unheard of, it was no worse than any other council estate in London at the time. Then the 1980s had arrived and drugs become prevalent. Around the same time, crime became an almost endemic way of life for a number of the estate's residents. These days it was something of a no-go area. Only a few months ago, a retired former police inspector had been found murdered in a squalid flat a couple of streets from where she was now walking.

She found the flat she was looking for on the third floor of a grim grey concrete slab of a building overlooking a playpark. As she passed the entrance to the staircase, she spotted needles in the grass and dog mess by the swings. Who would want to bring up children here, she thought?

But people did. They did because they had no choice. London was one of the most expensive cities in the world for accommodation. If you weren't rich, you had to take whatever you could get, including somewhere like this.

She took the stairs to the third floor, not trusting the lift, assuming it worked. The door to number six was painted green, the same as all the others in the block. After a moment's hesitation, she knocked on it, fully expecting to be told where to go. A moment later the door was opened by a skinny woman in a T-shirt with a baby in her arms. 'What do you want?' She wasn't unfriendly, just wary. Sensing trouble.

'I need to speak to Dylan,' Molly said. 'Is he in?'

The woman eyed Molly for a moment. 'You filth?'

'It's important I speak to him. I'm not here officially and he isn't in any trouble. The opposite, in fact. I think I might be able to help him if he agrees to talk to me.'

The woman seemed to weigh it up in her head. Realising she probably had nothing to lose, she let Molly in. The baby gave Molly a puzzled look, as though the woman's sense of curiosity had somehow rubbed off on it. Molly was led down a narrow hallway to a dingy sitting room at the back of the flat. A bloke, who was almost as skinny as the woman who'd shown Molly in, was lying on an old sofa in a grubby sweatshirt, watching some rubbishy gangster film on television. His right arm was in a sling and there were the dark remains of bruises fading on his face.

A thin pair of curtains were drawn in an attempt to keep out the light.

Dylan Lee glanced up when Molly entered. ''the fuck's she?'

'Old Bill,' the woman with the baby said. 'She wants to talk to you.' She looked at Molly, not menacingly, but with an air that said she wasn't prepared to take any shit. 'I don't want no trouble. We've had a bellyful of your lot lately. Why can't you give him a break?'

She shot Dylan a withering look then left the room, the baby still clinging to her hip.

The room stank of dope and unwashed nappies. Molly didn't sit down and Dylan didn't ask her.

'It's about Blair and Connor Heaton,' she said. 'The two men who assaulted you. I need to ask you a few questions about them.' She tried for a reassuring smile. 'You're not in any trouble, Dylan.'

'Oh yeah?' He sounded sceptical. Understandably so.

'Why did they assault you? The real reason.'

He shrugged. 'They're a pair of psychos. They claim we did over their mum's house. It's bullshit, man.'

'Look, I'm not interested in the robberies. That's no longer my case. I need to know what they said when they assaulted you. It's very important, Dylan.'

He stared at the television, pretending to be transfixed by the flickering images on the screen.

She walked over to the coffee table and picked up the remote control, pressing the button that turned off the television. She then stood between him and the telly, ensuring she had his full attention. 'I'm not going anywhere until you've answered my question. And believe it or don't believe it, but I'm on your side.'

He sat there, looking up at her, then sighed. 'Their old woman was gaga. I mean, not completely, but she didn't know what was going on half the time. I knew who those boys were, I'd heard rumours about what they was up to.'

'Go on.'

'The house was being used to stash gear.'

'Drugs?'

'Nah, nicked stuff. Phones, cameras. Laptops. That sort of shit.'

'You're telling me Mrs Heaton was a handler of stolen goods?' She sensed he was feeding her a line. Her patience was beginning to wear thin.

'Not her. Them. Her lads.'

'Blair and Connor?' She remembered what Anna had said about the Heatons: *From what I can gather… they were fencing stolen goods, that kind of thing.* 'You're saying they used their mother's house to store stolen goods?'

He nodded slowly, as though he were talking to an idiot. 'You catch on quick.'

She took a moment to digest the information, repeating it to make sure there was no mistake. 'Blair and Connor Heaton were using their mother's house to store stolen goods? Without her knowledge?'

'Well, she hardly knew what day it was, so it's unlikely she knew what they were doing. Mind you, she was a game old bird. After we pushed our way in, she was quick enough to twig what we were up to. She tried to stop us – even managed to put up a bit of a fight. We knew there was several grand's worth of gear in one of the upstairs bedrooms, and we weren't leaving without a sizeable chunk of it.'

'So you hit her?'

He dropped his gaze to the floor. 'That was an accident. Someone grabbed her to stop her phoning the cops. She lashed out, kicked him on the leg, and then she fell over. She fell against a table or something and hit her head.'

'That didn't stop you robbing her house. According to the crime report, a number of personal items were taken from the house, not just the stolen goods you're alleging the Heaton brothers were storing there.' She looked at him and sighed. He was pathetic and hopeless, and Anna Klein was right about one thing: people like him would never change, even though she hated herself for thinking it.

'But, that's not why I'm here.' She sighed again. 'Like I said, I'm no longer part of this case. All I'm interested in is what the Heaton brothers said to you.'

'They wanted the stuff back. Obviously they couldn't tell you lot we'd taken some of it. They wanted to know where it was as they had people lined up to buy it. Some of it was good quality gear: top of the range electricals. I think it had come from a warehouse job a couple of months back. We'd flogged some of it down The Lydon Arms and one or two other places. The rest was stashed in Bryn and Paul's place.'

So that was why Paul Chitterly was so worried. He was sitting on someone else's stolen stash. 'Did you tell them this?'

'I told them we'd flogged some of it, but I said we'd give them the money. I didn't tell them about Bryn, I swear. I dunno how they found out about her.'

She didn't know if she believed him. It was entirely possible he'd dropped Bryony in the shit without a moment's thought, as he squealed in his terror and tried to save his own pathetic backside. But it was more than likely too late for Bryony anyway. Jason Hart's gang got to her first; their needs were greater and their ruthlessness less restrained, albeit probably not by much. Whatever the case, Bryony Allen was destined to fall foul of some dangerous men who cared more for material goods than human life. She was someone Molly did feel sorry for. Life was just going to shit on her whatever way she jumped.

'If we arrest the Heaton brothers, you might have to make a statement.'

'No chance. I'm not having those fucking psychos coming after me again. You don't know what they're like. They'll kill me. Or worse. Look what they did to Bryn.'

She was going to tell him the truth about Bryony. Then she thought again. Perhaps it was better to let him believe the Heaton brothers had murdered Bryony. If nothing else, it might encourage him to at least think about trying to sort his life out, although somehow she doubted it.

'If you tell us what you know, we can offer you protection. Besides, if we can prove the Heatons were responsible for handling stolen goods as well for assaulting you, they'll be going down for a long time. It would get them off your back.'

But judging by the unhappy look he was giving her, she very much doubted he was going to cooperate.

Chapter Fifty-Three

Brompton Cemetery was sandwiched between the fashionable enclaves of South Kensington and Fulham in West London. It had been consecrated by the Bishop of London in 1840 and was apparently the final resting place of several noted people. Denning had a vague recollection of someone telling him Emmeline Pankhurst was buried somewhere in its grounds, as well as Samuel Cunard, the founder of the famous shipping company.

The cemetery was bordered on its western edge by a branch of the West London Line, and to the north by the busy thoroughfare of Old Brompton Road. Denning had decided to take a taxi to the meeting place, as parking around that part of London was likely to be a problem, and he hadn't wanted to waste time searching for an elusive space.

The taxi had dropped him off by the cemetery's impressive arched entrance on Old Brompton Road. As soon as he entered the grounds it was like setting foot in a different world. The distant din of traffic was instantly reduced to a muffled throb, interspersed with the sound of birdsong. A wide road stretched in front of him, lined by trees that were dotted between rows of weathered tombstones. Tall crosses and stone angels silently observed him as he checked his bearings and made his way to the meeting point.

Denning was still unsure he was doing the right thing in agreeing to meet Myerson. The whole situation was ringing mighty great alarm bells. He should have played this by the book, and notified DCS Ross, or Neeraj or Molly Fisher of his intentions. But they would probably have talked him out of it. Talked him out of the insanity of planning to meet up with a corrupt police officer who had been linked to several murders and was part of a dangerous drugs gang. But there had been something in Myerson's voice when he'd phoned that made him think there might be something else going on here. Callaghan had seemed so sure Myerson was straight. As had McKenna, and he trusted her judgement.

Myerson had texted the time and place they were to meet. Denning checked his watch. He was a little early, but if he took his time wandering around the gravestones, he would get to the meeting place more or less at the time Myerson had said.

As Denning headed along the road, a man approached him; muscled, with a neat beard and wearing a way-too-tight T-shirt, he was walking a tiny chihuahua on a thin lead. He smiled at Denning as he passed; Denning nodded politely in response but continued walking. The man obviously wasn't Myerson.

But what if this whole thing was a trap? An ambush? He was unarmed and unprepared. McKenna was still missing in action. He didn't want to end up the same way.

Denning followed the road, heading towards the domed chapel in the centre of the grounds: the agreed meeting place.

There was no one else around, the man with the chihuahua having disappeared into some other part of the cemetery.

He waited by the stone steps that led to the entrance to the chapel, quickly checking his phone for any new messages. There weren't any.

All he could do now was wait.

'It's rumoured that Beatrix Potter used some of the names on the gravestones for characters in her books.' A gruff man's voice came from behind him.

Denning turned round. There was a man standing a few meters away. He was dressed in a pale blue polo shirt and black jeans, and looked slightly dishevelled. Denning recognised him as the man who had punched him when they were in Jardine's house.

'Terry Myerson.' The man nodded at Denning but there was no suggestion of a handshake. 'You're pretty much as Lizzie described you. Though she did use the word "wet", which may not have been entirely fair.'

Denning tipped his chin towards the man, still wary. It was strange hearing McKenna referred to as Lizzie, but then she and Myerson had once been close.

'She's staying at a friend's cottage in Norfolk,' he said, answering Denning's next question before he'd had a chance to ask it. 'She's fine, by the way. Just needs a bit of time to herself.'

Denning wanted to believe him, but still wasn't sure how much he could trust the man standing opposite him. Myerson had a boxer's build: a shaved head and a couple of tattoos. But he had something more. A presence. Just looking at him, you could tell he was the kind of man who had a natural air of authority about him.

'She's safe, though?' Denning asked.

He nodded. 'I suggested she got away for a bit. She'd come dangerously close to being in the wrong place at the wrong time.' He nodded at Denning's cheek, where the bruise was already starting to fade. 'Apologies for the sore face the other day. I had to make it look convincing. And you did turn up unexpectedly. Collateral damage.' He smiled.

Collateral damage, Denning thought. Like Bryony Allen and all the others who'd got in the way, including the unfortunate lorry driver on the A21.

'It'll heal,' Denning said. 'But something tells me you didn't ask to meet to apologise for smacking me. Or have I completely misread the situation?'

'I wasn't sure if you would agree to meet me. I appreciate you're taking a big risk. And, it goes without saying, you probably don't trust me. And I wouldn't blame you.'

They stopped by an ancient statue of an angel with a trumpet. Myerson leant against it and lit a cigarette. He offered one to Denning, who shook his head. The man with the chihuahua walked past again, slowly watching Denning and Myerson, either suspicious, or just simply curious.

'All right, mate?' Myerson asked, throwing the bloke a cheesy smile.

The man smiled nervously and walked on, the tiny dog trotting along at his heel.

'This whole thing must feel like a set-up.' Myerson said as soon as the man and dog were out of earshot. 'It isn't, by the way.'

'So why me? Why not arrange to meet up with Callaghan? He's your handler.'

A throaty laugh, followed by a sharp drag on the cigarette. 'I have a feeling I ain't exactly flavour of the month with Dougie Callaghan at the moment.'

'Do you blame him? He's the one who's got to answer to the Home Office for the balls-up with the lorry yesterday. It's understandable if he feels the trust he placed in you has gone unrewarded.'

'Jason sussed me,' Myerson said coldly. 'Well, OK, maybe not sussed, but he had a pretty good indication of the direction the wind was blowing. That's why he fed me the crap about where and how that consignment was coming in. He lied about the route the drugs would be taking and dropped unsubtle hints about where he reckoned the worst spot for a police ambush would be. Like a twat, I fell for it.' He paused. Looked into the distance and sighed. 'I reckon someone's warned him that he's got someone in the team he can't trust.'

'And you think he knows it's you. That's why he knew you'd pass the information onto Callaghan?'

'I think it was like a test. He obviously suspected me. Probably not of being a cop, but I could tell there was a lack of trust that hadn't been there before. I'd spent many months getting Jason to trust me. And he did, more or less. Then another bloke muscled his way in, kept whispering shit in Jason's ear. Dripping poison. At first, I thought he just wanted me out the way so he could become Jase's right-hand man, and to be fair to him, that's exactly what I did when I joined the club. But now, looking back, I think he sussed I was undercover. Or was at least suspicious.'

They walked a bit further, passing an elderly couple carrying flowers. 'It can't have been easy, trying to get close to someone like Jason Hart.'

He shrugged again. 'It wasn't that difficult, actually. He's a nice guy, Jase. OK, he's a ruthless psychopath, and he's not someone you'd ever cross in a hurry, but away from all that, he's a good laugh. We used to go go-carting together. Well, me, him and a few of the others. That's his thing: go-carting. He's been into it ever since he was a kid. He likes his music too, and his football. And he's loyal to those around him. He looks after his friends. The closer I got to him, the more I saw that we had loads of stuff in common. I even found myself quite liking the bloke.'

'None of which detracts from the fact he's murdered at least six people. Or at the very least, is responsible for their murders.'

'That was just business. At least as far as he sees it. None of it was personal. Like I said, Jase isn't someone you wanna cross.'

Denning guessed that was possibly why Myerson had been chosen for the job, despite his questionable history. Someone who could click with Hart and make the whole thing seem natural. And it had obviously worked, up to a point…

'So, that's when Hart started suspecting you? After this other man pitched up on the scene?'

'Around then. I thought at first he might be another undercover cop that they hadn't told me about. I voiced my concerns to Callaghan but he assured me there was no one else undercover. We did a PNC search on this bloke, but nothing came up: no previous or anything.'

'What *do* you know about him?'

'Very little. He belonged to a rival gang. They were lifted by us. He migrated towards Jason's lot. Earned his spurs.' He looked crestfallen. 'He was the one responsible for Kelvin Moore and Adie Carter. He knew them. He as good as told Jase he wanted me on the job. I had no choice: it was either go along with the hit or raise Jase's suspicions. I justified it in my head by reminding myself they were drug dealers. It's easier if you can dehumanize them. That was how the average Nazi coped when ordered to murder Jews, or anyone else they disapproved of: don't look upon them as human beings.'

'That doesn't make it any less wrong.'

'The set-in-stone absolutes of right and wrong become very tinged with grey when you're doing my kind of policing, Denning. It's always easier to judge these things when you're on the outside looking in.'

Denning couldn't miss the way he'd stressed 'my kind of policing'. He was making it clear this was something way beyond the run-of-the-mill murder investigations Denning was engaged in. So much boiled down to the fact Denning and Myerson were two very different coppers. Denning had joined the Met straight after university. He'd been fast-tracked for promotion. He reflected the modern police force. Myerson was old school, trading on instinct and split-second decisions, regardless of the eventual outcome. Perhaps this was another reason why Denning felt uncomfortable? But he had to acknowledge that Myerson had a point. He had been placed in an extreme situation and had had to make a near impossible decision. Denning shouldn't judge him, and yet despite his claims to there being several areas of grey, his decision seemed to have been very black and white.

'So, you helped to murder two men in cold blood to protect your identity?'

'It worked. For a while. Jase was convinced I was on his side. It was just later. He started doubting me. The cock-up with the raid was the proof he needed.'

'What happened to the drugs?'

'Transferred to a warehouse in north Kent. They're probably out for distribution now: clubs, bars and county lines.'

'And McKenna?'

'She'd been sniffing round. Talking to my ex-wife. My ex and I haven't been in contact for a while, but every now and again I give her a call, just to make sure she and our boy are doing OK. She mentioned in passing that Lizzie had phoned her a couple of times asking about me. By then, Jase was getting more and more suspicious. I had to start limiting my contact with Callaghan. We were using an encrypted phone, so the risk was always minimal, but Jase was watching me more and more closely. There was a real danger he would find my phone and check my call log.'

'What about McKenna?'

'I arranged to meet her. I told her the score, explained how she was putting me in potential danger, as well as herself. I was sure Jase had someone on the inside passing on information. If he found out McKenna was asking questions about me, and discovered we used to be close, there was a danger he could go after her too.'

'And Bryony Allen and Robert Jardine? What were they? Collateral damage?'

'Jase wanted to get to Jardine, but nobody knew where he was. Except Bryony, or so we thought. I wasn't involved in that. At least not directly.'

'Just how "indirectly" were you involved?'

'We grabbed Bryony from outside the Lydon. We'd been watching the place waiting for either Jardine or her to show up. Jase pays the barmaid to keep him to speed with what's going on there. We wanted Jardine, but he'd gone to ground. According to the barmaid, Bryony was our best bet for finding Jardine.' Myerson was staring into the middle distance when he spoke, finding the words difficult to speak aloud. 'We put her in the back of a car and took her to a lock-up Jase uses in Walthamstow.

It became pretty obvious pretty quickly that she didn't know shit about where Jardine was, but Jase and his goons wouldn't stop. If anything, I think he was making a point. Jardine would get to hear what had been done to his bird and it would scare him into cooperating. Except it didn't. It took a couple of days to track Jardine down. Bryony didn't know where he was, but she told us he had a caravan in Southend where he used to take her sometimes. That's where we found him. Hiding. Shit scared because he knew what was coming his way. We took him back to London… You know the rest.'

There was silence. Denning could hear the birds overhead and the sound of traffic filtering through the greenery. It was a beautiful place: peaceful. And yet here there were discussing something ugly.

'That's how Jase operates,' Myerson continued. 'He's without compassion or sentiment when it comes to getting what he wants. I had to turn a blind eye to what they were doing to that poor kid. And to Jardine. OK, he was no angel, but he didn't deserve what happened to him.'

'And Karen Penfold?'

'Jase was sure she was double-crossing him. He'd got wind she'd been talking to an Albanian gang. She denied it, but when Jase starts, it's like something else takes over. It's almost as though he gets off on watching people suffer. And besides, once we'd started on her it wasn't like we could then just let her walk out of there. Not that she was in much of a condition to walk anywhere by then…'

'So, you quietly sat back while they tortured and killed three people?'

'Like I said, Denning – it's very easy to judge when you're not in my shoes.'

Denning just shook his head. There wasn't much else he could say. 'Why won't McKenna answer her phone? She must have known I was concerned.'

'She's staying at a friend's place on the Broads. There's almost no signal. It's what she wanted: to be isolated and forget about all the shit that's going down. She just wanted a break from everything, including you.'

'Right, where to now? We need to get together with Callaghan and the people from Border Force and find a way to stop Jason Hart.'

Myerson looked at him. His face suggested he was unconvinced, but eventually he nodded. 'Jase thinks he's untouchable. Let's show him that's not the case.'

Chapter Fifty-Four

Molly had wrestled with her conscience. It wasn't as though she had a personal gripe with Anna Klein. Quite the opposite. Perhaps, under different circumstances, she could have imagined the two of them being... well, if not friends exactly, then certainly two people who could share a drink and a chat about work whenever she felt like unwinding after a tough day.

If she was being honest with herself, she probably felt a bit sorry for her. She hadn't been exaggerating when she'd said the job was all she had. She was one of those officers, like Betty Taggart, who had invested so much in the job that it was difficult to switch off from it at the end of a shift. And sometimes you didn't switch off. Sometimes you took the job home with you, slept with it and woke up with it the next day. So many partners would struggle to understand that. There were certainly times Jon did, though he tried his best to show that wasn't the case.

She would try her best to keep the DS's name out of things, but if Anna Klein ended up losing her job over this, then she was determined not to lose any sleep over it.

The arrest hadn't been difficult. They were to be found where they were always to be found: at the seedy snooker hall in Dalston. CID hadn't allowed her to be present when they were arrested, but she was still hanging around

Islington nick while the arrest was processed. Both Paul Chitterly and Dylan Lee had agreed to make a statement. Paul had been the easiest to persuade – she'd kept mentioning Bryony and how she deserved justice. Somewhere in his mind he'd associated that with the Heaton brothers being arrested. Or maybe he hadn't. Maybe he just wanted to know that someone else was getting smacked around by life for a change and it wasn't him. It had been Paul who'd persuaded Dylan to make a written statement confirming who it was who'd assaulted him and why.

Anna Klein had phoned in sick that day. It was, her DI had commented to Molly, very out of character.

Molly watched as Blair and Connor Heaton were led into the custody suite in handcuffs, then guided into separate interview rooms. Blair was taking the lead as usual, demanding his solicitor and instructing Connor to keep his mouth shut and stick to 'no comment'. She continued watching them being led down the corridor towards the interview rooms. She knew Connor was the weaker link; given enough pressure, he was likely to spill the whole sorry saga.

A search of their respective properties, along with a warrant to search their late mother's property was underway. CID also had The Lydon Arms in their sights. Good luck speaking to Deena Jackson, she thought to herself. She'll be one tough nut to crack, but if they could get hold of Kelly-Ann it would be a different story. Molly was beginning to wish she'd listened to her in the first place.

She hadn't missed the look Blair Heaton had shot her before he was taken down to the interview rooms. A long, lingering look that was intended to intimidate. She smirked back at him, trying to feign a confidence she didn't feel, but damned if she was going to let him think he had the right to scare her. She knew about his reputation, and knew there was always the risk of reprisals.

But as she heard the interview room doors close, she allowed herself a little smile.

That just left one outstanding problem: what to do about Anna Klein...

Chapter Fifty-Five

If Callaghan was unhappy to see Denning sitting opposite him in his office, he was even less pleased to find himself facing off Myerson from across his desk.

Marsh was sitting next to Denning, keeping his mouth shut and staring at the ceiling.

A chainsaw would have struggled to cut the atmosphere in the room. Two men eyeballing each other like something out of a spaghetti Western. It was clear that Callaghan's earlier claims to have trusted Myerson had been as much an attempt to convince himself as everyone else. At some point over the past couple of days the penny had finally dropped for Callaghan that his trusted attack dog had turned on him and bitten him on the arse. Denning hadn't heard how things had gone when Callaghan had been forced to face his senior officers, but judging by the look on his face, he hadn't come out of it smelling like roses.

'It's the best offer on the table, Doug. You haven't got a hope in hell of bringing Jason Hart down without my help. I accept it's risky and I can't guarantee it'll work, but it's all we've got right now.'

Callaghan was glowering at Myerson from the other side of his desk. It reminded Denning of McKenna and how she looked at him when the pressure was on. It had no effect on Myerson. Several months of dealing with a headcase like Jason Hart would have toughened him to the point where a stare-off with his SIO would be a walk in the park.

'I don't even know why you're here,' Callaghan barked. 'Either of you.' He looked at Denning, but Denning knew his real ire was reserved for Myerson. The man he was still convinced had betrayed him; had made him look a fool in front of his fellow officers, and who had presumably been responsible for Callaghan's arse being dragged over the carpet by his bosses at the NCA. The humiliation would linger for some time. Callaghan looked like the kind of man who took failure personally.

'I know him, Doug,' Myerson argued. 'I've been working alongside the bastard for over a year now. I know how he thinks. I've still got a connection to him. And let's be honest here, chaps, I'm the only tosser who has the first idea of where to look for him.'

Myerson had a good point there. Hart had excelled at keeping one step ahead of them all this time. They now had his strongest asset sitting in an office trying his best to convince his senior officer that he was sincere.

'Convince me why I should trust you,' Callaghan said. 'Why should I believe a word that comes out your mouth?'

'You haven't got much choice, have you? Look, I sense I'm fucked whatever the outcome. You've already convinced yourself that I deliberately dropped you in it by passing on false intel on the drugs raid. There's nothing I can say to convince you that wasn't the case. At least not right now. If I bring you Jason Hart then at least you'll know I haven't dropped you in it.'

Callaghan looked like he wasn't convinced. 'On the other hand, you could just tell us where we could find him. We go in mob-handed and arrest him.'

'You've got to get it into your head, Callaghan: Hart isn't like your average shit-for-brains, corner-of-the-street dealer. He's clever, and he's shrewd. And he'll see you coming a mile off if you go after him with all guns blazing. Someone like that: you've got to play him at his own game.'

'OK. Impress me. Talk me through this crazy plan of yours.'

Myerson sat down. 'Up until now you've been chasing Hart and he's always remained one step ahead. From now on, we take the fight to him.'

'I'm listening.'

'Hart uses a warehouse in Chatham to store the gear. It's hidden in containers at the back of the building. The warehouse is officially used for storing farm equipment, but that's purely a cover. Its main purpose is to store anything that's going to be distributed around the South East, including London. But it's only used as a central storage unit. The drugs will be divvied up into smaller bundles then passed around various local distribution hubs. That's why he needed Jardine's list of contacts. They handle this in return for a hefty percentage. All Hart has to do is ensure he can meet the constant demand.'

'"Distribution hubs"? What the fuck are they?' Callaghan was struggling to hide his scepticism.

'Anything from seedy dumps like The Lydon Arms to properties being used for county lines. Any gear that's too pure will be cut with other substances. And that's as much for the users' benefit as for Hart's profit margins.'

'You what?' Callaghan's eyebrows shot towards the ceiling.

'Anyone not used to pure cocaine or cannabis can have a bad reaction,' Myerson explained. 'That's why it's cut with other stuff: soap powder, talcum powder, stuff like that. But yes, it all helps with profit. Everyone receives a percentage: from the dealer on the street, to the suppliers further up the line. It's profit share: encourages motivation. If anyone crosses Hart... Well, I don't have to tell you the end result. Just ask Denning. It's not pretty.'

Callaghan was shuffling awkwardly in his chair. 'I'm not happy about any of this. I need to speak with upstairs and arrange to get a team in place before we even think about going after Hart.'

'There isn't time,' Myerson bellowed. 'It could take days for them to agree to a full-scale operation, assuming they agree at all, which isn't looking terribly likely from where I'm sitting. Besides, I think Hart may have someone on the inside passing on info. The fewer people who know about this, the better. Hart's due to move the remaining stuff out tomorrow evening. We need to strike then, or he risks getting away. He's already getting jumpy and there's a rumour he's going to move the whole thing to another warehouse. If there's even the faintest chance he thinks we're on to him, he'll dive for cover, change his modus operandi and we're stuffed.'

'Then he'll want to move the drugs,' Denning said. He looked over to Callaghan, who was rubbing a hand over his chin. 'Myerson's right. We have to go after Hart tomorrow.'

'I'm still not convinced by any of this. There are proper procedures for this kind of thing, and they're there for a reason...'

'If we want to grab him,' Myerson said, 'we need to do it before the drugs are moved on to the distribution hubs. This is when they'll do it. We need to move tomorrow, and it needs to involve as few people as possible. And I'm looking at the three of you.'

'You're crazy,' Marsh said. 'Three of us against a drug gang, probably armed. You're taking the piss now, Tel.'

'Agreed,' Callaghan echoed. 'There's no way I can authorize anything that risky. We go in mob-handed, or we don't go in at all. I don't want another fuck-up on my watch.'

Myerson lowered his voice. 'No one will be armed. It'll just be three of us: me, Hart and one of his goons. He doesn't trust anyone else. You make this official and Hart gets wind of it, it *will* be another cock-up, and there will be someone else's arse grooves on that chair, Doug. And faster than you can blink. We have one window: tomorrow night, and that's it.'

Myerson sat back on his chair as soon as he'd finished speaking. He looked at Callaghan, who just shook his head slowly, as though all of this was still not sinking in. Marsh was looking between the two men, unsure which way to swing, clearly weighing the options up in his head. 'I don't think we have much choice here, boss,' he said eventually. 'I know it's risky, but if we don't move quickly and he shifts his base of operation, we'll never catch him.'

It didn't matter what Denning said. This was always going to be Callaghan's call. Three pairs of eyes were fixed on him, waiting for his answer. He clearly wasn't happy and Denning just knew his gut instinct was telling him to go through the official channels here. His career couldn't afford another cock-up.

'OK,' he said. 'We'll do it.'

Denning wasn't sure what he was potentially letting himself in for here. He wasn't trained in this sort of thing. Hart was clearly dangerous. The body count was sufficiently high to be of serious concern to Denning regarding the consequences. At the very least, he should discuss this with someone senior in his MIT, run it past DCS Ross. But there clearly wasn't time. Hart was an unconventional criminal and it was likely he could only be taken down by unconventional means. This was going to be dangerous and something totally outside of his comfort zone. As he left the room, he wondered what he had just got himself into.

Chapter Fifty-Six

Anna was in a contrite mood. Molly had called round at her flat. She'd had to blag the address from Denning, but she'd promised there was only one loose end left to tie up, and that loose end was Anna. Denning had sounded tired on the phone, as though his thoughts were elsewhere. She'd heard rumours about some fuck-up involving Denning and the NCA, but he hadn't offered any details and she hadn't dared to ask. Anna refused to open her door to Molly at first, but she'd made it clear she wasn't going to leave until they'd spoken, and was quite happy to stand on the pavement pressing the button on Anna's intercom all night if she had to. Eventually, her neighbours would call the police and Anna would have to explain the whole situation whether she wanted to or not.

After a few minutes, the door gave a reluctant click and Molly pushed it open. Anna was standing at the top of the stairs that led to her flat, arms folded. She looked like she'd been crying.

'What do you want, Molly? I thought we'd said all there was to say the other day. You've obviously made up your mind to drop me in it.'

'Can I come up?'

Anna looked at her for a few seconds then shrugged. 'Suit yourself. But there's nothing left to say.'

'Nice flat,' Molly said when she entered the small but pleasantly furnished sitting room. A little place like this would have suited her down to the ground if she didn't live with Jon.

Anna sighed heavily, as though she could sense she was running out of places to run. 'Do you want a drink?'

There was a bottle of pinot grigio sitting open on the little breakfast bar that separated the kitchenette from the living room. 'A glass of that would be nice, thanks.'

Anna opened a kitchen cupboard and removed a glass. She poured a decent amount of wine into it and handed it to Molly. She then topped her own glass up. This was clearly not her first glass of the day. In fact, Molly suspected it wasn't even her first bottle.

'How are you?' She looked awful. A combination of guilt and a hangover, she suspected.

'I think I've got flu,' she said. *In June?* Molly wanted to say, but if Anna was trying to sell this as flu, then who was she to refuse to play along?

Molly took a sip of the wine. The bottle had obviously been out of the fridge for a long time as the wine was at room temperature. 'You'll have heard by now,' Molly began, 'Blair and Connor Heaton have been arrested.' She waited for Anna to say something, watching her as she sipped her wine, looking defeated. 'They've been charged with handling stolen goods, as well as the assault on Dylan Lee. Apparently there was a significant number of stolen goods in the spare bedroom at their mother's house.' She took another sip of her drink. 'So far, I've kept your name out of it. Though I can't promise what Blair Heaton will do.'

Anna nodded slowly. 'I can't begin to say how grateful I am, Molly. I really thought you were going to drop me in it.' She gave a half-smile. 'I probably would have done in your shoes.'

Molly wasn't sure if she was joking. She wasn't sure she even cared anymore.

'Yes,' Molly said calmly, 'I expect you would have. That's where we're different, Anna. I believe in giving people a chance. You just see it all in terms of black and white. Good and bad. There's nothing in the middle.'

She knew if she'd reported Anna she would have been consumed with guilt. It wasn't like she'd never fucked up herself. She didn't tell Denning about her part in Bex's murder, when she'd been working on a case that had turned out to have a direct bearing on what had happened. She'd been given a second chance and was only in the job now because Denning and Betty Taggart had decided she was a good officer who shouldn't be punished for something that had happened years ago and wasn't her fault. But all the same, she hadn't broken the law the way Anna had. Molly wasn't going to let her off the hook that easily.

'I didn't tell your DI about your involvement with Blair Heaton because it's only fair that it comes from you.' Molly wasn't drinking. She stared at her wine, then looked up at Anna. 'But if you don't tell them, then I will.'

There was a silence that quickly filled the space between them. 'I can't...' Anna was still clutching her drink, her eyes wide. 'I thought we'd agreed. Why have you changed your mind?'

'I haven't changed my mind. I told you how I felt. It's not so much about your relationship with Blair Heaton – we've all been involved with shits like that in the past – it's to do with your behaviour potentially jeopardising a

serious investigation. If you can't do the job we've under-
taken to do, then you shouldn't be in it.'

'But they had nothing to do with the murders, and
Dylan Lee was never going to press charges. OK, the
stolen goods, I admit I was wrong to cover that up, but
I told you why I did it. I would have reported Blair
eventually. I just needed to find the right time and make
sure there was nothing that would backfire on me. I had
to make sure I'd covered my own arse.'

Molly shook her head. 'If you explain the background,
perhaps they'll go easy on you. I can only speak from
personal experience, and honesty is always best. These
things have a way of coming out when you least expect
them to. At least this way it gives you a chance to put your
side of the story forward first.'

'You'd really do that? You'd really drop me in it? I
thought we were friends, Molly. I thought we had a
connection. I was clearly wrong.'

'A friend would be honest with you, Anna, and that's
what I'm being. You've got to do what's right here, and
you know it.'

Molly finished the wine and thanked Anna. She left
her to think things over. She'd had enough for one day.

Chapter Fifty-Seven

It was already dark, which meant it was late. They were sitting in a people carrier on the outskirts of an industrial estate just off the A289, a dual carriageway to the north of Chatham. The warehouse they were interested in was one of half a dozen on the estate. A couple of security guards patrolled the area, along with a German Shepherd on the end of a metal lead. But the guards looked like they were simply going through the motions and the dog looked like it just wanted a nap.

The guards had been briefed that the place was under police surveillance, but the details had been kept deliberately light. With so much at stake, it was difficult to know who could and couldn't be trusted.

Apart from the security guards, the place was deserted.

Callaghan was in the front of the vehicle, Marsh beside him. Denning was in the back.

'I'm still not convinced by this,' Callaghan said. 'Not convinced by a long chalk.' He still didn't trust Myerson, and Denning was only there on sufferance. They needed the extra bodies, he'd said, the expression having failed to reassure Denning. Adding to his woes, Denning had heard on the grapevine that Callaghan had been hauled over the coals by his superiors for the fuck-up on the A21, rumours about which had slowly begun to leak on out on social media. There was still an official news blackout surrounding the incident, but that wouldn't stop the rumours spreading, and gaining momentum as they did so. It had also made it harder for Callaghan to persuade his superiors to allow this latest operation to go ahead. They had agreed, reluctantly. They were relying on intel from someone who had let them down in the past. Someone who had yet to prove he could be trusted. There was now a considerable amount at stake.

Myerson had insisted this had to be low-key, and Callaghan had reluctantly gone along with his wishes. If Hart got even a hint of what they were planning, they would be finished. To the end, Callaghan had argued that this should have been handled properly: a team of NCA officers along with armed back-up would go in mob-handed and drag Hart and his gang out.

They sat in silence for several minutes, no one speaking and nothing happening.

'We should have arranged back-up,' Marsh said. 'This whole thing is too risky.'

'You can always stay here if it scares you,' Callaghan said. 'Besides, you were all for it yesterday.'

'It's not that, boss. We've only got Tel's word that they won't be armed. And if they are, what have we got? An Asp and Taser. We'll be sitting ducks.'

'Look, there's only two of them. There's going to be four of us,' Denning said.

Callaghan guffawed loudly. 'That's assuming you trust Myerson. Otherwise the odds aren't so cosy.'

'A couple of days ago, you were the one insisting you still trusted Myerson,' Denning said.

'That was before I was hauled over the coals by my Director and two suits from the Home Office in the light of Operation Cock-Up.'

'I trust him,' Denning said after a pause. Except he didn't. Not entirely. It amused him that there had been a switch around in their positions, with Denning now the one insisting Myerson should be given a chance, while Callaghan was expressing doubts.

Callaghan's bosses had agreed to armed back-up if it was deemed necessary and there had to be significant risk attached to that. Denning knew there was great risk here, but Callaghan had, at Myerson's request, insisted on keeping it low-key. The whole thing made Denning nervous. If anything were to go wrong their arses weren't being covered here.

'I assume Hart knows Myerson is aware of this place?' Callaghan said. 'I mean, if he does suspect Myerson…'

'We don't know for certain that Hart suspects him,' Denning said. 'But we have to assume if he's nervous about there even being the possibility of having a spy in his camp, he'll want to cut and run. Myerson's right; we either move quickly or we risk the whole thing coming crashing down around our ears and we'll never catch Hart.' He was concerned all the time that this was about so much more than just bursting open a dangerous drugs' gang. Hart was a murderer, and one who was likely to escape justice if they didn't move to stop him.

'If the shit hits the fan, we can call for armed back-up,' Callaghan said.

'Christ, you're having a laugh,' Marsh shot back. 'By the time they get here we could be brown bread. We have to assume at least some of Hart's gang will be armed, and we shouldn't be taking any chances, not after what happened last time.'

He knew if there was another fuck-up his career would be well and truly on the line. They had to get this right. Callaghan was taking a massive risk.

The silence continued, Marsh checking his watch every few minutes and glancing out the window at nothing. Callaghan stared straight ahead, hands gripping the steering wheel.

Denning was in the back thinking things over in his head.

Eventually, a state-of-the-art Range Rover arrived. The blacked-out window gave it a sinister look. It pulled up at the entrance to the warehouse. Three men stepped out.

'That's Hart,' Callaghan said, pointing to the shortest of the three men. They were all dressed in black, but Denning guessed the other two were Myerson and the other man who had been with him at Jardine's house, but it was impossible to tell which one was Myerson.

One of the men unlocked the door and the three of them entered.

'What now?' Steve Marsh asked.

'We've got two choices,' Callaghan said. 'We either go in there now, or we wait until they come out and grab them then.'

Neither option appealed to Denning. Both came with a high risk. Luckily, it was Callaghan's call and not his.

'We go in,' Callaghan said after a moment. 'He's fucked us around enough already. But I give the call.'

Marsh went in first, Denning immediately behind him with Callaghan alongside. The warehouse was cavernous. At least two storeys high. Although the lights were on, it was dark inside. A couple of strip lights near the rear of the building cast shadowy illumination over most of the interior. Callaghan shouted over to Hart: 'Jason Hart, I'm arresting you for...' but before he had a chance to continue, all hell broke loose. Hart's goon pulled a semi-automatic handgun from his jacket and aimed it at Callaghan. Myerson dived on him just as he pulled the trigger. Callaghan fell to the floor. It looked like he had taken a bullet to the shoulder. Marsh ran over to him checking he was OK, and radioing for an ART and an ambulance. Myerson was struggling with the gunman.

Hart was running for the back of the warehouse. Denning took off after him. He didn't have a chance to see what was happening with the others, but he heard another shot go off.

Hart had legged it towards the rear of the building, then he disappeared. Denning still didn't know if Hart was armed. Marsh had radioed for back-up, but it would be several minutes before they got there. Hart could have legged it by then. He could be out of the county by this time tomorrow.

Denning heard a noise, spun round and saw Hart was thundering up a metal staircase that headed towards an upper level of the warehouse. Denning quickly glanced over towards his colleagues, but it was too dark to see what was happening. He could hear Marsh shouting down the radio and Callaghan insisting he was all right. There was no word from Myerson. Or the bloke with the gun.

Denning only had a split second to make a decision. He ran to the foot of the metal staircase and headed up it after Hart.

The staircase led to a raised area on the upper level of the warehouse, off which were a couple of what looked like offices. The whole area was dimly lit, and Denning had no idea where Hart was. He heard a voice calling him from the lower part of the warehouse, but in the confusion, he couldn't tell if it was Marsh or Callaghan. Or Myerson. He knew he couldn't risk letting Hart get away.

He reached for his Asp, and cautiously pushed open the door to the first office: there were a couple of desks and a filing cabinet. Loads of boxes littered the floor. Drugs already packaged and awaiting distribution? Denning didn't have time to think about it.

He pushed open the door to the next office. It was in darkness. He reached out for a light switch, vaguely aware of footsteps coming up behind him on the metal staircase. Suddenly, from inside the darkened office, someone leaped out at him, swinging what looked in the dim light like an iron bar. He ducked out the way as the iron bar thudded against the wood of the doorframe. A moment later, Hart pushed past him, knocking the ASP from his hand. It rolled off the metal walkway and landed with a metallic thud on the concrete floor twenty feet below.

Hart was running towards what looked like a fire escape. Denning got to his feet and followed him.

Hart pushed open the fire door and disappeared through it. The door closed behind him with a click.

Denning ran after him. The door led to a metal walkway that connected the warehouse with the one next to it. At the far end was a fire escape. There was a full moon overhead, casting pale light over the scene. In the distance he could hear sirens, but they were still a long way off.

If Hart got down it and reached his Range Rover, he'd be gone. Denning ran after him, slipping slightly on the floor of the walkway, twisting his ankle as he went down; the pain tearing through his ankle like a red-hot knife.

Hart was almost at the far end. Then he stopped, turned and faced Denning. He still had hold of the metal bar. Denning gripped the railing that ran along the walkway and tried to stand. Hart was running towards him now, the iron bar held in his right hand, a look of raw hard rage on his face. He swung the iron bar in Denning's direction just as the moon disappeared behind a cloud.

Chapter Fifty-Eight

Denning was standing on the edge of the walkway trying not to look down. His eyes had quickly adjusted to the dim light. The pain in his ankle was still agonising. Either he'd broken it, or he'd pulled a tendon. In the dim half-light, he could see Hart running towards him from the far end of the walkway, holding the iron bar above his head. Denning couldn't run. He couldn't move. They were about twenty feet above the ground. If Denning jumped, he'd have more than a broken ankle to worry about.

The moon reappeared from behind the cloud. He could see Hart clearly now. Almost on top of him. Denning reached for his Taser, but he wasn't quick enough. Hart swung the iron bar before he could get the Taser out of its holster. Denning ducked. The metal bar clanged off the handrail, missing him by millimetres, the noise reverberating round his head like a clanging bell.

Denning knew he wouldn't miss a second time. Hart raised the iron bar. Denning tried to make himself as small as he could, waiting for the iron bar to smash his skull.

Then from behind him came a crash. The fire door had been kicked open. Enough to make Hart pause. Denning tried to turn round, but he couldn't move. He stayed focused on Hart. The distraction only lasted for a fraction of a second, then Hart raised the iron bar for a second time and swung it at Denning. A shot rang out from behind him. Hart fell back, dropping the iron bar, which clattered to the ground below, landing with a distant clang. Hart was clutching his right arm, blood on the walkway and on Denning. Warm in the cool night air. Another shot rang out and Hart fell backwards, losing his footing and trying to grip the rail with his left hand. Denning reached out, grabbing his leg, steadying him. He wasn't going to let Jason Hart fall. He wouldn't allow him an easy death.

Then Myerson threw himself on Hart. Denning could see he had dropped the handgun by the fire door. He guessed it was the same one Hart's goon had used to shoot Callaghan.

As the two men struggled, Denning scrambled to his feet, trying to ignore the excruciating pain in his ankle. He reached over for the gun, just as a scream echoed out into the night. He turned to see Hart falling over the railing and plunging to the ground below.

Myerson was standing by the railing, an impassive look on his face. An accident... It *was* an accident? Denning hadn't seen, but it must have been. The walkway was narrow and slippery, the two men struggling. What else could it have been?

Myerson helped him to his feet, insisting Denning used him to support his weight. Myerson was covered in blood. Denning didn't know if it was his own, or Hart's. Denning could feel Hart's blood on his face, see it on his jacket. Myerson took the gun from him, ensuring the safety catch was on and then put it into the pocket of his leather jacket.

Agonising step by agonising step, they headed towards the fire escape stairs at the far end of the walkway, neither man saying a word.

He glanced down to see several squad cars approaching the entrance to the industrial estate. An ambulance was approaching too.

Back on the ground, Callaghan was being led into the back of an ambulance. It was a flesh wound, deep but not life-threatening. When the paramedics had finished checking over Callaghan, they examined Denning. He told them the blood wasn't his and, apart from his ankle, he was fine. Marsh was going to accompany Callaghan to the hospital in the ambulance but Denning was happy to be driven to the nearest hospital in a police car to be checked over. Callaghan was more of a priority.

He was more interested in Myerson, who was talking to one of the senior armed officers from Kent Police. He was some distance away, so Denning couldn't hear what they were saying. Hart's body was lying under the walkway between the two warehouses. He would lie there until forensics had examined him. There was no word on what had happened to the other gang member in the warehouse, the one who'd shot Callaghan.

There would be an official inquiry into Myerson's role in Hart's death, but for now he was a hero. He'd saved Callaghan's life and Denning's too, for that matter. Denning should have felt more grateful. Yet something was niggling away at him. He couldn't quite say what it was.

Denning wiped Hart's blood off his face with a handkerchief. He noted with some irony that it was the same one Jardine's neighbour had given him after Myerson had whacked him that time. He'd washed it and had meant to return it to the man sometime. Instead, it had somehow ended up in his pocket. His jacket, he noted, would have to be dry cleaned.

He still didn't know what had happened on the walkway. In the split second when he had turned to pick up the gun, it had all been over. A little too quickly and, he couldn't help but feel, a little too conveniently.

Myerson had finished talking to the officer from Kent Police and came over to Denning. 'They'll want a full statement in due course. This is their patch, after all. They call the shots.' He gave Denning a wry smile. 'No pun intended.'

He seemed calm. Almost too calm. Shock, maybe. The full significance of what had just happened had yet to sink in. Perhaps this was how Myerson coped. Pretend it was all a joke. He'd been an undercover officer for a long time and was a very different kind of detective to Denning. He'd seen things and done things Denning couldn't even begin to comprehend. That was why the nature of undercover work appealed to people like Myerson and not Denning.

Calm under pressure…

'I should thank you for saving my life up there,' Denning said. His voice sounded throaty as though it belonged to someone else.

Myerson laughed. 'You were brave going after Hart by yourself. Stupid but brave.' Another wry grin. 'At least I know I can rely on you to cover my arse about what happened up there.'

With that, a uniformed officer appeared, telling Denning he'd been instructed to take him to the local hospital to have him checked over. Denning turned back to speak to Myerson, but he was already walking away. He'd said all he'd needed to. Denning had his back. He'd made sure of it.

Chapter Fifty-Nine

There was a palpable sense of relief in the room. Not quite celebration, as that would have felt out of place, but certainly a general air of satisfaction that things had worked out for the best, especially when everything had been taken into account.

McKenna was in her office. She wasn't officially due back from her leave until the following week, so this was more of an informal visit.

'Where's the fucking parrot?' McKenna laughed at the sight of Denning.

Denning was hobbling along on crutches. He'd torn his Achilles tendon, which was going to involve a six-week recovery period, at least half that time spent on crutches. He'd be confined to office duties.

McKenna was looking well. The break had clearly done her good.

'I was off my nut with boredom most of the time,' she said. 'The cottage was in the middle of nowhere with nothing to look at except nature.' She grimaced. 'And I fucking hate nature.'

'Nice to see you're back to your old self, though,' Denning said. He'd managed to hobble as far as one of the chairs opposite her desk and was making an effort to sit down.

'Seriously, it was just what I needed. I was starting to think I was going mad. This whole thing with Myerson. For a while, I really did think Terry had sold out. To be honest, it wouldn't have entirely surprised me.' She sat back in her chair and gave him a warm smile. 'And I didn't want you getting too comfortable. It took years of graft to earn this chair, I'm not ready to hand it over yet.'

'That's good,' he said, 'because I'm not sure I want it. At least not quite yet. There's still a lot to be said for being hands on when it comes to a serious case.'

'Not that you'll be all that hands on for a while.' She nodded at his crutches. 'However, under the circumstances, it could have been a lot worse.' She was quiet for a moment. 'Hart would have killed you. By then, he had nothing left to lose. Terry saved your life.'

He'd never doubted that bit. It wasn't as though she needed to reiterate it. It was everything else that was refusing to fit together so easily. 'What will happen to Myerson now?'

She shrugged. 'That's up to him. I suspect his days of undercover work are over, and that's no bad thing. He's getting too old for it now, if nothing else. It's a young nutter's game.' She steepled her fingers under her chin. 'Like I said, Matt, I did have my doubts about Terry.' She shook her head. 'No, not doubts. At least not serious ones. It's just…'

'Go on,' he prompted her.

'I met up with him. I expect he told you that. He'd changed. Become jaded, cynical. I mean more so than the average cop.'

'Understandable, perhaps. Doing what he did, covert policing. It changes you.'

'It wasn't that.' McKenna looked uncomfortable, as though she was reluctant to continue with the line of conversation she'd started. 'He was the one who insisted I took myself off somewhere. He said it was for my own good. For a moment it felt like it was issued as some kind of threat. Stupid, I know. He only had my best interests at heart. But I remember thinking he was different, somehow. As though he just wanted me out the way.' She shook her head again. 'What about Callaghan? Any word on how he's doing?'

'Out of hospital. Bullet wound to the shoulder. Another one who owes his life to Myerson. And it's a good result for him. From what I've heard, the NCA has successfully dismantled Hart's entire operation. There was quite a bit of valuable intel in the office in the warehouse. The list of local dealers that he got from Jardine's house still hasn't turned up, though. Shame, as that would have been useful. We've located the lock-up Hart and his gang used in Walthamstow. It's being checked over by Forensics as we speak. Considering what was done to those poor sods, they're bound to find something.'

'And the rest of Hart's gang?'

'That's the NCA's call now. If and when we get evidence linking any of them to the murders, we can have a go at them, but the NCA has top priority until then.' She smiled. 'It's a victory, Matt.'

'If ultimately a small one,' he said 'OK, so Hart's gang has been busted wide open, but we both know there will be someone else along to fill the vacuum. It's pausing the supply chain rather than eradicating it.'

McKenna nodded her agreement. 'We can only do what we can. The more we interrupt the supply chain, the harder it is for people like Jason Hart, and all the others who come after him. The NCA reckon there's enough evidence to bring Hart's gang to court. A lot of them are not much more than foot soldiers and will more than likely end up with a token custodial sentence, but it's still a result.'

'And with Terry Myerson's evidence...'

'Unfortunately we can't rely on that,' McKenna said.

'No?'

She sighed. 'There's been some debate over the past few years about the ethics of using undercover police officers to get information. It's desperation on the part of defence barristers, but it means the CPS are cautious about attaching too much importance to their evidence.' She sat back in her chair. 'And then there's the whole thorny issue of Myerson's involvement in the deaths of Carter and Moore, not to mention his links to the others. If it gets out that a serving police officer – albeit an undercover one – has blood on his hands, the press would have a field day.'

'Hopefully it won't come to that.'

'What about the two bodies found in Bromley? Did Myerson have anything to offer there?' McKenna asked.

'He's still being deliberately vague about that. But he's probably just protecting his own backside there. He admits he was involved in their murders but insists it was down to Hart, on his orders. However, he is still responsible and we can't escape the fact there's forensic evidence to link him to the murders.' This was as much as Denning knew. Myerson was the NCA's problem now. If they wanted to haul him over the coals for his behaviour while he was undercover, then that was up to them. But Denning thought it was unlikely. Myerson had got them a result: a major player off the streets, and a drugs cartel broken up. Even if it could be comfortably proved that he had been directly involved in murder, he couldn't see his bosses at the NCA pushing for a prosecution. It was a dirty game and Denning was glad he had only been involved around the edges.

McKenna suddenly leapt up from her chair. 'Look, I shouldn't even be here.' She gestured to the empty chair. 'This is yours for another few days.'

'Actually, I was going to pop out to the main office,' he said. 'I'd like a word with the team.'

McKenna was halfway to the door, then stopped. She made her way back over to Denning. 'Would you like a hand, hop-along?' She handed him his crutches and supported his elbow whilst he climbed out of the chair. 'Oh, and I meant to say – thanks for stepping up to the plate while I was away. I appreciate it wasn't the best timing in the world, but I really did have to get my head together. However, if I ever hear that you've been rifling through my knicker drawer again, I really will have your bollocks on a kebab skewer...'

—

The team was keen to relax. Denning wanted a word with Neeraj, to thank him for standing in and holding the fort while he was running around with the NCA boys. However, Neeraj was deep in conversation with Kinsella, so he decided to wait.

He spotted Molly standing by the water cooler and made his way over. She smiled when she saw him approach. 'I heard about the Heaton brothers. Well done. That's a major loose end tidied up.'

'Thanks. I know it wasn't directly connected to the Bryony Allen murder investigation, but I didn't want them to get away with what they'd done. Islington CID have raided The Lydon Arms and arrested Deena Jackson and Sam Okojie. Apparently both are refusing to speak, but there's a good chance CID will find enough to charge them. Certainly for allowing criminal activity on the premises, perhaps more if they look hard enough.'

Denning smiled. 'I appreciate it wasn't easy working with Anna. And I also appreciate your discretion about... About anything she might have said. Or implied.'

Molly smiled back at him. 'I don't think either of us will be bothered by Anna Klein again for a while. I have a feeling she's going to be keeping her head down.'

'There is another matter I need to bring up with you...' He looked at her. This was a time to celebrate a good result. He didn't have the right to bring her down. 'But it can wait.'

She refilled her plastic cup from the water cooler and returned to her desk, giving him another little smile as she went. He was tempted to ask her what she meant by her last comment, but he knew it was better to try and appear unconcerned by the whole Anna Klein scenario. Sarah would be back from New York soon, and he would be very happy to forget his brief friendship with DS Anna Klein had ever happened.

There were still the unanswered questions about Myerson and his true role in Hart's gang. Had he been tempted to go rogue, then changed his mind at the last minute? Or had Hart really sussed him, and it was only a matter of time before they would have found Myerson's mutilated body in a public place? Hart's death was certainly convenient; a potentially awkward situation averted by his elimination. The only other possible witness who could cast doubt on Myerson's true intentions was also dead, a couple of bullets pumped into his body as he wrestled with Myerson in the warehouse. An accident, Myerson had claimed, just like Jason Hart's death.

Denning glanced out the window at the car park at the rear of the MIT building. McKenna was getting into her Megane. Even she had had doubts about Myerson in the end.

And what *had* happened on the walkway that night? Denning had backed up Myerson's version of events. He'd even put it in writing. If it were to go before the IOPC, Denning would probably stick to the same story. But was that the truth? Could he go to his grave knowing he'd done the right thing?

He shivered slightly at the thought, and then tried to put it out of his mind.

Chapter Sixty

When Molly returned home that evening she could feel the pleasant alcohol-induced haze beginning to wear off. She'd persuaded Trudi to join her for a couple of pints in their local. She had briefly thought about suggesting the wine bar in Dalston, just for somewhere different. She'd found herself quite liking it in the end. It was plastic and fake, but there was something comforting about it, as though it couldn't be bothered trying very hard to be something it wasn't. But she would always associate the place with Anna, and that was one brief friendship she was keen to forget.

Molly was home now. The house was quiet, for the first time in ages. Jon and Rowan were out. There had been a wedding rehearsal earlier in the day and Jon had decided to visit his ex-father-in-law straight afterwards. Barry was too ill to attend the rehearsal, so Jon was determined to tell him all about it. Jon was now at least on speaking terms with his ex-wife, which made the wedding less of a daunting prospect. However, Molly suspected hostilities were likely only paused for the time being for Rowan's sake. Feuding parents never looked good on anyone's wedding pictures. But still, it spoke volumes about the direction of travel for Jon's relationships. If she did agree to marry him, how long would it be until she was adding her name to the list of ex-Mrs-Kavanaghs?

She and Trudi had discussed their respective relationships. Trudi – once again – advising Molly to leave Jon. Echoing the words of Anna Klein...

She had so many decisions to make: about whether to report Anna Klein to her superiors, even though it would signal the end of her career in CID; about her relationship with Jon and where it might be heading in the long term.

Denning had confirmed what she'd already suspected. Jon had told Helen Tranter what she'd said about Bryony's body. It had been enough to convince the journalist there was something more to the story, and had set her on a road that could have ultimately jeopardised their case. She knew the importance of ensure it was the police that dictated the narrative of a murder investigation and not the press, whose need to sell stories so often got in the way of solid detective work.

It was her fault for blurting out something in the heat of the moment that she should have kept to herself, but equally, he knew what he was doing when he shared that information with a journalist. Perhaps he thought it was a way back in with the *Echo*. She'd heard the paper had recently been taken over by a consortium and there was always the possibility that Jon saw that as a chance for him to return to a career he loved. But it proved she couldn't trust him, and if a relationship wasn't built on trust, then it was built on sand.

It was always difficult to balance doing the right thing with what felt easy and comfortable.

She had deliberately failed to mention Anna Klein's role when telling Denning about her involvement in the arrest of Blair and Connor Heaton. She still wasn't sure what to do about Anna. It was looking less and less likely she was going to do the decent thing and report herself, but Molly was unsure. She suspected Anna was going to need some prompting, and that was going to have to come from her. She had the number for Professional Standards in her pocket. She could make the call anonymously, protect her arse from any comeback. But that wasn't her style. She'd be upfront about it. That was only fair.

She took her phone out of her bag and stared at it for several minutes.

Right now, she wasn't sure she could decide what was right and what only felt like it should be. She scrolled through her Contacts' list and found the number for Islington CID, then asked to speak to DI Gillies, Anna's immediate senior officer. Once she was put through, she explained who she was and how she'd been working with DS Anna Klein on the recent burglary cases. Then she told him about Anna and her connection to Connor Heaton. Ultimately it would be Anna's DCI's decision to report her to IOPC and make the complaint official. It had been a tough decision, but she was in the mood for making tough decisions at the moment.

Anna would get a fair hearing along with a chance to put her side of the case clearly. Molly wasn't motivated by anything vindictive. She knew she had to live with her conscience.

She knew she should listen to her gut. Right now, her gut was telling her to get something to eat. Decisions were always harder on an empty stomach, and Molly's had been rumbling noisily all the way home from the pub.

She was distracted by the sound of the front door opening, immediately followed by excited voices in the hallway. Jon and Rowan were back from visiting Barry. A moment later, the sitting room door opened.

'Hey, babe; you're back,' Jon said. Rowan was behind him, smiling at Molly. 'Everything went well. Fingers crossed, Barry should manage to get to the wedding.'

'Great. I'm glad.' She was now sick of hearing about the bloody wedding. She knew she should be happy for Rowan. None of this was her fault. She just wanted her day to be perfect. And who could blame her for that?

'It's a lovely evening,' Jon said. 'Why don't we open some wine and drink it in the garden?'

Jon and Rowan disappeared into the kitchen. Molly heard a cupboard door open and the chink of some wine glasses being lifted out. A few seconds later, the back door creaked open.

She texted Trudi to confirm that it was still OK to stay with her and Charys, then headed upstairs to their bedroom and took the large suitcase from the top of the wardrobe. She would pack what she could then come back for the rest at a later date. She glanced out the bedroom window and saw Jon and Rowan chatting at the garden table. Her grandmother had always told her that if a decision was a difficult one to make, then it was probably the right one.

She began filling the suitcase.

Chapter Sixty-One

The team was in the pub. It was always good to unwind once a case was officially over and they could let their hair down. McKenna was unofficially in charge of proceedings. She'd started a tab at the bar but hadn't stayed for long, insisting she had things to do.

Denning did briefly wonder if she was beating a retreat because she'd not been around so much during the investigation, but it didn't matter. He had spotted Molly and Trudi chatting in a quiet corner, both looking serious. He'd been trying to get Molly on her own for a moment to ask about Anna Klein. He'd heard on the Met grapevine that Professional Standards wanted to speak to her, and there were rumours her career was finished. Whatever she'd done, he felt sorry for her. She was a good police officer, in spite of any shortcomings. Maybe he would give her a call, offer a sympathetic shoulder to cry on. Then again, perhaps it would be better to back off and give her some space to get her head together.

And if he was being honest, he had other things on his mind.

Sarah had returned from New York the previous evening. She'd been shocked to see his injury, and had joked about suing the Met for a work-related injury.

And then she'd dropped her bombshell. She'd been offered a permanent job with the bank in New York.

Apparently the bank wanted her to head up their US investment portfolio. It was good money, she'd insisted, as though that was the only consideration.

He'd struggled to take it all on board. The expectation that he could just abandon his commitment to Jake and give up his job without some serious discussion was not something he had had the headspace to consider. Even now, sitting in the pub, enjoying a beer, he wasn't entirely sure about it. Sarah had said they didn't want an answer straight away, but it wouldn't be fair to keep them dangling indefinitely.

Sarah's career had always been something he'd just accepted rather than something he'd ever really given serious thought to. She earned the big bucks that paid for their flat and other luxuries they took for granted. He couldn't deny her the chance to take up an offer like that. But equally, he couldn't just up sticks and move to another continent.

At least he'd finally agreed that Claire was right about Jake. It made sense to send him to a school that would be able to cope with his needs, at least for the short term. He was determined to play a bigger role in his son's life. It was always going to be difficult balancing a demanding job with the role of being a part-time parent, but he had to make it work, for Jake's sake. He remembered Liam Allen and the look of defeat and regret on his face when he'd been informed of his daughter's murder. He had clearly wished he'd done more for her, but circumstances and life had played out the way they had and somewhere along the line he'd made the wrong choices. Denning didn't want to make the same mistake.

If Sarah was determined to go to New York, then there was a real chance she would be going without him. But then what did that leave? The job?

He thought about McKenna, her half-empty flat and how the job and her life had so quickly merged into one. He didn't want that either. The job wasn't his life, but it was an important part of it. The thought of giving it up to start afresh in America just didn't appeal to him.

He watched his team laughing and joking and he knew this was the life he wanted. Right here.

Difficult decisions lay ahead.

A letter from Graeme

Hello, and so many thanks for choosing to read *Run For Cover*, the fourth outing for Met detectives Matthew Denning and Molly Fisher. The joy of writing a serial crime series like Denning and Fisher is that by now I feel as though I really know my main characters, and have the confidence to push them headlong into situations which test their mettle.

Run For Cover was inspired by real-life stories of undercover police officers and what happens when they become so involved with their undercover work it literally starts to take over their lives.

If you've enjoyed reading *Run For Cover*, please mention it to your friends and family, as a word-of-mouth recommendation can really help make a book. And do please leave a review – it can be as long or as short as you like. I'd be very grateful.

There are more Denning and Fisher stories to come, and I'm already working on Book 5...

I love hearing from readers, so feel free to get in touch, either via my website: www.graemehampton.com, or you can say hello on Twitter at ghamoo1. I can also be found on Instagram at graeme_hampton, but that's mostly just me posting pics of my two Siamese cats (Bella and Raffles) and my Dachshund (Peggy)!

Graeme Hampton

Acknowledgments

So many people help to bring Denning and Fisher into the world, and I'd like to take this opportunity to thank them. Firstly, to everyone at Hera and Canelo for publishing the books, and a huge shout out to Keshini Naidoo for steering the book in the right direction, and Dan O'Brien for always being around to answer my endless questions and help soothe my constant anxieties about all things publishing related. Another shout out to my fellow Hera authors, who are a great source of support and encouragement on social media.

A massive debt of gratitude is owed to Jennie Ayres and Andrew Bridgmont for their editorial input, and to the readers and book bloggers who make the whole writing process feel worthwhile.

Thank you to Alan Phillips for some much-needed information on firearms, and Graham Bartlett for providing me with excellent advice on police procedure and other policing technicalities about which I was surprisingly ignorant. Graham offers an invaluable advisory service to authors of crime fiction, and can be contacted at: www.policeadvisor.co.uk or at twitter.com/gbpoliceadvisor.

A huge thank you too to Christine Warrington for casting her fine eye over the manuscript, and to Barry

Kemp for reading over the book and offering valuable feedback.

I have to thank Gary Metalle for providing me with advice on all things technical, and (along with Julia Knowles) for managing to get caught up in a real-life police raid, which provided the inspiration for the 'big scene' in Chapter 48. The A21 is a real road, but the exact location where the incident takes place exists only in my imagination.

Rob Evans and Paul Lewis's excellent book *Undercover: The True Story of Britain's Secret Police* was both a valuable research tool and an engaging read. If you are interested in reading about the reality of undercover policing, I can't recommend this book highly enough.

Finally, this book is dedicated to my late uncle, Charles Hampton, who sadly passed away just before Christmas 2021. He had always been an enthusiastic supporter of my writing, even when it looked like it was never going to get anywhere. He will be hugely missed by everyone who knew him.